BURY THEM DEEP

JAMES OSWALD

BURY THEM DEEP

WILDFIRE

First published in 2020 by WILDFIRE
An imprint of HEADLINE PUBLISHING GROUP

3

Cataloguing in Publication Data is available from the British Library

Hardback ISBN 978 1 4722 4996 8
Trade Paperback ISBN 978 1 4722 4997 5

Typeset in Aldine 401BT by Avon DataSet Ltd,
Bidford-on-Avon, Warwickshire

Printed and bound in Great Britain by Clays Ltd, Elcograf S.p.A.

MIX
Paper from
responsible sources
FSC® C104740

HEADLINE PUBLISHING GROUP
An Hachette UK Company
Carmelite House
50 Victoria Embankment
London EC4Y 0DZ

www.headline.co.uk
www.hachette.co.uk

For all the people who work behind the scenes.
Without you nothing would ever get done.

Sawney Bean was a Lothian man, who left his home and the honest profession to which he was born. He took up with Black Agnes Douglas, a woman of low morals. Both unsuited to work, they travelled the land as beggars until they made a home in a cave on the Ayrshire coast. Sawney provided for his wife by robbing travellers through the nearby woods, and soon realised it was better to murder them than risk being identified, caught and hanged. And how better to dispose of the bodies than by eating them?

This gruesome trade he continued nigh on twenty-five years. The couple had many children and incestuous grandchildren, all nurtured on human flesh and hidden away in their deep, dark cave. That which they didn't eat fresh, they pickled in salt, and anything left they threw into the sea. Many a local stumbled across grizzly finds washed up on nearby shores. A hand, a foot, mayhap a whole leg.

And so it might have continued, had Sawney not accidentally allowed a man to escape. His tale reached the ears of King James himself, and a party of men and dogs searched the woods and the coast for this savage attacker. Even then, the true horror might have gone unfound, but the dogs entering the cave gave up a great cry.

Sawney, Black Agnes, children and grandchildren were taken away to Edinburgh for summary execution. There was no trial, for there was no doubting the horror and evil madness of the whole Bean family, no hope for them as had no souls. And besides, they all remained unrepentant throughout. They were taken to Leith, where the men had their hands, feet and testicles cut off, left to bleed to death while the womenfolk and children were burned at the stake.

Or so the story goes. As with all these things, it is short on verifiable detail and high on horrific sensationalism. There is no record in the historical archives to corroborate the tale either, and it thereby begs several pertinent questions. What could possibly turn a man, even one so base as Sawney Bean, to cannibalism? How did he manage to elude capture for so many long years? Why, when finally discovered, was he not taken to the nearest Sheriff Court at Ayr, but dragged back to Lothian and the place of his birth? And why, truly, were he and his entire brood summarily executed without trial?

Barnaby Fortnum, *A History of Scottish Myths and Legends*, Edinburgh, 1935

1

She hates herself.

All the way from work, back to her compact top-floor flat, she feels the loathing in her gut, even as she feels the excitement too. It's always this way, the tug of war between the self-loathing and the desire. Showering away the grime and sweat of the day doesn't help either. The filth is deeper than skin, resistant to soap. And, besides, she doesn't want it to be washed away. She wants to wallow in it. That's part of the allure.

The clothes she picks out are her disguise, and with each layer the disgust fades, the excitement builds. It's been over a month now, the anticipation growing like a tumour in her stomach. The ache of longing.

One last look in the mirror before she goes. Her transformation is so total she can almost believe none of her colleagues would recognise her in the street. But then that's the whole point. If they knew, she'd be out of a job. She needs that other life too much to risk losing it. Not so much for the money as for the calm, the certainty. This other world, this other her, is about excitement. It's about risk and the sweet, sweet pleasure it brings.

A quick check of her phone confirms everything is set for this evening. A little flutter of nervous anticipation tickles her throat as she readies herself to leave. At the door she almost forgets the package, grabbing it at the last minute, slipping it into the pocket of her long leather coat. Swiftly down the stairs, out the back door, across the broken pavers and concrete drying green shared by the rest of the tenement. Through the gate that leads out to the back lane. This is the nervous time, when she might be seen, recognised, challenged. But no voice calls out, no curtain twitches. Nobody knows who she is. Who she really is.

The drive across town takes longer than she'd like, traffic jamming the roads around Cameron Toll. She's about to turn off onto the Braid Hill road when the text comes in. Police presence at the car park. She'd laugh if she wasn't so hyped up already. There's another meeting place, not somewhere she's been before, but not far either. Satnav shows her the route.

It's getting dark by the time she arrives. Not many other cars about, but that's hardly surprising. She finds a suitable spot, under some trees, away from the road. Engine off, crack the window down a little, switch on the passenger compartment light. Wait.

The first tap at the window comes after less than a minute.

2

A low morning sun streamed in through the glass window wall of his office, painting the whole room orange-red with the threat of unbearable heat later on. Unless the weather broke of course, although that seemed unlikely. What was the children's rhyme? Red sky at night, shepherd's delight. Red sky in the morning, shepherd's warning. Well, it was certainly red, and certainly morning. Way too early for anyone with any kind of sense.

Detective Chief Inspector Tony McLean shuffled the papers he'd been pretending to read, case notes, staff rotas and all the other things he needed to know for that morning's briefing. Except that he didn't really need to know any of it. There were detective inspectors who could deal with the planning, detective sergeants to shout the orders and detective constables to carry them out, moaning all the while. He sat close to the top of the pyramid, the gritty details of each investigation so far away he'd need spectacles to see them. Or perhaps a telescope. His life revolved around strategy meetings, budget reconciliation, juggling egos. It was almost enough to make a man cry.

'You got a minute, sir?'

The question came at almost exactly the same time as a light knock at the open door. McLean looked up to see Detective

Inspector Kirsty Ritchie standing in the doorway, a worried crease across her forehead. Lately she'd taken to cropping her strawberry-blonde hair short, almost a boy's cut. It suited her better than the frown.

'A minute, an hour. What's up?'

'Operation Caterwaul. I've been going over the security clearances for the admin staff.' Ritchie stepped into the room, and now McLean could see the thick wedge of papers she was carrying. More adorned his desk, an endless tide that threatened to drown them all.

'Any problems?' He had to ask, even though he knew there must be or Ritchie wouldn't have been here.

'Nothing serious. Just had a couple of kickbacks from the NCA. I guess their vetting's a bit more serious than ours. They're talking to the Feds too.' She handed the papers to him with a half-apologetic shrug. McLean took them and leafed through the pile. Records for a dozen of the many civilian workers who kept the station running almost smoothly. It was yet another thing to worry about, although normally the support staff had sufficient security clearance to work on most investigations. Clearly Operation Caterwaul was considered more risky, although not so risky it couldn't be given a stupid name.

'We've got enough cover though?' He handed back the files, noting Ritchie's shoulders slump slightly. If she'd been hoping he'd take the problem off her hands, she was going to have to learn to live with the disappointment.

'If everything goes to plan, aye. You know the saying about plans and first contact with the enemy though.'

'Ah well. If it goes tits up, they can send some of their own people over to pick up the slack. Not sure why we're involved in this anyway. It could all just as easily be run out of the Crime Campus.'

Ritchie stepped clear to let him out of the office, then fell in alongside him as they both walked to the operations room. 'Most of it is, to be honest. We're just coordinating the financial stuff, seeing as how Edinburgh's the financial centre.'

McLean said nothing to that. He'd far rather deal with a violent crime, a burglary or even the drugs and sex-trafficking rings that popped up more quickly than you could knock them down. Financial crimes, corporate fraud and all that kind of thing gave him a headache. Sure, the crimes needed investigation and the criminals to be punished, but money bought politicians and brought pressure from above. Sweep it under the carpet, or clear it up as quickly and quietly as possible. Neither option sat well with him.

'We got the go-ahead to start yet?' he asked as they both entered the small room given over to the operation. It was relatively empty for a change, a couple of detectives, some uniformed officers and admin staff all hand-picked by the suits at the National Crime Agency. Trustworthy, dependable, unlikely to talk to the press.

'Started already, sir. We raided a firm of accountants yesterday morning. Lofty Blane's going through their books with the forensic accounts team.'

McLean scanned the room, and sure enough there was the giant form of Detective Constable Blane lurking in the corner, his shoulders round, whole body hunched to make himself less of a looming presence over everyone.

'Must have missed the memo.' Or more likely he'd been distracted by a hundred and one other memos all needing his immediate attention. 'Guess I'd better rally the troops then.'

'Morning, everyone. Quiet it down now.'

McLean watched while DI Ritchie brought everyone to attention. Not that the room was exactly packed; that was the whole point. Operation Caterwaul was so clouded in secrecy even he didn't know what the full objective of it was, only that it

5

involved co-operation with the NCA, Interpol and several other foreign law enforcement and intelligence agencies. High stakes didn't begin to cover it, which was probably why it was being compartmentalised so thoroughly. Why everyone in this room had been vetted and vetted again.

Ritchie finished her warm-up act swiftly and efficiently before stepping aside to make way for him. McLean hadn't brought any briefing notes with him; it wasn't that kind of investigation. All he needed to do was frighten them all into line. Not something he was particularly comfortable doing, but sometimes that was the job.

'I don't really need to tell you that everything said in this room is classified, but I will anyway.' He cleared his throat, not quite sure what to do with his hands since he had no papers to rustle.

'This investigation is extremely sensitive. Word gets out about what we're doing and not only will the whole operation collapse, we'll be in a very sticky diplomatic situation. So speak about it to no one. Not your colleagues in the canteen or locker room, not your significant other at home, and certainly not any of our friends in the press. If any of this gets out without authorisation, we will find the leak, trust me. And it won't just be a sacking offence. You could end up in jail.'

He paused to let that sink in, took the opportunity to survey the crowd. As well as DC Blane, he could see DC Harrison in the small team, and Grumpy Bob had found himself both a comfortable chair to sit in and a mug of coffee.

'As you'll know, we raided the offices of Smail and Associates yesterday morning on the pretext that they've been laundering drug money.'

'That's actually true, sir.' DC Blane spoke softly, but the room was quiet enough and empty enough for his words to be heard.

'It is?' McLean asked.

6

'Preliminary analysis of the records we confiscated show they've been putting drug money through a number of small businesses in the region. Pop-up shops, nail salons and a couple of online stores. It's quite sophisticated.'

'Really?' McLean knew it wasn't what the operation was looking for, but once you got DC Blane started it wasn't easy to stop him.

'Aye, they sell stuff through the major online retailers. Amazon, eBay, a couple others. Only it's not real. Second-hand books for a thousand quid, but they're just old paperbacks no' worth pennies. Sale goes through, no goods change hands, but the cash comes out clean enough. They even pay tax on it. Well, some.'

'That's fascinating. But it's not what we're here for, is it?'

Lofty's head drooped, bringing it down to the same level as most of the other people in the room. 'Aye, well, no.'

'Don't worry. I don't expect you to close the whole operation before it's run a week. It's good that you've found something though. Helps to keep our real targets in the dark.'

'Are we allowed to know what the real target is, sir?' Another question, this time from one of the support officers.

'When it's all done, the objective will become clear. That's all you need to know right now. You've got your jobs, people, so get to them. The fact that you've been selected for this operation means you're the best of the best in this station. I'd like to think we're the best of the many teams working this operation across Scotland. Let's prove me right on that one, eh?'

3

McLean watched the assembled officers and admin set to their tasks like a well-choreographed dance troupe. This was the part of any investigation that he liked the best. Right at the beginning, before all the problems had started to surface. People knew what they had to do and got on with doing it.

'Think that went OK.' DI Ritchie cradled a mug of coffee in both hands as she approached. McLean raised an eyebrow, then noticed Grumpy Bob following on behind. Wherever Detective Sergeant Laird was, fine coffee would not be far away. How they'd all cope when he retired at the end of the month was anyone's guess.

'It's a good team.' McLean nodded his head towards the bustling room. 'Surprised not to see any of our NCA colleagues at the briefing though. Didn't think they trusted us enough to fly solo yet.'

'They're coordinating with Aberdeen at the moment. Need to tread a lot more carefully up there for now.'

'I guess so.' He looked past Ritchie to where one of the admin support staff was waiting patiently to ask a question, a young man with a pale, freckled face and wiry ginger hair. For a moment McLean struggled to remember his name, but Ritchie came to his aid.

'You needing something, Ben?'

'Aye, ma'am, sorry to bother you. We've no' had the Holmes 2 terminal access sorted yet.' He turned slightly, indicating the line of computers arranged along one wall of the room, all their screens blank.

Ritchie frowned. 'Can't you ask Anya? She's usually on top of that sort of thing.'

'Aye, I would, but she's no' here.' Ben shrugged.

'Anya? Not . . .' Ritchie looked at her sheaf of papers, but didn't flick through them. 'She should be. She's on the list. Couldn't not be. For something like this.'

'Anya?' The question was out of his mouth before McLean realised he knew the answer already. 'Oh, Renfrew. Yes.' He shouted to DC Harrison as she walked past. 'You seen Renfrew, Constable?'

Harrison stopped in her tracks, began to do the same meerkat routine, then shook her head. 'No, sir. Is she part of the team?'

'Should be.' Ritchie finally gave in and leafed through the stack of papers until she found her list. 'Anya's probably got better security clearance than any of us.'

'Bet she's been poached by one of the other investigations,' McLean said. 'I'll have a word with McIntyre and see if we can't get her back. This is exactly her sort of thing.'

'You want me to speak to the duty sergeant, sir?' Harrison asked, all eagerness to help, as ever. 'She's maybe just off sick.'

'Anya? Sick?' Ritchie's laugh startled a couple of junior constables nearby. 'Don't think I've ever known her take a day off.'

'May as well ask anyway,' McLean said. 'And if she's not, find out where she is, OK? I'll be in my office.'

Harrison nodded once, then scurried off like a busy mouse. He watched her go, then turned back to Ritchie and Grumpy Bob.

'You got everything under control here?'

'Reckon so. Anything comes up, we know where to find you. More likely to be a problem out there than in here though.' Ritchie waved a hand at the window, indicating the wider world beyond the walls of the station. McLean had to admit she was right; inside the investigation room the most that could go wrong was them missing some link in the paper trail. He had to hope that her mention of problems wasn't an omen of things to come.

The coffee machine at the far side of his office yielded something rather less appealing than the fine brew Grumpy Bob usually managed to rustle up. Nevertheless, it was warm and wet and the drinkable side of disgusting. McLean refilled his mug, splashed too much milk in it, and retreated to his desk. The visit to the operation room and his short pep talk to the team had been no more than a brief, welcome break from the grind. He had no choice now but to get on with the budget reconciliations and staff allocations. At least until something else came up to provide a legitimate distraction.

It arrived sooner than he was expecting, in the form of his mobile phone vibrating away in his pocket. He pulled it out and stared at the screen, a number he didn't recognise. Normally he'd let it ring through to voicemail; if it was important they'd leave a message and he could call them back. On the other hand, if he answered it, then he didn't have to worry about the meaningless spreadsheet in front of him for at least the duration of the conversation. Thumbing the green button, he lifted the handset to his ear.

'Detective Insp— . . . Detective *Chief* Inspector McLean.'

'Oh, ah. Hello.' A woman's voice on the other end. Young, if he was any judge. Edinburgh accent, even though the call hadn't come from a city number. She clearly hadn't been expecting him to answer.

'Who is this?'

'Oh, yes. Sorry. My name's Millicent. Millicent Graham. Doctor Millicent Graham.'

A pause, which McLean found himself uncharacteristically compelled to fill. 'And what can I do for you, Doctor Millicent Graham?'

Another pause, and he considered hanging up. Although as crank calls went, this didn't really fit the bill.

'It's . . . well. It's a bit complicated. I work at Bestingfield? The secure psychiatric hospital?'

A chill ran down McLean's back. He hunched forward, phone pressed harder to his ear now. There weren't many reasons why someone from Bestingfield would be calling. Even fewer good ones. 'Go on.'

'I work with some of the long-term patients. Those with the most well-formed delusions. We can't hope to cure them, as such, but we can stabilise them, make their lives a bit easier. And ours.'

'I'm sure you do your best for your patients, Doctor. I'm not exactly sure what it's got to do with me though.' Except that he was sure. He just didn't want to have to face the fact of it. All the paperwork in the world would be preferable.

'Well, one of my patients is here because of you.' Dr Graham paused again, then started up before McLean could reply. 'I'm sorry, that came out wrong. He's here because of what he did of course. But you were the one who caught him.'

'You're talking about the man who claims to be Norman Bale.'

'Claims to be . . . Oh, yes.' McLean heard a shuffling of papers over the line that suggested Dr Graham's desk was every bit as chaotic as his own. 'That's right. You said he couldn't be Norman Bale because Norman Bale died when he was six years old. Leukaemia, wasn't it?'

11

McLean remembered the case all too well. How many years ago was it? Not that many. Not nearly enough for it to be coming back to haunt him now. 'It was, and he did. I knew him when he was a boy. The man you're treating is not him, whatever he might claim. That's a delusion you really should be tackling right now.'

'Ah.'

There was something about the way Dr Graham said that one, short word that made McLean shiver all over again.

'Ah?' he asked. 'I don't much like the sound of "ah".'

'You'll recall Norman's parents were found in his . . . their house?'

The faintest hint of a question at the end of her words, but McLean did indeed recall. The dining room where he'd shared meals with the young Norman, watched over by the boy's stern mother. That same woman many decades older, and many years dead, sitting in that same dining room across the table from her equally dead and equally well-preserved husband. Not a thing a person could forget easily, even after a blow to the head with a short scaffolding pole.

'I thought you'd have seen the report, what with you being the arresting officer and everything.' Dr Graham's voice banished the image from McLean's mind.

'Report?' He looked over his desk. There were so many.

'Yes, the pathologist took DNA samples from the two bodies in the house. They match Norman's. They're his parents.' The doctor paused a moment, and this time McLean left the silence hanging.

'I'm sorry,' she said eventually. 'I assumed you knew.'

'No. I didn't.' He stared blankly across the office, out through the window wall to where a beautiful morning had just turned hellish. But then it occurred to him it didn't matter if Bale was who he said he was. The man was insane and had murdered at least five people. There was no way he was ever leaving the secure psychiatric unit alive.

'So why are you calling me?' he asked. 'Not to tell me about DNA tests, I'm sure.'

'No. Not at all. I'm sorry. I had no idea you didn't know that.'

'What then?' McLean asked, even though he knew.

'Norman has issues, as you well know. But he's much improved over the past year. He's far more lucid, and he acknowledges that what he did was wrong. He talks a lot about his childhood, about his only real friend when he was a boy. He wants to talk to you.'

And there it was. What he'd known it would be all about the moment the doctor had told him where she worked. Well, it wasn't a hard decision to make.

'I'm sorry, Doctor Graham. I can't help you. There's nothing I want to say to that man, and nothing I need to hear from him.'

McLean stared at the blank screen of his phone, reflecting the square ceiling lights back at him as it lay on top of the paperwork he'd been reading. Trouble always had a way of finding him, but he'd never have expected it to come in quite such a form. Norman Bale. He'd not thought about that case in a while, not followed it up once the man himself had been committed indefinitely to the secure psychiatric unit. That was the end of it, or at least it should have been. There was no cure for the sickness that festered in his head. No doctor would ever pronounce him sane enough to stand trial for his crimes. He'd murdered at least five people, probably many more. There was no way he'd ever not be a danger to the public.

But the news about his DNA results, the confirmation of the identity he claimed, that was a shock. Norman Bale had taken ill that last summer before McLean was sent away to his hated boarding school down in England, not yet seven years old. Norman Bale had died from childhood leukaemia some time during that first term away from home. Norman Bale was buried in the graveyard of McLean's local church, the headstone smoothed by more than forty years of Edinburgh weather. Was that a lie? Was that grave empty?

The graves of his parents were, so why not his? It was a disquieting thought, that graveyard filled with empty coffins. The dead still wandering the streets. It brought to mind another case, another unidentified body, a shadow in a dead man's house, and something McLean tried very hard not to think about.

A knock on the open door helped. He looked up to see DC Harrison standing there, a worried frown on her face.

'You OK, sir? Look like you've seen a ghost.'

'Probably not the best choice of words.' McLean shook away the strange feeling that had settled over him. 'Sorry. I'm fine. Just had an interesting phone call. Not sure what to make of it.'

'Wasn't Anya Renfrew, was it?' A little light of hope flickered in her eyes.

'Ah, no. I take it you've not tracked her down.'

'She's not phoned in sick, no. And she's no' answering her phones. Home just rings and mobile's going to voicemail.'

McLean picked up his own phone and slid it back into his pocket. 'Get a squad car round to her place, aye? And while they're doing that, have a word with anyone here who's friends with her. It's irregular and unexpected, but I'll not panic yet. Probably a perfectly good reason we can't find her.'

Harrison looked unconvinced, and McLean couldn't blame her. His internal alarm was ringing now, and not just because of his conversation with Dr Graham. That call and the missing admin support were two completely different things, after all.

'I'll ask around, see who knows her best. Should have next-of-kin contacts on her personnel file too.'

'Let's not go phoning her folks before we have to, OK? Don't want to cause any undue alarm.'

'Aye, sir.' Harrison nodded once, then turned and left. McLean went back to staring out the window, over the rooftops to Salisbury Crags. People moved about Holyrood Park like tiny ants, unaware they were observed. Edinburgh was in its fourth week of sunny weather, much to the delight of both the tourist board and the ice cream industry. And yet for all the heat and light, he couldn't help feeling a horrible, dark chill of foreboding, deep in his gut.

4

The quiet buzz as he entered the room told McLean that things were ticking along nicely. It was way too early for any great breakthroughs, and anyway this whole investigation would be a piecing together of many small nuggets of information. A puzzle with no reference picture and no idea how many pieces there were. It beat running around after a psychopathic serial killer with a God fixation though. And for now he'd take quiet busyness over growing panic.

Ritchie approached from the far corner, where the row of computer screens still stood unattended and blank. 'We're hoping to have a senior-officers meeting later this afternoon if you're free. Go over initial results.'

'Not sure we've got any, have we?'

'There's Lofty's money laundering stuff. And the Aberdeen team have emailed us everything they dug up too. The trick will be working out how to use it without tipping someone off as to what we're doing.'

'I'm happy to let the NCA team deal with that side of things. It's their baby, after all.'

'Aye, and you know who'll get the blame if it's dropped.' Ritchie's retort had a hard edge to it that gave McLean pause. She had a point of course. Edinburgh CID were a small cog in a big machine with this operation, but he was old enough and wise enough to see how they might get the blame should anything go wrong.

'So cynical for one so young.'

'Flattery will get you everywhere.'

'Yes, well. Don't get too used to it. I had an interesting phone call this morning you might want to hear about.' McLean told her about Dr Graham and Norman Bale.

'The actual fuck?' Ritchie's face might have heralded a coming storm, and her outburst sent a ripple of anxious quiet across the room. Eyes turned from whatever it was they had been concentrating on, fixed on her and McLean.

'Pretty much my reaction too. The DNA results have got me puzzled, I'll agree. No way I'm going to get an exhumation order for any of the graves though. Not now. Not sure I'd want to either.'

'So, what? You're just going to leave it? Walk away?'

'Don't see what else I can do. He can ask to speak to me all he likes, but I'm not about to go down there. No. As far as I'm concerned, the man claiming to be Norman Bale can stay where he is. And the longer the better.'

'Amen to that.' Ritchie began to reach up to her neck, but the silver crucifix she had worn for a few years wasn't there. McLean watched as she disguised the movement by rubbing her thumb against her fingers and changing the subject. 'Any word about Anya?'

'Not answering her phone. I told Harrison to send a squad car round to her place. Knock on her door. I don't think there's any need to panic just because she's late.'

Ritchie's face suggested otherwise. 'This is Anya Renfrew we're talking about, Tony. She's never been late in her life.'

'OK. I'll get her next-of-kin details from personnel and look into it. Sure there's nothing to worry about.'

'Anyone checked the hospitals? She might have been in an accident.'

McLean suppressed the sigh that wanted to escape. True enough, it was out of character for Renfrew to simply not turn up, and the failure to answer her phones was troubling. She was a grown adult though, quite capable of looking after herself without the entire station worrying about her. On the other hand, she had high security clearance. She'd worked on some very sensitive enquiries and probably knew secrets about important people they'd rather weren't in the public domain.

'I'll chase it up. Meantime you need to deal with this.' He nodded past her, towards a young uniformed constable standing behind Ritchie, clearly waiting to ask some vital question. 'We can compare notes at this riveting senior-officers meeting later on.'

Everyone else was already there when McLean hurried into Deputy Chief Constable Stephen 'Call-Me-Stevie' Robinson's office. Not that everyone was a large number of people. The nature of Operation Caterwaul meant that few had the security clearance necessary to be told exactly what was going on. He had a sneaking suspicion there was more sensitive information even the senior officers weren't being told. Maybe the chief constable knew, but if so he wasn't telling.

'Sorry I'm late. Still trying to track down a missing admin.' McLean took a seat beside Detective Superintendent Jayne McIntyre. She said nothing to his excuse, giving him no more than a raised eyebrow.

'Missing? Not one of ours, is it?' Deputy Chief Constable Robinson sat at the head of the table, as befitted his seniority. That he was part of the operation at all spoke volumes about how important it was, even if his input was only a small part of that. He managed to inject what McLean felt was an unreasonable note of panic into the question.

'If by "one of ours" you mean assigned to Operation Caterwaul, then, yes, she is. I don't think that's a cause for concern though. She's reliable. Well, she was reliable.'

'Who are we talking about, Tony?' McIntyre asked.

'Anya Renfrew. Didn't show up for the briefing this morning, not answering her phone and she's not called in sick.'

McIntyre's concern was more measured, which somehow made it worse. 'That's not like Anya. I don't think I've ever had a problem with her. Been working here, what? Must be twenty years now.'

'Twenty-one. She came to us straight out of university, never worked anywhere else. I spoke to HR earlier. They're sending over details. I've also asked a squad car to drop round her place and knock on the door, just in case she's had an accident over the weekend.'

'Even so.' Robinson cupped his hands together, resting them on the unblemished pad of notepaper on the conference table in front of him. Said nothing more.

'I'm sure there's a perfectly reasonable explanation, sir. And we've barely started on the operation so far. I don't think this is a security risk.'

'Don't you? I wish I had your confidence, Tony. You don't know as much about Caterwaul as I do, how far it reaches. We can't afford to have anything go wrong with our part of the operation.' Robinson picked up his pen, wrote something down on his pad that McLean couldn't read from where he was sitting, underlined it twice. 'I want this woman accounted for by the end of the day. Whatever's happened to her, wherever she is, we need to know. Top priority, understood?'

'Yes, sir.' McLean nodded, stayed in his seat. The meeting had barely started, after all, and there was much else to discuss. The DCC clearly had other ideas.

'Well, get to it then, man.' He closed his notepad, put away his pen and pushed his seat back before standing. Surprised, everyone else did the same.

'The meeting?' McIntyre asked.

'The meeting can wait. Right now I need to make a couple of difficult phone calls.' Robinson looked at McLean. 'Find this woman before I have to make any more.'

5

It is over all too soon. The last trouser pulled up, the last fly zipped. The men disappear into the gloom as quickly as they came, a few even quicker. Car lights spear the darkness, engine noise upsetting the silence as the sated depart. She can only wish she was one of them. For a while she was lost in the moment, the grinding and sensation. But now the shame returns, and the self-loathing grows as the night silence closes in on the scene of her degradation.

She sits for a while in the driver's seat of her car, door open and her legs out through the opening. Knees wide as she feels the soreness deep within her. A cold breeze blows up, sweeps across the car park and rustles the heavy canopy of the trees. It chills her skin, the sweat and other fluids, sends a shiver through her that sparks her back into action. Time to clean up. Time to go home.

There's a supermarket plastic bag on the back seat, and she spends a few moments picking up used condoms that litter the ground at her feet. So many. She can't remember ever having seen so many before. They slither and slip and slide as she drops them into the bag, and unbidden she remembers the song, Monty Python's *Meaning of Life* and all those Catholic children dancing around the streets to a musical number. 'Every sperm is sacred, every sperm is good . . .' It forces a half-chuckle, half-sob from her mouth. She'll dump the bag in a bin somewhere on the way home. It's time to go.

She pulls the mask off, wipes her face with a couple of moist towels. Can't do anything about the stains on her blouse, but it'll be going in the bin soon anyway. Car door closed, she stares into the darkness for a moment, feeling the weird elation drain from her. She knows that it's wrong, and yet she can't help herself. All she can think of is next month and doing it all again.

Or maybe she won't. Maybe this will be the last time. Perhaps she can seek help, therapy. Find a normal life. The ghostly reflection of her face in the windscreen thinks otherwise, and who is she to argue.

She reaches for the starter button, foot pressed on the brake pedal.

Nothing happens.

She presses it again, the stirring of fear in her throat as the lights in the dashboard flicker. Outside, the darkness pulls in around her like a tide. The headlights fade, then go out altogether.

Shit.

She reaches for her bag, tucked away under the passenger seat, scrabbles through the contents in vain hope. Key fob's there where she put it, so's her phone. Does she dare call for help? Like this?

It's cold outside, so she grabs her coat, slings her bag over her shoulder. Her shoes aren't the most practical for walking, but she dare not take them off. Underfoot are loose stones, broken twigs, dirt. She totters around the car park, searching desperately for any stragglers. Normally there'd be a few other cars, and at least someone else in the scene might help without judging her. But she's not in one of her usual spots, and there are no other cars. No other people.

In desperation, she switches on her phone. It takes an age to come to life, the light of its screen only making the darkness beyond it deeper. The tiny icon in the top corner shows empty. No signal.

That's when the full weight of it hits her. She doesn't know how to get home from here on foot, even if it wasn't miles away.

She's all alone in the woods at night.

And then something in the trees goes crack.

6

The bungalow sat at the end of a cul-de-sac, halfway between Musselburgh and Portobello. It didn't have a sea view, but it was pleasant enough, and quiet. McLean parked his Alfa Romeo in front of the narrow driveway and stared through the windscreen for a moment. No net curtains twitched, not even in the neighbouring houses.

'Squad car said it came past at eleven hundred hours, sir. No answer at the door and they couldn't see anything through the windows.' DC Harrison hadn't made any move to get out of the car when he'd switched off the engine, clearly waiting for his signal.

'Eleven hundred hours? Is that what they said?'

'Aye, sir. Wrote it down.' The detective constable fussed at her jacket pocket until she managed to persuade her notebook out of it, then flipped the pages until she found today's. 'Eleven hundred hours.'

'So they swung past, probably no closer than the road end. That's if they came here at all.'

'How d'you reckon that, sir?' Harrison's face was all innocence. But then she was young too. Maybe a little naïve.

'Call it old man's cynicism, but if I hear a policeman say "eleven hundred hours" rather than "eleven o'clock" in anything other than a formal report, I know he's making it up. It's too much detail too. That's always a good sign someone's lying.' He unclipped his seat belt and opened the door. 'Never mind. We're here now. Let's go see what we can find, eh?'

A warm breeze blew in off the nearby Forth, whispering around the houses and kicking up dust from the gutters in miniature tornadoes. The sun hung in a cloudless sky of that perfect pale blue you didn't see anywhere other than Edinburgh. McLean closed his eyes and turned his face to it for a moment, feeling the warmth on his skin. How nice it would be to just lie somewhere sheltered and soak up that heat. Except that he had a tendency to go as red as a cooked lobster more quickly than you could say factor 30.

Anya Renfrew's bungalow was as unassuming and unremarkable as the woman herself. Grey harling clung to the walls under slates baked dry by the sun. Overhung by an open porch, the front door had been painted fairly recently in a deep gloss green that looked strangely out of place. Beside it, a single button produced a loud 'ding dong' inside when McLean pressed it. No other sound followed. He tried the door handle, unsurprised to find it locked.

'Any sign of a key?' He looked around, but there were no flowerpots on the gravel path that surrounded the front of the house, nothing hanging in the eaves of the porch. The front garden wasn't much to look at either, mostly paved over although weeds were doing their best to reclaim it through the cracks.

'Nothing I can see.' Harrison walked along the front of the house towards the corner, peering through one of the front windows as she did so. 'Looks pretty empty in there too.'

'I'll see you round the back then.' McLean went the other way, pausing at the window on his side of the door. He cupped his hands against the glass to block out the glare, but it was still almost impossible to make out anything beyond the thin net curtain. A couple of sea-washed sticks lay on the windowsill, treasure from the nearby Portobello Beach, he assumed. The smooth wood was silvered and cracked, gnarls and knots worn almost shiny so that they looked a bit like miniature dragons guarding the house from intruders.

There were no windows on the side of the bungalow, only a path wide enough to wheel a bin between the house and the boundary wall. McLean found the bin around the back, but when he lifted up its lid, there was nothing inside.

'When's collection day?' he asked Harrison as she appeared from the other side.

'No idea, sir. I can find out.' She had her notebook in hand, flicked it open and scribbled something down. 'Any particular reason why?'

McLean looked out over the back garden. It was tidy enough, a small area of browning lawn, a couple of dwarf apple trees at the bottom end. The wall that ran between this property and the next ended at a concrete garage that must have opened up onto a lane at the back. 'We're sure this is the right address? It feels . . . I don't know . . .'

'Like no one actually lives here?'

'Exactly. See if you can find a key anywhere around the back door. I'll go and have a wee look in the garage.'

He followed the short path down the garden and peered through a spider-webbed window into a largely empty space. A potting table, shelves and a few garden tools piled against one wall suggested this was used more as a shed than as somewhere to park a car. The door was locked with a hasp, the shiny padlock the newest thing McLean had seen since arriving.

'If she's left a spare key it's well hidden, sir.' Harrison stood by the back door when he returned. 'There's a kitchen and a bedroom at the back. Both look like they've not been used in a while.'

McLean started to look for himself, then realised it wasn't necessary. 'When was Renfrew last at work?'

'Friday, sir. You spoke to her in the incident room, remember?'

He did of course. But that was the thing about Renfrew. She was anonymous. Competent enough that you could give her a task and know it would be completed. So reliable you came to rely on her completely, and then forgot all about her until she presented you with the work she'd done. Beyond that he knew absolutely nothing about her, and he couldn't deny that made him feel a little guilty.

'OK then. I guess we'll have to see if any of the neighbours have seen her recently.'

The first two houses they knocked at were as empty as the one they'd come to see. Waiting for doors to be answered at both, McLean could tell they were lived in though. Little things like a wooden box for milk bottles at the front door of one, flowers in pots on the windowsill of the other. Peering through windows, he saw empty coffee mugs on a low table, magazines strewn about, a television remote and a couple of games console controllers. Signs of life, but the people gone. Mid-afternoon, they were probably at work.

The doorbell on the third house made a similar 'ding dong' to the one in Renfrew's, but instead of silence after it, a small dog started yapping furiously. Then someone shouted: 'Quiet, Brandy', followed by a singsong 'Coming.' They waited patiently as first a scrabbling noise began at the door, then the lock clunked and it swung open.

McLean was ready for the furry bullet that shot out of the gap, but Harrison clearly had less experience. She jumped back with a little shriek. Stooping, McLean caught the dog around its middle and scooped it up into the air. A Jack Russell terrier if he was any judge.

'Och, thank you. He's a wee terror for running out like that, but he just loves everyone.'

McLean looked past the small furry face and tongue that was trying to lick him, to see an elderly lady standing in the doorway.

'He's certainly a handful. Friendly chap though.' McLean handed the wriggling dog to its owner, then went to his pocket for his warrant card. 'Detective Chief Inspector McLean. This is my colleague Detective Constable Harrison. I was wondering if we could have a word?'

The old lady peered at the card, then at McLean. He had a horrible feeling he knew how this was going to play out, but then again, at least he was away from the station and his desk groaning with its load of reports.

'Of course, of course. Why don't you come in. I'll put the kettle on for a cup of tea.'

Her name was Sandra Guilfoyle, and she'd lived in the cul-de-sac since it had been built, fifty-two years earlier. She'd thought about moving when her husband, Alastair, had died a few years back, but the memories kept her there, and the people. McLean learned all this and more as he sat on a sofa that had most likely also been there fifty-two years, with Brandy the terrier shedding beige and white hairs all over his lap. Harrison remained unusually quiet, clearly feeling the same way about small dogs as did Grumpy Bob. At least the tea was nice, and the biscuits well within their sell-by date.

'I wanted to ask a few questions about the bungalow at the end of the road,' McLean said when he finally managed to get a word in. As if affronted by his rudeness, the terrier leaped from his now hairy knees and padded over to its mistress.

'Oh aye? What about it?'

'I was wondering when you'd last seen its owner, Anya?'

'Anya?' The old lady scratched absent-mindedly at her

terrier's head, eliciting a wag of the tail and playful bite. 'No' this month, for sure. She drops by every so often, but it's usually old Bill the gardener who keeps an eye on the place.'

'Not this month?' McLean felt that familiar sense of dread creeping into his stomach like ice. 'You mean she doesn't live there?'

'Och, no. Nobody's lived there since old Grace went into a home – what? Two years back?' Mrs Guilfoyle raised a wrinkled hand and shook it in the air, index finger pointing crookedly at McLean. 'She was a detective too, wasn't she?'

'Anya works in admin. She's not a police officer as such.'

'No, no. Not Anya, Grace.'

'Grace? Grace Renfrew?' McLean couldn't recall an officer by that name, certainly not in plain clothes. The first name gave him pause though.

'Now you mention it, no. She went back to her maiden name when her husband died. Long before she moved in down the road, mind you. What was it now? Oh dear, my memory's not what it was. Not Renfrew, but something similar.' Mrs Guilfoyle made a clicking sound with her tongue. Either that or her false teeth were coming loose. 'Ach. I can't remember it now. She was always just Grace. Such a lovely lady. It was a shame when she took a tumble. Old bones can be so brittle. And to think she was lying there a whole day before anyone knew.'

'I'm sorry, Mrs Guilfoyle. You're saying that a detective named Grace lived in that bungalow and Anya looked after her? Where is she now?'

'Grace? I heard she was in a care home. Anya would be able to tell you which one.'

'Of course.' McLean felt it unnecessary to let the old lady know Anya was missing. There was something she might be able to help him with, even if he hoped that she wouldn't. 'This Grace, Anya's mother. Her maiden name's not Ramsay, is it?'

Mrs Guilfoyle blinked a couple of times before breaking into a smile that was too perfect white to be natural. 'Och, you know her. Well, of course you do. She'd be a fair bit older'n you, mind, but you'll have worked together, maybe?'

'I did indeed work with Detective Superintendent Ramsay when I was a junior officer. I have . . . memories of her.'

'Such a lovely lady. Not been the same round here since she left. You only ever see the other folk at the weekends. Everyone works so hard.'

'It's the curse of modern living, I'm afraid. And none of us are exempt. You've been very helpful, Mrs Guilfoyle, but we have to be getting on.' McLean stood up, placing his still half-full mug on the tray. Well trained, DC Harrison did likewise, although she'd managed to finish hers.

'There was one thing, sir. Before we go?'

McLean thought for a moment Harrison was going to ask for the bathroom. Her actual question to Mrs Guilfoyle was much more helpful.

'You said that the house was mostly looked after by the gardener. Bill, I think?'

'That's right, dearie. Bill Bradford. He does a lot of work around here.'

'You wouldn't happen to have his number, by any chance?'

7

'That was a good call, Constable. I'd forgotten about the gardener.'

McLean sat in the driver's seat of his Alfa, the window wound down to let the breeze through. Mid-afternoon sun baked the leather interior, and he was tempted to start the engine, switch on the air conditioning. That would be a waste of petrol though, even if he could hardly say the car was environmentally friendly in the first place. All 2.9 litres and 500-plus horsepower of it. Should really get himself something electric.

'Easier than breaking down the door, if he's got a key. You were planning on having a look inside, right?'

'Makes sense, since we're here. He say how long he'd be?'

Harrison had phoned the gardener as soon as Mrs Guilfoyle had handed her the card that had been pinned to the note board above her hall telephone. Fortunately for them both, Bill Bradford was working in the area and agreed to come right over. That had been twenty minutes ago, and McLean was beginning to feel the tug of guilt from those distant piles of paperwork back at the station. On the other hand, there was something strange going on here, and he wanted as much information as possible before going back to the other senior officers. After the ultimatum he'd been given by the DCC, he wasn't about to take any chances.

'I didn't know Anya's mum was a detective super, sir,' Harrison said after the silence had stretched beyond her threshold.

'I didn't either, which says something, I guess. A lot of things really.'

'But you know her?'

'Knew would be more accurate. Detective Superintendent Ramsay retired about two years after I made plain clothes. She was never much of a one for rubbing shoulders with the junior detectives, and when she did . . .' He paused a moment, partly because it had all been such a long time ago, and partly because he'd been raised to say nothing about a person if there was nothing good to say. 'Let's just say her management style was of its time.'

'Must have been tough as old nails, to make it to detective super back then.' Harrison's words carried a tone of awe and respect in them that didn't quite square with the woman McLean remembered.

'I'm not that old, Constable.'

'Sorry, sir.'

Movement in the rear-view mirror stopped the conversation from descending into petty insults. McLean saw a van turn into the cul-de-sac, then park outside Mrs Guilfoyle's bungalow. A tall, wiry man climbed out and scanned the area as if searching for someone.

'Looks like our gardener is here.'

McLean opened his own door and swung out, enjoying a fuller breeze on his face as he stood up. 'Mr Bradford?'

The wiry man turned to face them, looked McLean up and down, but barely seemed to register Harrison. 'Aye. You'd be the polis then.'

'Detective Chief Inspector McLean. This is my colleague Detective Constable Harrison. She's the one you spoke to.'

'An' you're wanting into the Ramsay place? That right?'

'Miss Renfrew has gone missing. We're trying to find her. When was the last time you saw her?'

Bradford screwed his face up with the effort of recalling. His skin was tanned with the dark hue of a man who spent most of his time outdoors, the wrinkles deep like caverns. He crossed the short distance from his van to McLean's Alfa, then did another double-take.

'Giulia Quadrifoglio.' He let out a low whistle. 'Don't see many of them about. I bet she goes like stink, aye?'

'Anya Renfrew, Mr Bradford. You were telling us the last time you saw her.'

'Oh, aye. What's it the day? Monday, aye, Monday. Would've been last week some time. Wednesday evening mebbe?'

'And that was here?'

'Aye. No' much mowing going on what wi' this dry weather, but I tidied up out back a bit. Usually spend a couple hours each Wednesday sorting out the gardens here. Old Mrs Guilfoyle's place as well as Miss Renfrew.'

'And you have a key?'

'That I do.' Bradford shoved a hand in his pocket and pulled out a large ring with at least a dozen smaller ones on it. He fumbled through them for a moment, then carefully unclipped a couple of latch keys and a larger mortice key. 'I suppose you'll be wanting in then?'

'Should I, you know, be asking for a warrant or something?' Bradford asked as he stood by the now-open door. McLean had the distinct impression it had only just occurred to the man.

'Miss Renfrew works for the police,' he said by way of a non-answer. They were treading on dodgy ground here, but he didn't think she would object. It seemed to have the desired effect on the gardener, who simply nodded.

33

'I'll leave you wi' the keys then. Need to get back to the job I was working on. You can give them to Miss Renfrew when you see her, aye?'

Had he not already spent some time in Bradford's company, McLean might have thought the man was joking. He seemed to view the world in a very simple and straightforward manner though. One in which Anya Renfrew was simply another client he would see again soon. The fact that two police officers were here searching her house, that she was missing, hadn't yet dislodged that conviction from his mind. McLean had met gardeners who had encyclopaedic knowledge, business acumen and a work ethic that put him to shame. One of them looked after the grounds around his own house. William Bradford was clearly cut from lesser cloth.

'I'll make sure she gets them, Mr Bradford. Thank you.' McLean patted the gardener on the shoulder, which seemed the right thing to do. Bradford nodded, then walked away back to his car, leaving him and Harrison alone to look over the bungalow. He followed her inside, closing the door behind him.

Beyond a narrow porch, the hallway was remarkably similar to the one in Mrs Guilfoyle's house. The furniture might have been more eighties than seventies, but it was laid out in much the same way. A narrow table held an old landline phone, no sign of an answering machine anywhere nearby. Above it, a cork note board held a couple of takeaway menus not unlike the ones in McLean's kitchen on the other side of the city. In one corner, a faded square of paper listed a half dozen phone numbers, including the one Harrison had dialled to summon Mr Bradford. Anya's was there too. McLean pulled out his phone and took a photograph. Chasing down those numbers would be just one of many actions he could see beginning to stack up for when they returned to the station.

'Are we looking for anything in particular, sir?' Harrison stood at the far end of the hall, where a partially open door revealed a bathroom beyond.

'Signs that Renfrew actually lived here would be a good start.' He pushed the door fully open and stepped into a small bathroom. The mirror-fronted cabinet above the basin was empty, and there were no toothbrushes or toothpaste anywhere to be seen. The bar of soap sitting between the taps was cracked and dry with age. 'Not looking good in here.'

While Harrison checked the front rooms, McLean went first to the kitchen. The cupboards were stocked with dried goods and tins, some of which had been around a while, if their use-by dates were anything to go by. The fridge was on though and contained a few relatively fresh vegetables, some cheese that wasn't mouldy and a tub of spreadable butter. No milk, and no alcohol either, but it was at least evidence that Renfrew had been there.

A small utility room led to the back door, and here he found a few more signs of recent use. A tub of washing powder stood on the countertop above the washing machine as if it had been hastily brought out and not put away again. Pulling out the little drawer, he dabbed his finger in the powder tray and it came away wet. This had been used fairly recently, although there was no evidence of what might have been washed.

'Living room looks like something from an eighties sitcom. Don't think anyone's been in there in years. The telly's like, half a metre thick.'

For a moment McLean couldn't work out what Harrison was talking about, but then it occurred to him she might not remember the old cathode ray tube televisions he'd grown up with.

'What about the bedrooms?'

'Front one's empty. No bed, nothing in the cupboards. Looks

like she uses the back one when she's here. There's a few clothes in the wardrobe, could be Anya's, could be her mum's.'

McLean followed Harrison into the room in question. Its window looked out over the garden, and it was a decent size given how small the whole bungalow was. The queen-sized bed had only one bedside table, an old alarm clock radio showing the time in bright red LED lights, a lamp with just a bare bulb and no shade, and a dog-eared copy of *Persuasion* by Jane Austen. He picked up the book, flicked to the front page. Scrawled inside the cover were the words 'Anya Renfrew, Year 6' and a doodled love heart with AR and LB written either side of it.

'LB?' Harrison asked, peering around his arm.

'Schoolgirl crush, at a guess. I don't think it's the clue that will tell us where she's gone. Or what her game is.'

'It is odd. This is definitely the address on her personnel file.' Harrison pulled out her mobile phone, tapped at the screen. Moments later the telephone in the hall started to ring. 'And that's the phone number too.'

McLean walked out to the hall and picked up the receiver just to be sure. Harrison said a cheery hello, then hung up.

'Looks to me very much like she stays somewhere else, but comes here from time to time. We know if she's got a boyfriend she might be living with?'

Harrison's shrug was answer enough. 'Don't really know her that well.'

McLean glanced at his watch. If needs be they could have a more thorough look later, but right now this was something of a dead end. And the day was marching on. 'OK. Let's get back to the station then. She's doesn't live here, so we're going to have to widen the search. Get a team out to go door to door with the neighbours when they're not all out at work.'

'Later tonight, or first thing tomorrow?' Harrison asked. McLean was tempted to get it done with, but then he remembered what day it was, and a promise he'd made that he couldn't break. Didn't want to break.

'It'll have to be tomorrow.' And if that upset the DCC, then so be it.

8

'Get on to Renfrew's mobile provider. We need to track down her phone. And ask around the station. I want to interview anyone she's friends with. All of the admin staff on the last two cases she worked, for starters.'

Harrison nodded her understanding and hurried off. McLean set a more leisurely pace as he made his way down into the basement. The Cold Case Unit lived in what might once have been a storage room, deep in the old Victorian bowels of the station. He liked to think that maybe it had been a drunk tank; a holding cell for many minor offenders, who would most likely be let off with a stern word of caution and sent home after a few hours' sober – or not so sober – reflection. Its arched stone ceiling rose to a decent height in the middle, but became more claustrophobic the closer to the walls you moved. Since that was where the desks had been arranged, he was glad his position as officer in charge was more nominal than actual.

That role fell to ex-Detective Superintendent Charles Duguid, one time bane of McLean's life, now a grudging ally. His desk was at the far end of the room, and centred so that the light well up to the car park at the back of the station at least had a chance of giving it some illumination. The chair behind the desk was empty when McLean entered, but a mixture of cough and growl from the bank of filing cabinets at the other end alerted him to where Duguid was.

'Looking for me, or are you just hiding from the angry mob upstairs?'

It didn't surprise McLean that Duguid knew what was going on. That had always been his skill, even before he retired. It didn't hurt that Grumpy Bob was settling into a similar role in the CCU either. Nobody had a better handle on station gossip than the old detective sergeant.

'A bit of both actually.' He closed the door and glanced around to see whether anyone else was there. As far as he could tell it was just the two of them. 'What do you remember about Grace Ramsay?'

'Ramsay?' Duguid rattled the filing cabinet closed. He paused for a moment. 'She's not dead, is she?'

'Don't think so. Least I hope not. I'd quite like to talk to her.'

'She retired when I was still a DI. Must be twenty years ago now. Can't say I've seen her since, don't think I've heard anyone mention her much either. Why do you want to know?'

'Seems our missing admin is her daughter. Did you know that?'

McLean didn't really need to wait for the answer to see that Duguid didn't.

'I knew she had a daughter, but Anya Renfrew? She kept that quiet.'

'That's not the only thing, I'm finding out now. Seems our Ms Renfrew has been leading us astray.' McLean told the ex-detective superintendent all he'd found out so far, what little it was.

'Ramsay lived out Joppa way. I remember that much. We were in different departments, didn't often cross paths. That was back in the days when we had enough detectives to spare, mind you.'

39

'Do you remember anything about her then?'

'Aye, a bit. She didn't suffer fools, had a bit of an obsessive streak. Good enough detective, but she rubbed most people up the wrong way.'

A mental image formed in McLean's mind. A slim, middle-aged woman in a severe dark suit with a face like licking piss off a nettle, tearing several strips off a hapless young detective constable who'd made the mistake of being two minutes late to a morning briefing. He still had the scars. 'Yes, she could be a bit prickly. Not that I had much to do with her when I started, and she was retired before I made DS.'

'What's your plan then? Want me to ask a few of the old guard what they know?'

It was such an uncharacteristic act of helpfulness that at first McLean thought Duguid was joking. Then he noticed the empty room again, the desks clear. Not much going on in the Cold Case Unit at the moment, it would seem.

'That would be helpful. I've already asked HR to send me Renfrew's complete file and I'll see if I can track down her mother too. Apparently she's in a nursing home, so it shouldn't be too difficult.'

'I'll get right on it. See if I can't persuade Grumpy Bob to give me a hand when he gets back.' Duguid looked at his watch. 'Not much of the day left, mind.'

'Couple of phone calls ought to do it. Don't want you wasting a lot of time.' McLean stared at the filing cabinet, then looked pointedly at Duguid's clean desk. 'Unless you want to of course.'

'Actually, I was thinking of heading off early. Might drop by the Police Club on my way home though. There's always one or two retired detectives in there of an evening. Might even be someone who remembers Grace Ramsay more fondly than the rest of us.'

★ ★ ★

The climb from the basement up three flights of stairs to the operations room left him surprisingly out of breath. McLean paused at the open door, gathering his thoughts as best he could. The quiet emptiness over the threshold did little to reassure him as he entered. He had a nasty feeling things were about to get complicated. Even more complicated than usual.

'Chief Superintendent McIntyre was looking for you, sir. Wanted an update on Anya.' Newly promoted Detective Sergeant Sandy Gregg bustled up the moment she saw him. From the way she spoke, it sounded like they all wanted an update. He'd not have minded one himself.

'You've worked with her a lot, haven't you?' he asked.

'Aye, pretty much. She's one of the team, you know? Even if she's no' an officer.'

'Did she ever mention her mother at all?' McLean wondered whether this conversation wouldn't be better in a more formal setting, complete with note taking, but he'd started now.

'Mother?' Gregg tilted her head like a confused pet. 'Not that I remember, no. She's not really the kind of person talks about her personal life. Just the work, maybe her choir.'

'Choir?'

'Well, mebbe more like a singing club. Folk stuff. I was talking to her about it just last week, right enough. Thought I might tag along one time.'

'You sing?' McLean tried to make the question as innocent as he meant it, but it came out more disbelieving than interested.

'Aye, and I'm no' half bad.' Gregg looked for a moment like she was about to break into song, but her gaze shifted past McLean towards the door, worry in her eyes.

'There you are. Where the hell have you been, Tony?'

McLean didn't need to turn to know that Detective Super-intendent Jayne McIntyre had entered the room. He did anyway, since she wanted to talk to him and he had much to tell her.

'I'll need to interview you more formally about Renfrew,' he said to DS Gregg, before she could scuttle away. 'Everyone else who's worked with her too. You might all want to have a wee think about what you can remember, aye?'

Gregg nodded her understanding. 'I'll put the word out. You want to start this evening?'

'Tomorrow will do. Most of them will be away now anyway. We'll get started first thing.'

'I heard you were wanting to speak to everyone who's worked with Anya. That doesn't inspire me with much confidence.' McIntyre looked past McLean as she spoke, at the retreating back of the detective sergeant.

'Yes, well. I'm afraid things have got a little more thorny since this morning, Jayne.'

'In my office, not here.' McIntyre cut him off before he could get started. 'You can bring us all up to speed.'

McLean wanted to ask who 'all' of them were, at the very least to give himself a bit of time to mentally prepare. McIntyre didn't give him the chance, striding out the door with a purpose. At least her office wasn't far, and the same faces he'd seen at the meeting earlier that day were all there. A somewhat overawed-looking DC Harrison sat at the conference table with them.

'Janie's been bringing us up to speed, as much as she can.' McIntyre stalked across the room and took a seat. 'Perhaps you could fill us in on the rest of the details?'

McLean looked at the expectant faces, all turned towards him. He pulled out a seat next to Harrison, settled himself down.

'It would seem that Anya Renfrew has been living something of a double life. The address and landline number we have for her on file are her mother's house in Joppa. Some of you might remember her. Detective Superintendent Grace Ramsay.'

He let that sink in a little, although the only person who

reacted was McIntyre. McLean thought the DCC might have recognised the name, but if he did, he wasn't letting it show.

'I'm trying to find out where Ramsay is now. Her neighbour says she went into a care home about two years ago, and Anya's been looking after the house since then. Doesn't seem to stay there all the time, so we need to find out where else she might be living, whether she's got a boyfriend or something like that. We're pulling mobile-phone records, and I'll be interviewing all the staff here who've worked closely with her in the past. Meantime, her photo's with every officer in Scotland.'

'I'll get that sent nationwide. All ports too.' Robinson rubbed at his face with tired hands. 'But what the actual fuck is going on? I thought this woman was supposed to be vetted. High security clearance, the works. And you don't even know where she lives?'

McLean had to admit that, put like that, it didn't sound good.

'She's worked here for more than twenty years. Never done anything to raise suspicions. The address we have for her is hers, it's just not where she actually stays any more. I'm going to get a team round there for a proper search in the morning. We'll interview all the neighbours, and hopefully we'll have located her mother by then too.'

'The morning? You can't get it done now?' Robinson asked, as McLean knew he would.

'We could. If we had the budget and the manpower. It's un-likely anything we turn up there is going to speed up finding her though. There are better things we can be doing in the meantime.'

The DCC let out a noise that was part frustration, part resignation. 'At least tell me we've revoked her security access.'

'We have. And I've got the IT team tracing everything she's seen with regards to Operation Caterwaul.' McLean shook his head slightly. 'But I don't think this is a security breach, or a mole, or anything like that.'

'Well, what the fuck is it then?' Robinson almost spat the words out, then seemed to remember where he was, who was with him. 'Sorry.'

'I don't know. But think about it. If she'd been abducted because of her work, why the mystery about where she lives? And if she was planted here, or somehow turned against us, why disappear now, so early on in the operation? She'd have been far better staying put and finding out more, wouldn't she?'

'I wish I could share your optimism, Tony. We can't give this woman the benefit of the doubt just because she was our friend and colleague.' McIntyre had been largely silent until now, but her point was valid enough.

'It's not that, Jayne. Call it a gut feeling, if you must. I think she's in trouble, but not because of what she does here. I will find her, and we will get to the bottom of this.'

'You'd better. And fast.' Robinson's growl wasn't quite as effective as some of the senior officers McLean had worked under, but the note of desperation in it was. He could see the pressure the man was under, the stakes riding on a successful outcome to the operation. Well, he felt it too, if for different reasons. And at least it meant there'd be no problem with overtime.

9

'Sorry I'm late. It's been a hell of a day.'

McLean pushed his way into the kitchen, dumped his briefcase on the chair. Emma stood up from where she'd been reading something at the table, a faint scowl on her face. He'd texted to let her know, but that didn't excuse the fact. For all that he was trying his best to make it home at a reasonable hour every day, it didn't always work out that way.

'You been home long?' He made a conscious effort to give her a hug. She accepted it, albeit briefly. Still a work in progress.

'Couple of hours. I had a bite to eat already. Would I be right in thinking you haven't even had lunch yet?'

He could have lied, but his stomach had other ideas, taking that moment to let out a gurgle far louder than could be blamed on the Aga.

'Like I said, hell of a day.'

'You can tell me all about it on the way. We need to be gone in twenty minutes and you really need a shower.'

McLean lifted an arm and sniffed carefully underneath. She had a point. 'I'll be quick then.'

By the time he'd stepped out of the shower and towelled himself down, there was a change of clothes laid out across the bed, Emma nowhere to be seen. McLean probably wouldn't have chosen that exact shirt, but he wasn't going to get into an argument about it either. He was back down in the kitchen, dressed and more acceptably fragrant, with five minutes to spare.

'Toast?' Emma proffered a plate, the slices already buttered.

'You're too good for me, you know that?' He picked one up and took a bite.

'Aye, well.' She said nothing more, an awkward silence falling in the room. There were a lot of those these days. McLean looked around, eyes falling on the papers she'd been reading earlier. He couldn't help but notice the logo of Edinburgh University at the top of one sheet.

'Going back to school?' He meant it as a joke, but Emma's defensive posture suggested he was closer to the mark than he'd expected.

'Maybe. What of it?'

'Think it's a great idea. What were you thinking of studying?'

'Always fancied Forensic Anthropology. You know, buried bones and all that. On the job training's all good and well, but I want to get stuck into something a bit more challenging.'

'Hence tonight's lecture?' McLean asked.

'Exactly so. Professor Turner heads up the course, so I was hoping I might get a chance to speak to her afterwards.'

McLean couldn't remember the last time Emma had sounded so enthusiastic about anything. It lit up her face more effectively than a week of him coming home on time. It was certainly better than their less than successful weekend break on Skye, although that might have had more to do with Storm Griselda than any lack of effort on his part. He hurried to eat the second slice of toast, talking with his mouth full in a manner that would have earned him a smack across the back of his hand from his grandmother.

'We'd better get moving then. My car or yours?'

Emma grabbed her keys from the side table by the phone. 'Mine tonight, I think. That Alfa of yours terrifies me.'

'. . . mass graves in Rwanda were a more tricky proposition. Such was the extent of the genocide, there were few surviving relatives to make DNA comparisons worthwhile. Relatively few of the dead carried any form of identification either, and even where the bodies were found wearing jewellery that often couldn't help. We had some success with matching clothing, but again that relied on survivors being able to identify loved ones from their garments.'

McLean half listened to Professor Harriet Turner's words. It wasn't that the subject didn't interest him; raised by a pathologist and working as a detective, he had a morbid fascination with the subject of Forensic Anthropology, after all. It wasn't that Professor Turner was a poor speaker either. She treated the subject with the gravitas it deserved, but nevertheless had much of the audience on the edge of their seats. No, it was more that he couldn't stop his mind from going over the day's events. The lecture theatre was warm too, and it had been a long day.

'. . . greater success in establishing cause of death, number of victims, and the spread of gender and age. The church site revealed the machete to be the execution weapon of choice.'

Was she dead, Anya Renfrew? Harrison had circulated her details around all the local hospitals without any joy. There'd been a few bad car accidents since last she'd been seen leaving the station on foot on Friday evening, a couple of yet-to-be-identified mugging victims across the whole of Scotland, but nothing that matched their missing admin. On the other hand, he knew all too well that thousands of people simply disappeared every year.

'. . . more interesting are some of these signs on bone

fragments from the older grave pits that show distinct signs of cannibalism.'

The words cut through McLean's musing, and for a moment he thought the professor was still talking about Rwanda. He didn't recall that particular atrocity among the many that happened during that genocide, although he'd read reports about something like it in neighbouring Uganda under Idi Amin. A glance at the slide projection showed that the talk had moved on from Africa though. He looked at Emma, wondering whether he could ask her where they were now, but his finely honed sense of self-preservation kicked in when he saw the rapt look on her face.

'. . . cut marks any butcher would recognise where meat has been removed from the bone prior to cooking. Some of the larger bones, like the femurs, have been split for the marrow inside them too. These are human bones, although there are often cattle and sheep bones nearby.'

On balance, it was perhaps an odd way to spend an evening together, listening to a late-middle-aged woman talk about genocide and cannibalism to an audience of several hundred people. It had been Emma's idea though, and if she was serious about going back to university to study Forensic Anthropology, McLean was happy to support her however he could. It wasn't as if either of them actually needed to work.

Except that people went missing and he needed to find them. They lived double lives and he needed to work out why. There were drug dealers, money launderers, traffickers and a thousand other kinds of criminal out there who demanded his attention. He could no more give up the day job than voluntarily stop breathing. Something else drove Emma, but it was no less strong for that. Her obsession with finding the truth was what had brought them together in the first place, and he was damned if he was going to let it drive them apart.

The hall broke into applause, and McLean realised he'd almost dozed off, mind far away from the subject of the lecture. If Emma noticed, she said nothing, and soon enough they were out of their seats and making their way against the flow of departing people, towards the lectern and the professor.

'What did you think? She's a brilliant speaker, isn't she?' Emma took hold of his arm and steered him more forcefully.

'Yes. Fascinating,' he said, aware that it didn't sound terribly convincing. Fortunately he was spared Emma's further ire. Professor Turner looked up, cocked her head slightly quizzically, and then beamed a smile. Too late he saw that it was directed not at Emma but at him.

'Tony. What a delightful surprise. What on earth are you doing here?'

'Professor Turner. I . . .' McLean took the professor's outstretched hand to shake, then found himself pulled into a friendly embrace. Up close, there was something vaguely familiar about the woman, but for the life of him he couldn't recall where or when he might have met her.

'None of this professor nonsense. You used to call me Harriet.' She let go of him, took a step back, still smiling, and shook her head. 'You don't remember at all, do you? It's OK. It was a long time ago. I studied with your grandmother when I was doing my postgrad. Used to come round to her house for the odd weekend. I think you might still have been at school. Maybe gap year?'

Something clicked, and he saw the young woman in the older lady's face now. Back then she'd been Harriet Fairweather, which might also have explained his confusion. She'd cut her hair short, and it had gone almost completely grey. Laughter lines wrinkled around her eyes too. But the woman he remembered hadn't been all that much older than him, surely. Mid-twenties to his seventeen or so? When had they got so old?

A light cough reminded him that he wasn't there alone.

'Sorry. Harriet, this is Emma Baird. Emma's hoping to get onto your Forensic Anthropology course.'

'I really enjoyed the lecture, thank you.' Emma only got a handshake, not the full hug. 'I had no idea you knew Tony.'

'Neither did he.' The professor laughed. 'To be fair, it's been what? Thirty years? Maybe more. Where does the time go?' A wistful look spread across her face, and then she turned serious. 'So you want to be a forensic anthropologist. What is it you do at the moment?'

'Crime Scene Investigation. Photography mostly, but finger-prints, fibre analysis, whatever needs doing really.'

'And Tony's a policeman, so I hear. You two are well matched.'

'How is it our paths haven't crossed?' McLean asked, then realised he knew the answer to his question was going to land him in trouble. He tried to cover up his mistake by waving at the now blank projection screen. 'You've only just come back to Edinburgh of course.'

'Well, it's been a few months now, but busy ones. I'm getting a bit old for clambering about in mass graves. Time to teach the next generation.'

'You should come by some time. Gran died a while back, but I'm living in the old house.'

'I heard about Esther. Such a shame. She was a great lady. A fine mentor.' Professor Turner was about to say something else when a young man joined them, the anxious expression on his face one McLean had seen on many a press officer down the years.

'I think your adoring public wants you.' McLean nodded towards a line of people waiting patiently by a table stacked with books. Professor Turner looked around, bemused for a while, then finally understood.

'Oh, of course. Sorry. I need to get on with this. But it was good to see you, Tony. I'd love to drop by some time. Maybe help . . .' She paused a moment. '. . . Emma with her application for the course.'

'I'd appreciate that, Professor. Thank you,' Emma said, but the professor had already turned away.

'Seriously, Tony. Is there anyone in this city you don't know?'

'I think that's a bit unfair, don't you, Em? Professor Turner's been away for years, only just come back here. I don't think I'd even gone to university the last time I saw her.'

Emma sat on the other side of a small table in a busy Thai restaurant at the top end of Leith Walk, toying with the un-finished remains of her coconut pudding. They'd walked from the lecture theatre, enjoying the cooling air of evening after what had been another oppressively hot day. McLean couldn't remember whose suggestion it had been to find somewhere to eat, but their footsteps had led them to this place, somewhere he'd not been in a long time. It was pleasing to see that it hadn't changed at all, and the food had been as good as ever.

'Well, it's lucky for me, I guess. Can't hurt to have an inside track to the course.'

It didn't take his degree in psychology, or decades of getting into people's heads, to know what the problem was. McLean could hear it in Emma's voice. This had been her thing, a chance to break out and do something new. Something independent of him, without his support. And fate had gone and ruined that, however much it might also have helped.

'You don't need an inside track, Em. You're more than qualified already. What with the job you're doing at the moment, your work experience.'

Emma shrugged, took a sip of her drink and then went back to playing with her pudding. McLean had finished his, as well as

51

the very fine curry beforehand. It was so much nicer when it came on a plate and not in a little foil container. Of course, Emma had eaten before he'd arrived home late, so it was hardly surprising if she didn't have quite his appetite.

'This was where you took me on our first date,' she said out of nowhere.

He looked around the room, then out through the glass at the front to the street beyond. She was right, now he thought about it. This was where he'd taken her.

'As I remember it, I owed you dinner for proving I'd been framed. It wasn't exactly a date.'

Emma pouted. 'Can't imagine what I saw in you.'

'Whatever it was, I'm glad you did.' He cast his mind back to that time, and then fast forward through all the shit that had happened since. 'And I'm sorry for everything that happened because of it.'

'Everything?' She raised an eyebrow, smiled at her joke, then frowned. No doubt her thoughts were tracking through the same course as his. Eventually she shrugged, gave up toying with her pudding. 'It's been fun though, this evening. In a morbid kind of way.'

'Not the first subject I'd choose to listen to a lecture on, but yes. I know what you mean.'

'Do you really think I'll get on the course? It's a big step, leaving work.'

McLean reached across the table and took her hand in his. Her gaze flicked down, and for a moment he could see her tense, feared she might pull away. But little by little she relaxed.

'I know you want to do this on your own, Em. I can even sort of understand why. I'll keep out of the way if you want me to, but if you need help? Well, I'm not going anywhere.'

Emma said nothing, but she did smile, which was more than McLean had hoped for. He reluctantly released her hand after a few moments, nodded his head in the direction of her bowl.

'Now, are you eating that or what? I'd hate to see it go to waste.'

She laughed, which was something he'd not heard in far too long, picked up the bowl and passed it over.

10

She runs in the darkness, terror chasing her through the trees. Somewhere in the distance she has lost her high-heeled shoes, but she's so scared the pain in her soles barely registers the stabs of broken stick and sharp rock, the tear of thorns. Behind her, something large is crashing through the undergrowth, making no attempt at stealth. It wants to kill her, to rip the flesh from her bones and drink upon her still-warm blood. She does not know how she knows this, only that it is true.

Raw and exhausted from the evening's activities, she barely has the strength to run. Is this retribution? Punishment for her sins? The fear keeps her moving, makes her swallow the sounds of her sobbing even as she gasps for each breath. A small part of her knows this is irrational, knows she should stand and face whoever is trying to scare her. But the crash from her earlier high has left her vulnerable. Her tormentor knows it well, can smell the self-loathing on her, can smell the fright.

She should have stayed in her car. She should have locked herself in and hidden in the footwell. Waited until dawn and the chance of a passer-by. She shouldn't have shouted into the night when that first branch snapped like a pistol shot. Now she is too deep in the forest, no idea where the car park is, no idea where she is. The only thing she knows is that she is being chased, her life at stake. All the sick things she has done, all the bad men, they are all out there in the darkness, circling like jackals.

Another crack of breaking wood, and something screeches like a wounded animal. She ducks away, stumbles as the ground dips beneath her. Rough branches rip at her hands and arms as she reaches out to steady herself. Stops running for just a moment.

And then she sees the light.

It is faint, in the distance, barely a candle through the dark shadowy trunks of the trees. It disappears as quickly as it came, and for a moment she fears it's one of her pursuers. There must surely be more than one. Another step, and it reappears. Through the hammering of her heart and the lump in her throat, she realises the light has not moved, but been blocked by a distant truck. That screech behind her again, fading away in a series of low, guttural moans as if someone else has been caught and is now dying a slow, painful death at the claws of whatever great beast is chasing her. For a handful of seconds she wonders if she is safe, if the creature is sated now that it has caught its prey. Except that she was alone in the woods, no one else but her and the beast. It is toying with her.

At some point she stopped moving, but she doesn't know when. The cuts in her feet, her forearms and palms sting, blood sticky all over her. Eyes wide in the darkness, she strains to make out anything beyond the deeper blackness of the trees, but the light is all she can see now. She has to go to it, even if it is a trap.

A silence falls over the land. Not the busy quiet of a night-time forest, this is the silence of something terrifying, waiting for her to make a move. And yet she can't ignore the possibility of help. As quietly as she can, she takes a step forward, stops.

Nothing happens. No noise of attack. No screech of triumph.

Another step, and then another. Every movement sounds like

an explosion to her. She knows the beast is behind her, closing in on her, its teeth bloody, its breath foetid with the stench of other victims.

And yet the attack never comes.

Step by painful step, she approaches the light. And now she sees it hangs over the porch of an old stone cottage. The clearing between the trees and the door isn't wide, but stepping out into the open brings fresh terror. She can be seen here. Nowhere to hide. She wants to rush, but the pain in her feet is too great, her strength all gone now. It's all she can manage to limp across the sharp gravel, stumble up the step and jangle the bell that hangs from a little frame beneath the light. The noise sends another shiver of fear through her, but she is too tired, too weak to do anything but surrender to it.

Sounds of movement inside bring her a sliver of hope. She hears bolts being slid back, a key turned in a lock. The door swings open with a creaking of hinges that haven't seen oil in a generation, and she looks up into a face filled with alarm, and concern.

'Please.' The word sounds like it comes from someone else, not her. Not her voice at all. She tries to take a step forward, but then the ground comes rushing up to greet her.

11

The number of cars parked in the cul-de-sac had grown significantly overnight, which gave McLean a little glimmer of hope there might be people at home to interview. The bungalow at the end was still dark, but most of the others had lights on, even though it was early. Folk getting ready for the daily commute, another day of work. Had Mrs Guilfoyle spoken to any of them? It wouldn't matter. By the time his small team of constables was done, they'd all know the story well enough.

'You know the drill. One team to each house. Any details about Renfrew or her mother. We'll also need names and phone numbers for follow-up interviews. Try not to alarm anyone too much.' He'd briefed the team before they'd all come out, but it never hurt to say things twice. 'Quicker we're started, quicker these people can get on with their days, but if anyone's seen Renfrew in the past week I want to speak to them myself, OK?'

A nod of heads, and then they all set off. McLean motioned for DC Harrison to follow him as he went to the house closest to the empty bungalow.

'Someone at the door.' The shout came from the back of the house just moments after he rang the doorbell. A woman's muffled voice, it wasn't immediately answered. They waited patiently, McLean straining to hear any sound from within of feet approaching. He was just about to ring again when the door swung open, no sign of a lock or latch being undone. A scruffy young man stood there, barefoot and hairy-legged beneath a towelling dressing gown that probably didn't belong to him. He rubbed at his lightly stubbled face as he stared at them.

'What youse want? If you're sellin' God we're no' buying, ken?'

'Detective Chief Inspector McLean. This is my colleague Detective Constable Harrison.' McLean held up his warrant card. The young man sniffed, not even a little bit impressed.

'No' Jehovah's Witnesses then. So, what youse want?'

'You live here, Mr . . . ?'

'Opened the door, din't I?' He scratched at his cheek, sniffed a finger. 'What's this about then?'

'The house at the end there.' McLean jabbed his thumb over his shoulder. 'Miss Renfrew's place. Have you seen her recently?'

'Dinnae ken, mind.' The young man sniffed again, and for a moment McLean thought he might hawk out a gob of phlegm. Would that be grounds for arrest? Probably. The repercussions might not help his investigation though.

'Who is it, Johnny? An' why're you no' dressed yet?' The previously muffled woman's voice came closer and clearer. The young man looked round over his shoulder, then turned his back completely on them and stepped inside. He might even have closed the door had McLean not placed his foot in the way.

'It's the polis, Mum. Askin' about that hoose at the back, aye?'

'Go an' get dressed. We've to be at your gran's in half an hour. And do something about your face. You look like a tramp.'

The last of those words were directed at McLean, even though he knew they weren't intended for him. The door had opened again, this time to reveal a middle-aged woman. Johnny's mother, no doubt. She looked at him and Harrison with suspicious eyes for a moment before saying: 'What this aboot, eh?'

McLean went through the same introductions, the same question about the bungalow. 'Can you remember the last time you saw her, Mrs . . . ?'

'Russell. Agnes Russell.' The woman swung the door a bit wider, holding a hand out for them to come in. 'Sorry about Johnny. He's sixteen going on twenty-five. School holidays are a nightmare. Come through an' I'll put the kettle on. Youse lot all like a cuppa, right enough?'

McLean closed the door, followed Harrison and Mrs Russell through to a surprisingly large kitchen at the back of the house. By the time he arrived, the kettle was on, three mugs lined up on the counter.

'Grace liked her tea black as tar. That how you take it, Inspector?'

'Grace?' It took his brain a moment to catch up with his hearing. 'Detective Superintendent Ramsay, you mean.'

'She was always just Grace. Long as I can remember. Such a shame when she had to go into that home.' Mrs Russell paused a moment to pour boiling water into the mugs and mash at the teabags with a spoon. 'I must go and visit her some time. I feel so bad about what happened to her.'

'She had a fall, I understand.'

'Aye, that's right. Broke her hip in a couple of places. Osteoporosis, they told me. That's no' the worst of it, mind. She was lying there a whole day before anyone found her. Might have died.'

'You know where she is now?'

'Oh aye. It's no' far. Care home up on Deal Street. I helped Anya move her in.'

McLean sipped at his tea to give him time to gather his thoughts. No milk offered, and it had been over-brewed. The bitterness numbed his tongue. 'When did you last see Miss Renfrew?'

59

Mrs Russell cocked her head to one side, staring sightlessly at the light hanging from the middle of the kitchen ceiling. 'What's it today? Tuesday? Would have been last Thursday, I think.'

'Nah, Mum. She was in the house on Friday night, remember. For a while, at least.' Johnny Russell walked into the kitchen fully dressed. He'd dragged an ineffective brush through his hair, but stubble still clung to his face. Sixteen going on twenty-five indeed.

'Aye. That's right. Saw her car parked up, must have been about seven? She weren't there long, mind. Not more than half an hour. Probably picking up the post or something.'

'That's probably it.' McLean put the mug back down on the counter, unwilling to try and drink any more of the liquid inside lest it dissolve his throat.

'So what's the problem then? Why all the questions? Has she gone missing?'

'Sure it's nothing serious, but she didn't turn up to work yesterday, and she's not answering her phone. We're just trying to trace her movements.'

Mrs Russell raised a suspicious eyebrow, the tone of her voice unconvinced. 'A chief inspector?'

'As I say, probably nothing serious, but if you wouldn't mind giving some contact details to my colleague here. Just in case we have any more questions.' McLean nodded in Harrison's direction. 'Thanks for the tea. I'll see myself out.'

The bungalow was unchanged from when he had visited it the night before. McLean went in through the back this time, then walked through to the front door. Before unlocking it, he collected together the mail and flicked through it again. Nothing for Anya, only junk for her mother, and none of the little flyers that seemed to come these days even when there was no other post. He put them down on the little table in the hall, beside the phone. As he did so, he noticed a faded colour photograph on the wall he'd overlooked before. It showed a group of people, mostly men, sitting around a table in a pub garden somewhere. In the middle of them sat Detective Superintendent Grace Ramsay, quite a few years before she had retired. A small woman, she nevertheless dominated the picture, and the group. Clearly the one in charge of whatever investigation it was they had been celebrating. Or drowning their sorrows over. McLean peered at the faces, trying to put names to the detectives. He was fairly sure one of them was an extremely young Charles Duguid, and there beside him, DI Malcolm Duff. And was that John Needham hiding behind them?

He was reaching up to take the photograph off the wall when a knock at the door distracted him. Opening it revealed Harrison, along with DC Stringer and a pair of uniformed constables.

'That's everyone spoken to, sir. Looks like the only people who knew Anya were the Russells and Mrs Guilfoyle. Couple of houses further up have sold recently, and the rest of them only know her face. Couldn't say how often they saw her, or when that last was. Thought it was maybe an Airbnb or something.'

'So much for community.' He stepped aside to let the constables in. 'OK then. Let's go over the house methodically. If Anya's not staying here, she must have somewhere else to go. I want anything that might point to where that could be.'

They set about their tasks while McLean took himself through to the master bedroom. It was the same as he'd seen it the day before, but with still no contact from Anya, her mobile switched off and another fifteen hours of the clock ticked past, he needed to look a bit closer. Needed to think smarter.

The bed was neatly made, a thin floral duvet over clean white sheets. When she slept here, Anya favoured two pillows, it seemed, and aside from the alarm clock, light and copy of

Persuasion, no other distractions. McLean could find no phone-charging cable and wall transformer anywhere in the room.

A narrow dressing table sat in front of the window, its top clear. Its drawers held underwear, tights, a few pairs of socks. Nothing at all unusual. Hanging in the wardrobe, he found a couple of identical calf-length dresses with matching jackets in dark-grey cotton. Three neatly ironed white blouses hung alongside, and below them all a suspiciously sparse collection of practical shoes. This was the Anya Renfrew he recalled. Sensible. But where was the casual wear? The jeans and trainers? Sweatpants and hoodie? He couldn't imagine her taking off her work clothes and wandering the house naked. Except that now he'd thought of it, he couldn't help it. Only that didn't make sense. There were no blinds in the living room, no lace curtains to avoid embarrassing the neighbours. And none of them had said anything, least of all sixteen-going-on-twenty-five Johnny Russell.

Shaking the image from his mind, he kneeled down and looked under the bed, but apart from a spectacular collection of fluff there was nothing to see. Something was bothering him though. He stared at the bed, then the dressing table, the wardrobe and rickety wooden chair. Finally he went back to the wardrobe, pulled it open again. The clothes still hung from the rail, shoes lined up underneath.

And that's when he noticed the inside base of the wardrobe was higher than the outside. Crouching down, he saw that there was a drawer built into it, with no handle. Not exactly a secret compartment, but easily enough overlooked. The shoes covered a small hole, exactly the right size for a pair of fingers to reach inside and pull the whole thing open. And there, neatly folded, was something far more colourful than the dull grey suits hanging above it.

He had carefully taken out the garment and was holding it up to the light for a better look when DC Harrison came in through the door.

'Not found anything yet, sir – oh.'

'Oh?' McLean asked, which was perhaps a bit unfair since it was much what he was thinking.

'I . . . Er, that is . . .' Harrison's face began to redden. 'Not what I would have expected to find here, sir.'

An understatement at best. McLean carefully laid out the dress on the bed. Short, skimpy and a red so vibrant it was almost painful to look at, it was the polar opposite of all the other clothes in the wardrobe, or at least those not hidden away. There were more like it, all neatly folded in the large drawer, all garments he'd more associate with his time spent working in the Sexual Crimes Unit than with demure Anya Renfrew.

'Do you suppose, fancy dress?' Harrison offered.

'One maybe. But half a dozen? There's a box here too.' McLean bent down to fetch it out. At first he thought it might be a pair of boots; the box was large enough. It had a logo he didn't recognise embossed into the lid, and when he opened it, the smell of new tyre inner tubes wafted up to his nose. Inside was something as red as the first dress, but shiny, and heavy. His gloved fingers squeaked against the material as he gently lifted up and held out a full-body latex suit. The last time he'd seen anything like it was when they had raided an upmarket brothel in Stockbridge a few years earlier.

'Oh,' Harrison said again. 'That's quite something, isn't it?'

'Indeed.' McLean did his best to fold the garment back down into its box, but there was no way he was going to succeed. 'It seems there's rather more to Anya Renfrew than we thought. Wouldn't you say?'

12

'You've been working here for what, eight years now?'
McLean sat in interview room two, the one with a fresh coat of paint and windows you could see out of. Across the table from him, yet another of the station's admin staff shifted nervously in her seat. He'd thought that working with the police day in, day out would have lessened the impact of being interviewed, but so far that hadn't been the case. They were all nervous. Not because they were trying to hide something like the uncountable number of criminals he'd interviewed down the years, but because people were hard-wired to be nervous around authority figures. He'd never really considered himself to be one of those. Now, it seemed, he was. Particularly to Wendy Brown.

'Nine in August, sir. Started back when it was still Lothian and Borders. Filing and stuff mostly.'

'And you worked with Miss Renfrew all of that time?'

'On an off, sir. I was up at Gayfield Square for a while and Anya was here. We've both been based at this station for the past five years though.'

'So you know her quite well then.'

'I suppose. I mean, we chat in the canteen and that. Usually station gossip. What cases we're helping out with, who the good bosses are and who we'd rather avoid.' Wendy blushed as she spoke, but McLean merely smiled. He'd learned early on that the trick was to ignore the nervousness and do nothing to increase it.

'What about out of work? You ever go to the pub with her? Meet up at the weekend?'

'No, I don't think I ever did.' Wendy paused a moment, then sat up straight, a hand going halfway to her face like a schoolgirl knowing the answer to a question. 'Well, there's been a few times we've all gone to the pub. All the admins and the officers. When a case goes well. Or sometimes, when it doesn't.' The excitement dropped away as quickly as it had come on, the hand with it. McLean understood well enough. It was great when a case was solved quickly and easily. There were plenty of times in his career when he'd gone to the pub to celebrate, happily drinking beer paid for by the officer in charge. Nowadays it was more often than not him who put some cash behind the bar as a reward for a job well done, but there were times the drinking was in commiseration, not celebration.

'I think that probably counts as work, don't you?' he said after a moment's silence. 'So you never met Renfrew for lunch at the weekend, went shopping together, saw a film, something like that?'

Again, Wendy paused before answering. 'No. I'm sorry, sir. She's not like that.'

'What is she like then? I know she's good at her job, but how is she to work with?'

'Fine, I guess. She's just . . . Anya. She's always on top of things, seems to know how everything's meant to work, who to ask for what. If we ever need something, it's always Anya who sorts it. And she never complains. Don't think I've ever heard her raise her voice or speak a harsh word. Except maybe about some of the officers who like to get a bit too hands on.' Again, Wendy blushed. McLean stopped himself from asking if that happened often. Of course it did, and of course the mostly female admin staff wouldn't lodge a complaint unless it got completely out of hand. He wished they would, but he was old enough and jaded enough to know they wouldn't. And neither would the behaviour of the mostly male junior officers change. Not quickly enough anyway.

'She's a bit older than me, Anya.' Wendy took McLean's silence as an invitation to go on. Not exactly what he'd intended it for, but welcome nonetheless. 'And she's been working here for ever. Guess that's why we all look up to her. Almost like a mother figure, you know?'

McLean did. His own experiences of working with her matched the picture Wendy was painting. It didn't quite square with the rather risqué dresses and fetish wear they had found at her house that morning though.

'Well, thank you. That's all for now. But if you think of anything, however silly or inconsequential, do tell me. Or speak to one of the detective constables.'

Wendy nodded, then stood up to leave. She hesitated a moment at the door. 'She's going to be OK, isn't she? I mean, she's not in any trouble, right?'

'We're all concerned for her safety' was all McLean felt he could say. Wendy smiled uncertainly, nodded again, then left.

'You seen DS Gregg about, Constable?'

Fresh from interviewing admin staff, McLean had gone straight to the Operation Caterwaul control room on the third floor, hoping to have a quick chat with the detective sergeant. There weren't many people on his list left to talk to, and she had at least known something about Renfrew's life outside work.

'Think she's gone for lunch, sir. You want me to give her a buzz?' DC Blane had been sitting at one of the computer workstations. He had stood up as soon as he'd seen McLean, so now he loomed over everyone in the room. There weren't many of them, a distinct lack of activity that underlined how crucial it was they track down their missing support administrator.

'It's OK. Just wanted to ask her a bit more about Renfrew's fondness for singing.' McLean checked his watch. 'Might see if I can grab a bite myself.'

He didn't get far. DC Harrison stepped into the room before he was halfway to the door. The look on her face and printouts in her hand meant lunch would be a while yet.

'Hoping I'd find you here, sir. Just had this back from the phone company.' She handed the sheet to him as if that was going to help. Scanning it showed a list of times, all on the previous Friday evening, and alongside them a set of codes that probably meant something but he was damned if he knew what.

'Executive summary?'

'She used data somewhere in Joppa. That's round about the time Mrs Russell's son claims he saw the car outside Grace Ramsay's house. Something similar an hour later in the New Town or Leith area. Probably downloading emails, or maybe private messaging. There's another data blip near Liberton Brae at half ten, and then it goes dark. The phone's not reconnected with any towers since then. Must be switched off.'

'Any update on the car?'

'Aye, I spoke to the DVLA. Nothing registered to Anya herself, but there's a dark silver BMW X3 registered to her mother. That's the address in Joppa again.'

'Get the details out, and see if ANPR have anything.'

'Already done, sir. I'll let you know as soon as we get a hit. Presuming we get a hit, that is.' Harrison's tone didn't hold out any great hope.

'So what do we think about her movements? Where did she go after work? And what's happening in Liberton?'

'No idea about Liberton, sir, but going by the times on there and when she clocked off on Friday, she must have gone straight over to her mum's house first. Then to wherever it was she went in the New Town. My guess is she's got a flat there, maybe? Where she really lives. Jay – DC Stringer's going through the council records, see if we can get an address. Nothing coming up under Anya Renfrew so far though.'

'What about Ramsay? That's her mother's maiden name, but she might have adopted it too, if she was trying to keep things secret.'

'Good point, sir. I'll get right on that.'

'Thanks. You'll let me know as soon as you've got anything, right?' McLean knew the question was unnecessary, but he could feel the puzzle slipping away from him, not coming together as he would have liked. Each new detail they uncovered only added to the mystery.

'You don't know anything about this folk club Renfrew goes to every week, do you?' he asked before Harrison could escape.

She shook her head slowly. 'First I've heard of it, sir.'

'Never mind. I'll speak to Gregg, see if she knows any more than she told me yesterday. Ask around though, will you? Apparently they have an open mic night on a Tuesday. Might be worth a visit if we can find out where it is.'

There was no sign of DS Gregg in the canteen, and not much in the way of food left either. McLean nabbed a sorry-looking apple and a banana that was more brown spot than yellow, adding a healthy chocolate bar to the lunch haul at the last minute. He took his spoils back up to his office on the third floor, along with a mug of coffee that was less tarry than the stuff lurking in the bottom of his filter machine.

The paperwork arranged in neat piles around his desk and on the conference table across the room from it reminded him that there was a lot more going on than the search for Anya Renfrew. He found it hard to concentrate on anything else though, drawn in by the mystery of her disappearance and the double life it had revealed. It took a moment to find her personnel file in among the overtime sheets. He opened it out, staring at the scant information within. Fruit forgotten, he munched on the chocolate and washed it down with bitter coffee.

'Who are you, Anya Renfrew?'

He'd not been expecting a response, but no sooner had he asked the question than his phone buzzed in his pocket. By the time he'd put down his coffee mug, balanced the half-eaten chocolate on the edge of the personnel file and pulled out the handset, it had almost switched itself to voicemail. Something stopped him from letting that happen, and he thumbed the screen to accept the call.

'McLean.'

'Detective Chief Inspector?' The voice was familiar. 'It's Doctor Graham here. From Bestingfield?'

He tensed, knowing what was coming next. He didn't like being rude, but he would be if it became necessary.

'How can I help you, Doctor?'

'It's . . .' She paused a while, no doubt looking for the right words. 'Well, you know it's about Norman Bale, right? And I know you don't want anything to do with him. I've read the case notes. I can understand. And normally I'd respect that decision and not bother you again.'

There was a 'but' coming. McLean didn't need to be a detective of many decades' experience to know that. He let the silence grow. Dr Graham would fill it soon enough.

'He was very animated in this morning's session, you see. Much more so than normal. He's usually just, well, quiet and laid back. Serene, even.'

McLean couldn't quite square that with the man who'd tried to cut him open with a large and very sharp hunting knife. The lunatic who'd nailed a priest to a cross and hooked a man up to a machine that slowly drained all the blood from his body. Serene wasn't quite the word he'd have chosen.

'But this morning he was agitated. Asked me repeatedly if I'd spoken to you. Told me I had to make contact again, pass on a message.'

And so it goes. McLean rubbed at his forehead with his free hand. Part of him wanted to hang up and block Dr Graham's phone number, even though he knew that this wasn't really her fault. Another, smaller, part of him wanted to know what madly inventive idea the man who claimed to be Norman Bale had come up with, what insane story he thought would grab his attention. But then what? There was no way in hell he'd actually visit the secure psychiatric unit, and even less chance anything Bale did or said could change the fact he was going to die behind bars.

'His exact words were: "The scarlet woman is still alive, but her life is in danger." That's what he asked me to tell you. I wouldn't normally play along with these things, certainly didn't agree that I'd speak to you. But, well, I guess I'm speaking to you.'

McLean stared down at the open file in front of him. Anya Renfrew looked back in black-and-white, head on, unflattering.

'Is that exactly what he said?' he asked after an awkward silence. 'Those were the words he used.'

'I record all my sessions, Chief Inspector. Would you like to hear this morning's?'

'No. That won't be necessary. I don't know you, Doctor Graham, but I imagine you know how to do your job. You wouldn't bring this up if you thought it wasn't important. So tell me, why do you think it's important? Why does Bale think it's important, for that matter?'

'As I said before, normally he's quiet, introspective. Serene isn't a word I use lightly, but it fits. Bale's a man who seems to have come to terms with his situation, accepted it. He is deeply religious. Well, you know that he believed he was doing God's work when he killed those people.'

McLean bit back the retort he wanted to make to that. Telling a psychiatrist that their patient is nuts would be much like telling your father not to patronise you.

'I'm aware of his psychosis, Doctor. It's a poor justification for murder however you look at it.'

Dr Graham paused a while before answering, either calming herself or considering his dismissal. 'It's not my job to judge him. I've been working with him for over a year now and he's fallen into a pattern. That is, until this week. Something's got to him, but he won't tell me what. Just says he needs to speak to you.'

McLean tried pinching the bridge of his nose, closing his eyes, but the problem refused to go away. 'That's not going to happen, Doctor Graham. I hope you can find a way to break the news to him that doesn't upset his therapy. In the meantime, I'm going to need a list of all the people who've visited him in the past week, all the other inmates he's associated with, and who's visited them too.'

The silence that followed on from his words lasted long enough that McLean was tempted to take the phone from his ear and check the call was still connected. Finally, Dr Graham made a noise halfway between a cough and a gasp.

'There is someone missing, isn't there? A woman.'

'As I said, Doctor Graham. I'll need to see a list of all the people who've visited Bale, and who he regularly interacts with. If he's being fed information so he can go through you to get at me, then I need to put a stop to it.'

Another long silence, then the doctor spoke again. 'I'll see what I can find out for you, Chief Inspector. But, as far as I know, Bale's had no visitors in months. He has no family, after all. As to his fellow inmates, as you describe them. Well, I prefer the term patients. And they don't mix much. He's something of a loner. Doesn't really talk to anyone unless he has to. I'll ask around the nursing staff though. They'll know better the day-to-day goings on than me.'

'Thank you. I'd appreciate that. And please, if you can, keep this to yourself for now, OK?'

'I . . . Of course. I'd not talk about one of my patients with anyone who wasn't directly involved. I'll let you know as soon as I've spoken to the staff.'

'Thank you, Doctor Graham.' McLean started to say something else, but this time the line really had gone dead.

13

'So help me, Gavin Mason, if you're on that damned computer again, I'll have your da' chuck it in the bin.'

Wee Gav looks at his mate Bobby and rolls his eyes. It's the holidays. There's no homework. What's the point in having an Xbox if you can't use it? He can hear the heavy thump of his mum's footsteps on the stairs though, which means she's in a bad mood again. Probably been on the phone to Dad.

'We're no' doing anything, Mam.' He grabs the controller from Bobby's hand, shoves both of them under a heap of clothes on the floor and switches off the telly before the door swings open. That's the one good thing about his mam; she moves slowly.

'Whit're the two of youse doing? It's a braw day out there. Go on and get some fresh air.'

'Come on, Gav.' Bobby's on his feet in an instant, wiry thin in a way Gav will never be. 'We was just goin' out anyways, Mrs M.'

'I'm no' Mrs M any more, Bobby. You know that.'

He shrugs uncomfortably, and Gav knows why. It's weird calling your mate's mum by her first name. Disrespectful.

'Sorry, Sheila.' Bobby grins as he squeezes past and out the door. Gav has to endure a hand ruffling his hair and a quick hug as he follows.

'Dinner's at five. You be back in time, mind?'

'Aye, Mum. Nae worries.'

Bobby's outside, already straddling his bike when Gav catches up with him. 'What we gonnae do? Can't go back to mine.'

Gav fetches his bike from the garage, helmet swinging from the handlebars. 'I dunno. Could go up the glen mebbe? Go see if we can break intae the loony bin.'

'Aye, and they'll lock you up if they catch you.' Bobby laughs like he's mad, and then he's pedalling off at high speed. Gav shoves the helmet on his head, not bothering with the strap, and sets off after his friend. Bobby's a pain most of the time, but he's OK. As long as he doesn't take a turn.

It's probably better being out in the sunshine than shut away in his stinky old bedroom, but Gav wouldn't admit to that. He wouldn't admit to being less fit than Bobby either, but his pal's way ahead, and only stops when they get to the place they know they can hide the bikes and climb through a gap in the fence. No one's supposed to go into the old hospital any more. Not since the fires and the explosion that shook the town a few years back. That just makes it even more cool to come here though. They're not the only ones, judging by the litter strewn about, dog ends and worse.

'Sweet. Look what somebody's dropped.'

Gav's a bit out of breath by the time he reaches Bobby, and more than a little sweaty. His friend looks just like he always does, except for the light in his eyes, the expression on his face. He shows Gav something shiny lying in the palm of his hand. A metal box, engraved with some capital letters, and a date written underneath, but he can't read them. Not before Bobby snatches his find away. Gav knows what it is though. A lighter. A Zippo, that's what his da' calls them. Must be worth a bit.

'Where'd you find it?' he asks, but Bobby's too caught up in flicking open the lid, spinning the wee wheel and laughing at the flame every time it appears. Gav knows what's going to happen next. It always does when Bobby gets like this.

'Wannae see something mental?'

The question's not meant to be answered. They did something in school about that, Gav thinks. Can't remember what the word for it was. Doesn't matter anyways. He can tell this is going to end badly.

They're in a clearing, the mesh fence with its barbed wire top behind them. A few old trees loom overhead, but they're mostly dead or dying. Gorse bushes cluster around them, a narrow path barely showing through the spiky green thorns and those weird yellow flowers that smell of coconut.

'Bobby, gonnae no do that.' Gav's already stepping back towards the fence and the loose gash in it they squeezed through.

'How no?' Bobby's kneeling down now, hand stretched under the nearest bush. Gav hears the flick, flick, flick of the lighter, then wisps of smoke start to weave up through the thick spikes. There's a moment when he thinks it's just going to go out, then the dry stuff catches and the bush seems to explode in flame. Bobby falls back, laughing off his fear as he scrambles over to join Gav. The flames give off thick black smoke, like that time someone set fire to one of the old industrial units down by the river.

'Fuck, look at it go.' Bobby's voice sounds weird against the crackling roar as the flames take hold and rush through the bushes. Soon a swathe twenty feet wide is alight, spreading fast. The black smoke billowing up into the cloudless sky.

'C'mon, Bobby. We gotta go.' Gav grabs his friend by the arm. It's getting hot now, too hot. Bobby resists a moment, then the tension goes out of him, the madness passed.

'Aye, better split before anyone sees us.' He pushes past Gav, through the gap in the fence and away.

14

McLean stared at the personnel file, trying to focus on the words and failing miserably. His mind kept going over the conversation with Dr Graham, and the sudden, unwelcome, return of Norman Bale into his life. He was contemplating ringing the doctor back when a knock at the door startled him into dropping his phone. He looked around to see DS Gregg standing half in, half out the open doorway, wide-eyed in sudden surprise.

'Everything OK, sir?'

'Fine, fine.' He closed the file, picked up the phone and slid it into his jacket pocket.

'Heard you wanted to see me. I take it this is about Anya?'

'Indeed it is. Come in.' He got up and walked over to the conference table, pulling out a chair for Gregg to sit in.

'Would you say you know Renfrew well?' he asked once she'd settled herself. The detective sergeant wasn't normally ill at ease around him, not since he'd carried her unconscious husband out of her house moments before it exploded from a gas leak a few years past. Now she seemed if not nervous then certainly uncomfortable.

'I wouldn't say well, sir. No. Don't think any of us really do.'

'You've been talking about her with the other officers and

support staff, I take it? Comparing notes, things she's said in the past.'

'Aye, and that's the thing, see?' Gregg shifted on her chair as if she had piles. 'The more you speak to people, the more it's like none of us ever knew her at all. I mean, she's good at the job. Always want to have Anya on your team when there's a complicated case unfolding.'

'I've heard she's very well organised.'

'Och, it goes beyond that, sir. She knows the Holmes system better'n anyone. She knows who to speak to at the council, Holyrood, all the other stations in Lothian and Borders. If there's anyone who knows more about how we work than Anya, then I don't know who.'

For some unfathomable reason, McLean didn't find this in the least bit reassuring. 'But nobody knows anything about her life outside work, I take it.'

Gregg shrugged. 'Not much. Judy down in Accounts said something about her mum being in a home after she'd fallen and broken her hip. Didn't know any more details than that. Pete in Records said he'd asked her out once. Got a refusal that was a bit more explicit than he was expecting. Someone told me she broke PC Carter's fingers when he tried to grab her backside once, but that might just be gossip. Oh, and I told you before about her singing.'

'That's actually what I wanted to ask you about. You don't happen to know the name of the club she went to, do you?'

Gregg frowned in concentration for a minute. 'Don't think she ever mentioned the name, but I'm sure she mentioned the Old Town, so it'd have to be Fanny's or the Croon Club, I reckon. Maybe something in the Vaults?'

'Any of those meet regularly on a Tuesday night?'

'I don't know. Can find out soon enough if you want.'

McLean glanced up at the clock on the wall, surprised to see another day heading fast towards evening. 'Thanks. Let me know how you get on. Might be paying a wee visit to a folk club tonight.'

'You got a minute, Jayne?'

Like McLean's own office, Detective Superintendent McIntyre's door was always open. She looked up from a desk even more cluttered than McLean's own, peered at him over the top of a pair of half-moon spectacles.

'Of course, Tony. Come on in. News about Anya?'

McLean thought about remaining on his feet, but it felt a bit awkward towering over his boss. He dragged a chair over from the far wall and sat down before answering.

'I'm not sure.' He told McIntyre about his recent conversation with Dr Graham and the message Norman Bale had insisted she pass on. It made no more sense for the telling a second time.

'He's trying to play with you, that's all.' McIntyre took off her spectacles, carefully folded them and placed them in front of her. 'Best thing you can do is ignore it. Tell this Doctor Graham not to bother you with any more messages. If Bale wants to bend her ear, well, that's what she's being paid for.'

'Don't you think it strange though? That he should know we're looking for a missing woman?'

'Come on, Tony. You know as well as I do just how many people go missing every day. At least half of them are going to be women just from pure statistics. You have Bale's exact words, and they're no better than some sensationalist stage show mindreader. A couple of deliberately vague statements for you to hang your own experience on.'

Put like that, he had to admit McIntyre had a point, and yet his gut instinct told him otherwise. Either that or he was suffering from too much coffee and not enough lunch.

'The timing of it bothers me though. Why now? He's been

locked up for years, so what's set him off? And he didn't just say woman, he said scarlet woman. He's not the sort of person who wastes words.'

'As I recall, the man's a complete nutter. He might just have woken up one morning with a thought to make a nuisance of himself.' McIntyre picked up her spectacles again, fiddled with them but didn't put them on. 'If you want, have a DS look into it. Grumpy Bob's not got much on his hands right now, what with him winding down to the end of the month and all. Why don't you ask him to go and have a word with the hospital staff, see what they have to say about Bale, who he speaks to, who's been to visit. You'll probably get a better picture if he asks rather than your friendly Doctor Graham.'

'Good idea. I'll see if I can prise him out of the basement. Sometimes I reckon he thinks he's retired already, the way he's always in there helping out Dagwood.'

'I'm just happy to have his expertise still available. We've few enough experienced officers as it is.' McIntyre let out a weary sigh that McLean could well appreciate. Budget cuts and restructuring were the only things you could rely on these days.

'But enough of that. How are we getting on with tracking down Anya Renfrew?'

It was McLean's turn to sigh. 'I've a horrible feeling it's going to be one of those complicated cases. The more we find out about her, the less sense it all makes. I've spoken to pretty much all of the staff who worked with her, and it seems she's the very definition of a recluse. Hardly ever socialised with work people out of the office. It's like she lived a completely separate life away from here. One that's the complete opposite of the woman we all thought we knew, if what I found at her house in Joppa is anything to go by.'

'Oh aye?' McIntyre leaned forward, elbows on the desk, spectacles clutched in both hands like a rosary.

'For a start, it looks like she only stays there occasionally. Then there's the stash of . . . How can I put it? . . . unusual clothing we found hidden in the bottom of her wardrobe.' McLean told the detective superintendent about the revealing dresses and the red latex bodysuit.

'You sure they're hers and not . . .' McIntyre trailed off as she realised what she was saying.

'Like I said. It's getting complicated. We're following up on her phone records though. Reckon she might have a place in the New Town somewhere she's been living. I've a couple of DCs looking for it.'

'Keep me up to date on that then. Any other leads?'

'Seems she's a regular at a folk club in the Old Town. DS Gregg's trying to find out which one. I'll pay them a visit.'

McIntyre nodded slowly to herself for a moment, then looked him straight in the eye. 'Normally I'd tell you to get a sergeant to do that, but this is too important. Operation Caterwaul's at a standstill until we know what's happened to her, and you can imagine how popular that is with the top brass. It's costing a fortune, for one thing.'

'Understood. I'll let you know as soon as we have anything.' McLean stood up, put the chair back where he'd got it from and then left the room. Detective Superintendent McIntyre was right, there was a lot at stake. But as far as he was concerned the budgetary worries of the bean-counters and politicians were of much less concern to him than the well-being of one missing woman.

15

'This the place then? Doesn't look like much.'

McLean stood at the top of a long flight of stone steps leading from the Royal Mile down towards Waverly Station, one of the many narrow closes that criss-crossed the Old Town. A dozen steps down, a nondescript plywood door in bad need of a lick of paint was propped open with a mop bucket, nothing to indicate what went on behind it other than an antique wall lamp that looked too out of place to be original.

'It's early, sir. Place probably won't really wake up till ten.'

DC Gregg still wore her work clothes; a sensible trouser suit and white blouse that wouldn't be out of place in any office within a mile of where they stood. And yet somehow she managed to look like she was off duty. It took him a while to realise that she'd untied her hair and let it drop so that it hung past her shoulders. So much for being trained in observation skills.

'Well, I hope there's someone here. Bit of a wasted trip otherwise.' He checked his watch, not quite eight yet. He'd already texted Emma to let her know what was going on, but he'd rather get this over and done with, head home at a reasonable hour.

The door opened onto a narrow lobby with an unmanned counter to one side. A sign on the wall above it read 'Fanny's Folk Club' in gaudy painted letters laid over a picture of a smiling woman's head. Her fifties hairstyle and bright-red lipstick made McLean think this might not be his kind of joint.

'Think it's this way, sir.' Gregg pointed to a set of stone steps leading down into a basement. He followed her, ducking under the narrow, arched ceiling. How on earth could a place like this be legal? It was a health and safety nightmare, surely.

Another door at the bottom of the stairs opened onto a large room with a vaulted ceiling held up by fat stone pillars. A low stage at one end faced a bar at the other, intimate tables arranged in between them to give the place the feel of a 1920s speakeasy. All it needed to complete the image was for someone to turn the lights down. And a few more people of course.

'We don't open till half eight. Sorry. You'll have to come back then.' A young woman dressed in the kind of clothes McLean imagined Fanny on the sign upstairs would wear weaved a path through the tables from the far side of the room towards them. She smiled, and pointed a finger at the ceiling. 'You can get a drink in the pub if you want.'

'Actually, we're not here for the club.' McLean showed the woman his warrant card. 'I was wondering if I might ask a few questions about one of your regulars. Anya Renfrew?'

He'd been hoping the name might spark a look of recognition, but the woman merely frowned. 'Not sure I know her.'

'Perhaps this might help?' Gregg held up a photo, a copy of the head shot in Renfrew's personnel file. The young woman peered at it a moment, then took it from the detective sergeant and held it under a nearby light. Finally something like recognition dawned.

'Oh aye. That's Grace, so it is. Never seen her look so dowdy, mind. Where's this photo from?'

'That's not important.' McLean took the photograph away. 'You say she calls herself Grace? Do you know what surname she uses?'

The young woman frowned in concentration again. 'Not off the top of my head. It'll be in the register though, I'd imagine. She was here last week and everyone who sings signs in.'

She set off towards the bar without telling them to follow. McLean did anyway, catching up with her as she stepped behind the counter and bent down to fetch out a heavy leather-bound notebook. Licking an absent-minded finger, she flicked through the pages. 'Last Tuesday, last Tuesday. Ah. Here we are.' The finger traced down a list of names, all written in different hands. 'Grace, Grace, Grace, yes. There. Grace Ramsay. Knew she'd been here. Great voice has Grace. Always popular with the punters.'

'And she's a regular, is she?'

'Fairly, aye.'

'Does she come alone? Or is she part of a group?'

'I couldn't say really. See this place in half an hour or so, it's heaving. We really need to move to a bigger venue, but this is where Fanny started it all, so here's where it'll stay. I'm that busy checking them all in, keeping an eye on the numbers and that. Don't exactly pay attention to who's coming wi' who.'

'What about the other names on the register next to Ren— . . . next to Ramsay's? They regulars too?'

The young woman looked back at the book. 'I see where you're coming from. I'm no' sure I should be giving out these, mind. Isn't there some data protection or something?'

'I could get a warrant, if it helps. This is kind of important though. She's gone missing, you see. Grace, that is. We urgently need to find her.'

'Well, you can wait here and she'll like as not walk in through the door before nine.' The young woman gave a little laugh that died on her lips almost as quickly as it was born. 'She's no' coming tonight, is she?'

'How's about I stay, sir?' Gregg said in the awkward silence that followed.

'What?'

'I can stay. I'll stand behind the counter with . . .' She waved her hand at the young woman.

'Dolores.' She rolled her eyes. 'And before you ask, yes, that's my real name.'

'Well, I'll stay here with Dolores, and she can introduce me to anyone who knows An— . . . Grace.' Gregg turned to the young woman. 'That OK?'

'Knock yourself out.' She looked at her watch. 'They'll be starting soon enough.'

As if on cue, a grey-haired man appeared through a door on the far side of the room, followed by a couple more carrying cases McLean assumed contained musical instruments. It being a speakeasy, they could have been hiding something else entirely though. Dolores went to speak to them, taking the ledger with her.

'You sure about this?' McLean asked of Gregg.

'Aye, it'll be fun. Might even have a go myself.'

'Well, I hope you won't be too upset if I don't hang around for that. And don't stay out carousing into the wee small hours. I'll need an update before tomorrow morning's briefing.'

The band started tuning up as McLean was leaving the club for the short walk back to the station. They sounded professional enough, but the music wasn't really to his taste. In truth, Gregg had done him a favour, even if her approach to the investigation was somewhat unorthodox. This way he could get home at a decent hour, earlier even than he'd promised Emma. Their fragile relationship seemed to be on the mend, but he had a hunch the search for Anya Renfrew was going to be one of those difficult cases leading to late nights and earlier starts, weekends something other people experienced. He'd been doing his best to be there for her, to spend time together, go out and do stuff of an evening. It wouldn't take much though to undo all the hard work he'd put in over the past few months.

He had climbed into his Alfa and was reaching for the starter button when a tap at the window stopped him. He looked round to see a man standing by the passenger window, bent down so that he could peer in. Despite the hour, it was still light enough for McLean to know that he'd never seen him before. They were in the station car park though, which meant he probably wasn't some random stranger looking for a lift.

'Can I help you?' he asked, once he'd found the right button for the window and wound it down a few inches.

'Detective Chief Inspector McLean, I presume.' American accent, difficult to place beyond that. Even so, it wasn't hard to work out why he was here.

'I'm on my way home. Can it wait until tomorrow?' McLean knew it couldn't, but asked anyway.

'Just wanted a chat. Won't take long.' The man stood up straight, waved a hand at the Alfa's swooping bonnet, then leaned back to the window. 'Nice car. Always did like the way Italians make 'em.'

Suppressing the annoyed sigh he knew wouldn't help the situation, McLean leaned over and popped open the passenger door. 'You can chat while I drive then. How you get back's up to you.'

The man climbed in, pulled on his seat belt and clunked the door shut as McLean started the engine. The bass rumble of the V6 brought a smile to his passenger's lips.

'Yeah. That's what I thought. Much sweeter than anything we make.' He leaned around and held out a hand. 'Brad Fenwick.'

McLean looked at the hand, then at the man. It would be rude not to shake it, he supposed. And probably not wise.

'What can I do for you, Mr Fenwick?'

'Drive home, for starters. Don't want to keep your missus waiting.'

McLean let that one slide, for now. 'I take it this is about Anya Renfrew, your precious Operation Caterwaul.'

Fenwick held up his hands in mock surrender. 'Hey, that's your code name, not mine. I'm just concerned it's all going south before it's even started.'

'I don't think Renfrew's disappearance is anything to do with the operation.' McLean pulled out into the traffic, resisting the temptation to accelerate hard and shake up his unwanted passenger.

'Yeah, that's what your superintendent told me you'd say. Not quite sure how you come to that conclusion though.'

'My gut?' McLean waited for a sarcastic comment, but none came. 'Look, I know there's a lot tied up in this operation.'

'You have no idea.'

Something about the way Fenwick said the words made McLean a little more sympathetic towards the man. He knew that put-upon feeling all too well. 'So what's the story then? You CIA?'

'Best you don't ask. The point is, I've been sent over to keep an eye on you poor little small-town cops, make sure you're doing your job properly. That's what my bosses want, and they don't care how patronising it sounds. You guys don't need my help and certainly don't want me looking over your shoulders the whole time. But this missing clerk of yours? That's got people worried.'

'It's got me worried, but for her safety, not the operation.'

'Yeah, well. All I'm saying is, don't be surprised if people start leaning on you hard. The types I work with, they want results and they want them now. Earlier if they can. They'll also be lining up someone to take the rap if it all heads south.'

'Why are you telling me this, Mr Fenwick?'

The American said nothing for a while, which McLean took as a good sign. Easier to blurt out a prepared lie than work out the best way to tell the truth.

'What do you know about Operation Caterwaul?' he asked eventually.

'Not as much as you, I'd guess. We're logistical support more than anything, and the whole thing's being run on a need-to-know basis. I do have sufficient seniority to know that it's a multi-agency investigation into money laundering and tax evasion on a massive scale. Billions of pounds, or dollars, or whatever.'

Fenwick laughed. 'I'd heard that about you, McLean. Can I call you Tony?'

'If it keeps you happy. It's my name.'

'You know as well as I do what we're dealing with here. Dirty money, most of it Russian, but some of it from South American drugs. All being funnelled through certain corporations and banks, back and forth until it's almost impossible to tell where it first came from. And up at the top of the pyramid, there's some very powerful and influential people. The sort of people who don't think twice about permanent solutions to their problems, if you get my meaning.'

'That why we raided the accountants in Aberdeen? You think this money's going through some of the big oil companies? Or would it have more to do with the leisure industry? Golf courses and luxury hotels?'

'That's above both of our pay grades, Tony.' Fenwick pointed to the roadside up ahead. 'You can drop me off here. I'll make my own way home.'

16

McLean watched the spook walk away down the road in the direction of Morningside until he disappeared out of sight around a corner. A few moments later a black Mercedes with tinted windows and diplomatic plates glided slowly past, so clearly Brad Fenwick was as much showman as spy. The message was no less worrying for that.

It didn't exactly surprise him that the Americans were jittery about Operation Caterwaul. McLean wasn't nearly senior enough to have the top security clearance, but it didn't take a genius to see what they were really after. Money laundering on a national scale meant state operators. That the initial fact-finding accountancy raids had taken place in Aberdeen and Ayr suggested a target he didn't particularly want to think about. Profiles didn't get much higher than that, and neither did stakes. No wonder they were nervous about Renfrew's untimely disappearance.

He had pulled over to the kerb not far from the church. It was only a hundred yards or so to his front gate, home and Emma waiting. And yet McLean found himself turning off the engine, settling back in the leather seat. He stared sightlessly out of the windscreen and let his thoughts roam, free from the distractions of the station, the worries of his personal life.

Despite what everyone thought, the Americans included,

he wasn't convinced that Renfrew's disappearance had anything to do with the operation. She was too junior, too peripheral to compromise anything. That didn't mean it was any less urgent they track her down. She could well be in trouble, and she certainly had some questions to answer about her double life. Why was she pretending to be her mother? What was she trying to hide?

McLean drummed his fingers idly on the steering wheel. The inside of the car had been cool while the engine was running, chilled by the air conditioning. Now it was rapidly turning into a sauna, cooked by the evening sun and the reflected heat off the stone wall that separated the graveyard from the road and kept the dead from escaping. He reached forward to tap the button that would bring the V6 engine back into life, then stopped. Something had caught his eye and it took a moment for him to focus on what it was.

The air was thick and warm as he stepped out of the car, closed and locked the door. No other traffic moved along the road, and if it hadn't been for the background roar of the city, he might have been in a well-to-do village in the middle of nowhere. The church wall came up to his shoulder, topped by iron railings. Beyond the church boundary, these gave way to thick laurel hedge, only recently trimmed. A few leaves still scattered the pavement where the gardener hadn't tidied up properly.

Except that there was no gardener looking after the grounds around that particular house. Nobody had been in there for at least a couple of years, as far as McLean was aware. He walked up towards the gate that opened onto the house where Norman Bale had lived, and stared up at the empty building. The window frames had been painted, the ivy cleared from the walls, the lawn mown. A lot of effort had been put into making it presentable. Given that Bale himself was unlikely to be returning any time soon, that could only mean one thing. He couldn't imagine who would want to buy the place, not with its history, but it was clearly about to go up for sale.

McLean retraced his steps, then carried on past his car and up to the house on the other side of the church. If anyone knew what was going on, it would be the minister. And if she wasn't in, he could put a detective constable on to Bale's solicitor for answers. It was too much of a coincidence that the man should resurface now, eager to speak to him.

'Tony. What a nice surprise.'

Mary Currie wore a flour-dusted apron over her black shirt and clerical collar. A patch of flour smeared across her forehead where she'd pushed away her grey hair without thinking, and McLean found it hard not to stare.

'It's been a while,' he said. 'I trust you're well.'

'As well as anyone can be in this heat. And someone thought it would be a good idea to have a bake sale to raise funds.' The minister shrugged to indicate that the someone had been her. 'Would I be right in thinking this isn't a social call? I notice Emma's not with you.'

'I was just on my way home actually. Couldn't help noticing they've tidied up the Bale house.'

Mary Currie's smile disappeared, the flour creasing on her forehead as she frowned. She paused a moment as if making a difficult decision, then stepped to one side and indicated for him to enter.

'Why don't you come in for a cup of tea, eh?'

McLean remembered the last time he had been in the rectory kitchen all too well. It was a comfortable room, well lived in, if a little warm given the weather. Mary Currie had opened the windows wide, letting a lazy breeze in from the graveyard beyond, but it didn't do much to cool the air.

'You've been busy.' McLean indicated the large table, covered in enough scones, cakes, shortbread and other baked goods to feed an army. The smell was enough to make his mouth water.

'The bring-and-buy's on Saturday morning, if you and Emma would like to come.' The minister filled the kettle and plugged it in, searched in the cupboards for mugs and tea bags.

'I'll see what we can do. Been trying to get out and about a bit more.'

He was all too aware that they were skirting around the subject. The minister had been involved in the Bale case too, had seen up close and personal the horror of his madness. He'd sat at this very table, sharing tea and platitudes with one of her prayer groups while sizing up his next victim.

'Do you hear much from Daniel?' he asked after the kettle had finished its noisy boiling.

'Bits and pieces. The bishop found him a nice little parish up in the Perthshire hills. Keeps himself to himself. He took a long time to heal physically. Mentally, I think that's still a work in progress.'

McLean could only imagine what being crucified in your own church would do to your mental state. He could remember the sight all too well. At least that had been the end of Bale's killing spree.

'There's been painters and workmen at the house for a couple of weeks now. Surprised you didn't notice before.' The minister placed a mug of tea on the table in front of him, pulled out a seat and sat down. McLean paused a while before doing the same.

'My route to work takes me the other way. And you know I don't really do church.'

Mary Currie smiled at that. 'Not unless you have to. I know. Your gran was the same.' She took a sip of tea, stared at the endless baked goods for a moment, but didn't succumb to temptation. 'The man clipping the hedge today said it was going on the market next week. Reckons somewhere north of two million pounds, if you can believe that?'

McLean could. The property market in Edinburgh had exploded in recent times, especially at the top end. Where all the money was coming from was another question. Although maybe the constant cuts to public services had something to do with it.

'Bale's tried to get in touch with me recently. I can't help thinking this is no coincidence.' He explained the details to the minister, wondering as he did if this counted as some kind of confession. Wrong denomination of course. For her part, Mary Currie gave him the time and space, not interrupting as he unfolded the tale. Only when he was sure he'd finished did she speak.

'I know I'm supposed to give people the benefit of the doubt. It's kind of the job description really. Second chances and redemption, atonement for sins. That said, I share your scepticism with regards to Norman.' She took another sip of tea, perhaps waiting for McLean to say something. When he didn't, she carried on.

'It's possible all this, selling up the family home, reaching out to you as his last link to childhood, all of it might be his way of seeking forgiveness. But if that's the case, then who is he asking it from? And why now?'

'That's the first thing I thought of too. I checked with the psychiatric hospital. He's in good health physically, not had any recent brushes with death to remind him of his mortality. If something's set him off, I've no idea what it is.'

'What do you remember about him?'

'Apart from the fact he was a complete nutter?' McLean shook his head, knowing that wasn't what Mary Currie meant. 'He was obsessed with saving peoples' souls. At least that was the reason he gave for killing all those people. Something about apotheosis.'

'He believed he could see when a person was blessed, that

God directed him to such people precisely so that he could hasten their journey to heaven before they became corrupted again.' The minister looked into her empty tea mug for inspiration, found none. 'As you say, a complete nutter. But he was absolutely certain he was doing the right thing. Until you stopped him.'

'Do you think he wants revenge then?' McLean followed the thought out into the many different ways a man of Bale's capabilities could make his life a misery. It wasn't a happy trail.

'No. Not revenge. That's not the Norman I remember. He considered himself above such things.'

'So if not revenge, then what does he want?'

The minister shrugged. 'I don't know, Tony. But I'd hazard a guess that whatever it is, it's not about you or the house. No, if I know anything about Norman at all, it's that he's only ever really been concerned with himself.'

McLean found Emma sitting at the kitchen table when he let himself in half an hour later. She looked up almost guiltily, eyes wide with surprise.

'Hello, stranger. Wasn't expecting you home for hours yet.'

A quick glance at the clock showed that she was being a little unfair, but there was no hint of scorn in her voice this time.

'I'd have been a bit earlier, but I stopped off at the vicarage.'

'Oh yes? Something I should know?' That was more of the old Emma. A slightly sarcastic and joking tone he'd missed in the months since her miscarriage. She stood up as she spoke, but didn't come to give him a hug. Instead she started clearing up the teapot, mugs and plates scattered around the table.

'Visitors?' he nodded at the collection.

'You first.'

'Fair enough.' He told her about Norman Bale and the house for sale on the other side of the church. It occurred to him as he did so that she'd been away for the whole of that episode, travelling the world in search of answers to a question he still didn't quite understand himself.

'I noticed them working on that house. Wondered what was going on. Can't imagine anyone wanting to live there though. Not after . . .' She trailed off, not needing to elaborate.

'Well, we caught Bale in the church, and the minister knew him. Knew his parents too, for that matter. It was a useful chat. I think.' He helped her with the last mug and plate, carrying them over to the dishwasher as she started to load it. 'Oh, and she's having a bring-and-buy on Saturday morning. Coffee and cakes sort of thing. If you're interested?'

'Are you asking me out to church on a date, Tony McLean?' Emma nudged him in the ribs, and her smile was a welcome sight after months of frowns.

'That depends on who you've been secretly inviting round to tea.'

'This?' She held up the last mug before bending down to put it with the others. 'Just Professor Turner dropped by. She helped me with my application for the postgrad course, which is probably against the rules or something. We got chatting about forensics and the afternoon just disappeared.'

'And of course she didn't tell any tall tales about me at all.'

Emma stood up straight, leaned in and gave him a peck on the cheek. 'Your name might have come up. Once or twice.'

She walked away, out through the kitchen door. McLean watched her go, a little bemused and a little pleased. Her mood was much improved, and if it took her finding out embarrassing secrets from his youth to do that, then it was a price he was happy to pay.

17

She awakes in darkness and in pain. Her whole body aches as if she's been tumbled down a hill a mile long. Breathing sends little jabs of agony through her chest, like knives sewn between her ribs. Her face burns from a thousand cuts, each daubed with acid. She tries to reach up and feel her cheeks, certain they must be scarred and hideous, and that is when she realises she is trapped.

The panic only brings more pain as she struggles against unseen bonds. Something holds her down, keeps her arms tight by her sides, her legs pinned together. Only her feet are free to move, and bare with it. Wherever she is, it is cold enough that her toes have gone numb. And it's dark, so dark. She can see nothing.

'Help.'

Her voice sounds like someone else. Someone turned hoarse by shouting, husky by decades of cigarettes and whisky. It's a voice that reminds her of her mother more than anyone. Certainly not herself.

'Help. Please.'

She tries to move again, but the pain brings flashes of light to the darkness, swirling and darting around her like maddened faeries. The stabbing in her chest grows worse, the swaddling that holds her down making every breath a strain. What happened to her? Where is she? How did she get here?

She remembers the car park in the woods. The men and their insatiable needs. Her own insatiable needs too, the guilt she has to burn out of herself with sin. Was it one of them who did this to her? No. It was the car. Battery dead. And then the trees, the forest, something chasing her, getting closer. The panic that had gripped her then begins to swell once more, and she thrashes around heedless of the agony. For an instant that is a lifetime, she imagines some great beast, some spider from myth, has caught her, poisoned her, wrapped her tight in a cocoon of strongest silk. Even now the toxins pumped into her body are dissolving her from the inside, and soon the great beast will return, drink her dry.

How long she lies in the darkness she cannot know. Time has no meaning here, and all she has is her pain. If she drifts off to sleep it is fitful and no release. The pain of her dreams is indistinguishable from the pain of her waking. She is dead, she knows. This is hell, her punishment for a life of lies and depravity. It will never end.

And then she hears footsteps, muffled by distance or some kind of door. For a moment she considers shouting, but the jabbing in her chest stops her. That and a realisation that it's far more likely whoever brought her here is returning to see whether she has woken. It seems unlikely they're here to rescue her.

Faintest light flickers in her peripheral vision, enough to show a rough stone wall close by, arching over her head to a low ceiling. She strains to move, tilts her head backwards until she can make out the shape of a door lined by brightness. There is a jangling of keys, one slotted into a lock. It clicks and the door swings open. She can't focus on the figure that stands in the doorway, and the burning in her chest is too much to keep her head tipped back so far.

'You're awake. Thank the Lord. We weren't sure if you'd make it.'

The voice sparks a memory. Knocking on a cottage door in the dead of night. Why is she here and not in a hospital?

'Please –'

'Shh. Don't try to move. You were badly injured. Don't want to risk a rib puncturing one of your lungs now.'

A man's voice, soft and low. She can't see him as he shuffles into the room, but the light spreads from outside, showing more of her surroundings. The stone is covered in thick white paint. It vaults overhead, the highest point marked by a bare bulb in a light fitting that is as old as the man crouching beside her. He reaches out, and she catches a whiff of something from him that she can't immediately place. Whatever it is, it wakes a primal fear deep inside her. She struggles, tries to move away from him before he can touch her face. But the blankets wound around her are too tight. She is trapped, helpless.

'Don't.' His tone is chiding, like one might admonish a child. As he speaks, his fingers brush over the skin of her cheek, her forehead, feeling the scars on her face. She cannot recoil from it, head pushed hard into the pillow as she tries. He examines her for what feels like hours, his fingers gentle but probing. There's a skill to his touch, a familiarity that isn't medical.

'Here. You need to drink. Clean out your system so you can heal.' He presses a cup to her lips, and as the liquid trickles into her mouth she realises she is parched. She drinks as deep as she can, each swallow a little less painful than the last. Too late, she understands there is something in the water to take away the pain. Something to lull her off to sleep. No refuge there from the demons that haunt her.

18

They shouldn't be here. Wee Gav's heard stuff about these woods, how they play tricks on you. Folk get lost and are never seen again. He didn't want to come here, but Bobby dared him, and he doesn't want to be called feart. Still, he'd rather be home playing on the Xbox.

'Hey, Gav. Look.' Bobby's in the car park, his bike leaning against a tree. Gav doesn't really want to look, but he pedals up anyway.

'What?'

'Rubber johnnies. They's thoosands of them.' Bobby has a stick, and he's prodding at the little plastic blobs strewn around the base of the tree like some weird rotting fruit. It smells of piss and something else. Like that tramp Gav saw last time he was in the city. Young bloke wrapped up in a filthy sleeping bag. Big old dog lying beside him. Mum had dragged him away muttering something under her breath about druggies and wasters. Didn't seem fair on the dog.

'That's boggin'. Come on, Bobby. Let's go. Ah dinnae like this place.'

'You a wee feartie, Gav? Come on. It's just a johnny.' Bobby hooks one with the end of the stick, picks it up and twirls it around.

'Aye, but someone's used it, right? That's been on someone's cock. There's some bloke's cum in there.'

'Eww. Ya dirty bastard.' Bobby whips the stick around, trying to fling the slimy little parcel at Gav. It shoots off the end, but misses, disappearing into a nearby bush. And, anyway, Gav's ducked.

'Fuck off, Bobby, ya wee fud.' He shoves a foot in the pedal, kicks off and bikes away as quick as he can. Only when he's made a bit of distance between himself and his friend does he realise he's going the wrong way.

'Hey. What's that over there?' Bobby's caught up already, over-taking and speeding through the gaps in the trees. Gav follows even though he doesn't want to. Doesn't want to be on his own even more. He's heard the stories about these woods. More'n the folk who left the johnnies behind. His da' told him about when they found bones buried under an old oak tree. Human bones. Gav reckons it's just his da' trying to stop him coming here. Grown-ups lie like that all the time. He still disnae like it.

'Whoa. Check this out.' Bobby's stopped now, alongside a parked car, tucked away in a spot that's more clearing than car park, deeper in the woods. Before Gav can say anything, he's reached out and pulled the handle. 'It's no' locked, see.'

Gav approaches more slowly, staring into the trees and all around. The car's owner's got to be somewhere near if they've not locked it, surely? But there's nothing. The only sound is the birds, and there's not many of them. That's another reason he disnae like these woods. They're too quiet. Dead quiet.

'See me, I can drive.' Bobby's dumped his bike now and climbed into the driving seat. Gav's expecting an alarm to sound or something, but it doesn't happen.

'Come away, Bobby. They'll be back soon. Don't wannae get caught.'

'Ah ye wee chicken, Gav. There's naebody here. Must've gone off intae the woods for a shag. Dirty bastards.'

'An' left the car unlocked?'

'Aye, well, there's nothin' in here 'cept this wee bag.' Bobby reaches over to the passenger footwell and comes back with his prize, opens it up and peers inside. 'Aww man, that's fuckin' boak.'

Gav's not so lucky this time, as Bobby chucks the bag out of the car. Fair's fair, he probably wasn't trying to hit him but the bag smacks his leg with a wet slap and a handful of used johnnies fall out over his foot. It stinks of rubber and something else, and the stains darken the blue of his jeans.

'Fuck man, what ye doin'?' Gav falls over in his haste to get away, tangling in his bike frame as he goes. Bobby's no help, the wee fud. He just laughs like it's the funniest thing. Then he falls quiet, a dark grin spreading over his face as he steps out of the car. He shoves a hand in his pocket.

'Let's torch it.' He pulls his hand out again, holding the lighter he found up at the loony bin.

'You fucking mad, Bobby? Let's just go. I wannae get these jeans off, ken?' He points at the slimy mess dribbling down one shin. 'Proper boggin' it is.'

'Aye, and the wee fuckers who left it in here need telt.' Bobby clicks the lighter, the flame reflecting the eager madness in his eyes. He's Gav's best mate, is Bobby, but he's a right mentalist when he gets like this.

'No' havin' anything tae dae wi' it, man.' Gav grabs his bike back up, swings his leg over the crossbar and starts to pedal off towards the road. Home's half an hour away and he already feels sick at the thought of what's on his leg. Bobby overtakes him after less than a minute, screaming like a total nutcase as he whizzes past. Gav looks over his shoulder for a second, sees black smoke already billowing out of the car. How the fuck do they burn so easy?

19

A dull headache squatted like a malevolent toad at the back of McLean's head as he tried to concentrate on the screen of his laptop. True to her word, DS Gregg had left a detailed report of her evening's activities for him, but he was having a hard time making sense of anything. Not enough sleep and too many things on his mind. He'd have liked to have been able to blame it on the whisky, but he'd not touched a drop of alcohol the night before. Another one of Emma's ideas that, while sensible, wasn't much fun.

'Something you should see, sir.' McLean looked up to see DC Harrison standing in the doorway, bright-eyed and bushy-tailed as ever. Only the worried expression on her face ruined it. That and the printout she was carrying.

'Good news, I hope.' McLean tried to inject a little sarcasm into his voice, not difficult given the way he felt.

'It's a report from the IT department. They've been collating a list of all the system access carried out recently by Anya's login.'

'Let me guess. She's been selling our secrets to the Russians.'

Harrison frowned in confusion. 'The Russians?'

McLean reminded himself that the detective constable was almost half his age. The Cold War was a footnote in her history books, not something lived through. 'It's an expression. Not literal Russians, just people who shouldn't have access. What's she been looking into then?'

'Actually, that's all fairly innocuous. Nothing she shouldn't be doing. At least not as far as they could tell.'

'So why do I need to see it then?'

Harrison moved further into the room, offering the printout as if it would make any more sense than the words on his laptop screen. 'It's more the number of systems she has access to, sir. I mean, I know she's worked here a long time, but she seems to have higher security clearance than most of the DIs. And she's got linked accounts on a lot of external systems too. CCTV feed, DVLA database, some of the council records. There's a bunch of others I didn't even know existed.'

McLean took the sheet of paper, rubbing at his forehead as he tried to focus on the tiny print. It was a list, as Harrison had said. It was a very long and comprehensive list too. It brought to mind something that had come up regularly when he'd interviewed the other support staff; that Renfrew was the person you went to if you had a problem, the person who always seemed to know how to sort it. That was the innocent explanation of course.

'Do we know when these were last accessed?' he asked, then noticed a column in the table. A few of the entries were recent, but they weren't particularly sensitive. Most of the rest either hadn't been accessed for months or years, or had nothing logged against them at all.

'Not all of the systems monitor access like that. She could have logged into some of them on Friday and we'd never know.'

'How much of this is relevant to Operation Caterwaul?' McLean stared at the page again, not taking any of it in.

'I'm not sure, sir. That's a bit above my pay grade.'

He let out a weary sigh. This was a smoking gun, if ever there were one. And yet he still didn't believe Renfrew's disappearance was anything to do with the operation. That gut feeling was getting harder to trust as the evidence against her mounted up though. Might she be a mole? Or maybe someone was blackmailing her? Found out about her secret life and was using it to make her do their bidding. No, that was stupid. This wasn't some spy thriller, and Renfrew wasn't important enough to be worth the effort. Except that she did seem to know a lot about everything.

'These accesses have all been revoked now, I take it?'

'Aye, sir. First thing IT did.'

Well, at least that much was going by the book. He handed the list back to Harrison. 'Get that to the operations room, will you? They can pass it on to the other partners. Stakeholders, I should probably say.'

Harrison managed to muster a smile at that, but she looked as worried as he felt. 'What about the senior officers?' she asked.

'Let me worry about them. I want you to go and find Grumpy Bob. He'll probably be in the CCU down in the basement. Think we're going to need to set up an incident room. Start treating this disappearance like the major investigation it's turning into.'

The detective constable brightened immediately at the prospect. Renfrew going missing had upset the whole station, McLean realised. Taking control of the search for her like this would hopefully boost morale as much as improve their chances of finding her.

'I'll get right on it, sir.' She turned to leave.

'One more thing, Constable. You don't know if DS Gregg's in, by any chance?'

'Aye, sir. Saw her heading for the canteen not five minutes ago. You want me to go find her?'

McLean stood up, doing his best to ignore the twinge in his hip as he did so. The coffee machine on the other side of the office hadn't been switched on yet, and still contained the cold tar of yesterday's last brew.

'No, it's OK. I'll go find her myself. Could use some exercise and a half-decent coffee. Besides, I only want to talk to her about singing.'

As Harrison had promised, he found Detective Sergeant Gregg in the canteen, standing in line for breakfast. For someone who'd stayed out late in a folk club, then written up a report and emailed it to her boss, she looked surprisingly chirpy.

'Good time last night, was it?' McLean asked as he joined the queue. He didn't have time to eat anything, but a coffee might help shift the headache, and he could always shove one of those healthy muesli bars on the tray for later. Or some chocolate.

'Oh, it was amazing. Can't wait till next week. I'm going to take Barry along.'

The last, and first, time McLean had met DS Gregg's husband had been a few years back, when he'd carried the unconscious man from their gas-filled house just a few moments before it exploded.

'He a big folk music fan then?' he asked.

'Och, no. But it's so much more than that. Besides, he never goes out much. Just sits and watches telly all evening. Mebbe reads a book if there's nothin' much on. Can't be doing wi' that.'

McLean thought it sounded idyllic, but decided not to say so. 'What about the other regulars then? Any of them know Anya?'

'Grace, remember. She's been using her mum's name. And, aye, there were a couple used to talk to her. Got their names and contact details. It's all in the report I emailed you.'

'Busy morning. I've not had a chance to do much more than skim it so far. They say anything about her we didn't already know?'

'Funny you should mention that, sir. They mostly said what we've heard from everyone else. She kept herself to herself, didn't share much. But there was one – Val Robertson. She didn't really know Grace any better, but she says she lived not far from her. Next street over. Used to see her walking to the corner shop sometimes. A nod and a smile if they passed each other, that sort of thing. Only, she doesn't live in Joppa. Val, that is. She lives in Pilrig.'

McLean shuffled further along the queue, waiting while Gregg ordered an enormous fry-up. Tempting though it was to join her, there really wasn't time. His hand hovered over something made of nuts and fruit that claimed to be delicious. He'd learned the hard way never to believe that sort of claim, and grabbed a couple of chocolate bars instead. Paying for his spoils, he shoved the bars in his pocket and carried the coffee over to where Gregg was already pouring brown sauce over her breakfast.

'This Val Robertson. I don't suppose she gave you an address?' He pulled out a chair, then decided sitting wasn't such a good idea. There was too much else he needed to be doing.

'She wasn't sure exactly which one it was, but it was one of the tenements on Spey Street. Said she'd call me this morning once she'd had a chance to walk down there and have a look.' Harrison chewed a mouthful of bacon and egg for a moment before adding, 'I'll give her a call soon as I've had my breakfast, if that's OK. Shift doesn't start for another half-hour.'

McLean glanced up at the clock on the wall, surprised to find it was still so early. On the other hand, he'd left home before six, Emma fast asleep and with a day off to look forward to. How much nicer it would be to be spending it with her.

'No, that's fine. She's probably not even up yet. Don't rush your breakfast, you'll only regret it later.'

20

'I don't need to tell you that this is very serious, Tony.'

McLean stood on the wrong side of the deputy chief constable's desk, hands clasped behind his back like a schoolboy awaiting detention. It wasn't the first time he'd stood in this office in a similar manner, and neither was Robinson the first senior officer to vent their frustration at him. He'd learned a long time ago, back in his hated boarding school in the south of England, that it was best just to take whatever was said, get it over with and get back to the job. Also best to say nothing unless it was strictly necessary.

'I've had three different ministers on the phone this morning, including the First Minister herself. She at least was polite, but it's clear that this setback's got everyone on edge. You do realise what's at stake here?'

That one had to be answered, McLean knew. He couldn't help but recall the words of the CIA spook, Brad Fenwick, the previous evening. 'I know that some very powerful and influential people are nervous about what Operation Caterwaul is doing, if that's what you mean, sir? There's a lot of egg to go around, a lot of faces.'

Robinson raised a single eyebrow. 'You have a very reserved way of saying things sometimes, McLean. Egg on faces is one thing, but we're talking national reputation on the line here. The kind of people implicated in this investigation will do anything to protect themselves and their interests. They consider themselves above the law.'

'And you honestly think that they'd what? Kidnap a member of the admin staff in one of the many stations and teams giving support to the operation? An operation that's barely begun and which very few people know about. Even I don't know the whole picture.'

Robinson leaned back in his chair. 'Oh come on, McLean. You know who we're really after with this one, don't you?'

'I can guess. And I can understand how Renfrew going missing might get a few people worried, but we'll find her soon enough. I don't believe she's the security risk everyone thinks she is either. I'm more concerned for her welfare.'

Robinson rocked forward so swiftly McLean had to stop himself from flinching. 'That's always the way with you, isn't it? Everyone else is concerned about a threat to national security and all you can think about is some poor wee girl.'

'With respect, sir. She's forty-five, she's not a wee girl. She's worked for the police all her life. Longer than most of the officers here. Ask around the canteen, anywhere in the station. You won't hear a bad word spoken about her.'

'From what I'm hearing she's spent all those years hacking her way into our secure systems. Sounds very much like someone playing a long game. Who knows what sensitive information she's been hoarding? Who she's trying to sell it to. Maybe Operation Caterwaul's the one she's been waiting for. Cashing it in for a nice early retirement.'

McLean closed his eyes, shook his head ever so slightly. He might have reached up and pinched the bridge of his nose, but the self-preservation instinct kicked in before his hand got halfway.

'That's not what's happening here, sir. I know we've got spooks from the NCA and the CIA kicking around, but if you think Renfrew is some kind of spy, you couldn't be more wrong. She's got more security clearance than is perhaps wise for a civilian, but it's only because she's been here so long and is good at her work. And because we're rubbish at revoking access once a job's done. Really, you should read the report from the IT team. Our security protocols are a joke. Renfrew's done us a favour pointing that out to us.'

'Christ, I wish I had your optimism. What about this double life she's been living? Could someone be blackmailing her? I heard there was some kinky stuff involved. Do we need to get Vice in on it too? Christ knows, the budget's been buggered five ways till Tuesday already.'

'Again, my instinct says no, sir. We've locked everything down anyway, so even if someone's trying to use us to find things out, they're not getting anything more.'

Robinson slumped back in his seat, pinched the bridge of his nose. McLean could almost hear the silent prayer.

'We any further on with finding out where she's been living?'

'DS Gregg's chasing up a lead on that, sir. Should have something more by midday, hopefully.'

'Well, keep me up to speed, OK? I need all the ammunition I can get to keep the bloody politicians happy.'

'You'll know as soon as I do, sir.'

The deputy chief constable opened his mouth to say something more, but a light knock at the door stopped him. McLean walked over and opened it before Robinson could react. A slightly bemused-looking DC Harrison stood on the other side.

'Ah, sir. They told me you were here. There's something come up and I thought you needed to know ASAP.' She pronounced the abbreviation as a word, McLean noticed. An affectation that reminded him of the CIA agent, Fenwick.

'Is it about Renfrew?'

'Possibly. We've a report in from Penicuik. Car on fire in a remote spot near Gladhouse Reservoir. Don't think it would have come our way, except that it's the same make and colour as Renfrew's. BMX X3. Dark silver.'

'When did this come in, Constable?' Robinson was on his feet and round his desk with far greater speed than might have been expected from a man of his years.

'Just now, sir. There's a fire crew at the scene, but we've had an all-ports out on the car since we found out about it. First officer on scene called it in. Can't be more than twenty minutes ago.'

McLean glanced at his watch. Mid-morning and all he really wanted was a mug of coffee. 'Get on to the squad car out there, see if they've any better identification for the car. A partial plate will do. If it looks like it might be Renfrew's car, then I want you to head out there and see what's going on. Take Stringer with you if you want, and call in Forensics if necessary.'

Harrison nodded her understanding, and hurried off down the corridor.

'Actually, I think you should head out there yourself.'

McLean turned back to the DCC, surprised by the suggestion. 'Sir?'

'I know, I know. It's not the sort of thing a detective chief inspector should be doing. Your job's to oversee the investigation, it's up to the sergeants and constables to do the legwork. Yes, yes, yes.' Robinson flapped one hand about in a vaguely dismissive manner. 'All that's true, but this is not a normal situation. And besides, you'll end up going out there anyway.'

All too aware of how narrow the road was, McLean parked his Alfa some way back from the scene and walked the last couple of hundred metres. The drive out had been a pleasant one, cocooned in air-conditioned cool, but the distant city shimmered under a fierce midday sun. The stench of burning plastic hung in the air like a threat, a haze of thin oily smoke still wafting up out of the trees at the end of the reservoir. It tickled his throat and pricked at his eyes, reminding him of the dull headache he'd woken to that morning.

Searching for the faintest hint of a breeze and the fresh air it might bring, he stared out over the mirror-smooth waters of Gladhouse Reservoir. It had been years since last he'd been out here. A body in a culvert on the northern bank. All that madness with John Needham and Donald Anderson, peeling back the scabs that had formed over that old wound and letting the bloody memories flow free. Christ, what was the woman's name? He must be getting old if he couldn't remember that. McLean shook his head to loosen the memory, turned away from the reservoir and stepped into the relative shade of the trees.

The car park was empty, save for a couple of police cars. One he recognised as a pool car from the station, which DCs Stringer and Harrison must have used to get there. The other bore the logo of Police Scotland, two uniformed officers leaning against it and chatting. As he approached, the older of the two noticed him and stood up straight. He was equally tall as DC Lofty Blane, his short-cropped hair turning grey, face ruddy with a summer spent as much outdoors as in.

'Detective Insp—... Chief Inspector McLean, sir. Beg pardon. Sergeant Donaldson. We met a few years back. Body in the water in Roslin Glen.'

McLean shook the outstretched hand, tried and failed to recall anything about the sergeant. 'Donaldson? Were you involved in the case at the other end of the reservoir too? What was that poor woman's name?'

'Audrey Carpenter? Aye. That was old Sergeant Needham, wasn't it?'

'Indeed it was. A sorry business all round.' McLean winced at the memory, tried to move the conversation on to less painful things. 'I hear you've got a car we're interested in?'

'Up through the trees, sir. Just past the fire engine. You can't miss it. The two detective constables are already up there.' Donaldson pointed into the trees where dappled shade was making a good job of camouflaging everything. It couldn't hide the stench of burning though.

'You're maintaining a cordon, I take it?' McLean asked, aware that no other vehicles had come near since he'd arrived. This spot was remote, tucked away even from the road that ran around the perimeter of the reservoir.

'Aye, sir. Sent a car up the ways the stop people coming down from the western approach. Not that we'd expect any. Constable Green and me were just about to head out to the east and set up a block there.'

'What about the woods? There's tracks through here, surely? We'll need to keep walkers away.'

'I doubt it, sir. Not these woods. Folks don't come here.'

McLean found it hard to believe that. He was fairly sure he'd been this way on his mountain bike, back in the days when he used to take exercise. 'They don't?'

'Not often, no.' There was something about the way the sergeant said it that convinced McLean he was telling the truth, or at least some part of it. But if that was the case, then what the hell was Anya Renfrew doing out here?

The cloying reek of oil smoke grew steadily stronger as McLean followed his nose across the minimal car park and through the trees. A fire engine blocked the narrow track leading to the clearing, and beyond it stood a blackened hulk of steel, broken glass and melted rubber. Steam rose from the body where a lone fireman trained his hose, but the fire had been put out. DC Stringer stood close enough to look on, but far enough away to breathe without needing a face mask. He turned as he heard McLean's footsteps on the hard-packed gravel and earth.

'BMW X3, sir. Number plates melted before anyone got here. Could only get a partial index. We've managed to read the VIN now the fire's out. It matches the one we're looking for.'

'This is definitely the car?'

'According to the database, aye.'

McLean approached the burned-out mess with caution, then backed off again as the close canopy of the trees concentrated the smell, making the air thick and noxious. At least the fireman had a breathing mask. A few of his colleagues stood at the rear of the fire engine, rolling up hoses and putting kit away.

'You any idea how long since it was set alight?' McLean asked after he'd introduced himself.

'It was pretty well ablaze when we got here. Say an hour maybe? There's nobody inside, if that's what you're worried about.'

McLean glanced back at the blackened bulk of the car. The seats had burned down to their frames, a skeletal mess that nevertheless was all metal, no bone. He'd not smelled the telltale stench of charred flesh either, just the chemical reek that was making his head ache.

'Any idea what set it off?'

'Not had a chance to look at it yet, but I'd say it wasn't an accident. Modern thing like that wouldn't just set itself on fire. Not where it's parked, least ways.'

'How do you mean?'

'See the ground here?' The fireman kicked at the gravel with his boot. 'We get called out the whole time in the summer. Cars parked in fields of dry grass. If it's too long, it catches fire on the exhaust and the whole car goes up. But here?' He shook his head. 'Nothing to set it off. No idea how long it's been parked there either. There weren't any other cars when we got here. Don't think many folk come out this way.'

'Who reported it then?'

The fireman shrugged. 'You'd have to speak to Control about that.'

McLean thanked him, then walked back towards the car. The metal bodywork clinked and pinged as it cooled down, little spirals of grey-black smoke still chimneying upwards from the corners. All four tyres had melted, the body lowering itself down onto the ground. The windscreen had cracked and fallen inwards, but the rest of the glass was surprisingly intact. He'd not noticed before, but the driver's side door hung open.

'Was it not locked?' McLean asked the question as he looked around for someone who might know the answer. The fire crew had gone back to packing away their kit, chatting among themselves as if this was just another working day.

'Did you want something, sir?' DC Harrison scurried over from the far side of the clearing.

'The car door's open. Doesn't look like it's been forced.'

'It was like that when we got here, sir. I didn't really think anything of it, but if the fire crew had cut it open you'd know about it.'

McLean strode back to the fireman he'd talked to earlier. 'The door. It was like that when you got here?' He waved a hand in the general direction of the burned-out wreck.

'Aye. Handy that. Saved us a lot of time cutting it open.'

'So it can't have been locked then.'

'I guess no.'

McLean turned back to DC Harrison. She'd followed him over and was putting her Airwave set away. 'Think we're going to have to get Forensics in on this one.'

'Already on their way, sir.'

'And you might want to get on to the station too. We'll need to search these woods, and that's going to take a lot of people.'

21

Now that the fire had been put out, the headache-inducing smell began to dissipate. It was still too pungent close to the car, but at least McLean could start to get his head around the scene. The deputy chief constable would want an update soon, and there was much to do before the forensics team arrived.

'Anyone run the index through ANPR yet?' he asked DC Stringer as the two of them stood at the edge of the clearing. It wasn't much of a hope. The cameras logged vehicles at key transport points, like the Queensferry Crossing, and the major roads out of the city. This place was as close to the middle of nowhere as you could get without starting to come out the other side.

'I think Harrison's on that.'

'Check it, will you? And get on to the insurance company. Some of these vehicles have trackers fitted nowadays. Might be worth following up.'

Stringer nodded, hurried off to do his bidding. McLean stared at the car, the trees, then turned full circle. Had he come out here on his mountain bike, back in his student days? It was possible, although he couldn't remember it. Nor could he remember how far the woodland stretched into the hills. Thick stands of Scots pine and larch trees, plantation woodland that had been allowed to grow wild.

'What was she doing out here?'

'Sir?'

McLean twisted around a little too fast, a twinge of pain shooting up into his hip. Somehow DC Harrison had managed to sneak up on him unawares. His question hadn't been intended for anyone other than himself.

'Just thinking out loud. You get anywhere tracking the car from the city?'

'They're working on it. Doesn't seem likely though. We didn't get a hit on Monday, and this has probably been here since before then.'

'You reckon? Someone would have reported it, surely? I mean, this place is remote, but it's not like nobody ever comes here. Look at the litter.' He waved a hand at the base of a nearby tree. The little holes formed by the roots were filled with all manner of rubbish. Crisp packets, discarded drinks bottles, cigarette ends, little foil squares ripped open, their unsavoury used contents not far away.

A horrible thought began to form in his mind, a connection between what he was seeing now and what he'd found in Anya Renfrew's wardrobe. McLean walked over to the tree, looked down, counted. Three used condoms scattered around the base of the trunk. He crossed the car park to another large tree, three of them there too. A few yards away from the open door of the burned-out car, a supermarket-branded plastic bag lay under the low branches of a rhododendron bush. He crouched beside it, used a stick to gently tease it open and peer at the contents. Just as gently let it close again.

'Something up, sir?' Harrison asked.

'A theory. What if the car was never reported because the people who were out here didn't want anyone to know where they'd been?'

'How –?' Harrison's question cut short as she joined the dots. 'Oh.'

'Oh indeed.' McLean saw the scene in a different light now. Set back from a road that was already narrow and largely unused, the main car park was well secluded. This secondary car park, tucked even deeper into the woods and not much more than a natural clearing, was exactly the kind of place to go if you didn't want to be seen or disturbed.

Through the trees, McLean could see a large white van pulling into the lower car park, its diesel engine spoiling the peace that had settled around them. The first of the forensics team to arrive. He'd no doubt there would be more along soon. This case was going to have everything thrown at it, after all.

'Is your flatmate likely to be working this site?' he asked. Manda Parsons often joked about getting all the shit jobs, but this was maybe taking it a step too far.

'No, she's on leave. Gone to see her folks for the week. Any reason why?'

'Because I'm about to ask Forensics to do something for me, and I'm not sure I want to lose another friend.'

The forensics team descended on the scene like a well-rehearsed dance troop. McLean knew better than to get in their way, even if the conditions for preservation of evidence beyond the car itself weren't ideal. Taking out his phone, he wandered off to a quiet part of the car park as he placed a call through to the Sexual Crimes Unit. It took a while to be answered, longer still to be patched through to Detective Chief Inspector Jo Dexter. From the background noise, she was either at a crime scene herself, or more likely in the smokers' shelter at the back of the station.

'Heard you were up shit creek, Tony. If you're looking for a transfer back to Vice I'm not sure I can help you.'

'It's not that bad, Jo. Not yet, at least. Could actually have a lead on our missing support staff.'

Dexter made a noise that might have been a cough to cover an expletive. 'At least you've actually got some support staff to lose.' There was a short pause during which McLean was convinced he could hear the crackle of burning tobacco as she inhaled a lungful of smoke. 'Ach, that's unfair. We're all being squeezed, and Anya's one of the best. Remember working with her when I was still a DS. That was a while ago.'

'I should probably interview you about her then. I've been trying to talk to everyone who knows her.'

'Was that why you called? Because I don't really know her out of work.'

'It seems nobody does. And I'm coming to the conclusion that was exactly how she wanted it. So, no, that's not why I called. Not entirely anyway. I wanted to ask if you knew anything about dogging.'

The silence might have been another long drag on her cigarette, but this time it felt different. Not so much the crackle of burning tobacco as the grinding of internal gears.

'That's a hell of a question to ask a girl, Tony.' Dexter coughed again, and McLean could almost smell the smoke even though he was a good fifteen miles away from the station.

'Seriously, Jo. There's a scene in the city, right?'

'Christ, yes. There's a scene in every city. Every town in the country. The things people do for kicks, eh?'

'So where do people go to get their kicks these days? And before you ask, no, I'm not looking to spice up my sex life.'

'I'm no expert, but last I heard the Braids car park was popular. That's not far from your place.'

'Jo, I'm serious. I think this might be Renfrew's secret. Why she never socialised with us, and possibly why she's disappeared. What about the car park at the south end of Gladhouse Reservoir?'

'Not that I've heard of. It's not impossible though. I mean, we tend to ignore it unless it gets out of hand or someone complains.

Shut them down in one place, they'll just find somewhere else to go. It's all organised on the internet these days. I can ask the team, but out there you'd probably be better off talking to Penicuik or Dalkeith. Local beat bobbies will have a much better idea of what's going on.'

'I'll do that, thanks, Jo.' McLean hung up before the DCI could start on at him again.

It took McLean a while to find Sergeant Donaldson. Most of the people at the crime scene itself were forensic technicians, Detective Constables Harrison and Stringer trying their best not to get in the way. A short walk back to the narrow road and the banks of the reservoir answered the question of where all the locals had gone. Four of them clustered around a squad car, three constables listening hard to whatever it was the old sergeant had to say. He loomed over them like a great bear, fully a head taller than them and broad across the shoulders. McLean was glad he was on their side; he didn't much fancy his chances against Donaldson in a fight.

'Wondered where everyone was,' he said as he approached. The nearest constable had his back turned, and almost ruined his uniform as he jumped in surprise. Half of his mug of coffee went flying.

'Jesus fuck! What the hell do you – ah. Sorry, sir. Didn't know it was you.'

'You might want to stick that hand under cold water. Scalds can be nasty. Maybe go shove your hand in the reservoir for a while, aye? Ten minutes should do it.'

The young constable looked at him with a mixture of uncertainty and fear. He probably thought McLean was taking the piss, had no doubt been on the receiving end of a good many pranks in the few years since he'd joined up. It couldn't be more than a few years, given how young and fresh-faced he looked.

'Better do what the detective chief inspector tells you, son. Might sound stupid, but the best way to treat a scald like that's to stick it in cool water for a good long while.' Donaldson gave his young colleague a reassuring pat on the back. 'And you two, back to maintaining the cordon. Coffee break's over.'

McLean watched them all do as they were told, the youngest picking a careful path down to the water's edge, while the other two set off in opposite directions up the single-track road.

'Sorry about Josh, sir. He can be a bit of a handful at times, but he's dependable. Think he was more shocked the coffee was hot than anything.'

'I should know better than to creep up on people like that. I was hoping to have a word with someone who knew the local beat well.'

'Born and raised in Penicuik, sir. I did a stint over on the West Coast, but I've been back home almost fifteen years now. If there's anything I can't tell you, reckon I know who to ask.'

'That car park, up at the back. You know what it's been used for, right?'

'Aye. I noticed that when I first saw the car and called it in. Folk can be strange, you know, but doing it with strangers, out in the open?' The sergeant shook his head as if the endless variety of human sexuality was a mystery to him.

'Is there much of that sort of thing in these parts?'

'Not here, no.' Donaldson paused a moment as if trying to remember. 'You might get the occasional couple enjoying the seclusion, mind. But it's too remote for the dogging scene. You're more likely to find them just off the main road. There's a big car park at the back of the industrial estate's popular late at night. A couple of the warehouses hired a security guard, but he spent most of his time just watching them at it, filming it all on the security cameras. We move 'em on if we find them, but mostly it's only what they leave behind gives the game away.'

'So this place isn't a regular dogging spot.'

'No' really. I don't know if it's too far for them. Like I said, nobody comes here much. Might be the stories about the place.'

'Stories?'

Donaldson looked a little embarrassed at having brought the subject up. 'Aye, well. Folk tales mostly. They say these woods are haunted, that people go in there and are never seen again. Or go in young and come out old, even though they've only been gone a day or two. Folk tales, aye.' He shook his head at the madness of such things.

'I'd guess things like finding Audrey Carpenter's body at the head of the reservoir don't help either.' McLean stared out over the water towards the far end, but the view was blocked by the two small tree-covered islands that rose from the surface a few hundred metres away.

'No, you're right there. And there's been others drowned here too. There was a brother and sister, what, must be twenty years ago now. Skinny-dipping at night, so they say. Got themselves into trouble. Found their bodies in the reeds there where Constable Harker's gone.' Donaldson pointed down the bank to where the young man crouched, awkwardly swishing at the water with one hand while he slapped away mosquitoes with the other.

'Well, whatever put them off before, looks like someone's found this place and decided it'll do nicely.'

'Aye, I see that.' The sergeant glanced briefly into the trees, then back at McLean. 'Can I ask a question, sir? What's so important about that car it gets a DCI out to look at it? And the full forensics works too? Soon as I called it in all hell broke loose.'

'The car belongs to one of our support staff. She went missing last weekend and we're very anxious to find out where she's gone. I can't tell you why, apart from the most obvious reason that we're concerned for her safety.'

The sergeant looked away into the trees again, an expression on his face McLean couldn't quite read. When he spoke, his voice was quiet. 'Don't much fancy her chances if she's got lost in the woods. The trees go on for ever, and there's all manner of things in there. Old mine workings, borrow pits, abandoned rail lines and God knows what else. If you wandered off in there in the dark, fell down a shaft, you could be lost for days. Might never be found.'

McLean followed the sergeant's gaze, but there was nothing to see except endless forest. 'In which case I hope you like overtime, because we're going to have to search them.'

22

The car was up on a transporter when McLean walked back through the trees to the crime scene. One of the forensic technicians poked carefully around the area that had been underneath it, but when she saw him she beckoned him over.

'Detective Chief Inspector. What do you make of this?'

He recognised the voice, but just to confirm it, the technician pulled her hood back to reveal a severely short crop of greying hair. Dr Cairns had a reputation for being overly protective of her crime scenes, so he hung back in case he inadvertently contaminated something just by existing.

'It's OK. We've done all we can here. I'll no' shout at you for not wearing a bunny suit. No' this time.'

Suitably reassured, McLean came closer, not sure what he was meant to be looking at. The fire hadn't quite turned the car into nothing but a metal shell, but it had made a hell of a mess of it anyway. The tyres had melted, welding it to the ground until the crane had arrived to lift it onto the transporter. Now he stared at a rectangular patch of ground, a dark black divot at each corner.

'It's very dry underneath,' he said after a moment. Cairns gave him a withering stare, as if she thought him an idiot. But then she gave that stare to everyone, so it was hard to be sure.

'Of course it's dry. It's been baked by the heat. And we've not had any rain for a month either.'

McLean looked around the rest of the car park. The ground here was a mix of hard-packed dirt and gravel, unlike the crumbling tarmac nearer the road. Tracks criss-crossed the area, made by the cars that had driven in and out. Deeper indentations marked where the truck had backed in to pick up the burned-out wreck. It was less easy to see, but he could still make out the route the car had taken as it pulled in to park, the ends of the tracks marked by little puddles of sticky, melted rubber. And nestling in one track, roughly where the driver's seat would have been, something shiny and metal glinted in the light filtering through the trees.

'We've photographed this, but I thought you'd want a look at it before we move it.' Cairns crouched down beside the object, and McLean stepped carefully up to join her. Closer in, he instantly recognised the familiar shape of a Zippo lighter. Clean and shiny, he could just about see the marks of something etched on the side. He knew better than to try and pick it up though.

'What's that engraved on it?'

'Think it's initials. And a date. We'll get a better look when we check it for prints. More important is where it's sitting.'

'Under the car?'

Cairns rolled her eyes. 'Obviously under the car. But look more closely. It's not been crushed down into the gravel, see? It's just resting on top.'

'So it was put there after the car was parked.'

'Exactly so. I'd hazard a guess that this was used to set fire to it.' Cairns produced a clear plastic evidence bag, then picked up the lighter and slipped it inside. She sealed it with a practised ease and handed it to McLean.

'This?' He laid it in the palm of his hand. Closer up he could see the engraving, some impossible-to-read initials and what looked like a date. 'Seems a bit low-tech, doesn't it?'

'Car fires are hard to investigate. You know that as well as I do. They've a tendency to go up like a bonfire doused in petrol. Mostly because they are full of petrol. At least this one was relatively new, which means some of the materials inside it had been treated to make them less combustible. There's enough of it left to indicate the fire started somewhere around the dashboard on the driver's side.'

McLean handed the bag back to Cairns, then stood upright, somehow managing not to make a groaning sound as he did so. Up on the transporter, he couldn't see into the car properly any more. 'I'll take your word for it, but what are you suggesting?'

'I think that whoever set fire to the car used that lighter. I don't know if you've ever seen a car being set alight, but it goes up much more quickly than you might expect. If they'd been sitting in the driver's seat and scrambled out in a hurry, they could easily have dropped that lighter. It bounced under the car, and then when the tyres melted the whole thing settled down on top of it.'

'That's . . .' McLean began to protest, but the more he thought about it, the more sense it made. 'But why set fire to it like that? I mean, why set fire to it at all?'

'That's your department, not mine. I can tell you how it was done, but why's a different matter altogether.' Cairns dangled the bag with its lighter inside. 'I'll do my best to find out who this belongs to. Maybe you can ask them.'

'Thanks. I hope it's that easy.' McLean shoved his hands in his pockets. He'd been coming to ask the forensics team to do something, but Cairns's revelation of the lighter had been a distraction. 'There was one other thing.'

'Aye?'

'This place. It's been used as a site for dogging. Recently, I'd say. Do you think that might be why the car's here?'

Cairns cocked her head to one side as she considered the

question. 'Again, the why's not my department. But given the plastic bag full of used johnnies we found over there, I'd say it's a fair guess.' She pointed to the spot under the rhododendron bush he'd looked at earlier. The bag was gone, replaced by a crime scene evidence tag.

'Ah, you found those. I was going to mention it. I was hoping you might be able to –'

'Collect up all the condoms and run DNA tests on the contents? Way ahead of you there.' Cairns interrupted him before he could finish. She waved a hand over towards the far side of the car park, where a couple of white-suited technicians were crouched down beside a tree. One held a handful of plastic evidence bags. McLean watched as the other held up something slippery between finger and thumb, then dropped it into a waiting bag. 'Those two thought they could get away with cutting corners on site contamination protocols. That's not something they'll do again in a hurry.'

As encounters with the senior forensic technician went, that one hadn't been too bad. McLean knew better than to push his luck though, and beat a hasty retreat from the immediate area. He found Detective Constables Harrison and Stringer down at the road, deep in discussion with Constable Harker. The young man was holding his scalded hand as if it were broken, not lightly poached by a drop of hot coffee, and as he came closer McLean could see the blotches on his neck and face where he'd reacted badly to mosquito bites.

'How's the hand, Constable?' he asked, once he was satisfied the young man wasn't going to jump out of his skin.

'Fine, thank you, sir. A bit sore maybe.' He reached up and scratched at his neck. 'Not as bad as these bastard midges.'

'Well, if you need something to take your mind off things, I've a job for you.'

'Sir.' Harker stood to attention as straight as any soldier. McLean had no idea how old he was, but at a guess it wasn't far north of twenty. Fresh out of school and into training.

'I'm sure Sergeant Donaldson's already told you why we're so interested in that car. It's empty though. There was nobody in it when it was set alight, and the driver's door was wide open. That means we're going to have to search these woods.' He glanced over at the trees, their heavy canopy of leaves rustling gently in the late-afternoon breeze. Nights were short at this time of year and it wouldn't get dark for hours yet. Even so, it would be too late to start today whatever his gut instinct told him. Whatever the deputy chief constable might want.

'You do know how far these woods go, sir?' Constable Harker said.

'I've an idea, yes. And I know they're not easy to get through. So we need to be clever with how we go about it. Which is where you come in. You and all the other local officers. I want every house, farm, bothy and building in a three-mile radius of here checked as soon as possible.'

The constable scratched at his neck again. 'That's . . . that's going to take a lot of time. Sir.'

'Aye, I know. Which is why the quicker you get started the better. I'd suggest working from this point outwards. Stringer and Harrison here can draw up a plan, but there's nothing better than local knowledge when it comes to these things.'

'I'll get right on it, sir.'

'You do that, Constable. And keep us up to speed with any developments.'

McLean watched as the young man bustled off about his duties. As the heat slowly began to drain from the day, so the midges were venturing farther from the water's edge, and he began to feel them buzzing around his head. Harrison seemed impervious to them, but Stringer was suffering too.

'You want us to run things from here, sir?' he asked.

'For now. At least until the forensics team are done. We've set up an incident room back at the station, but you might as well be running the search from Penicuik. It's closer and we'll be using as many of their officers as we can.' He shoved his hand in his pocket and pulled out his key fob, then checked his watch. 'I'm going to drop past the control centre on my way back, see if I can't have a listen to the 999 call. If nothing else comes up, we can have a catch-up briefing at six.'

Stringer nodded his understanding, almost poking out his own eye as he slapped away a midge at the same time. Immune to the little buggers, Harrison gave voice to the thoughts McLean was trying not to pursue too deeply, at least not yet.

'It's not looking very good, is it, sir? Last time anyone saw her was Friday, and it's Wednesday now. What are the chances of her surviving out there in the woods for the best part of a week?'

23

McLean could remember when Bilston Glen had still been a working coal mine. Childhood trips to the borders had taken him out past its twin towers and utilitarian buildings. He'd been away at boarding school when the miners' strike had virtually closed the place down, and had somehow managed to miss the news of its decommissioning and demolition a few years later. For a long while the site had been a wasteland, the derelict and half-demolished sheds daubed with graffiti, the ground littered with broken Buckfast bottles and dog mess. It was only fairly recently the whole place had been cleaned up and turned into a mixed industrial and business park.

Police Scotland's main Area Control Room and Service Centre, as it was somewhat pompously called, was a nondescript building in the middle of all the regeneration. It might have been mistaken for the regional offices of some multi-national corporation, or an insurance company's call centre. He had no need to actually visit, but since it was on the way back from the burned-out car, it was as easy to pop in as call. He could pick up a haggis from the MacSween's factory next door while he was at it too.

'We weren't expecting anyone, sir. You'll have to sign in.' The receptionist handed him a clipboard with a poorly photocopied visitor register that was quite at odds with the high-tech interior of the control centre. McLean signed it, then pinned the hastily printed name badge to his lapel. By the time this was all done, a young woman had appeared to take him through to the main centre. She wore a badge with 'S. Dalton' written on it, but introduced herself as Shirley.

'I realise I should have called ahead. Probably could have done this with an email anyway, but I was passing.' For some reason McLean felt the need to justify upsetting the routine of the place.

'It's no bother, sir. Quite nice to put a face to the name sometimes. Not sure how many times I've spoken to you, and never met you before.'

McLean looked at the young woman more closely, although how that would help he couldn't say. He didn't much recognise her voice either, but it was perfectly reasonable to assume they'd spoken in the past. Everything came through this building, after all. That was why he was here.

He'd been expecting to be shown into a large hall full of headset-wearing phone operatives, but instead Shirley took him to a small meeting room. 'You wanted to know about the treble-nine call. The car fire this morning, is that right?'

'Aye. When was the call first logged?'

Shirley went to a computer terminal set up at a side table. A couple of seconds of tapping at keys, and a screen appeared with all manner of details on it.

'Ten fourteen and twenty seconds, according to the computer. Janine took the call. You'll be wanting to listen, I expect?'

'If I can.'

Shirley tapped a couple of keys, and a pair of speakers McLean hadn't noticed before crackled into life.

'Emergency services. How may I direct your call?'

'That 999, aye?' A young voice, male, but quite high-pitched.

'That's correct. How can I help?'

'There's a fire, aye? A car.' The boy sounded hesitant, perhaps a little fearful.

'A car on fire? Can you tell me where this is?'

'It's up Gladhouse, ken. End o' the reservoir in the trees. Youse need to send the fire brigade oot quick like or the whole forest's gonnae go up.'

'There's a car on fire at Gladhouse Reservoir, is that what you're telling me?'

'D'ye no' ken English, hen? Tha's whit I just said.'

'Of course, of course. I'm just checking. Can I take your name, please?'

'Why'd you need that?'

'If you'd rather not say, that's fine. But it helps us if we need to follow things up. Can you tell me when you saw this fire?'

'Jes' now.' The boy's voice wavered a little. 'Well, mebbe ten minutes ago. But I had to get tae a phone. That scunner Bobby nicked mine an aw.'

'So you went to the payphone at Temple. You know the area well then?'

'Temple? Naw, I'm no . . . How'd . . .' The line went dead.

'That's all of it. I'll get a copy of the recording made up for you.'

McLean said nothing for a while, still staring blankly at the screen and trying to make sense of what he'd heard. Eventually Shirley's words sunk in.

'Oh. Thank you. Yes, that'd be great.' He pulled out his notebook and flipped to an empty page. 'So the call came in at a quarter past ten, from the call box in Temple, right?'

'Aye. Number confirmed it. Not sure Janine should have mentioned that, but we weren't sure if it was just a crank call. You've no idea how many of those we get every day. Worse in the summer holidays when the kids are all kicking around with nothing to do. It's always payphones though. They're smart enough not to use their mobiles.'

'Or their friend Bobby's nicked it. I take it you asked a patrol car to go out and check the fire anyway?'

'We did, aye. Turned out it wasn't necessary though. There was another call a couple of minutes later. Farmer working up that way spotted the smoke and called us. You want to hear that one?'

McLean couldn't say he wasn't tempted. Any time spent here was time away from the senior-officers meeting, time away from the endless questions and strategising and searching for someone to blame. On the other hand, if it wasn't him, then they'd pick on someone else.

'Not just now. If you could send it over with a recording of that one I'd be grateful.'

'I'd have thought it was bloody obvious, wouldn't you?' The deputy chief constable's face, normally calm, looked like it might burst open at any minute. 'She's done a runner, hasn't she. Driven out to the sticks and torched her car. Probably picked up by whoever's been paying her all these years. I bet she was on a flight out of the country with a fake passport before the bloody thing had stopped burning.'

McLean said nothing. He'd learned over the years that it was easiest not to provoke people when they were under pressure. The inevitable shouting never really helped, and only led to resentment later on. Detective Superintendent McIntyre wasn't so diplomatic.

'I think you're jumping to way too many conclusions there, Stevie. A burned-out car doesn't make a conspiracy. There could be any number of reasons why it's there.'

'Really?'

'I'm not saying it's impossible, just unlikely. It doesn't fit her profile.'

'That's the whole point though, isn't it, Jayne? Her profile is wrong. She doesn't even live where we thought she did. Has anyone done any security checks on her at all?'

McLean decided it was time for him to step in. 'Actually, yes, sir. We have. She's undergone several routine security screenings in the past ten years and nothing's flagged as suspicious.'

'So our security screening is rubbish. That's great. One more thing to explain to the minister. Along with how we've single-handedly ruined a multi-agency, multi-nation operation that's been years in the planning. Oh, she's going to love that.'

'Operation Caterwaul hasn't been compromised, sir. Renfrew hadn't even begun working on it when she went missing.'

Robinson looked at him as if he was an idiot. 'We don't know that, Tony. We can't know that, and they can't risk it.'

McLean didn't ask who 'they' were. It didn't really matter. He let it lie, giving the DCC a chance to calm down from his initial frustrated anger. It was understandable enough, and better to vent it here, in a meeting of senior officers, than out in the operation room or somewhere else even more public.

'If she's not some kind of spy, then what's the story with the car?' Robinson asked eventually. 'What do you think she was doing out there? And where is she now?'

McLean waited a moment before answering. Partly to gather his thoughts, but mostly because it was an uncomfortable matter to broach.

'I'll admit it's conjecture, based on minimal evidence, but I think I know why she was out in the woods. We're working on proof, but it might take a little time.'

'Go on,' McIntyre said. Somehow that was worse than the DCC asking.

'I think the reason Renfrew lives a secret double life is that she has a . . .' What could he call it? Hobby? Peccadillo? '. . . rather unusual way of spending her leisure time. I think she might have been active in Edinburgh's dogging scene.'

'Dogging?' Robinson asked.

'Meeting up in semi-secluded places for public sex with strangers is, I understand, the commonly accepted definition,' McLean said. Across the table Detective Superintendent McIntyre let out an unprofessional snort of laughter.

'We know what it means, Tony,' the DCC continued. 'But what makes you think a long-standing member of our support staff, someone who's the daughter of a retired detective super no less, would do something like that?'

McLean leaned back in his chair, composing his thoughts before speaking. All eyes were on him now, but at least nobody was shouting.

'As to why a person feels compelled to indulge in such acts, I have no idea, sir. I could speculate, go into psychological reasons, look for evidence of past abuse. It's not all that important really. What I do know is that the area where we found Renfrew's car had an unusually high concentration of used condoms, most relatively fresh, if you'll excuse the term. I've asked the forensics team to run DNA analysis on the contents.'

'You've what?' Robinson's voice didn't quite rise an octave, but it wasn't far off.

'If we get a hit, then we can bring them in for questioning. If nothing else, it should help us confirm Renfrew was there when we think she was.' McLean leaned forward, elbows on the table. 'I've asked the Sexual Crimes Unit to pass on any recent intel about the scene they've got, and I'll put a couple of our IT people on to checking the sites these people use to organise themselves.'

'This is all going to cost a great deal of money.' The DCC broke the awkward silence. 'Not to mention the time it's going to take to get your results, McLean.'

'Would you prefer we not investigate, sir?'

'That's not what I –'

'Good, because I've already drafted in uniformed officers from the regional stations to help search the woods and all the nearby buildings. We'll be starting at first light tomorrow morning. I'd have liked to have done some searching this evening, but we couldn't get the dog team out and the woods are tricky terrain.'

'Where are you going with this, Tony?' McIntyre asked. 'What's your theory?'

'At the moment there's too many unknowns. I'm fairly certain Renfrew went to those woods for sex, it's what happened afterwards I'm not sure of. If her car had broken down, she'd have found a way of getting home, even if it was just walking to the nearest bus stop. But if someone fancied a little one on one, maybe without consent . . .' He let the rest of the idea hang in the air. There was every possibility that Anya Renfrew was dead, buried in a shallow grave somewhere, or shoved under a rhododendron bush. At least if that was the case they'd find her with the dogs in the morning.

'Of course, without a body we can't know either way, and I'm not completely dismissing the idea she's been stealing intel from us and passing it on to persons unknown. Could be for money, or it could be because someone's blackmailing her. If that's the case then she may have disappeared simply to get away from whoever's doing that. Torching the car to throw them off the scent. As you see, sir. We've too few facts and too much conjecture right now. We need to find her first, then worry about what she's done.'

The deputy chief commissioner knew it, even if he wasn't happy with the situation. He gave McLean the most imperceptible of nods. 'Use what you need to get the job done,' he said. 'But please keep an eye on the cost, eh?'

24

The plaque on the wall outside the Deal Street Care Home advertised it as a Dee Foundation property, which sent an involuntary shudder up McLean's spine as he read it. The foundation did good work, providing halfway-house accommodation to youngsters making the transition from care home to employment. They helped homeless people and also looked after the elderly, it seemed. They also owned and ran Bestingfield and the secure psychiatric unit where Norman Bale was held. He couldn't deny that there was a need for the services they provided, but neither could he square the charity with its founder and funder, Jane Louise Dee. It bothered him that in some small way she was looking after an elderly retired detective, even if he couldn't say exactly why it bothered him.

'Detective Chief Inspector McLean. I'm here to see Grace Ramsay?' He presented his warrant card at the smart reception desk that sat in one corner of an elegantly furnished hallway. Unlike many old people's homes he'd visited, this one didn't have the odour of urine and cleaning fluid he'd been expecting. Maybe it would be beyond the double doors opposite the entrance, where the large bunch of flowers arranged in a vase couldn't overpower it.

'Of course, sir. We've been expecting you.' The receptionist didn't even look at the warrant card, instead reaching for the phone on her desk. She quickly informed someone in the building that he was there, then fixed him with a smile that was a credit to her dentist. 'If you'd like to take a seat, one of the nurses will be along in a minute. Can I get you a coffee?'

He was about to accept the offer when he remembered who ultimately owned the care home. For some reason the idea of accepting any kind of hospitality from Jane Louise Dee was anathema. 'Thanks, but I'm fine just waiting.'

In the end he didn't have enough time even to sit down, let alone drink anything. The double doors swung open and another young woman stepped through. She took a moment to see him, even though there was nobody else there apart from the receptionist.

'Detective Chief Inspector? Hi, I'm Anne. Please, come with me and I'll take you to Grace.'

Grace, he noticed. Not Detective Superintendent, nor even Ms Ramsay. The woman he remembered wouldn't have stood for such casual informality. McLean hurried to catch up with the nurse as she went back through the double doors. Beyond them, a long corridor stretched towards a distant window, light reflecting off a polished linoleum floor so shiny as to be almost dazzling. More doors opened off the corridor, and he caught the occasional glimpse through glass panels of what went on behind them. A dining room was laid out with round tables, their tops covered in white cloth but otherwise empty. Along from it, another room appeared to be some kind of physical therapy gym. Other doors had name plates or numbers on them, but there was a distinct lack of people. It was eerily quiet too.

'How long has Ms Ramsay been here?' McLean asked as the nurse led him through another door that opened onto a stairwell. The only option was up, no basement here.

'Och, must be about two years now. She's one of our oldest

clients. Both in age and how long she's been a resident.'

'And does her daughter visit often?'

The nurse paused, her hand hovering over the rail. 'More often than some. Less than others. People don't like to confront their own mortality, Detective Chief Inspector. That, sadly, is what this place is all about.'

There wasn't much answer to that, so McLean said nothing. He followed the nurse up to the second floor, then along another corridor to its far end. It was only when they reached the last door that she spoke again.

'I've told Grace you've come to visit, so she's expecting you. She asked for tea, and it's all there ready. I should warn you though, she's very frail. The fall nearly killed her, you know.'

McLean nodded his understanding, even if he wasn't sure why he was being told. Maybe the nurse felt a warning was necessary. She knocked on the door and then pushed it open without waiting for an answer from within. They both stepped into a large, airy room with a high ceiling and tall windows looking out onto a small garden, bright in the summer sun. A table similar to the ones in the dining room downstairs sat in the middle of the room, a tray with teapot, cups and all the other essentials in the middle of it. At first he thought the room empty, but then movement at the window resolved itself into a figure in a wheelchair. The person sitting in it was struggling with the mechanism, face in shadow but frustration evident in every move.

'Here, Grace, let me help you with that.' The nurse bustled over, taking control of the chair and wheeling it to the table. As it passed from shadow to light, so McLean saw the occupant properly. Even if he'd not known who she was already, he'd still have recognised the irascible detective superintendent in the old woman before him.

'You know I said earlier about someone coming to pay you a

visit?' The nurse's tone was that of a teacher admonishing a young child for their forgetfulness, another thing he couldn't imagine Grace Ramsay enjoying. 'Well, he's here. Say hello to Detective Chief Inspector McLean, won't you? And I'll see about pouring the tea.'

'Knew a detective constable called McLean once. Runty wee fellow. Always apologising for other people's mistakes.' The old woman stared at him with slightly clouded eyes. She sat up straight in her wheelchair, waited for the nurse to pour tea and then leave before speaking again. 'Not you though. He was much younger. Thinner too.'

McLean sat in his uncomfortable chair and tried not to stare too hard at the woman Grace Ramsay had become. She was tiny, in that way very old people seemed to shrink in on themselves. But despite that, and the wheelchair, she was very much the same terrifying detective superintendent he had known so many years before.

'Well, we're all of us a little older now. And I wish I was as thin.'

Ramsay cocked her head to one side, quizzical for a moment. Then her expression changed, a hint of a mischievous smile. 'So we are, Detective Constable. So we are.'

McLean considered correcting her, but decided it didn't really matter. 'I had a few questions I wanted to ask you, Detective Superintendent ma'am. That's if you feel up to it?'

'Questions about what?'

'About your daughter, Anya.'

Ramsay reached out with a shaking hand and picked up the cup of tea from the table in front of her. McLean was sure she'd spill it, but somehow she managed to take a sip and replace the cup in its saucer without a drip. She said nothing all the while, waiting until her hand was back in her lap and firmly clasped by the other one before speaking again.

'Anya. Yes. What has she done now?'

'I was thinking you might be able to tell me that, ma'am. When did you last speak to her?'

'Oh, I don't know. A week ago? Maybe ten days? She doesn't come as often as she should. Why do you want to know?'

How much to tell? McLean would normally do his best not to worry a relative in such a situation, but Ramsay had been a detective, knew exactly how the job worked. It wouldn't take her long to realise what was going on.

'You know she works for us. Police Scotland that is. In admin support.'

'She wanted to join the army, but she couldn't pass the physical. Didn't like front-line policing, so she went into admin. So dull.' Ramsay took another sip of her tea, her hand more steady this time. 'When did she go missing? I assume that's why you're here.'

'She didn't show up for work on Monday morning. Last anyone saw her was Friday evening. We found her car – your car, I should say – out in the woods south of Gladhouse Reservoir.'

Something in Ramsay's demeanour changed at those last two words. The tremor came back to her arm, and this time she clattered the cup back into its saucer, tea spilling over her hand. 'Gladhouse? Oh. Oh no. What has she done?'

'Are you –?' McLean began to ask, but Ramsay had already begun fiddling with the brakes on her wheelchair with hurried, unhappy movements. She finally worked them off, pushed herself backwards until she was clear of the table, then hurriedly applied them once more. He had assumed she was unable to walk, but she levered herself out of the chair and onto unsteady feet. Standing only showed how much she had shrunk, and she favoured one side. Presumably it was the other hip that had

139

broken. The same, McLean noticed, as himself. He went to her side, offered an arm for support.

'Oh. Thank you.' She laid a hand on his and led him back to the window she had been staring out of when he'd entered the room. 'Gladhouse. I never thought.' She looked up at him then, eyes like skimmed milk fixed on him as if she had made some difficult decision. 'What do they call you, Detective Chief Inspector? I expect the constables still call you "sir", but mostly it's all first names these days, isn't it?'

'McLean to my face, or Tony. What they call me behind my back is best I don't know.'

'They used to call me Ramrod Ramsay, which shows there's nothing quite so unimaginative as a copper.' The merest flicker of a smile ghosted her face, chased away by a darker frown. 'But Gladhouse is not good. People who go missing there aren't often found again. If Anya's . . .' She left the sentence unfinished.

'What's so special about Gladhouse?' McLean knew all too well about the discovery of Audrey Carpenter's body, and Sergeant Donaldson had mentioned two youngsters drowning there twenty years or so earlier. Neither of those seemed to fit what the retired detective superintendent was talking about.

'Who's still in CID these days?' Ramsay shook her head slightly. 'No, you're not CID any more, are you. All that nonsense with Police Scotland and the like. Glad I retired. Is Duguid still about? I heard old Mac Duff died of the cancer. And of course Needy went mad.' She looked up at him as she spoke the last. 'That was you, wasn't it. Picked up that rock and found the nastiness living underneath it.'

'Duguid retired a year or two back, but he's working with us in the Cold Case Unit. He's a lot easier to live with now he's not in charge.'

Ramsay took a couple of steps back towards her wheelchair. She leaned one withered hand on the arm for support, but didn't sit down. 'Well, ask old Dagwood about his cold cases. Ask him about the ones out by Gladhouse and Penicuik. The ones that have got my name on them as SIO.' She shook silently, and for a moment McLean imagined that it was her age wearing her down. But then he understood she was fighting back tears. She leaned too heavily on the wheelchair, its brakes not properly locked. He caught her as gently as possible as it began to slide away from her, but instead of thanking him, she shook him away. Tottered back to the table and lowered herself into the chair McLean had vacated minutes earlier.

'Stupid bloody thing. Stupid bloody body.' She shook as she rubbed at her eyes, smeared tears over her wrinkled cheeks. 'Just when I need to be strong. Need to find my wee girl.'

A noise at the far side of the room distracted them both. McLean glanced across to see the door open and a nurse enter. She took one look at them and hurried over.

'Goodness me, what's happened here?' She spoke like a mother to a young child, and McLean couldn't help notice the way Ramsay stiffened at the words. Nevertheless she allowed herself to be treated in a manner Ramrod would never have suffered.

'I'd best be going.' He dipped his head to acknowledge the reprimand. 'I'll speak to Duguid as soon as I can. And we'll find her, ma'am.'

'You'll try. I remember that much about you, McLean. Tenacious wee bugger, that's what the other detectives used to say.' Ramsay turned to face him as the nurse brought the wheelchair over to her. 'Go. Go find my Anya. Or whatever's left of her.'

25

Dawn came early at this time of year, but even so the light had that fresh, new quality to it as McLean pulled in to the car park at the south end of the reservoir and silenced the V6 burble of his Alfa Romeo. Stepping out of the car, he might have expected quiet, the plaintive cry of a curlew across the water perhaps, the distant gossiping of ducks. Instead he was greeted by the sound of a couple of dozen uniformed officers grumbling about the hour.

'Come to help have you, sir?' Grumpy Bob sauntered over, dressed in a lightweight coat against the morning chill that couldn't hope to last, a bright orange bobble hat pulled down over the tops of his ears.

'Thought I'd maybe give everyone a pep talk then bugger off. Isn't that what DCIs are supposed to do?' McLean popped the boot lid of the car and pulled out his walking boots. He'd found a Police Scotland fleece jacket for protection against thorns, and decided not to bring a hat, knowing full well that it would be sweltering before nine. All the same, he'd do his best to help with the search, and more importantly be seen to be helping.

Half of the station seemed to be waiting for their orders, kitted up and ready in the hidden car park. Three police Transit vans had brought them, along with as many uniformed officers from nearby Penicuik and Dalkeith as could be persuaded to take the overtime. Given the area they needed to cover, it didn't make for as big a search party as McLean would have liked. Still, they gathered in a bunch around him, attentively quiet when he called.

'For those of you who don't already know, we're here because one of our admin support officers went missing a few days ago, and her burned-out car was found here just yesterday.' McLean glanced past the collected officers to the patch of ground darkened by the fire. Forensics had been and gone, but a few of their markers still lingered.

'I'm sure some of you think you know why she was out here, but we're not here to judge, only to gather whatever evidence we can find and hopefully the woman herself. Best guess is she's out there in the woods somewhere. She may be injured, may be simply lost. It's a big area and easy to lose your bearings. Your sergeants will explain the search pattern. Pay attention to them. I don't want to lose any more officers, OK?'

That got him a few nervous laughs, which was perhaps better than no comment at all. 'Right then. Sooner we get started the better. We're looking for any sign of recent activity. If you see something and you're not sure, then flag it with your sergeant. I'd far rather mark something and come back to it than miss it altogether.'

McLean left the gathered constables to find their maps and further instructions, heading over to the nearest Transit van, where Grumpy Bob had set up a base of operations. As usual, the detective sergeant had managed to find the only decent mug of coffee in the area and was guarding it like the Crown Jewels.

'One of these days I'm going to pull rank on you, Bob.' McLean pointed at the mug. Grumpy Bob swivelled in his seat, reached behind it and pulled out a disposable cup with a plastic lid on it. Not exactly environmentally friendly, but at that exact moment McLean found it hard to care.

'You'll need to hurry up then, sir. I'm retiring at the end of the month, remember?'

'How could I forget?' McLean took the cup, popped off the lid and sniffed the fine aroma from within. He took a welcome sip, then looked down at the map spread across a fold-out table. From his point of view it was upside down, but he could see easily enough the reservoir and the woodland spreading south into the hills. The scale of it didn't fill him with much hope they'd find anything unless it was close by.

'There's a series of short paths through the woodland close by here. They're marked with coloured posts, see?' Grumpy Bob jabbed a fat finger at the narrow lines on the map, barely visible in the gloom of the car park. Then he pointed away from the van towards the trees. McLean hadn't noticed before, probably because it was hidden by the fire engine, but now he could see a short wooden post with yellow, green and red bands painted around it at waist height. Beyond it, a gap opened up into the woods.

'Has anyone walked the paths yet?'

'PC Harker and his mates did yesterday, while the forensics team were here. Didn't find anything, but we'll walk them all again. Reckon the best thing we can do is transect the woodland between the paths first, see what we find. If there's nothing, then we'll spread the search further in blocks. If we don't keep it systematic then we'll be as lost as poor Anya.'

'What about the dog team? They here yet?'

'Over the far side of the car park. They're not happy though.'

McLean looked in the direction Grumpy Bob had indicated, seeing the telltale ventilation fans on the tops of two vans.

'They say why?' he asked, then shook his head. 'No, don't worry. I'll go speak to them myself.'

★ ★ ★

McLean remembered the dog team from the case over at the derelict Rosskettle lunatic asylum a few years back. Two highly trained cadaver spaniels had sniffed out rather more dead bodies than anyone had been expecting, including that of a recently deceased member of the Scottish Parliament who was supposed to have been lying in rest in the family mausoleum in the city. His abiding memory of the dogs was their focus and sense of purpose; they were disciplined and eager, but went about their work in silence until they found something. So it was with some surprise he heard whining from the first van, the occasional angry bark from the second.

'Constable Brewster?' He approached the nearest van, where a short woman was leaning around from the driver's seat, trying to calm down the animal in the back. She started at his voice, then relaxed when she recognised him. With a gentle command to her charges to calm down, she climbed out of the car.

'It's no good, sir. I cannae get him to settle. Something's no' right here.'

'DS Laird said there was a problem. What's up?'

'Wish I knew. They both started acting up soon as we pulled into the car park. Jim's no' had any better luck than me.' Brewster hooked a thumb over her shoulder in the direction of the second van, where another constable leaned in through the open rear door. Another couple of loud barks were followed by low whining.

'Did DC Harrison bring you the clothes?' McLean had asked the detective constable to fetch anything she thought might have Renfrew's scent on it from the bungalow in Joppa.

'Aye, she did. Pity it was all laundered. Something out of the dirty washing basket's usually better. Thought we'd got something when the two of them set off up that path there.' Constable Brewster pointed to a narrow opening between the rhododendron bushes. 'Further up we got, the more nervous they were. Never seen anything like it. All they wanted to do was come back to the vans.'

'Any idea what might have set them off?' McLean wasn't a dog person particularly, but he knew people, and he knew Brewster was equally embarrassed at her failure and concerned for the welfare of her animals.

'If I didn't know better, I'd say they're afraid of something. Terrified even.' She looked up and around the clearing, visibly shuddering. 'Fair gives me the willies too.'

He knew what she meant. McLean wasn't given to superstition, but there was something about the trees that pressed in on him, a niggling sensation at the back of his mind that he'd really rather be somewhere, anywhere, else. Some of the other officers clearly felt it too, although by no means all of them. He could tell by the way the waiting search teams had clumped into groups, some chatting noisily while they waited for the off, others standing quietly, faces glum.

'Best get them away from here if something's upsetting them.' He turned back to Brewster, nodded at the van and its whining canine occupant. The constable's tension eased at his words, although the look of worry and embarrassment stayed on her face.

'I'm sorry, sir. Thought we'd be more help'n this.'

'It's no matter,' he said, even though it was. 'We'll just have to do it the old-fashioned way.'

26

Beyond the car park and the short network of paths, the woodland soon became a tangle of thick undergrowth and uneven ground. Sergeant Donaldson had warned them all, but as the day progressed McLean began to wonder whether he hadn't been understating the difficulty of the terrain. In some places the leaf canopy blotted out almost all available light, and there the going was a little easier. Nothing about the search was remotely easy though. As the morning turned to afternoon and the sun rose higher in the sky, so the temperature began to rise too. It wasn't long before McLean could see constables stripping off coats and tying them around their waists. Not exactly protocol, but neither was he going to make anything of it. He'd already unzipped his own fleece in a vain attempt to get some airflow, but the trees damped what little breeze there had been and the undergrowth snagged at everything. The air here grew increasingly thick and hard to breathe, the smells of the forest threatening to overwhelm them all.

'To think I used to bike out here from the city. Up into the hills and on down to Heriot. For fun.' McLean stood at the top of a steep bank, leaning against an ancient, moss-covered oak tree as he watched DC Harrison struggle up towards him. Her face was almost as red as the seats in his car, and sweat beaded on her forehead, her cheeks, a drip of it dangling precariously from the tip of her nose. She stared at him with a look he found hard to read, too breathless to comment as she finally reached the summit beside him.

'Not sure I ever came through here exactly, but if memory serves there's an old drover's road about a mile west, a couple of abandoned bothies too. Someone must farm the moorland, own these woods.'

'Lofty was going through the Land Registry records, sir. Looks like he made the better call, staying at the station.' Harrison produced a water bottle from her pocket, drained about half of it then offered the rest to McLean. He shook his head even as he cursed himself for not coming better prepared. How the hell Renfrew could have come through here he had no idea, was beginning to suspect she hadn't.

'Chances are it all belongs to the Duke of Buccleuch, or someone like him. It's more who actually lives here, works here, comes here regularly. They're the ones we need to talk to.'

'Aye, I know. It's so quiet though. So remote. Who'd 've thought you'd find somewhere like this so close to the city.'

As if hearing her words, a shout of alarm broke the stillness. McLean started towards the sound, not far off at all. Either a constable had found something or they'd slipped and fallen down one of the many narrow gullies that criss-crossed the woodland. Harrison stopped him before he could move more than a pace.

'One moment, sir.' She reached into her pocket and pulled out a short piece of blue and white crime scene tape. The lowest branch on the tree was too high for her to reach, so she handed the tape to him. 'Loop that over the branch so we know where we were, aye?'

McLean did as he was told, suppressing the urge to ask her if she'd ever been a Girl Guide. No doubt the sergeants running the search teams would have briefed everybody about this, and handed out tape at the same time. He'd been too busy chatting with Constable Brewster and the dog team at the time. And, besides, as a DCI he should know all that stuff anyway.

Half a dozen officers had converged on the source of the shout by the time McLean and Harrison arrived. A young female PC squatted by a half-rotted fallen log, and in front of her lay a small canvas carry-all not unlike the one Emma used as a handbag. The PC looked up as the group surrounded her, then stood and took a step back as she recognised McLean.

'It's exactly as I found it, sir. Haven't touched anything.'

'Good work, Constable. Get this place marked on the map.' McLean pulled a pair of latex gloves out of his pocket as he turned to the other members of the search team. 'You lot, spread out around this point, see if you can spot anything else.'

They did as they were told as he kneeled down beside the bag. It wasn't big, and it felt almost empty as he picked it up. The top opened with a thin leather strap, unbuckled. Inside, he found a folding hairbrush, a small compact with 'No. 7' written on it, a lipstick in gaudy red, half a dozen police-issue latex gloves, a handful of condoms still in their wrappers, a packet of moist tissues and a small velvet eye mask of the kind you might wear to a fancy dress ball in a period drama. There was also a mobile phone. Lifting this last one out, McLean tapped at the button to turn it on, but it was as dead as the log under which the bag had lain. He went through the outer pockets for anything that might yield a clue as to who owned it. There were only a set of house keys, an electronic fob with a BMW logo on it and a small roll of cash. Nothing whatsoever to identify whose bag this was. That more or less confirmed it for him.

'You think it's hers?' Harrison asked, squatting down beside him.

'I think it is, yes. We need to get that phone to the IT team.' McLean held up the keys. 'And I've a suspicion Sandy Gregg's going to tell me where the front door these unlock is soon enough.'

McLean left the complicated matter of electronically tagging the spot where they had found the bag to those officers more technologically savvy than him. DC Harrison had produced an evidence bag from her voluminous pockets, and he'd put their discovery inside it before the two of them cut a route back through the searched forest to the car park. When they arrived, Grumpy Bob still sat at his command post; the general overseeing his battle from well behind the front line. Police Sergeant Donaldson sat beside him, two time-served officers who knew how to avoid the hard work.

'Heard you found something, sir.' Donaldson had the decency to stand as they approached. Grumpy Bob took a little longer to rise out of his seat.

'Not me. One of the constables from Penicuik, I think.' McLean placed the evidence bag with its contents onto the table. 'We'll need to get this to Forensics pronto. Pretty sure it's going to belong to Renfrew though. Quite far back into the woods too, which is a worry. No sign of anyone being dragged through there, so it looks like she must have dropped it.'

'Aye. I was just marking things up here on the system, see?' Alongside the map he'd been using earlier, Grumpy Bob now had a laptop set up, displaying something similar on the screen. It took McLean a moment to work out what he was looking at, as the scale was much smaller than the paper version. A couple of points hovered over the woodland, GPS locations of things of interest to the search. As he watched, a new one appeared. Marking the point where the bag had lain, he assumed. Grumpy Bob peered at the screen, then picked up a pen and drew a small circle on the paper map in roughly the same position. High-tech, indeed.

'These other points are where we found these.' The detective sergeant bent down and lifted up two clear evidence bags from under his table. Each contained a battered high-heeled shoe, one missing its heel and neither suitable for woodland walking. He put them back down again, then tapped a heavy finger on each of the marks in turn, dragging it along to the point where the bag had been found. 'Not quite a straight line, but no' far off it either. And if you trace it back . . .' He didn't finish the sentence, didn't need to. They could all see the point where Renfrew's car had burned out.

'Why go that way though? Was she being chased by someone?' Harrison asked. 'And where does it go?'

McLean squinted at the map, the contour lines like a migraine halo under the green of the forest canopy. There were all too many mine workings, hidden monuments, old cairns and the like marked around the area, and then everything rose up towards the moorland and the hills. But there was one small cluster of buildings close to the imaginary straight line that speared away from where they were, through where they had found the bag and on to infinity.

'What's that place?' McLean obliterated it with a finger, turning to Sergeant Donaldson.

'Woodhill Farm? That's Sandy Bayne's place. But it's miles from here. No way someone would walk that far through these woods.'

McLean wasn't so sure. Desperation and fear could do strange things to a person. 'We should check it out anyway.'

'Already done, sir. Josh – Constable Harker – paid them a visit last night.'

'On his own? Or did he have a search team with him?'

The old sergeant looked puzzled for a moment. 'He had another constable with him, but –'

'I'm sure they're both very competent, but in the light of this

151

discovery, I think we should visit again. Take a team out with us.'

Donaldson said nothing for a moment, his silent stillness betraying some inner argument eventually won by the side of reason. 'I'll get it sorted.'

'Thanks. Let me know when you're heading over there. I'd quite like to tag along.'

Donaldson stared perhaps a moment longer than was strictly necessary before nodding once. 'Aye, sir. It'll no' be today, mind. We need to get this search done so I can have my constables back, aye?'

'Fair enough.' McLean checked his watch, glanced back at the trees. The afternoon heat made the forest oppressive, no longer as attractive an alternative to being back at the station with the paperwork as it had been first thing. 'Give it a couple more hours, and if you've not found anything else relevant we'll call it a day.'

27

'Aw no, man. I've fuckin' lost it.'

Wee Gav's about to take a bite out of his piece, but Bobby's words stop him. From the smell of it, his mum's made fish paste sandwiches again, so he's not exactly missing out.

'Lost what?'

'Fuckin' lighter. It was in here, I swear.' Bobby's got his rucksack off, one hand inside it throwing stuff around. Gav has no idea what shit his friend keeps in there. Trophies mostly, he guesses. Stuff Bobby's found lying around, or nicked more likely.

'When did you last see it?' He asks the question even though every time his mum does the same it pisses him off. It seems to have much the same effect on Bobby.

'Fuck should I know? When we torched that car mebbe?'

Gav lets the 'we' in that sentence go. It's been a couple of days now, and he still worries about the call he made from the phone box. Stupid really. He knows well enough they can track a mobile; that's why he didn't use his. Well, that and the fact Bobby'd 'borrowed' it to play games on and run the battery down. Of course they'd know exactly where he was calling from. Same way the number shows up on the landline at home.

'You no' use it since then?' Gav dumps the uneaten fish paste sandwich back in his lunch box, poking around in the hope that there might be a Mars Bar in there he didn't notice before. It's still just the spotty yellow apple and the wrapper from the bag of crisps he ate already. Even the juice is gone, and this heat's making him thirsty.

'Ah fuck it. Must've dropped it. Bollocks.' Bobby throws his rucksack onto the grass bank and slumps down beside Gav. 'You no' eatin' that?'

Bobby's taken the sandwich and bitten into it before Gav can even answer. He doesn't mind really. At least his mum made him a piece. Bobby's mum hardly even remembers to shop for food half the time.

'What we gonnae do this afternoon then?' Bobby asks through a mouthful of sliced white and too much margarine.

Gav shrugs. 'I don't know. What you wannae do?' It's the same old conversation they've had a hundred times before. If it was up to him they'd be back home, in his bedroom, playing on the Xbox. But his mum sent them off with a warning not to come back until four. Why can't she be like the other mums and not let her kids out of her sight?

'We could go see if there's anything in the old bothy, aye?'

Last time they'd been there, Bobby had found a half-full bottle of whisky and dared Gav to drink some of it. He almost had, but as soon as they opened it they could tell it was piss. Gav still had a suspicion Bobby had known all along and was just waiting for him to take a swig. Wee tosser.

'Can't we just hang out here? It's too hot to walk all the way up to the bothy.'

'Aye, you're right.' Bobby grabs his rucksack and goes back to searching in it for something. 'Boring as fuck, mind. An' I thought school was bad. Holidays suck.'

Gav has to agree. It wasn't so bad in the winter, when there was no excuse to go outside. If either of them had any money they could catch a bus into the city, but that's not going to happen. So here they are in the middle of nowhere, up a dirt track out of sight and out of mind. Nothing to do but stare at the sky. Wait until it's late enough to go home.

'Here, check this out.'

He smells the smoke at the same time as he hears the words. Confused, Gav rolls over to see what Bobby's done this time. Maybe he's found the lighter after all.

'What you doing?'

It's a stupid question. He can see well enough what Bobby's doing. He's got a magnifying glass that looks a lot like the ones they hand out in biology class. The ones that are all carefully collected at the end of the lesson. He uses it to focus the sunlight onto a patch of dry grass. The smoke appears almost instantly, and then seconds later it bursts into flame.

'Cool, ain't it.' Bobby scrunches the sleeve of his hoodie into his hand to protect his palm, then rubs out the burning grass before it can spread. 'You want tae try?'

Gav knows he shouldn't, but it's kind of cool. And it's not as if they've got anything better to do. He takes the magnifying glass, kneels down and looks for a good spot. They're at the edge of the moors here; there's heather and that spiky grass he doesn't know the name of. Everything's bone dry, baked by weeks of sun and no rain. Still, it's not like he's going to set the whole hill on fire.

The focused point of light is almost too bright to look at, the sun so strong it's easy to get that hot spot and move it around. He's not done this for ages. Not since he was a wee kid. Dad used to show him how to do it. Use the burning light to carve his name in a piece of wood. But Dad fucked off to live with Abby, and Mum's too busy working to ever play.

'Fuuuck.' Bobby's voice is full of admiration, and Gav realises he's let his mind wander, left the magnifier burning too long on a piece of heather. White smoke billows out from the tangle of stems and roots, too much to pat out with his sleeve, and anyway he can't see where the flame is. A moment later and it's every-where, exploding out of the ground like it was soaked in petrol. Gav springs away, trips, falls on his backside, unable to take his eyes off the growing fire.

'Gav, pal. We gotta split. Come on.' A hand on his shoulder breaks the spell, and Gav scrambles to his feet. Bobby's already got his rucksack over his shoulder, Gav's bag in one hand. They slither down the bank to the track and their bikes, the sky darkening overhead as smoke begins to blot out the sun that started it all. Fuck, but he's going to get in trouble for this if they catch him.

As he pedals like fuck to catch up with his mate, Gav can't tell whether the noise is the clattering of his bike chain or the crackling of flames.

28

Thick black smoke palled the southern sky as McLean drove around the bypass, heading for the forensics labs and the remains of Anya Renfrew's BMW. Harrison had called him twenty minutes after he'd left the scene, a wildfire on the moors not far from the woods that were currently being searched. Or more accurately, where the search had been called off because it wasn't safe and every trained officer in the vicinity was needed for something more urgent. The long, hot spell had left everything tinder-dry, so it wouldn't have taken much to spark it alight. In many ways they'd been lucky the burning car hadn't set the forest ablaze the day before, but he didn't much fancy its chances now.

Dr Cairns met him in Reception as he was countersigning the chain of evidence form for the handbag. He'd brought it in mostly as an excuse for coming to the labs rather than going back to the station. There wasn't much Forensics could do with it, and the phone would need to go to the IT labs. He'd probably need the keys too. If DS Gregg had managed to find an address for Renfrew's place in Pilrig.

'We've done what we can with it, but there's only so far you can go when something's been burned. Fire's not the best way of preserving forensic evidence.' Cairns led him through to the workshops at the back of the building. The burned-out hulk had been placed in a separate bay at the far end, where the stench of it wouldn't put everyone off their lunch. McLean hadn't thought there was much of a breeze at the woodland car park where they'd found the car, but it had been enough to shift the worst of the smell. Here in an enclosed space, even with the roller shutter wide open, it was eye-watering.

'Christ. That's strong.'

'Here. Pop this on. It'll help.' Cairns handed McLean a face mask.

'How am I supposed to ask questions with this over my mouth?' he asked. Her smile suggested that she rather hoped he wouldn't.

'Let's just make it quick, aye?' He held his hand up to his mouth and nose, to little useful effect. 'What's the verdict?'

'As good as we can tell, the fire was started by a flame applied under the dashboard on the driver's side. To the right of the steering wheel, so either they were leaning in to do it or they're right handed and sitting in the driver's seat.' Cairns walked around the car as she spoke, pointing at things McLean found hard to focus on through watery eyes.

'The worst of the damage is on that side, and it's fairly well contained to the interior. These things are more reluctant to burn than they used to be, which makes our job a little easier. We've pulled the satnav out. It's got a tracker function, so there's a chance we might be able to pull recent routes from it if it's not been totally fried by the heat. I wouldn't pin too many hopes on that though. Electronics don't like being cooked.'

'Anything else?'

'Aye. Like I said at the scene, the car wasn't locked. We can't get anything from the inside, but the door handles front and back have both got usable prints on them. Passenger side's best, where the fire didn't do too much damage.'

'Prints?' McLean hadn't really considered the possibility. 'Any matches?'

'We're running them at the moment. They're only partials, and chances are they'll be mostly the owner's. You've got hers on file, I take it?'

'Should have. She works for us.' McLean couldn't remember whether admin support staff were routinely fingerprinted these days.

'We'll find out soon enough. She wasn't particularly small though, was she? Have kids?' Cairns continued her journey around the car as she talked, coming to a halt at the front passenger door.

'Small?' McLean did his best to picture Anya Renfrew in his mind without thinking too hard about the exotic clothing they'd found at her home. The woman he remembered from countless investigations was probably about the same height as he was. Slight, maybe, but not small. 'Not especially. Why?'

'We got the cleanest prints from the passenger door handle here.' Cairns crouched down and pointed, but McLean was happy to keep his distance. 'They're too small for a normal adult though. If she had a child, maybe picked up from school or something, that'd explain it.'

'No, she doesn't have any children. Well, not that we know of.'

Cairns shrugged. 'We'll run them anyway. Might get a hit. Might match the ones we pulled from the lighter.'

'What, the one you found under the car?' McLean raised an astonished eyebrow.

'Oh ye of little faith, Chief Inspector. Come. Let's get out of this stinking garage and I'll let you see.'

The air was much sweeter back in the main laboratory building, although McLean still caught whiffs of burned plastic every so often. Either the taint had infused into his suit or it was one of those smells that was going to follow him around for a while. Dr Cairns led him along a corridor that wouldn't have looked out of place in his old school science block, and in through an open door to a well-lit room kitted out with expensive-looking machines. Over on a far bench a plastic evidence bag held the small, silver Zippo.

'We've taken everything off it we can, but best you wear gloves anyway.' The forensic scientist handed him a pair from a nearby box. By the time McLean had struggled into them, she had snapped on her own pair and removed the lighter from its bag.

'We managed to lift quite a few prints off it in the end. They're all only partials, badly smeared, but we'll see what we can do with them. Like the car door handle, they're mostly small though. Either an adult with tiny hands or a child.'

'The 999 call was made by a child. Could be his, or his friend's?' McLean searched his memory for the name. Bobby, that was it. 'You said they're mostly small? Not all of them though?'

'Aye. We managed to get a good print off the inside where you put the fuel, look.' Cairns took the lighter back from him, flipped the lid, then pulled the strike wheel assembly away from the body. It slid out to reveal an inner sleeve. 'We found a full thumb on one side, partial finger on the other. Definitely adult prints. If they're in the database we'll know who last refilled it at least.'

'I'm impressed.' McLean waited while Cairns reassembled the lighter and gave it back to him. He remembered having one like it when he was a teenager. Not that he'd ever smoked, but it was the sort of illicit possession that raised your cool quotient at school. His hadn't been engraved though.

'I don't suppose you've any ideas about the inscription.' He held the lighter up to the light, angling it so that he could make out more clearly the initials etched into the shiny surface. 'J.D.F.' And underneath that a date, '22nd July 1997'.

'No idea. Someone's birthday, maybe? Whoever J.D.F. is, I'd guess. Probably a twenty-first or eighteenth or something. It's a fairly standard Zippo otherwise. Nothing special.'

McLean turned the lighter over, studying it for clues, finding none. If it came down to it, he could get a constable to run the date through the system and see if it came up with anything, but the fingerprints were a better bet.

'I don't suppose you've got any update on the DNA samples yet.'

Cairns gave him a look that perfectly described how stupid a question that had been. 'You'll get the results as soon as we have them. Can't do any better than that. There's more than a hundred of those slippery wee things, you know? Christ only knows what was going on in those woods.'

'Still, at least they were using protection, eh?' McLean said, and the withering stare Dr Cairns gave him suggested it was most probably time to leave.

The black smoke still hung over the southern sky as McLean drove back from the forensics labs to the station. Cocooned in air-conditioned luxury, he couldn't smell it, but the short walk from building to car had brought the faintest whiff of bonfire. Far more pleasant than the acrid stench of burned plastic, but unlikely to be much fun for the many fire crews who would be out tackling the blaze. What had the uniformed sergeant from Penicuik said? There'd been a spate of fires in the area, always were when the weather turned dry like this. Had this one started simply from a badly parked car? Or was it no coincidence it was only a short distance from the woods they'd been searching?

A squad of constables were climbing into the back of a Transit van as he parked his Alfa and squeezed through into the building. Empty spaces showed where yet more vans had left already. McLean didn't need to ask where they were going. He even toyed with the idea of offering to help, except that he'd more likely get in the way than anything else.

There wasn't much point going to either the control room for Operation Caterwaul or the small incident room across the corridor from it that they'd set up for the Anya Renfrew investigation. The first had been on hold following her disappearance, and it looked like the second was going to be on hold at least until the fire on the moors was under control. How much else that buggered things up was anyone's guess. He went instead to his own office, took one look at the piles of folders on his desk, and continued on to see McIntyre. Her office door stood open, so he knocked once on the frame and stepped inside.

'Ah, Tony. I was wondering where you'd got to.' She was sitting at her desk and smiled when she saw him. McLean almost relaxed, but then he noticed the figure with his back to them both, staring out the window. Well, he was going to have to break the bad news to the DCC some time, so why not now?

'What the bloody hell's going on, McLean?' Robinson didn't turn away from the view as he spoke, which on balance was not a good sign. The window didn't face south, but even so a smear of dark smoke could be seen drifting across the distant sky.

'Wildfire on Oakhill Moor, sir. We don't know what started it yet. Everyone's more concerned with getting it under control.'

Now the DCC turned, and his face was as dark as the smoke. 'I know that, dammit. And I know it's only a mile from your search site. I suppose you think that's a coincidence, do you?'

'To be honest, sir, I've not given it much thought yet. But, if you ask me, something like this was bound to happen sooner or later. We've had no rain in well over a month now. It's hot as hell

162

out there and we know from up north that these fires are getting more frequent now a lot of the moorlands aren't managed for grouse any more.'

'Grouse?' Robinson's angry bluster evaporated in the face of his confusion. 'What the hell are you talking about?'

'The moors, sir. They used to burn them regularly. It encourages new heather growth, gets rid of the old, woody stuff. Perfect for grouse, and sheep. If you stop controlled burning, then the old vegetation builds up. Lots of dead wood, dried grass, that kind of thing. Once it gets going, it's almost impossible to put out.'

The DCC stared at him for a moment, then shook his head slightly. 'What about the missing woman then? I suppose you've called the search off.'

'We had to, sir. It wasn't safe, and the officers we drafted in from Penicuik and Dalkeith were needed. We did find a bag though. It could belong to Renfrew. Forensics are going over it now.'

'What makes you think it's hers?' McIntyre asked. McLean told her about the contents. The wad of cash, the mask and condoms, the set of keys he hoped Gregg might have an address soon for him to try them on.

'Not much we can do right now, which is frustrating. But we should be in better shape in the morning. Provided the fire's under control and we haven't lost half our officers to smoke inhalation.'

'Christ, that's all we need,' Robinson said. 'So what's the plan of action, then? Give me something I can use to keep the minister off my back.'

McLean glanced at his watch, surprised at how late it was getting. He'd hoped to have got home early, given the unreasonable hour he'd left in the morning. Well, he'd find a way to make it up to Emma somehow. And if he could keep the DCC from losing his temper again, it might not take too long to come up with something for the minister.

'Give me an hour, sir. I'll have a situation report done and you can send it straight over.'

'You've got half an hour, McLean. So I suggest you get a move on.'

29

McLean didn't recognise the car parked on the driveway beside the front door. The number plate suggested it was brand new, as did its shiny clean paintwork. He wasn't anything like as knowledgeable about cars as he had been in his teenage years, but he recognised the Jaguar badge on the front. The cable plugged into the side by the house, and an extension reel snaking to the part-open back door told him it was the new electric model. It looked sleek enough, modern and sophisticated, but he preferred his Alfa Romeo.

The empty kitchen smelled of fine cooking. His stomach rumbled as he put his briefcase down on the table, reminding him that he'd managed to forget lunch again. Well, there'd been a Mars Bar and an apple, but he'd thrown the apple away after the first bite.

'Thought I heard a noise.' Emma appeared at the kitchen door. She was dressed in clothes rather more elegant and formal than the jogging bottoms and hoody she usually wore around the house, and when she came over to give him a hug, she smelled of delicate perfume.

'Important visitors?' McLean asked as Emma released him and went to the Aga. Steam billowed out of the opened oven door, a scent of warm herbs and garlic blotting out whatever

Chanel number she was wearing. 'Only, I can't help notice they're stealing all the electric.'

Emma said nothing for a moment, too busy checking on whatever was cooking. When she clanged the door shut and turned to face him, McLean saw the look on her face was no longer quite so friendly.

'You forgot, didn't you. Honestly, Tony. You're hopeless.'

'Forgot?' He searched his memory for anything, but came up short. Either senility was setting in or this was genuinely not his fault. He knew he'd get the blame either way though.

'Professor Turner? Dinner?'

It really didn't spark a memory at all. He opened his mouth to ask if she was sure she'd told him about it, then closed it again before he made things worse. It was just as well he'd managed to manipulate Robinson into accepting a hastily drawn-up report, otherwise in all likelihood he'd not have been home for another hour yet.

'Never mind. Come through to the library and say hello. Food won't be ready for another twenty minutes anyway.'

He did as he was told, following Emma along the corridor, out into the hall and then through the open door to the library. The room was tidier than he'd seen it in a while, and the French windows had been opened, letting the warm evening air in from the garden. A scent of burning wood tinged the air, the fire on Oakhill Moor making itself known to the city.

'I'd heard you were something of a workaholic, Tony. Dare say I shouldn't be surprised.'

McLean turned to see Professor Turner – Harriet, he reminded himself – standing by the fireplace. Another woman stood close beside her, their shoulders almost touching. He couldn't be sure, but he thought he might have seen her at the lecture a few nights back. Certainly her thin face and grey curtain of shoulder-length hair seemed familiar.

'I'm so sorry. Em must have told me, but I completely forgot. It's been a busy day.' McLean held out a hand, as he had before, only to be engulfed in another hug.

'Your grandmother was just the same. Happiest down in the mortuary with the dead, quite forgetting the niceties of dealing with the living.' Professor Turner smiled at her own joke, then frowned. 'But I'm forgetting myself. This is Meg, my wife.'

Something about the way Meg smiled as she shook his hand put McLean on his guard. He'd not been prepared for guests, and the day's events still crowded in on his mind.

'Hattie's told me so much about you. I feel as if I've known you for years.'

'She has?' McLean asked. 'Hattie?'

'Your grandmother always insisted on Harriet.' Professor Turner butted in to the conversation. 'Or latterly Doctor Fairweather, which made me sound very important. I've always been Hattie though. When I'm not berating students. And I was so tired of the jokes about my name I decided to take Meg's when we got married.'

McLean started to say something about that, then realised that he was probably going to regret it. Fortunately Emma came to his rescue, whether she intended to or not, by choosing that moment to interrupt.

'Now Tony's finally home, shall we go through to the dining room and eat?'

He didn't need to be a detective to see that Emma was trying her hardest to impress Professor Turner. McLean could have told her it wasn't necessary, that the professor wouldn't have accepted the invitation if she'd not already made up her mind about her. It was fun to watch though. If nothing else, he couldn't remember the last time Emma had been so bright and vivacious.

'Tell me, Tony. What does a detective chief inspector get up to on the average day?'

He turned away from Emma to look at the woman next to him, Harriet's wife, Meg. The oval dining table was far too large for just four people, so they sat in a cluster at one end. McLean would have been far happier in the kitchen, but that didn't fit Emma's ambitions well enough.

'I'm not sure there's ever an average day. It very much depends on what's going on.'

Meg stared at him with eyes that were hard to read. He wasn't sure, but it was possible she was wearing tinted contacts. There was certainly something other-worldly about her. She was an artist, he knew that much, and his first impression was that she was the complete opposite of the professor. He was old enough and wise enough not to trust first impressions though.

'What's going on at the moment then?' she asked. 'It must be something very important for you to forget all about this evening. Emma's absolutely raging at you.'

McLean risked a glance at the woman in question, deep in conversation with Professor Turner. Given the way she'd treated him in recent months, this evening felt like warmth and joy. Not rage at all. When he turned back to Meg, she had a grin on her face like the Cheshire cat.

'Made you look. Made you stare.'

Made you lose your underwear, McLean didn't say. 'How is it you and Harriet met?' he asked instead.

'Oh, now there's a story.' Meg reached for her wine glass and drained almost half of it. 'Was it Rwanda? Or was it Kenya? I forget. Somewhere hot, anyway. Hattie always was swanning off to the least desirable places to look at the most horrendous things.'

'I can't begin to imagine what her work is like, and I've seen some disturbing stuff in my time. But what were you doing there? You don't sound like you're from Africa.'

Meg drained the other half of her glass, holding it in her hand without saying a word until McLean had reached for the bottle and given her a refill. 'I'm not. I grew up not a half a mile from here. Went to the Glasgow School of Art. Tried to be a portrait artist, but I'm not really a people person. And not all art's lovely landscapes and what's on the outside, you know.' She waved the now perilously full glass at the paintings on the dining room wall. He'd not given them much thought before, but they mostly fell into the 'lovely landscapes' category, he supposed. There were a couple of paintings that his father had bought before McLean had been born. His grandmother had hung them in this room because she didn't much like them but couldn't bear to put them in a cupboard somewhere. They were modern, and that was as far as his artistic sensibilities went. He was on firmer ground teasing meaning out of people when they were trying to be enigmatic.

'You paint pictures of genocide. The mass graves and things like that.'

Meg smiled, then punched him lightly on the shoulder. 'Knew you'd get it.'

'So you were out there painting while Hattie was trying to put names to the dead.'

'We met at a dinner party. Not unlike this one really. Except that Hattie had been dragged along by one of the other doctors on the dig. I think he was hoping she might sleep with him. I went along at the last minute as a favour to a friend. Which just goes to show good deeds do sometimes go rewarded.'

McLean raised his own glass to that, although the mouthful of wine he drank was considerably smaller than Meg's. The alcohol didn't appear to be having much effect on her though, despite her having put away at least a bottle already. Hattie was clearly the designated driver for the evening.

'So, Detective Chief Inspector,' she said after half another glass was gone. 'Tell me. How did you and the lovely Miss Baird come to be together?'

He picked up the bottle, topped up Meg's glass and then emptied the rest into his own. 'That,' he said, 'is a very long story indeed.'

Long hours later, McLean sat at the kitchen table, staring at the Aga and Mrs McCutcheon's cat as she cleaned herself. One leg in the air like a ham hock, tongue making a noise that could put a deaf man off his pudding. He was dog tired, and tomorrow was going to start early. A weary glance up at the clock confirmed that tomorrow had already started. He should really go to bed, sleep for at least a little while. But he needed to get his head straight about all the things that had happened. Being bounced into an evening of socialising, however pleasant it had turned out to be, had thrown him.

'Well, I think that was a success, don't you?'

Emma clumped into the kitchen, hands laden with crockery from the dining room. It could have waited until the morning – later in the morning – but he had just enough self-control not to say so. Instead, McLean levered himself to his feet and intercepted her on her way to the sink.

'Here, let me.' He held out his hands, but Emma shook her head and carried on.

'I can manage, Tony. Honestly, you should go to bed. You look done in.'

She sounded like his gran, but in a good way.

'It was fun. Can't say I'm not tired, true enough.'

'So why do I get the feeling you're thinking about sitting in that old chair of yours in the library with a dram to keep you company into the wee small hours?'

He stifled a yawn, even though the thought had occurred to

him. 'Meg's an interesting person,' he said out of nowhere.

'Changing the subject, I see, Chief Inspector.' Emma rinsed the plates before stacking them in the dishwasher, something McLean had never quite seen the point of doing.

'A bit. Maybe. Just not sure what to make of her, that's all. I guess I was a bit surprised. The Harriet Turner I remember didn't seem . . .' He shut up before his tired brain got him into trouble. Emma's expression suggested it might have been too late for that.

'I'd 've thought having seventeen-year-old boys perving after you would be more than enough reason. Honestly, Tony. I thought you were the open-minded one.'

McLean rubbed at his face with tired hands. 'Sorry. I didn't mean . . . Well. Sorry. And for forgetting they were coming. I'd have tried to get home earlier if I'd remembered.'

'Tried?' Emma's eyebrow arched towards her hairline, and for a moment he thought he was going to get an earful. Not that she shouted often; theirs was a more silent form of argument in the main. Then her shoulders slumped a little and she half smiled, half frowned. 'Actually, I'm being unfair. It's very possible I forgot to tell you I'd invited them. It was a spur of the moment thing after they'd dropped round for tea yesterday. Then you were gone so early this morning, and I was so wrapped up in applying for the course, persuading work to let me take a sabbatical . . .'

'I don't think you need to worry too hard about being accepted. Even without your background and qualifications, she likes you. Meg said as much.'

'You two seemed to get on well.' Emma pulled out a chair opposite him and sat down. For a moment McLean thought there might have been a challenge in her words, but it was only his tired brain seeing things that weren't there.

'Don't think I've ever met someone who can put away quite

so much drink without it having the slightest effect on her. Well, outside of the police, maybe. She's got a new exhibition of her work at some gallery over in the West End tomorrow evening. Said she'd put us on the guest list for the opening.' He stifled a yawn, the long day catching up.

'You don't have to go if you don't want to,' Emma said, mistaking his tiredness for a lack of enthusiasm.

'No. I'd like to. I think it could be fun. Well, interesting at least.' He stretched, then yawned again. 'But right now I'm going to bed.'

30

She wakes from a sleep so deep and dreamless it is almost as if she didn't exist until this moment. Thoughts tumble through her mind, a confusion of memory and sensation so that for a moment she doesn't know who she is, what is happening. Something cold and wet scrapes against her skin, the rough tongue of some unimaginable beast. She lies motionless, frozen in terror.

'. . . Soon have you all cleaned up, won't we now . . .'

At first she's not sure that she has heard the voice. All noise is muffled, as if she is underwater, her ears stopped up with wax. That tongue still licks at her skin though, cold and harsh. And as she focuses on it, she remembers the pain, the cuts on her arms and legs and face. She remembers the night in the woods as if it were a lifetime ago, the panic as she was chased by something wild and hungry.

Something that licks at her now.

'. . . What a mess you've made of yourself, dear. Still, it's understandable given . . .'

The voice is a little clearer, a woman, old. It makes no sense. How can there be a woman nearby when the beast is softening her up to eat? That cold, rasping tongue working its methodical way along her arm, her skin puckering and stretching with each stroke.

Other sounds filter through, the trickle of running water, the creaking of metal. She can't see anything, still enveloped in total darkness. But no sooner has she noticed this than she realises it is because her eyes are closed. She tries to open them, but nothing happens. Though the paralysing fear has begun to ebb away, she still can't move a muscle.

'. . . Such a long time since last someone was called to us. Beginning to think we had fallen from God's grace . . .'

The old woman's voice is closer now, near her head. The tongue reaches her shoulder, pauses a moment before starting again on her neck, her breasts. And that's when she understands it isn't a tongue but some kind of cloth. She isn't being licked but washed.

'I . . .' She tries to speak, but like everything else her voice is paralysed. She can still breathe though, and the word comes out as a sigh that gains an instant response. She feels a pressure on her lips, a finger perhaps although it's hard to tell.

'Shhh, dear. Don't fret. We'll get you all clean and presentable in time.'

The tongue-cloth resumes its rough licking, working its way over her body with ungentle thoroughness. She is naked, she knows, and no part of her is spared the cleaning. It should be soothing, to be washed this way, but it is far from that. With each waking moment, each chafing rub against raw skin, the memories build. How long has she been asleep? How long since she stumbled through the forest to what she thought was help? The empty hollowness at her core is something beyond hunger. When did she last eat?

With each passing moment more sensation returns. The sounds of washing and the woman's breathy muttering are less muffled now. She can smell something foul, thankfully distant. A mixture of human ordure and rot that reminds her of dead animals in a farmyard. And there is something else mixed in, a spicy smokiness she can't place. It sparks a fear in her, another fear among the many terrors she is helpless before.

'That's much better.' The cloth has finished at her feet, and she hears the sound of it splashing into a bucket nearby. A hand runs over her damp body, fingers splayed over her naked flesh, feeling for something as they work back up to her head, softly caress her cheeks like a mother might quieten a frightened child, like a lover might express their devotion. Then the fingers pinch, forcing her mouth to open. Liquid trickles into her mouth, reflex making her swallow it down. It is water, but sweet and fresh. Only then does she realise how thirsty she is, how parched her throat.

'Good, good. Drink it all down.' The woman's voice has a soft burr to it that might be soothing in any other circumstance. Her words don't reassure though, quite the opposite.

'God will free you from all your sins, my child. But you must be clean before He can enter fully into you.'

31

The lightest haze of smoke coloured the morning air as McLean walked across the car park and into the station. Normally he would have expected a breeze off the Forth to clear it away, but there was none, the utter stillness threatening another sweltering day ahead.

There were few officers about as he climbed the stairs to the third floor and his office. It was early, but even so he would have expected more of a buzz. Clearly the fire had kept everyone busy throughout the night. It gave him a tiny pang of guilt to think that he'd been eating fine food and drinking fine wine while his colleagues were putting in the extra hours, but the feeling was short-lived when he realised he'd have to spend most of the morning trying to sort out the mess that would have been made of the budgets by so much unplanned overtime.

He was coaxing the coffee machine into action, putting off the inevitable struggle with the paperwork, when a light knock at the open door provided a different distraction. Detective Inspector Ritchie stood on the threshold, her normal slightly worried expression deepened by weariness. Her cheeks and forehead had a slightly sunburned hue to them, accentuating the pale lines where her eyebrows had never quite grown back after she had rescued McLean from a fire some years earlier. Clearly she'd been close to the flames again, which surprised him. It was one thing to send as many uniformed constables and sergeants out to help, but a detective inspector?

'Out on the moors last night, were you?' McLean pulled two mugs from the tray beside the coffee machine. Ritchie looked like she needed one.

'Aye. Not my idea of a great night out. See if I find the wee . . .' She swore so quietly McLean couldn't quite make out what she said. '. . . I'd throttle the life out of him, so I would.'

'You reckon it was deliberately set?'

'Like as not. There's been a spate of fires around that area recently. Can't all be accidental.'

McLean recalled his conversation with the sergeant from Penicuik. He'd said much the same thing. 'They got someone looking into that?'

'Funny you should ask. Jayne just handed it to me this morning. Of course, it might all be nothing. Ground's as dry as anything up there. It's all dead heather and gorse too. Goes up like you wouldn't believe. And the smoke.' Ritchie stifled a yawn that turned into a cough. Thumped at her chest a couple of times.

McLean poured coffee, then realised he had no milk. Shrugging, he carried both mugs over, handing one to the detective inspector. 'There you go. That'll wake you up.'

Ritchie looked at the black liquid, grimaced. 'You know they say people who drink their coffee black are more likely to be psychopaths?'

'What about people who forget to buy milk on their way in to work?'

'Definitely psychopaths.' Ritchie drank, grimaced again, then drank some more.

'What if it's kids?' McLean asked, the thought popping into his head almost from nowhere.

'What, psychopaths?' Ritchie's brow furrowed, her missing eyebrows disappearing almost completely.

'No. Setting the fires, I mean. You've had, what? One at Rosskettle, the burned-out car and now the moorland. All in the last week. What else has happened in that time?'

Ritchie stared at him as if he were mad, then something clicked. 'School holidays.'

'Exactly. And it was a child who called in the car fire. Mentioned his friend Bobby. What's the betting they started it in the first place? Probably didn't think it'd go up the way it did. Our helpful caller found a conscience and headed for the nearest phone box.'

Ritchie cocked her head to one side. 'It's plausible, I guess. How long's it take to get from the burned-out car to the phone box?'

McLean was about to answer that he wasn't sure, but it was worth working out, when another light knock distracted the two of them. He looked past Ritchie to see Detective Constable Harrison standing in the doorway. Like the detective inspector, her face bore the rosy hue of someone who'd been standing too close to a source of heat for a while. Had the entire station gone out to help fight the fire while he went home?

'What is it, Janie?' DI Ritchie asked before McLean could speak.

'Call just came in from the moorland fire. It's pretty much out now. Certainly under control. But see, they've found something.' Harrison was a little breathless, and McLean wondered if she'd inhaled too much smoke, or simply run to his office from wherever she'd been when she learned this clearly important news.

'Something?' he asked. 'What sort of thing?'

'It's bones sir. In the ground. Human bones.'

★ ★ ★

McLean gazed over the blackened moorland, grey-white smoke still drifting up in places like dry-ice fog in a horror movie. The more hardy shrubs had been reduced to skeletons by the fire, and scorched boulders poked up out of dry earth like the skulls of the dead rising. The destruction spread from the road a good 200 metres up the hillside, where a low drystone wall had held back the flames. He dreaded to think what might have happened had it not been there.

A lone fire engine stood in the lay-by, firemen packing up the last of their gear. Police cars and forensics vans clustered around it like piglets at a sow. Just as well they'd closed the road; there was no way anyone would be able to get through.

'Any idea where it started?' McLean asked, after showing his warrant card to the first fireman he could find who wasn't obviously busy.

'Down by the old farm track's our best bet.' The fireman waved a hand over the blackened, smoking ground towards a point a few hundred metres downhill. 'There's been a few fires around here in the past couple of weeks. Could just be coincidence of course. Everything's so dry it doesn't take much to set it off.'

'Control said something about bones?'

'Aye. The forensics folk are setting up over there.' The fireman pointed to a spot a bit further up the road where a couple of technicians were standing outside a scene-of-crime tent. McLean thanked him and set off towards it. Out here, away from the city, the air was normally sweet, but now the smoke tickled his throat, threatening a nasty headache for later. The heat of the sun overhead felt amplified by the burned earth, and the still air only added to the sensation of being in some kind of hellscape. By the time he reached the tent he was sweating.

'Might want to put some overalls on, sir.'

McLean glanced at the young woman standing by the open

179

rear doors of a forensics van. He was about to protest, when he saw the condition of her own white paper overalls. Black knees and arms from the burned heather, ash all over her front. At some point she must have rubbed at an itch on her face too, smearing more black on her cheek.

'Thanks. I'm guessing you'll not find much recent forensic evidence here.' He took the overalls she offered him, and started to pull them on. They never fitted, and an extra layer in this heat was the last thing he wanted. On the other hand, his suit was clean on that morning. Emma wouldn't be best pleased if he came home stinking like a fire pit either.

Gazing out over the scorched earth, it was hard to imagine what this part of the hill had looked like before the fire. By the contours of the land, the point where the tent had been pitched was at the top of a natural gully, maybe a small burn in the distant past. No doubt the vegetation had been thicker there, hiding it from casual sight until it was scoured away by the fire. McLean followed the narrow path made by earlier feet, relieved to find a familiar face at the end. Dr Tracy Sharp was assistant to the city pathologist, Angus Cadwallader.

'Afternoon, Tracy. Angus in the tent, I take it?'

'He is, yes.' Dr Sharp gave him a friendly smile, then coughed. 'It's not so easy to breathe in there, and a wee bit on the warm side to be comfortable. I'm not really needed here, given the circumstances.'

'I'd better go see what's up anyway.'

'Aye, well. Suit yourself.' She stood aside, and McLean squeezed past, pulled open the tent flap and stepped inside.

Dr Sharp had been right about the heat. The inside of the tent was like an oven, and the smell of burned heather almost overpowered him. McLean wanted to tie back the entrance flap and let some slightly cooler air circulate, but he couldn't find any kind of tether. Best make it a quick inspection then.

'Morning, Angus. What have you got for me here?'

The city pathologist had his back to the entrance, kneeling in the ash-blackened dirt. McLean recognised the balding crown and grey-brown hair well enough though. At his question, Angus Cadwallader straightened his back and turned. As he did so, McLean caught the first glimpse of bones.

'Ah, Tony. Excellent. I'm afraid there's not much I can tell you about this poor soul. Or should I say these poor souls?'

'I was told it was a skeleton.' McLean edged carefully around the pathologist until he could see properly. He crouched down beside a shallow pit, scraped in the ground. What could only be described as a mismatched jumble of bones poked from the charred soil at all angles.

'Skeleton implies bones laid out as they would be in a body. These are more like dismembered remains. And from more than one person too.'

McLean stopped himself from rubbing at his forehead, remembering the young forensic technician who had given him his paper overalls, the ash smudges on her cheeks. The more he looked, the more he saw. Dozens of bones scattered around like rubbish from a seagull-scavenged bin bag. Small pieces that might have been from hands or feet, one end of what looked like a femur poking out of the dirt at a jaunty angle. Something that looked uncomfortably like the top of a spine, although there was no skull to be seen.

'They're all human though?' He sank gently onto his knees as a twinge in his own hip reminded him of what he was looking at.

'Far as I can tell. And there's more here than we can see. No idea how deep this pit is. We'll have to get the specialists in to excavate. I can tell you this much though. These people didn't die of natural causes, and these aren't all ancient either.'

McLean bent low, the better to see. He'd looked at far too

many bodies in the course of his career, and in varying states of decay. One thing he'd never struggled with before was identifying how the various pieces were meant to go together though. Normally it was the whole body, or a piece of it still held together by muscle, skin and ligament. The bones poking up out of the earth here were clean, not a scrap of flesh on them. And there was no smell of rotting either. Fair enough, mostly all he could smell was burned heather and ash, but he knew the smell of decaying body and it wasn't here.

'You've noticed it too, I see.' Cadwallader eased himself backwards before standing up with all the groaning someone of his years needed. McLean stared unseeing at the jumble of bones for a while longer before doing the same, only with a little less noise.

'I have indeed. These bones have had their flesh removed before being dumped here. Almost as if the bodies they belong to have been butchered.'

'Exactly as if they've been butchered, Tony. That's what we're looking at. This is no shallow grave here. It's a charnel pit.'

32

'It's not Renfrew. I can tell you that much.'

The faint whiff of burned heather and gorse still clung to his suit as McLean sat at the all too familiar table in Deputy Chief Constable Robinson's office. Detective Chief Superintendent McIntyre was there too, along with DI Ritchie.

'That's something, I guess.' Robinson didn't sound as if he meant it. 'So who is it then?'

'At the moment we don't even know how many people, sir. Let alone who they might be. The pathologist identified parts from three different bodies before he decided to call in help.'

'Help?' Robinson asked. 'What kind of help?'

'As it happens, the university has just appointed a new professor in forensic anthropology. She's had experience with investigating mass graves. If anyone can piece together this puzzle then it's her.'

'You know this woman?'

'She worked with my grandmother, a long time ago, sir.' McLean didn't feel the need to tell Robinson that the woman in question had also been around to his house the night before for supper.

'These bones. They're recent, you say?' McIntyre asked.

'From what Angus could tell, yes. At least, the ones exposed by the fire. We won't know how many and how old until Professor Turner's surveyed the site. She should be on her way if she's not there already.'

'Christ, what a mess.' The DCC rubbed at his face with both hands for a moment. 'OK. So we've got at least three dead bodies. Dismembered, buried in a remote bit of scrubland. And none of them are our missing admin support officer.'

'As far as we can tell, sir.'

'How far are they from the spot where we found her car?'

'About a mile as the crow flies. Two if you're going by road.' McLean had an OS Landranger map spread out on the table. He circled the spot at the southern end of Gladhouse reservoir in pencil, then marked the approximate site of the latest, grisly find. Green squares marked the forest, more than half filling the gap between the two.

'But none of the bodies is Renfrew.' The DCC made it a statement more than a question, as if the problem of multiple unexplained and very suspicious deaths was less bothersome than one missing admin support officer. 'What's your plan of action then?'

'Angus is coordinating with Professor Turner. He'll PM the bones we've already retrieved and give us a better idea of who they might belong to. And how long they've been in the ground. It'll be a day or two, Monday, I guess, given it's the weekend, before we get much back from that. Meantime I've some other leads to chase up on Renfrew. If we're lucky, the two cases are entirely unrelated.'

Robinson barked a humourless laugh, and McLean found he had to agree. Luck was rarely on their side, and something else was niggling in the back of his mind too. A conversation or something someone had said in his hearing. He couldn't remember.

'I'll have a word with Duguid and see if he can dig up any old Mis Per cases from that area,' he said after a moment's pause.

'I'm hoping DS Gregg's got an address for me by now too. If we can find out where Renfrew has been living, that might give us some idea as to where she's gone.'

'You wanted to see me, sir?'

McLean glanced up from the report he'd been trying to read to see DS Gregg standing in the doorway. Like most of the officers he'd seen today, her cheeks were rosy from having spent much of the previous afternoon out on the moors helping with the fire. He almost imagined he could smell the heather smoke coming off her, but he felt sure she would have washed and changed her clothes in the intervening time.

'I did indeed.' He closed the folder on the report, not sure he could even remember what it was about. 'I was wondering if you'd heard back from your contact about Anya Renfrew's flat over in the East End.'

'Oh. Aye. I'm sorry I didn't tell you earlier, sir. Only what with the fire and everything, it sort of slipped my mind.'

Gregg had a habit of retreating from the subject as soon as she was asked a direct question, McLean recalled. Some might find it endearing, but not him.

'So you have heard then, Sandy?'

The use of her first name brought her up sharp. 'Sorry, sir. Aye, the flat in Pilrig. It's on Spey Street, right enough. Top-floor flat at number seventeen.'

'You busy right now?' he asked.

'Always busy, sir. Nothing that can't wait, mind.'

'See about getting us a car then, can you? I'd like to head over there as soon as possible.'

'I'll get right on it.' Gregg stepped back out into the corridor, then turned and popped her head into the office. 'You want me to sort a squad car and a couple of constables too? In case we have to break in?'

McLean reached down and opened the drawer of his desk, pulled out the small evidence bag he'd been given by the forensics lab, and held it up for the detective sergeant to see. The keys that had been in the bag found in the woods.

'Don't think that'll be necessary. I've a hunch these will get us in.'

McLean didn't know Pilrig well. It had never been one of his beats, and somehow none of the crimes he'd investigated down the years – decades now – had brought him this way. He'd been close by, at the end of Leith Walk and up towards Trinity and Newhaven before, but Spey Street itself was new to him. Strange that he could live his whole life in a city as small as Edinburgh and still not know it all.

Gregg drove the almost-new BMW that was the latest addition to Edinburgh CID's pool. He could tell it wasn't long out of the dealers by the way there was no rubbish under the seats and in the footwells. That and the new-car smell that never lasted more than a month when detectives were involved. Pool cars were something of a luxury these days, the victim of ever deeper cuts. The disappearance of Renfrew at the start of a major investigation and the extra expense of dealing with the moorland fire were going to play even more havoc with the budgets. No wonder the DCC was so crabbit most of the time.

Number seventeen Spey Street was an unremarkable three-storey tenement building, overlooked by a more modern council high-rise on the other side of the road. Mid-morning there were few people about, and those that were ignored them as they parked at the bottom end of the street and walked back. Gregg said nothing as McLean produced the keys from his pocket and flipped through them until he found the one most likely to fit the front door.

'There's a possibility I'm going to look really stupid now,' he said before sliding the key into the lock. 'Please don't tell everyone if I am.'

Gregg frowned at him, then nodded her head in under-standing. He twisted the key and felt a mix of emotions as it clicked and the door fell open. There was relief that his hunch had been correct, but there was also sadness that this seemed to confirm their worst suspicions about Renfrew, and worry at the implications.

'I guess that answers that question,' Gregg said as they both stepped inside. The narrow hallway beyond led to a stone stairwell, a door on either side opening onto the ground floor flats. Apart from there only being three storeys, this was much the same as McLean's old tenement in Newington, over on the other side of the city. The stairwell even smelled the same, that unmistakable odour of damp and cat piss. A wave of melancholic nostalgia washed over him. Memories good and bad of the years he'd climbed those steps. Drunk and sober, with company or alone. He'd not realised how much he missed the place. Or was it the past that the place represented?

'You said top-floor flat, right?'

'That's what Val told me, aye, sir.'

'Val?' McLean struggled with the name, then remembered how Gregg had found the address. 'Renfrew's friend from the club.'

The detective sergeant nodded, but said nothing more. In-stead, she started up the stairs, leaving him to follow. The landing at the top opened onto two doors, but only one bore a name plate. Since it didn't say either Renfrew or Ramsay, McLean tried the keys in the other one. The lock clicked as swiftly as the main door downstairs. He pushed open the door onto a narrow hallway, sniffed stale air and a hint of something else. Across the sanded floorboards from the door, a narrow table held a phone, and beside it a turned wooden bowl filled with the sort of things you might want to get rid of as soon as you stepped indoors. There were no keys – he held those in his hand – but there were a few pound coins, a hairbrush, something that looked like a pac-a-mac still in its pac. And lying across the top of it all an ID badge on a lanyard, bearing the familiar logo of Police Scotland. He'd seen them countless times, the poorly printed photograph, the square where the chip was embedded, and the name printed in a large, bold font across the front.

Anya Renfrew.

'Gloves, I think.' McLean shoved his hands into his jacket pockets and pulled out a pair of latex gloves. DS Gregg still stood on the landing, eyes wide as she stared at the tiny hallway. McLean turned slowly, taking it all in, worried that she'd seen something he'd missed.

'Is there a problem?' he asked when he'd spotted nothing particularly out of the ordinary.

'No. Sorry, sir. Just a bit surprised.' Gregg shuddered slightly, like a dog shaking the water from its coat. Then she produced her own pair of gloves and pulled them on with rather more difficulty. The detective sergeant was good at administration, McLean reminded himself. Less so at investigation.

'We're going to have a look around. This isn't a crime scene, but I'd rather not upset too much just in case. OK?'

Gregg nodded her understanding, then followed him into the flat. McLean closed the door behind them to avoid an awkward conversation with the neighbours. They'd talk to all of the people who lived in the tenement in due course, but for now he wanted to see what this particular flat could tell him about Anya Renfrew. Or Grace Ramsay as she seemed to be calling herself.

'Looks like the kitchen's that way.' He pointed Gregg towards the back of the flat and an open door. 'Check the cupboards and fridge. If we're right, she's been away since last Friday, but this is where she lives most of the time. Should be milk, coffee, bread, that sort of thing.'

The detective sergeant gave him a look that suggested this wasn't her first rodeo, then she walked off in the direction he'd indicated. At the front of the flat, McLean found a decent-sized living room and a small bedroom that looked like it was more of a storage space than somewhere people slept. A compact bathroom separated them from the kitchen at the back and a second, larger bedroom.

He found nothing more sinister than a small tub of ibuprofen and a packet of disposable razors in the cabinet in the bathroom. The laundry basket held an assortment of clothes he'd associate more with Anya Renfrew than the assortment of risqué clothes they'd found at the house in Joppa. A couple of sensible white blouses, normal underwear, rolled-up tights. A small airing cupboard was mostly filled with a hot-water tank, but there was also room for some linen and a few towels. So far, so unremarkable.

The living-room floor hadn't been vacuumed in a while, the remains of a takeaway curry still lying on the low table between the sofa and the television. Turning his attention to the rest of the room, McLean was struck by the lack of any personalisation. The pictures could have been in any flat anywhere in the country. Any cheap hotel for that matter. There were no books, he noticed, and the only thing that looked like it might have meant something to the woman who lived there was a single framed photograph on the mantelpiece. It showed a man in military uniform and a woman, posed slightly awkwardly with a baby between them. The dated hairstyles and saturated colours reminded him of pictures his grandmother had kept in an old album. Family shots taken in the early 1970s, before his parents had caught that fateful flight from Inverness. He recognised one of the people in the photograph as Detective Superintendent

Grace Ramsay, although back then she would more likely have been a detective constable. The man must have been her husband, the baby young Anya.

'Nothing much in the kitchen, sir. She lived here sure enough, but it doesn't look like she ever had friends round.' DS Gregg joined him in the living room, saw the plate and foil containers on the table. 'More of a takeaway kind of person, I see.'

'Not a lot in here either. I don't know Renfrew well, but you'd think there'd be something here that showed a bit of personality, wouldn't you? The house in Joppa's a bit characterless too.'

'I see what you mean.' Gregg turned slowly, taking in the room. She walked over to the window, tugged back the lace curtain and looked outside, first down to the road and then up towards the top of the tower block that swallowed most of the light from across the way. Finally she went to the mantelpiece and picked up the photograph.

'Could have been taken forty years ago. More, maybe. It's almost as if she hasn't had a life since then.'

'There's still the master bedroom. Maybe we'll get lucky there.'

Gregg looked at him as if she couldn't quite believe what he'd just said. McLean wasn't sure he could either, hiding his embarrassment by striding out of the room and across the hall. The bedroom was a decent size for an Edinburgh tenement in this part of town, but not big by the standards of his own house. It was dominated by a double bed and an antique wardrobe that must have been fun to get up the stairs. The bed had been made, but a few clothes were lain out across it as if Renfrew had been deciding what to wear for her evening out in the woods and couldn't make up her mind. None of the garments were as racy as the ones they'd found in Joppa, but neither were they the kind of thing he'd have expected Renfrew to wear.

'These are a bit glamorous.' Gregg picked up a dress in a thin, gold material that shimmered like fine silk. She held it up to herself, but it clearly hadn't been cut for someone of her shape. 'Shame. It would fit in perfectly at the folk club.'

'Maybe not these two though.' McLean waved a hand at the other dresses. They'd not look out of place in Newcastle on a Saturday night. He walked over to the wardrobe, opened the first of its three doors to reveal several more outfits he'd associate with a high-end sex worker rather than a long-serving police admin support officer. Those clothes were behind the second and third doors. Anya Renfrew's two different lives laid out side by side.

33

'To be honest, Tony, this isn't really my area of expertise. Soft tissue, organs, that sort of thing. I'm more comfortable dealing with those.'

McLean stood in his customary position in the post-mortem theatre, watching as his old friend the city pathologist laid out a selection of bones on the central examination table. Unpleasant though it was to be there, it wasn't as horrible as some post-mortems he'd attended down the years, and there was none of the usual smell of decay. In its place, the faintest whiff of burning heather permeated the room, a reminder of the fire that had uncovered this grisly find.

'If it's any consolation, I'll not ask you for an estimated time of death.'

Cadwallader sighed at the joke, peered at a bone and then put it back in the white plastic container they'd all been brought to the mortuary in before selecting another.

'I couldn't even begin to hazard a guess. Some a lot longer ago than others. Right now I'm not even sure exactly how many people we're dealing with here. More than the three I thought it might be when I examined them in situ. And that's just what we found at the surface. Christ only knows how many more there are up there.'

McLean shuddered at the thought of it. Quite apart from the horror of finding so many dead, his mind was already spinning through the ramifications. It was only a matter of time before the press got hold of the story and ran wild with it. He didn't much relish broaching the subject of overtime costs with the DCC, but between this and the search for Anya Renfrew their understaffed team were going to have to put in a lot of extra hours. Beg a lot of favours. At least Professor Turner was happy to work the site with as many volunteer students as she could muster, but they still needed oversight.

'This one's probably the oldest. And the most interesting.' Cadwallader's voice broke through his musing, dragging McLean's attention from the central examination table to the next one along. The bones laid out on this one made the most obvious skeleton, although none of them were exactly complete. They'd not found any skulls, for one thing.

'Oldest as in age at death, or time in the ground?'

'Fair enough, I should be more precise. Longest in the ground, although none of these were buried particularly deep. And that's what's so fascinating about them.'

'OK. I know you're dying to tell me, so what is so fascinating?'

The pathologist looked at him with an expression that reminded McLean of his housemaster at boarding school. One of the few of the masters there who didn't subscribe to the ethos of corporal punishment, he had kept the boys under his care in line with a mixture of praise carefully rationed and a knack for making you feel utterly miserable when you had done something wrong. His disappointment could crush the hardiest of souls, the knowledge that you had let him down, let the house down and let yourself down too. Cadwallader had somehow managed to tap into that same vein of deepest dismay.

'What do you remember about the scene where these bones were found, Tony?' Even the pathologist's tone was the same.

Old Mr Hewitson come back to haunt him.

'Up on the moors, in a deep gully that would have been covered in thick vegetation before the fire scoured everything down to the peat and stones.'

'And we had no idea they were there, did we?' Cadwallader opened his arms wide to encompass all the examination tables with their assorted bones, the partly reassembled skeletons of long-dead people. 'Tell me, Tony. Have there been the occasional unaccountable human bone discoveries in the area recently?'

McLean understood where his friend was going with this. He should have seen it himself, straight away. 'These bones were on the surface, not really buried at all. If they'd been dumped as whole bodies or even chopped up, then the scavengers and carrion birds would have spread bits of them around. Someone would have found something, a hand or a foot maybe. Reported it. That's what you're trying to say, right?'

Cadwallader favoured him with a condescending smile. 'Exactly so. I suspected as much when I saw them in the ground, but now I'm sure of it. These bones were dumped, as you put it. Some might have been buried deep enough to keep animals away, but not all of them. Whoever did it was either too lazy, or didn't think it necessary because there wasn't a scrap of meat on them. No connective tissue, no cartilage, no flesh or skin. Nothing left to attract carrion feeders. Do you know the only sure way to remove all the flesh from a skeleton?'

'Beetles?'

The pathologist shook his head irritably. 'The only other way, smarty-pants.' He picked up one of the larger bones from the central examination table and held it under the light. 'Here, look at this.'

McLean stepped closer, realising as he did so that there had been no need for his more normal distance. There would be no dissecting of these bodies, no need for scalpels, no whine of electric bone saw as the skull was opened up. He wasn't familiar enough with skeletal anatomy to identify exactly what the pathologist was holding, but it had the look of a child's drawing of a bone about it. Long and thin, with knobbly joint lobes at either end. Its time in, or on, the ground had stained it dark yellow, and the fire had left soot marks in places. If it had come out of an ossuary he wouldn't have raised an eyebrow.

'It's a bone,' he said.

'It's a left femur from a middle-aged woman actually. More important are these marks on it here, see?' Cadwallader angled the bone to the light, pointing just below the joint. McLean strained to look closer, wishing his eyes weren't quite so tired. Maybe a trip to the optician's was overdue. He couldn't see anything beyond the stains and the soot. A crack up the length that must have happened after death. 'What am I looking at?'

'Here. These marks. Like chips in the bone. See them?' Cadwallader held the bone even nearer, so that McLean's nose was filled with the scent of burning earth and something much deeper. This close, he could finally see what the pathologist was talking about, a series of parallel lines etched into the surface an inch or so below the more shiny lobe of the joint. They were stained, so must have happened before the bone went into the ground. He recalled a recent lecture, a series of projected images.

'Knife marks?'

'Ten out of ten, Chief Inspector.' Cadwallader put the bone down on the examination table in roughly the space where a left thigh should be, picked up a right forearm. 'And see here? Much the same. All of these bones show similar markings. They've been cut. More accurately I should say they've been butchered.'

The cold sensation seeped into his gut as he studied the skeletons with new sight. 'And the best way to get flesh off a bone is to boil it. Like soup.'

The pathologist carefully replaced the bone in its place on the table, reached for another from the box. 'Soup would suggest cannibalism, Tony. It's possible these bodies have been rendered down simply to make identification impossible. We don't know what became of the soft tissues.'

McLean had to concede that Cadwallader was right. It didn't make him feel any better. 'And what about this one?' He pointed at the skeleton on the central table. 'You said this was the most interesting?'

The pathologist put the bone back down again, then crossed to the table and picked up another. 'This one might be useful for identification. See here?' He pointed at the surface, and McLean saw it immediately.

'It's been broken, then healed. Some time before death.'

'So you do pay attention sometimes. Excellent. Yes, she'd broken her right tibia. About ten years before death, I'd say. And it's set well, so she was looked after properly. Given plenty of time to heal. If you've got a twenty-five to thirty-year-old woman with a broken leg from her late childhood, reported missing maybe twenty, thirty years ago? Well, this could be her.'

McLean looked at the bone, not really seeing it any more. He remembered what he'd been trying to remember now, his conversation with Grace Ramsay. People going missing near Gladhouse Reservoir, she'd said. Ask Duguid about the unsolved cases where she'd been SIO.

'You've got that look on your face, Tony. Thought of something?' Cadwallader asked, breaking the moment.

'I have indeed, Angus. Something I need to follow up right away.' He looked once more at the bone, the telltale mark where it had been broken so many years before. 'But I've a feeling I'm not going to be popular for mentioning it.'

The cool air of the station basement was a welcome contrast after a sweaty climb up the hill from the city mortuary. McLean stood in the corridor outside the CCU room, enjoying the light breeze for a moment before he knocked on the door and went in.

Ex-Detective Superintendent Charles Duguid sat at his desk. His anglepoise lamp cast light on whatever he was reading and reflected brightly off the shiny bald top of his head. He looked up at the noise, pulled his spectacles down to the tip of his nose and peered over them.

'Here comes trouble,' he said, although not unkindly. 'Why do I get the impression you're looking for something?'

McLean ignored the half-hearted insult. 'I spoke to Grace Ramsay a couple of days ago. She said I should ask you about the cold-case files where she was SIO on the original investigations. That make any sense to you?'

'Nothing that woman says makes any sense to me.' Duguid took off his spectacles, folded them carefully and tucked them into the breast pocket of his jacket before standing up. He stalked across to the long row of filing cabinets at the far end of the room, ran his fingers down them one by one until he found what he was looking for.

'Missing-persons cases. She was always obsessed with them. Saw connections where there weren't any. Ignored obvious conclusions in favour of something much more complicated.' He pulled out a drawer, flipped through it, then fished out a slim folder. McLean had thought he was going to hand it over to him, but instead Duguid closed the cabinet and took the folder back to his desk before speaking again.

'Reminds me a bit of you really. Or maybe you remind me of her. That'd explain why I always thought you were so insufferable.'

'You do realise her own daughter's gone missing,' McLean said.

'Which is exactly why you should take anything she says with a fistful of salt. She's unreliable and emotionally attached. And bonkers with it.'

And you're not? McLean managed to keep the thought to himself. 'Well, we've got bones from at least three bodies up on Oakhill Moor, one of which shows signs of a pre-mortem healed fracture that could well be on a medical record somewhere.'

Duguid had opened up his new folder and was reaching for his spectacles again, but he gave up, sat back in his seat with a sigh. 'And you want me to look into it.'

'You as in the CCU, yes. Angus should have all the details to you by the end of the day.'

'As you can see, we're not exactly over-staffed here.' Duguid raised both hands, palms up, to indicate the otherwise empty room. 'I've even lost my loyal sidekick, and he's meant to be retiring at the end of the month.'

McLean shrugged. They were all short staffed, but this needed looking into. He'd work out how to pay for it once it was done.

'I'll see about getting you some help. But you need to go easy on the young constables. The last lot won't even look me in the eye any more.'

34

Leaving Duguid to his miserable loneliness, McLean walked the short distance along the basement corridor to the room given over to the IT forensics team, ever hopeful that they might have been able to do something with Anya Renfrew's phone. He didn't often visit, possibly because him and electronics were barely on speaking terms, and possibly because there was a certain aroma about the place. The only window was a light well, but the same could be said about the Cold Case Unit at the other side of the station, and that didn't smell like a teenage boy's bedroom. The underlying whiff of fried electronics didn't help either. At least the man who ruled this subterranean domain was dependable. And clean. Mike Simpson had been part of the support team in the station almost as long as Anya Renfrew.

'Bastard thing wasn't easy to crack, y'know.'

'But you managed, right?' McLean looked at the phone lying in a hastily cleared space on an otherwise cluttered workbench. It looked a lot like the old physics lab at school, far more 1970s and a lot less technical than he would have expected. The phone itself was by far the most modern piece of equipment to be seen.

'Oh ye of little faith.' Simpson reached for the phone, clicked a button on the side and the screen lit up. No passcode request, no invitation to read a thumbprint. Just a standard smartphone screen with remarkably few icons on display.

'Of course, it'd be a different story if this was an iPhone. They're not infallible, but they're a lot harder to break into. This would normally be easy, but whoever owns it knows their security.'

'Nobody told you who it belongs to?'

Simpson shook his head slightly. 'It's usually need-to-know. I don't, so I never ask. I was told it was important and needed doing quickly, but that's pretty standard too.'

'Can I?' McLean reached for the phone but didn't pick it up. The cable plugged into the charging socket looked rather more jury-rigged than standard and he didn't want to break anything.

'Sure.' Simpson tugged it out without a care, then handed the phone over. 'It's got a full charge now. Should be good for a while. We've mirrored the memory on this little thing.' He tapped a squat grey plastic box on the workbench. 'It's a full backup, so we can dig through the apps and settings without worrying about losing stuff.'

McLean tapped at the screen to wake it again. He should probably give the phone to one of the younger detectives to work through, but there was no harm in looking at the text messages, contacts and any photos that might be on it. The call log showed several attempts by Police Scotland to call the number since the previous Friday, but nothing outgoing. The standard texts were all about meeting up at Fanny's Folk Club, and none of them were less than a month old. They'd be followed up of course, but it wasn't exactly the breakthrough he'd been hoping for.

'Is this the only messaging service on the phone?' he asked, after peering at the screen for a while longer. He knew when he was defeated by technology.

'SMS?' Simpson took the handset from him and swiped at the screen a couple of times. Then he tapped at an icon and pushed his spectacles back up his nose to get a better look. 'Here we go.

Good old WhatsApp. Seems whoever owned this was part of a group calling themselves the GoodDog Group. Looks like they exchanged messages and arranged meetings. Ah. Ew.'

'What?' McLean leaned over so that he could see what Simpson was looking at. Then wished he hadn't.

'Is that what I think it is?' The technician angled the screen, leaned in close, then pulled back again. 'Ew.'

'WhatsApp's secure, encrypted and all that stuff, right?' McLean asked as Simpson handed him the phone as if it was a baby's soiled nappy.

'That's the one. If we'd not been able to get into this phone, we'd never have been able to crack those messages. Given that photograph I think that might probably have been a good thing. Not sure I'm going to forget that in a while, and I've seen stuff doing this job, let me tell you.'

McLean swiped away the image, unsure he'd be able to forget it in a while either. There were other messages in the conversation though, many dated from the previous Friday night. He scrolled down until he reached the last, thankfully text only this time. It came from somebody calling themselves JackieBigTits.

Police presence at BGC. New meeting site at this location. GoodDogs are go! JBTx

He tapped the underlined word, and the phone opened a mapping app. A message flashed up about no internet connection, but he didn't need it to connect to know where the meeting had been. The app was already centred on the car park at Gladhouse.

'Don't suppose we've any way of finding out who this person is?' McLean pointed at the screen, which Simpson seemed reluctant to look at again.

'There's a number associated with the account. We can try tracking it back to an owner, but if they've any sense it'll be a burner phone.' Simpson took the phone back, tapped away at the screen for a moment, then walked over to his computer terminal. Writing down the number on a slip of paper by the keyboard seemed somewhat low-tech to McLean, but he wasn't going to point that out if it worked. He waited while the IT specialist tapped and scrolled away. If all else failed, he could always try texting Jackie Big Tits, he supposed. Maybe even phone her. Or him.

'Well, what do you know?' Simpson stood up straight, angling the terminal screen so that McLean could see. A match for the number and an entry on the database. He read the name with a sense of disbelief.

'If this name and address are correct, clearly not as much as I thought. Thanks, Mike. This should make for a very interesting interview.'

McLean had never met Danielle Murray before, but he knew well enough who she was. Or at least he had thought he did. He'd read her reviews in the weekend papers, and even managed to wade through the first three chapters of her debut novel before something more interesting had distracted him. He'd seen photographs of her at posh literary events and never really thought much about what she looked like; it wasn't important, after all. Now, as she sat across the table from him in interview room one, he could understand the pseudonym she used for the GoodDog Group.

'I must say, this is most irregular, Detective Chief Inspector. The officers who brought me here refused to say why. Only that it was of the utmost importance and urgency.'

'That's because they don't know why. I thought it best to keep the circle of people who do to a minimum. It's just me at the moment. I expect you'll probably want us to keep it that way.' He didn't bother telling her about Mike Simpson, confident that the IT specialist wouldn't be the source of any leak.

'I'm sure I don't know what you mean,' Murray said.

'Perhaps the phrase "GoodDog" means something to you? Or maybe "Jackie Big Tits"?'

If he hadn't been trained in observing people, and with many years' experience behind him, McLean might have missed the tell. Murray didn't flinch at the words, but her expression remained just a little too bland. The second of the two phrases at least should have warranted some reaction from a woman of her stature. She stared at him impassively for a count of five seconds, then shook her head slowly.

'No. Can't say they do.'

'So you don't know anything about this message then?' He slid Renfrew's phone from its evidence bag, switched it on and tapped the icons until he found what he was looking for. Turned the whole thing around and placed it, screen up, on the table between them. 'It was sent from your mobile.'

Murray stared at the screen for a long while, and now the conflicting emotions played across her face like a cartoon. McLean gave her the time she needed to come to terms with what she was seeing.

'I don't . . . That is, I . . .' She picked up the phone. 'How did you get this?'

'It belongs to another member of your . . .' McLean struggled for a collective noun. ' . . . group? She was out at Gladhouse last Friday, same as you. Unlike you, she never made it home.'

'Oh.' Murray thumbed the screen, then put the phone back down again. 'Oh my God. Amazing Grace? What happened? Is she . . . ?'

Amazing Grace? Well, it made sense, he supposed. McLean leaned back in his seat, almost folded his hands across his chest too, but stopped himself at the last minute. 'So you do actually know about the GoodDog Group, and you are, in fact, Jackie Big Tits.'

As if to emphasise the name, Murray clasped her hands to her ample bosom theatrically. 'What can I say? My secret is out. Are you going to arrest me now?'

'What you do isn't illegal.' McLean held up one hand and waved it about. 'Well, not strictly speaking. It's a bit of a grey area, as I'm sure you know. That's why you relocated to Gladhouse last Friday, isn't it. "Police presence at BGC". That's Braids Golf Club, I'm guessing. We had a few complaints, and that's when having sex in public becomes an offence. When people are offended and complain to us about it.'

Murray said nothing, but he could see the look in her eyes. She wasn't stupid.

'So why Gladhouse? Who decided that was to be the place?'

'I've no idea. I was just given the details and asked to pass them on. It's quite a way off our normal patch, but this time of year, and this weather? We go where we can. Like you say, it's not illegal until someone sees and is offended enough to make a complaint. Everyone's much happier if that doesn't happen.'

Now that she had come to terms with the initial shock of discovery, Murray seemed surprisingly unashamed about her participation in the city's dogging scene. McLean supposed he should be glad, although the whole thing left him feeling ever so slightly unclean. Well, it would be time to go home soon. Then he could have a shower. A long, cold one.

'I don't suppose you could tell me who gave you the details?' he asked.

'His user name is Big Jim. That's all I know. Well, apart from that it's apt. Might recognise him in the street, but I've no idea what his real name is, or what he does other than . . . well.'

'Is there a meeting this weekend?'

Murray gave him a grin that could only be described as

lascivious. 'Why, Chief Inspector? Were you thinking of coming along? We do have one or two police officers who are regulars, you know.' She switched from playful to serious in an instant. 'But no. Not that I know of. I'm sure we're not the only group active in the city, but once a month's more than enough for me. Anticipation is a large part of the thrill, don't you think?'

He ignored that. 'Was there anything unusual about last Friday's meeting? Apart from the location, that is? Any new faces, unwelcome behaviour, that sort of thing?'

Murray thought for a moment before answering, always a good sign. 'Not that I noticed, although I wasn't necessarily paying much attention to the other people there. Well, some of them. Seemed to be a good evening. I probably left earlier than most. Had to file a review for the paper.'

For a moment McLean thought she meant a review about her experiences in the woods, then he remembered her day job. He glanced at his watch, aware that it was getting late and he had places to be. He gathered up the phone and put it back in the bag, picked up his unused notebook.

'Thank you, Ms Murray. You've been very helpful. I might have some more questions for you later, but that's enough to be going on with.' He stood up, and she did the same, a look of uncertainty coming onto her face now.

'This . . . It's just helping with enquiries, right? And the whole Jackie thing's just between the two of us.'

'I'm not interested in spreading malicious gossip, if that's what you mean. Until we find An— . . . Amazing Grace though, I can't promise anything. If we find her and something's happened, there'll be an enquiry. I can't predict what that will turn up, so let's just hope we find her soon, and well.' There was no point in asking her not to talk to the group about it. He knew that she would anyway, and who knew? Maybe that would shake something loose.

'Thank you.' Murray held his gaze for a little longer than was necessary. 'I've not met a detective before who was so . . . understanding?'

McLean shrugged. He'd have called it calculating himself. 'There was one thing I was wondering though. Why Jackie Big Tits? You don't look like a Kooks fan to me.'

Murray's frown suggested that she'd not got the reference. 'My mother's name is Jacqueline. Horrible prude of a woman, always sneering at people, spends most of her time in church these days. And, well . . .' She pointed at her chest with both hands, smiled. 'What else could I be?'

35

In the end the shower had been warm, and far too short for his liking. McLean had left the station at a reasonable enough time, but he knew better than to try and explain his late arrival home on bad traffic. Emma's pursed lips and tapping foot had been warning enough. She'd calmed down a bit once they were in the taxi and on their way, and by the time they arrived she was almost speaking to him.

The gallery where Meg Turner's exhibition was on display was a new one on him. Tucked away in a side street in the West End, it would have been easy to overlook the gap in the railings, and the tiny window looking onto a narrow light well promised a crowded room beyond. Hardly the best place to step back and admire some pictures.

'You sure this is the place?' he asked as Emma waited impatiently for him to catch up. He could see by her scowl it was the wrong thing to say.

'Bloody well better be. We're late already. Hurry up, Tony.'

As far as he was aware, they were maybe fifteen minutes past the opening time. If he knew anything about art establishments, it was that they were at least an hour early. If they were lucky, there would be no one to let them in yet, and they could nip around the corner to the pub. He wasn't feeling lucky though.

Sticky, yes, despite having showered and changed not long ago. The sun might have dipped behind the tall buildings now, but its heat still radiated from the stone.

Emma couldn't wait for him any more, descending a short flight of stairs and disappearing inside. He paused for long enough to read a small brass sign fixed to the rail at the top of the steps.

Galleria Subterranea – Fine Art Exhibitors

Beside it, a less permanent poster advertised that this was indeed the right place, and that tonight was the opening night of a week-long exhibition by the artist Megan Turner, a series of paintings and sculptures inspired by her visits to mass graves and other sites of genocide around the world. Taking a deep breath, McLean set off down the stairs. He hoped there would at the very least be wine to drink. Preferably lots of it.

'Tony, Emma. You came.' McLean had barely stepped inside the front door before he was being swept into a fierce hug. Professor Turner – Hattie, he reminded himself – was dressed in the same somewhat shabby manner as when she and Meg had come to dinner. Her wife, on the other hand, had made more of an effort. Her face was flawlessly made up, she wore an elegant black dress and had tied back her hair in a neat braid. Her necklace looked expensive, diamonds sparkling in silver, and she clutched a glass of champagne with fingers that couldn't quite keep still. Nervous at her opening night, perhaps.

'Tony, it's good to see you again.' She held out her free hand to be shaken, which McLean found he preferred to the hug.

'I hope we're not too early,' he said. 'I'm never sure with these things.'

'Punctuality is the politeness of kings. And of course it's easier to see the paintings when the gallery's not full.'

At the mention of paintings, Meg turned slightly, sweeping her arm in the direction of the main body of the gallery. The reception area was something of a mezzanine, more steps descending to a much larger room beyond, and McLean was surprised at just how large the room was, how far back it stretched under the tenements above. He wouldn't have thought that a vaulted basement would lend itself to such a use, but the stone had been painted white, and someone worth every penny of their fee had designed a lighting system that seemed to cast no awkward shadows. The paintings hung on stands either side of the space, sculptures dotted around the centre on daises of varying height.

A glass balustrade gave him a clear view of the exhibition floor, and, as he looked around, McLean could see that he and Emma weren't the first to arrive. The room would take ten times the number of people already there before it felt crowded though.

'I have to confess to having a bit of a dead eye when it comes to art.' McLean turned back to Meg, who was standing beside a larger version of the poster on the railings outside. It was dominated by a reproduction of one of her works, an abstract composition of mostly black and red, with here and there flecks of white like bone splinters. 'The subject matter's . . . interesting too.'

Meg laughed, an almost girlie giggle that was surprising yet fitted her perfectly. 'Truth be told, most of the people here have a dead eye for art. It's just that they like to be seen at events like this. Grab yourself a glass of fizz, Tony. Stand in front of any one of these pictures and just listen to what other people say about it. You'll be surprised, trust me.'

He tried to tell whether Meg was joking, but she was too well made up, and her eyes had that odd colour to them he

209

remembered from their dinner. Definitely contacts, or she was some kind of faerie. He glanced back to where Emma was still talking to the professor, hopeful of some moral support. The two of them were deep in conversation and quite oblivious to anyone else. More people were coming in through the door now too. Meg would need to greet them.

'I'll give it a go,' he said. At the top of the stairs leading down to the gallery, a table was laid out with glasses of champagne; orange juice for those who preferred their art sober. He considered it for all of a second before opting for something fizzy and, with a deep breath, descended into the fray.

'Fascinating how she blends the surreal and the horrific in a melange of sensual brushwork, don't you think?'

McLean stared at what to him looked like an abstract depiction of a coal hearth as the embers died down to nothing. Beside him a young man with awkward facial hair was talking to a woman in a kimono, who kept wafting herself with a fan like a geisha even though she was more likely from Tranent than Tokyo. Top marks for effort with her costume though.

'It all seems a bit brutal to me. The darkness crushes your soul, sucks it in and you become one with the oils.'

Definitely Tranent, by way of the Glasgow School of Art department of pseudo-intellectualism. He'd been just as much of a twat at that age of course; in his case a student trying to impress with his rather flawed knowledge of basic psychology, arrogant in his certainty that he knew all there was to know about a subject he'd only just begun to study. And at least they were both trying. If a little too hard.

Turning away, his attention was caught by a sculpture off towards the back of the gallery. He paused for long enough to allow a young waiter to refill his glass, and ambled over for a closer look. About a metre high, it was made from strands of rusted steel razor wire, twisted into something that might have been a horse's head in one of Picasso's more wild nightmares. There was no denying that it was a powerful piece of work, but he wasn't sure he'd want it in his home. Chances were he'd cut himself on it and end up with tetanus, for one thing.

'What are you thinking, Tony?'

He turned a little too swiftly, the familiar twinge of pain shooting up his hip where he'd broken the bone some years earlier. Meg had crept up on him unawares, something that wasn't too hard given the crowd now building in the gallery.

'Honestly?' he asked.

'Always.'

He looked back at the piece again, speaking to it rather than her. 'It's impressive, evocative. There's certainly pain in there, and terror too.'

'But you wouldn't give it house room.' Meg smiled.

'Your words, not mine.' McLean shrugged. 'But no. I'd be worried about tearing my clothes. Or worse.'

'You're probably right. The wire came from a concentration camp in Uganda. One of my darker periods, I think.' Meg's eyes lost their focus for a moment, no doubt seeing something that had happened long ago. Then she snapped back to herself with a jolt. 'Oh bugger. What's she doing here?'

McLean followed her gaze across the gallery towards the stairs down from the mezzanine. For a moment he couldn't work out who among the many women in the crowd such a heavily emphasised 'she' could refer to. Then he spotted her, leading from the front.

'Oh, isn't that Danielle Murray?' he asked.

'You know her?'

'Not exactly, but we have met. She's art critic for one of the broadsheets, isn't she?'

'She gave me a horrible review the last time I had a show up

211

here. Thought I'd told Robert to keep her name off the invitation list.'

'Do you think that would have helped?'

'Probably not. She'd just make up some snark anyway.' Meg drained her glass, looked around for a refill. 'I suppose I'd better go and talk to her, at least try to be civil.'

McLean spotted a passing waiter and managed to grab two full glasses off his tray before he disappeared. He handed one to Meg. 'Here. Why don't I come and give you some moral support.'

36

Who is she?

Light burns through the closed lids of her eyes, red like blood. For a while she is convinced it is the sun beating down on her like an abusive partner, flaying the skin from her face with its merciless heat. But she feels no warmth, only a deep bone-chill that sends spasms of shivering through her.

Who is she?

Movement is futile, impossible. The heavy weight of a coarse blanket pins her down without giving her any warmth. She can only lie shivering, sluggish thoughts picking around the central question of her identity. She doesn't know how she came to be here, where here is, what has happened to her. But she knows she cannot move. Or is it that she must not move? In case the monster sees her, comes for her?

Another spasm of shivering, and this time she instinctively curls in on herself for warmth. Foetal. It's only as she feels her bony knees against her arms that she understands she is not strapped down. Why did she think she was?

Fearful, she holds still in this new position, the light less bright on her tight-closed eyes. She strains to hear the beast approaching, but there is nothing save a distant trickle of water. She listens to it for a long time, not daring to move, but as she concentrates on the sound, so the pressure builds up in her bladder, the burn between her legs growing ever more insistent.

The light is not bright when she opens her eyes, but it hurts none the less. For a while all she can do is blink and squint, details slowly resolving themselves in her vision. A dirt floor, hard-packed. Stone walls painted white. She lies on her side on a narrow bed, the mattress bare and stained, the blanket too small, too thin. A pair of old tin buckets stand in the far corner of her cell, and as she sees them she realises that this is, indeed, a cell.

Who is she?

Reaching bare feet out, she shifts slowly into a seated position. She is naked, but clean. A memory of being washed, an old woman's voice, rough flannel like an animal's tongue on her skin. Cold. She looks at her arms, the scratches dark, the bruises yellowing at their edges. Running through trees, chased, terrified. She remembers it now, but it is almost as if she watched it happen to another person. She feels no connection to the events. No connection to anything.

Shivers run through her, chattering her teeth together as she hugs herself tight. But there is no warmth in her arms, and the pressure in her bladder is unbearable. She stands, sways, almost blacks out. A moment to gather herself, then she steps over to the buckets. One has a wooden lid, and underneath it is empty. The other holds water, that same rough flannel draped over the lip. She relieves herself in the first bucket, a sour smell filling her tiny cell until she puts the lid back in place.

It's only as she's cleaning herself with the wetted flannel that she realises how empty she feels. Beyond hunger, she is hollowed out. Weak from it, and so cold. She can't remember the last time she ate anything, but then neither can she remember how she came to be here.

Or who she is.

She walks slowly to the door, a heavy thing of ancient oak

planks and black iron nails. A small hatch at head height might look out onto whatever lies beyond, were it not covered over on the outside. At her feet, unnoticed in the gloom until now, she finds a tray with a cup and a jug. No food, only water. As she bends to pick them up, the world darkens even further, tilting dangerously so that she is forced to retreat to the bed, sit before she falls.

The water tastes flat, as if it has sat in the jug a long while. There's an odd bitterness to it too, that she only notices after the first cupful. She doesn't care, drinks it all just to feel some weight in her empty stomach. And then with sudden violence it all comes rushing back up again. She spews so hard she thinks she might have broken her ribs, spasms and chokes and retches. Somehow she has gone from sitting on the bed to crouching on the floor, hands pressed hard into the dirt.

She vomits until there is nothing left in her but bile. Then she vomits some more. A dark line marks the ground where the water has soaked in, reaching almost as far as the bucket in the corner. By the time the roiling in her stomach has settled she is so weak she can barely struggle back onto the bed. She hugs the useless blanket about her, curls up into as tight a ball as she can, shivering both at the shock and the cold. Somewhere deep down she feels this is penance, punishment for some terrible sin. But, as she drifts once more into frozen oblivion, she can't help but wish her hell was one of fire.

37

The call came in as he was driving across the meadows, breaking through the music McLean had managed to coax out of the overly complicated radio in his Alfa. Early Monday morning after a sort of weekend off. Sort of because while he'd managed to spend most of it at home, he'd still been working, much to Emma's annoyance. It wasn't as if he could go anywhere of course. Not with Renfrew missing, Operation Caterwaul in limbo, bones found on the moors and the budgets shot to pieces. But he was doing his best, and he wished she could see that.

A quick glance showed that it was the forensics lab, so he tapped the button on the big screen to accept it.

'McLean.'

A moment's silence, as if the person making the call hadn't been expecting an answer. Then the familiar voice of Amanda Parsons, forensic technician and DC Harrison's flatmate, cut in. 'Are you driving?'

'I am indeed, Ms Parsons. But it's hands-free, so you don't need to worry.'

'"Ms Parsons"? You sound like my boss. Call me Manda, please. If only to wind up poor Janie.'

'I thought you were on holiday, Manda.' McLean gave in, knowing that it would take longer for the forensic technician to get to the point than it would for him to drive to the station otherwise.

'Aye, I was. But someone asked us to DNA sample a couple hundred used condoms, so they called everyone in for a party. My fault for letting slip I wasn't leaving the country, I guess.'

McLean shifted in his seat, uncomfortable even though Amanda Parsons was many miles away. 'I did tell Doctor Cairns it wasn't highest priority. It could have waited –'

'Till I got back? Aye, you're all heart, Detective Chief Inspector. I was still going to be the one lumbered with the job.'

'I take it you've not called just to moan at me about it though? Seems a bit early for results already.'

'Aye, well. We've not run them all, and we've only done preliminary tests to weed out the duplicates. We've a couple potential hits off the offenders' register though. High enough confidence to be worth taking further, I'd guess. I've pinged them off to your team, but I thought you'd like to know soonest.'

More likely angling for some praise, possibly a favour. Maybe both.

'That's great work, Manda. Thanks.' He didn't tell her that since he'd spoken to Jackie Big Tits the DNA sampling to identify other participants at the dogging site had become less high priority. Mostly because he didn't want to upset her or Dr Cairns, but also because he'd forgotten all about it. Maybe he really did need a weekend off. A proper one.

'You've no right dragging me in like this. It's harassment, that's what it is.'

Even without knowing his background and arrest record, McLean reckoned he wouldn't have had much time for the man sitting across the table from him in interview room three. Dennis Johns wasn't the gift to mankind he thought he was. More of a pain in the arse. His nasal whine made him sound like he might burst into tears at any moment, and there was an odour about him that suggested being nervous upset his digestive system. There was plenty for him to be nervous about, unfortunately, and the window in the interview room didn't open. It did let in the sunlight, which was making everything uncomfortably warm as well as malodorous.

'Mr Johns. Would you have preferred it if we'd asked your employer for a room at work so we could interview you there? What sort of questions do you think they'd have asked once we'd finished?'

Johns opened his mouth to complain again, then his brain caught up. 'I've not done anything wrong,' he said, slumping back in his seat like a petulant schoolboy.

'That's not strictly speaking true now, is it, Mr Johns?' McLean leaned his elbows on the table and stared at the man over clasped hands. Beside him, Grumpy Bob sat motionless and staring. Detective Sergeant Laird was usually the relaxed and avuncular one in interview situations, but he could outstare a statue when he needed to. Now, with his arms folded across his chest and head tilted ever so slightly to one side, he was creating a dead zone in the room where Johns couldn't look for more than an instant. He didn't want to look at McLean either, but eventually he had no choice.

'I don't know what I'm supposed to have done. You've got the wrong man, aye?'

There was something of the confused ferret about Dennis Johns. His eyes were just too close together, his nose that little bit too long and thin. Perhaps a different hairstyle might have lessened the effect, but there was only so much a barber could do with what little hair the man had. As it was, his widow's peak gave him the look of a third-rate supervillain from a 1970s comic book. They'd picked him up on his way to work in a data warehouse down in Newhaven, and he was wearing some kind of company uniform that did him no favours either. Dark-brown nylon was never a good look.

'Seems you've moved on from grooming teenage girls now, Dennis.'

'I never –' he started to say, then shut up again.

'You were out at Gladhouse Reservoir week ago last Friday night. Enjoying the local wildlife.'

Johns went very still in his chair. 'I never . . .' he said again.

'DNA says otherwise. You should probably clean up after, you know? Amazing what you can get from a used condom. And, of course, we've got you on the database.'

'It's not . . . I didn't . . . You don't . . . There's no harm . . .' Johns's head twitched from side to side as he looked first at McLean, then at the space occupied by Grumpy Bob, then at McLean again, back and forth. It must have been sore on his neck.

'There's every harm, Dennis. It is, you did and we do.' McLean opened up his notepad and fished a pen out of his pocket, perhaps a little more theatrically than was necessary.

'Do I no' get a solicitor then?' Johns finally found some backbone in the jelly of his spine.

'Only if we charge you. Which depends on whether or not you cooperate. So. Tell us all about your little session, aye. How'd you find out about it?'

Something like relief passed across the man's face. 'Easy enough. There's websites and stuff tell you all about what's happening and where. I can give you the address if you're interested.'

'I think it's a bit more sophisticated than that, isn't it now, Dennis?' McLean put the pen down on top of the pad. 'You use secure messaging to arrange meetings, don't you? And if there's a crackdown somewhere, you all warn each other, arrange somewhere else to go. That's what happened last Friday, isn't it?

Heavy police presence at Braid Golf Course, so you all hightail it out to Gladhouse.'

'Why are you asking me this stuff if you know the answers already?'

'Perhaps you could tell me how it all works then.' McLean ignored the question. 'You head out to a car park in the woods, the back of some shopping centre, somewhere like that. And what? You just wait? Is there a signal? Do the . . . ladies come to you? Or maybe you just like to watch, aye?'

Johns bristled in his chair, taking this as the insult to his manhood that McLean had intended. 'It's all consensual. There's nothing illegal, right.'

'You want to ask a judge about that, Dennis? With your record?' McLean fixed the man with a steely glare to match Grumpy Bob's. The detective sergeant still hadn't said a word, which was the whole point of his being there of course.

'Going back to Gladhouse.' McLean pulled the evidence bag containing the eye mask out of his pocket and laid it carefully on the table between them. 'Did you see a woman there wearing this?'

He didn't need to hear what Johns had to say – the answer was written all across his weasel face. He reached out for the bag, but McLean pulled it away before he could pick it up.

'That what this is all about?' Johns asked. 'She in some kind of trouble?' He squinted, leaning forward to see better.

'Do you know her?'

Johns paused, the thoughts painting themselves on his face without subtlety. Every so often his gaze would dart to Grumpy Bob, then back again. McLean left him the time he needed. It wasn't long.

'Aye. Well, no. I ken that mask though. Older lassie wearing it, right? Tall, thin, dark hair going a wee bit grey? No' bad body, mind. Amazing Grace, they call her. But that's no' her real name. Mouth on her like a vacuum cleaner.'

McLean could have done without that last bit of information. 'What time did you leave? Was she still there then?'

'No' exactly sure. One in the morning? Maybe half past? And aye, she was still there. Finishing up the stragglers and the shy boys. What's this all about then? You know who she is?' Johns perked up a bit. 'She someone famous?'

'Who she is is no concern of yours, Mr Johns. When you last saw her, and who was still about, is all that matters now.'

'Aye, well. I wasnae the last one to leave, mind. A few of the other lads might've hung about a bit longer.'

McLean picked up his pen and flicked open the notepad. 'These lads have names?'

'You think it's wise, letting him off like that?'

Grumpy Bob stood in the doorway as he and McLean watched Dennis Johns being led away by a uniformed constable. They hadn't charged him; there wasn't much point really. It might have been possible to make something stick with his entry on the sexual offenders' register, but it wouldn't have solved anything.

'He's not going to disappear any time soon. And the list of names he's given us might be useful. You'll need to get someone to run them all through the system. Maybe pull any interesting ones in for a chat.'

Grumpy Bob checked his watch. 'Might be a wee while. I'm meant to be heading off to Bestingfield in a mo.'

McLean didn't need to ask why. 'Sounds fun. You taking anyone with you?'

'No' if I can help it. I'm only going to talk to the doctor and maybe have a chat with some of the nursing staff. Reckon I can do that on my own.'

'OK. Let me know how you get on.'

'You here, sir? If anything comes up?'

'No. I'm heading out to Gladhouse again. You remember Sergeant Donaldson? From Penicuik?'

'Big chap, aye. No' sure what to make of him, to be honest, sir.'

'Well, he's taking me out to Woodhill Farm. Should have gone last week, but the moors catching fire put a stop to all that.'

'You'll be taking Janie Harrison with you, I expect.' There was the slightest note of disapproval in the old detective sergeant's voice, something McLean had become accustomed to.

'Or one of the others. Stringer or Blane are both reliable. It depends entirely on who's hanging around looking like they've nothing better to do.'

'Aye, sir. Of course.' Grumpy Bob shrugged, then without another word he turned and walked off down the corridor.

38

It was as well Police Sergeant Donaldson had given them good directions to get to Woodhill Farm. Without them, and DC Harrison's expert driving, McLean might never have found the place on his own. The expression 'middle of nowhere' sprang to mind as they drove along a narrow, rutted farm track, plotting a complex path through the potholes that studded the surface like teenage acne. At least it was dry, parched by the hot weather and endless summer sun. Come the winter rains, he'd not much fancy his chances in a big 4x4.

The farmyard once they reached it looked like the sort of place a period drama location scout would drool over. Past an open-sided steel girder shed that was more rust than iron, the track took them through a set of old stone steading buildings with arched entrances far too small for any modern agricultural machinery. That wouldn't be a problem if the ancient David Brown tractor parked at the end of a hay barn was anything to go by. It was hitched up to a small trailer laden with bales, but there didn't appear to be anyone around to unload them.

Two cars were parked outside a house barely distinguishable from the grey whinstone steadings that formed the other three sides of a large courtyard. One was an elderly Land Rover, a series one if McLean was any judge. The other was a somewhat more modern Police Scotland BMW squad car, which at least meant Donaldson had already arrived. Where the constables who were meant to be searching the farmyard and surrounding buildings were, McLean had no idea.

'Quiet here, isn't it,' Harrison observed as she climbed out of the car. The only sound was the plinking of the engine as it cooled. McLean was about to comment, but the door to the farmhouse opened and Sergeant Donaldson stepped out.

'Thought you might be a little late,' he said by way of greeting. 'People always get lost the first time they come here.'

'Like your search team?' McLean asked.

'Oh, they've been and gone. Surprised you didn't meet them on the track, though it's as well you didn't, come to think of it. You can have a look around the old buildings yourself if you want to, but there's no sign of missing admin support officers, trust me. Sandy Bayne knows this farm like the back of his hand. He'd have seen Renfrew the moment she came out of the woods.'

Something about Donaldson's breezy certainty annoyed McLean, although not enough to have him call the search team back. A full week had passed since Renfrew had gone missing now, so if she had been in one of these outbuildings she would have been noticed. And if she'd died somewhere they ought to be able to smell her by now, which reminded him he needed to check in with the dog unit.

'You seem to know a lot about this place,' he said.

'That I do. Used to spend summers up here helping with the harvest. Sandy's my cousin. Well, something cousin removed, but family, aye?' Donaldson turned to Harrison briefly. 'Morag's in the kitchen making a cup of tea, Constable. Why don't you go in and introduce yourself. I'll take the chief inspector round to the fish house and find Sandy.'

'Fish house?' McLean asked.

'Aye, come with me. It's quite something.' And without waiting the sergeant set off towards the corner of the courtyard where
a narrow passage led between the side of the house and the
nearest of the old steading buildings. As he followed Donaldson
towards the end of it, McLean finally caught the sound of
something. Running water, a soft noise underneath it that might
have been someone humming. Flagstone steps at the far end
brought them down to another set of buildings and, more
surprisingly, a large circular pond. The trees came right up to the
edge of it on the other side, their leaves reflected in the mirror
black surface. As he watched, something broke through, a fin like
some ancient sea monster rolling through the water. Ripples
spread out from it, bouncing back from the edge in an interference pattern that took far longer to dissipate than he would
have expected.

'Oh, there you are, Andrew. And I see you've brought a
friend.'

McLean looked past the sergeant to see an elderly man, who
had just emerged from the low stone building at the side of the
pond. Slightly stooped with age, he was still a giant, easily a head
taller than McLean and proportionately big. No doubting he and
Donaldson were related. His face looked like leather, wrinkled
by age and years spent outdoors in all weathers. He wore clothes
from another, earlier, era: faded gingham shirt under a pair of
dungarees that were more patch than denim and frayed around
the ankles. McLean vaguely noticed that he was barefoot, but
mostly he was fixated on the enormous fish the man carried in
his hands, cradled like a sleeping baby.

'Sandy, this is the detective I was telling you about.' Sergeant
Donaldson made the briefest of introductions. McLean scarcely
noticed the rudeness – he was too fixated on the sight in front of
him.

'That's some fish,' he said, unsure what else he could do.

'Ctenopharyngodon idella. The grass carp. This one's nearly ready, but no' quite there yet.' Bayne walked over to the edge of the pond, kneeled and gently eased the fish into the water. Until it wriggled and swam away, McLean had assumed it was dead.

'Ready?'

'To eat, aye? If you're no' careful they just taste of what they've been eating. Mud and weeds mostly. A week or two in there and she'll be sweet as any trout you'll catch.'

'That's quite a lot of effort to go to. You must really like your fish, Mr Bayne.' McLean took in the buildings, the neatly edged pond and stone walls, all a great deal older even than the man himself. 'I don't think I've ever seen a setup like this before. Does it predate the farm?'

'In a manner of speaking, aye. There used to be an old monastery near here. The monks built most of this farm, and a few others besides. They built this pond for cleaning the carp too.'

'It's certainly not something I expected to find out here. I'd have thought there'd be fish enough in the river, and Gladhouse isn't far.'

'Well. The monastery'd been a ruin a couple of centuries before they dammed the loch to make the reservoir.' Bayne spoke as if he'd been around to see both things happen. 'And the monks didn't like eating the local fish. Brought their own with them when they came here from France. Least, that's what my father told me. There's some work gone into this pond too. See the far end there?' He pointed to a low stone structure. 'That's a natural spring. It drains at the other end. No burn fill here, no silt. Keeps it fresh and clear. The bottom's lined with flagstones, the sides too. You could swim in there if you didn't mind getting your toes nibbled.'

McLean wasn't sure if Bayne was joking or not. His face was so lined he seemed to have a permanent grin.

'Still, I'm sure you didn't come all this way to talk about fish, Detective Chief Inspector.' Bayne rubbed his hands on his dungarees, and for a moment McLean thought he was going to offer one to shake. Instead, he held it splayed wide, palm out to indicate they go back up the stairs towards the house. 'Come on up to the house, why don't you. I'm sure Morag will have the kettle on for some tea.'

They found DC Harrison inside, sitting at a scrubbed-pine table in a kitchen that probably hadn't changed much since the monks built it. An old woman busied herself at an equally ancient range cooker, barely turning to register his arrival, or that of the two enormous men behind him.

'Take a seat, please, Detective Chief Inspector,' Bayne said. 'I'll just away and wash my hands. Morag will fetch you a cup of tea.'

Morag shrugged her shoulders irritably at the instruction, but when she turned to face him it was with a genuine smile. She was the complete opposite of the tall man, short and round. She busied herself with an old teapot, pouring out something that made the canteen coffee back at the station look weak by comparison. McLean could smell the tannin from the other side of the kitchen.

'Janie's been telling me about your missing wifey. Pair of constables came through last week and had a poke around the buildings, but I telt them then we'd no' seen anyone. See, if she'd come here we'd have taken her in.'

'Do you see many folk up here?' he asked.

Morag shook her head slowly. 'We're a bit cut off. Like it that way, if I'm being honest. Mr Bayne sees the occasional walker up in the brae fields sometimes, but folk don't venture this way often.'

'Mr Bayne is your husband?' McLean had thought so, but the way she'd used his surname had thrown him slightly.

'Aye, fifty-three years now. What times we've seen. Cake?' She offered up a slice already on a plate, which made it hard to refuse. Donaldson was halfway through his, clearly as at home in this kitchen as his own.

'And have you farmed out here all that time?' he asked as Mr Bayne came back into the kitchen, rubbing his hands dry on what looked like an old rag.

'Aye, and my father 'fore me. His father 'fore him. There's been Baynes at Woodhill since before it was Woodhill.'

Looking at the man, McLean could believe it. There was something slow and measured about him, as if aeons meant nothing. He could well imagine him tending his livestock, patiently tilling the land, even preparing those fish for monks who would never eat them, all because that's what the family had always done. In many ways it was an intensely dull life, and that was its clear appeal.

'I don't suppose you –?' McLean began to ask, but he was interrupted by a squawk from Sergeant Donaldson's Airwave set. Behind him Morag tutted, but not with any great anger. This was obviously something that happened a lot.

'Excuse me a minute. Better see what this is about.' The sergeant stood up and strode out, already talking into the handset.

'You were saying?' Mrs Bayne asked, but before McLean could admit that he'd forgotten, Harrison's pocket made a similar noise to Donaldson's. She pulled out her own set, gave Mrs Bayne an embarrassed half-shrug, half-smile, then stood up and followed the sergeant out.

'It wasn't important,' McLean said eventually. 'Thank you for your time. And the tea and excellent cake. I should probably go and see what all this is about anyway. Then we'll get out of your way.'

Neither Mr nor Mrs Bayne said anything more, merely nodding goodbye as McLean stood up and walked out of the house. He found Harrison and Donaldson deep in conversation.

'Something up?' he asked.

'The prints on that lighter we found under the car, sir,' Harrison beat the sergeant to the answer. 'Finally got a match.'

'Have we brought him in for questioning?' McLean asked, then added: 'It is a he, I take it?'

'Dan Forbes,' Sergeant Donaldson said. 'He's a Penicuik lad. Just got nicked for attempted burglary. The alert pinged as soon as our custody sergeant put his prints on the system.'

'Well, I guess we'd better go and have a word with him then.'

39

Were it not for the sign outside, Penicuik Police Station might well be mistaken for someone's end-of-terrace house. With the same painted harling as the other buildings on the street, it blended in far better than McLean's own station back in the city. Donaldson had gone ahead, probably misusing his lights and siren to get back in time to make sure everything was ready. He buzzed them into the business end of the building, down a corridor to an empty interview room.

'I'll warn you now he's got an attitude, this one,' he said as they waited for the prisoner to be brought up from the cells. 'He's been on our radar a while. Never crossed the line until today.'

'Lucky us,' McLean said, although he wasn't sure he really meant it.

It didn't take long, and when he arrived, Dan Forbes was everything Sergeant Donaldson had warned them, and more. Not yet twenty years old, and already full of enough attitude to last a lifetime. Two uniformed constables escorted him into the room, and despite McLean asking him to sit, he had to be forced into his seat before he would comply. It was only when he noticed DC Harrison, sitting off to one side with a notepad on her knees, that he settled down. He placed his cuffed hands on the table in front of him before finally looking at McLean.

'She your bird then?'

So it was going to be like that. McLean ignored Forbes for the moment, directing his attention to the two constables who'd brought him in.

'Thank you. We should be able to handle him, I think.'

'You sure, sir?' the older of the two asked.

'Aye. Go get yourselves a coffee or something. Don't think we'll be long with this one.'

Forbes stared at the backs of the constables as they left, then at the door when it clicked shut. He looked around the room, at Harrison, over his shoulder to the window behind. Everywhere but at the detective chief inspector. McLean waited, saying nothing. Harrison was almost as good at being a statue as Grumpy Bob. The silence dragged for a whole minute before Forbes broke.

'What's this all about then? Draggin' me in here like this?' He lifted up his hands to show off the shiny metal cuffs. 'I've no' done anything, aye?'

McLean reached into his pocket and pulled out his phone. The forensics labs had sent him photos of the lighter, and he chose one that clearly showed the initials and date inscribed on it, held it up for Forbes to see.

'This is yours, isn't it.' Not a question.

Forbes frowned with genuine puzzlement. He bent forward in his seat and stared at the image.

'Where the fuck did youse find that? Been looking for it for ages like.'

'Is that confirmation that this lighter belongs to you, Mr Forbes?' Harrison asked. She had her pen poised, for taking notes.

'Aye. Well. Aye. It was my dad's, ken? That date's his twenty-first birthday. His dad gave it him an' all.' He slumped in the seat as far back as he could get without standing up. 'Where'd youse find it?'

'We've lifted your fingerprint from the inside. That's how we know it's yours.' McLean switched off his phone and put it away. 'Of course, if you'd not been stupid enough to try breaking into a warehouse in broad daylight, we'd never have had prints to match to it. So thank you for that.'

'Why'd youse ask then? If you knew it was mine?' Forbes reached up and scratched at his cheek, hooded eyes glowering at McLean in silent accusation. The look on his face would sour milk. His every movement, the slouch of his shoulders and the way he slumped in his chair, none of it was an act. Angry, bitter and resentful were the only things he knew. It didn't bode well for them getting any kind of cooperation from him.

'I wanted to see how you reacted.' McLean left a pause for Forbes to fill, but he wasn't playing that game. 'So, tell me. What do you know about the car park in the woods up by Gladhouse Reservoir?'

Again, McLean was met with a puzzled frown. 'Gladhouse? Car park? I don't even drive, pal.'

'How do you explain your lighter being found up there then? How do you explain it being used to set fire to someone's car?'

'Ain't got a scooby. Probably the same fucker who nicked it off me in the first place, aye?'

'So you're telling me you've never been up to those woods then?'

'Don't think so? Why?'

McLean countered the question with one of his own. 'Does the name "GoodDog" mean anything to you? Maybe "The GoodDog Club"?'

It wasn't easy to read much more than general surliness in Forbes's expression, but McLean could tell clearly enough that the man didn't have anything to do with the doggers. That would have been too easy.

'OK then. When do you last remember using the lighter?'

He may have been trying to think, or he might simply have had a bit of indigestion. Whatever it was, Forbes paused a moment before answering. If he didn't know better, McLean might have thought the man was considering the option of actually cooperating. Maybe even giving him a straight answer. Stranger things had happened.

'The fuck should I know?'

'OK then. What did you use it for?' McLean sniffed, but caught no scent of cigarettes off the man. 'You smoke?'

'Fags are for losers, aye? Got me one of them e-cigs.' He drummed a foot on the floor for a moment. 'Only you pigs took it away from me, right? Gasping, I am.'

'So what's the lighter for then? Setting fire to cars?'

'Told you I don't know nothing about that.'

'And yet we found it up at Gladhouse, with your fingerprints all over it.'

Forbes leaned in, elbows clattering on the table in what he probably thought was an aggressive movement. 'I told you I lost it.'

McLean had seen it all before, knew it was coming, and didn't flinch. Instead he held Forbes's gaze until the man backed down. It didn't take long this time.

'So tell me about when you lost it. Where were you?'

Forbes leaned back again, stared up at the ceiling, over at Harrison. His leg was drumming again, so maybe he really did need a nicotine fix, perhaps something a little stronger. Well, he was all out of luck there.

'OK. Was a few weeks back, ken? Know I had it wi' me cause I used it to light my way.'

'And where was this?' McLean asked, then added: 'And don't say somewhere dark.'

233

That got the ghost of a smile from Forbes, an easing in the tension that had filled the room since he'd first been brought to them. 'I wasnae doing anything wrong, ken? Just having a wee nosey. Place is fair spooky since the fire, eh? All them explosions and stuff.'

McLean didn't need to ask what Forbes was talking about any more. He knew well enough.

'Rosskettle? The psychiatric hospital?'

'The loony bin, aye.'

'What were you doing there? I'm surprised the place hasn't all collapsed.'

'Aw no, man. There's loads still standing. Fair creepy place, mind. I ken reading about it. All they dead bodies buried in the grounds. Tunnels everywhere. Ghosts an' shit.'

'So you were just "having a wee nosey" as you put it. And that was the last place you remember having the lighter.'

'Aye. Must have dropped it on my way out.'

Forbes seemed to relax now that he'd explained himself, which made McLean think he was probably telling the truth. Or at least mostly the truth. It was too far-fetched to be an out-and-out lie, but exploring the ruined buildings was most likely only half of the reason for going there. If he dug deep enough, he'd probably find that the man came from the sort of home it was best to get out of from time to time. Maybe he'd gone on his own, maybe he'd been with friends. It didn't really matter. He truly had lost his lighter long before it was used to set fire to Anya Renfrew's car. Another dead end.

Police Sergeant Donaldson appeared from a side room as the two constables led Dan Forbes away towards the back of the station. He'd almost certainly been listening in on the whole interview, but had to pretend he hadn't.

'Give you anything useful then?' he asked as he walked with

them to the front door. McLean saw no harm in indulging the pretense.

'Not much. Reckon he really did lose his lighter. He should probably have it back once we're done, not that they'll let him keep it where he's most likely going. Now all we need to do is work out who found it and why they took it up to Gladhouse to torch a car.'

'Can't help much with that.' Donaldson shrugged. 'Where're you off to next?'

'Back to the city. Might swing past Rosskettle on my way though.'

'Rosskettle?' Donaldson's lack of real surprise gave the game away. 'It's a nightmare keeping people out of there. You'd think the fact it might collapse at any moment would be enough, but no. That just makes it even more attractive. And the rumours about ghosts, secret tunnels, Christ only knows what else.'

'Were you there? When it blew up?' McLean remembered the event all too clearly himself.

Donaldson shook his head. 'Missed that one. Someone thought it was a great idea to send us rural bobbies over to Glasgow for some street time. Guess that's better than sending their lot over here.'

'The wonders of modern policing, eh?'

'Aye, that it is.' The sergeant paused a moment, hand reaching for the door to open it. Then he stopped. 'Forbes told you he lost his lighter out at Rosskettle, right? He say when?'

'Couple of weeks back, apparently. Why?'

'See, when you get there, the site's pretty well fenced off. You know as well as I do that's no obstacle to someone like your man Dan there. There's all sorts of folk've been getting in through a gap by the side of the old railway cutting. Go for a walk and you can't miss it. Big gorse fire there not that long ago.'

'You've been getting a lot of fires out here lately.'

'Aye, well. It's been a long hot summer. Doesn't help that the kids are out for the holidays either. Couple of them on bikes seen near Rosskettle not long before the fire too.'

'Kids?' McLean recalled his visit to the control centre at Bilston Glen, listening to a young lad tell them about the car on fire. 'Any idea who they were?'

Donaldson shook his head again. 'Could be almost anyone. Probably fairly local, but that hardly narrows it down.'

'What about the name Bobby? That mean anything?'

'Bobby? Can't say as it does, no.'

'Do me a favour and ask around, will you? Anyone who patrols this area regularly. School liaisons, PCSOs. Might be nothing, but someone might know something. If there's a young lad named Bobby who's come across their radar recently, I'd like to have a wee chat with him.'

40

She does not know how long she has slept. Does not feel as if she has slept at all, only been absent from herself while the minutes and hours and days tick past. Rather than waking, she comes to awareness slowly, reluctantly. The cold is everything, a numbing, sucking presence that makes it all but impossible to think. If anything, her thin blanket only makes it worse. A mockery of hope in this hopeless place.

Her memory is as sluggish as the chill that surrounds her, although it comes and goes with greater freedom than she has in her tiny cell. Sometimes she remembers a car park, men, the guiltiest of pleasures she is surely paying for now. In the quietest times she hears the voices of her workmates, even though she cannot recall their names. They ask her for help and she wants so much to be able to give them that.

There is more water in the jug by the door, the cup scoured clean. No food though, and the lack of it gnaws at her like maggots burrowing through her insides. Her ribs ache, and the sourness in her mouth reminds her that she was sick. There is no mark in the dirt now to show for it though. Only an insistent pressure in her bladder that seems unfair given how little she has drunk.

Shivering, she crosses the short distance to the steel bucket, lifts off its lid and squats. The smell is of sickness, and she mourns the heat it takes from her. She kneels, places hands on either side of the pail, but the meagre warmth inside it soon turns cold.

What is this place? Why are they doing this to her? Who is doing this to her?

She stands slowly, hugs the coarse blanket around her nakedness and looks back to the door. For an instant she imagines movement, the cover over the small window sliding closed. Was she being watched? Is there someone there?

'H-hello?'

Her voice is so small, so dry, it is hardly audible at all. She would rush to the door, but sudden movements leave her light-headed, the risk of fainting very real. She goes carefully instead, straining to hear any sound from outside. There is only the distant, constant trickle of water.

Resting her head against the unyielding wooden planks, she feels sobs of self-pity well up in her. Why is this happening? Is this hell? Eternal punishment for her sins?

'Please. Just let me go.' Even to her own ears it sounds pathetic, and the fists she raises to the door are too weak to hold up. She is spent, exhausted, beyond starved. It is all she can do to avoid knocking over the water jug as she slumps to the dirt floor.

She stares at it for a long while, wondering whether she dares drink. Eventually she can stand the foul taste in her mouth no more, pours water into the cup and takes a tiny sip. It is sweeter than any honey, but the chill as it goes down makes her shiver all the more. Far from slaking her thirst, it only makes it worse, and before long the cup is finished, another after it. A glance down at the jug shows it is empty.

Wiping at dry lips with the back of her hand, she sits and stares across the tiny cell. She sees nothing, all effort given to concentrating on her stomach. Any moment she expects it to squeeze tight again, violently expel the water she has just filled it with. Seconds tick by to the ragged beat of her heart and the regular spasms of shivering that rack her frame. It might be an eternity or it might be only five minutes, lost in her misery she can't tell. Only when the numbness in her backside begins to spread does she finally wake enough to move. Three short paces to the narrow bed, but before she can reach it, her world explodes once more.

It's not vomit this time, but that doesn't make things any better. She tries to reach the pail, lift off its lid, squat. She doesn't have the strength, and neither is there anything solid in her gut. Warm liquid gushes down her legs, then they give way and she falls, knocks over the pail, smacks her head against the stone wall. Too much to hope that the blow might knock her out.

Her ears ring, the noise echoing around the cell. She is battered and bruised, soiled with her own waste, cold beyond bearing and so hungry she can scarcely understand it. Her thin, useless blanket is soaked in piss and worse. There is nothing she can do. No end to this torment and no reason for it either. No half-remembered sin can possibly be as bad as to justify such punishment.

Collapsed in the corner, too weak to move, all she can do is shiver. She lacks even the strength to cry.

41

'It's not my favourite place in all the world, I can tell you that much.'

Early morning, before the sun had managed to warm the air to gas mark four. Grumpy Bob sat in one of the chairs around the conference table in McLean's office, nursing a mug of coffee and moaning about the world in general and his imminent retirement in particular. His trip out to Bestingfield psychiatric hospital the day before hadn't improved his mood, and it was taking a while to get the full story from him.

'It's a place we send people so we can forget about them, Bob. Not surprising nobody wants to know about it.' Except that wasn't strictly speaking true. Yes, there were people who went in and never came out again, and sometimes it really was the best place for them. But there were others who responded to treatment, recovered, returned to society as changed people. He knew which of those two categories Norman Bale fell into.

'Well, whatever it is, I'm glad I'll not be going back any time soon. Place fair creeps me out.' Grumpy Bob took a long slurp of his coffee and made a face. Fair enough, it wasn't the best.

'So, what did you find out then?' McLean asked. 'Apart from the fact that it's not exactly a holiday camp.'

'Your Doctor Graham's as keen as mustard, for one thing. I

can only assume she's not been in the job long. Still hasn't had the corners knocked off her. She seems to genuinely believe Bale isn't a lost cause.'

'He certainly seems to have her wrapped around his finger, if her messages are anything to go by. Did she say why he was so keen to speak to me?'

'I got the impression she was trying to understand his fixation on you. She doesn't really know why he's obsessed with you, but she feels that unless he can confront that obsession he'll never move on.'

'And the only way for him to confront it is for him to speak to me?' McLean picked up his own coffee mug reflexively, then put it back down again when he realised he didn't actually want to drink it. 'I know my psychology degree's a few decades out of date now, but that seems counterintuitive to me. If I jump in the car and drive down there to see him just because he's asking for me to do so, then that's only going to reinforce his obsession, not undo it.'

Grumpy Bob's expression suggested that he couldn't agree more. Still there was something else he'd not said yet, McLean could tell.

'I had a wee chat with some of the psych nurses and orderlies while I was there. They all say Bale's a model patient. Never does anything to upset anyone. He's well behaved, polite, does what he's told. Spends most of his time in his cell reading and writing.'

'Writing? He's not penning his memoirs is he?'

'No. He's been compiling a collection of old Scottish folk tales, of all things. Seems a suitably twisted thing for someone like him to do, I suppose.'

'Folk tales? What, like Kate Crackernuts? The milk-white Doo?'

Grumpy Bob raised an eyebrow. 'If I'd known you were an expert . . .'

241

'Hardly. My gran scoffed at all that sort of thing as nonsense, but Mrs Roberts, the old housekeeper, she used to tell me them to get me to sleep. Never read anything from a book. She had them all in her head.' He smiled at the memory, long forgotten. Then remembered what had brought it back. 'Do you think he's playing games with them all? Lulling them into a false sense of security?'

'I don't know. If he is, then it's a long game. Takes a lot to pull the wool over their eyes too. I think they mostly figure he's not doing any harm so they let him get on with it. Occupational therapy, I guess.'

'And yet he still wants to talk to me.'

Grumpy Bob let out a long sigh. 'He still wants to see you, aye. According to Doctor Graham he was asking for you in his last session, yesterday morning. Mind you, he asks every session. This time he also asked to pass on another message.'

McLean was sorely tempted to tell the detective sergeant to keep it to himself, but Grumpy Bob had already gone out of his way to check out the situation at the secure psychiatric unit for him. And Dr Graham was only doing her job. Might as well take the message; it wasn't as if he had to do anything about it, after all.

'Go ahead then. What has Norman Bale got to say that's so important?'

'Apparently he's been researching the legend of Sawney Bean. I'm guessing that's not one Mrs Roberts told you just before bedtime, aye?'

McLean shook his head, a horrible feeling growing in his gut. Too many coincidences, too many echoes. 'Was that it?' He had a feeling it wasn't.

'No. Here, I wrote it down.' Grumpy Bob pulled out his notebook and flicked through the pages. 'Apparently he wanted to tell you that Sawney Bean was an East Lothian man, even if he carried out his gruesome trade in Galloway. And that's why they brought him back to Edinburgh to face justice. So they could control what happened to him.' He snapped the notebook closed again. 'Does that make even the slightest bit of sense?'

McLean rubbed at his face with both hands, his eyes gritty all of a sudden. Everyone knew the legend of Sawney Bean, but it was just that, a legend. A man and his wife, their children and incestuous grandchildren, living in a sea cave on the Galloway coast and killing unfortunate travellers through the nearby forest for food. Twenty-five years and a thousand victims later, they'd been finally brought to justice by King James I himself. Or possibly King James VI, what was a detail of 150 years' difference in the dates, after all? The entire family had been dragged to Edinburgh, rather than the nearer town of Ayr, and put to death without trial. The story might have been inspired by some actual, long-forgotten case of cannibalism; there were some few historical records earlier in the country's history, after all. But the old wives' tale was too full of inconsistencies to be anything else.

'As I remember it, Sawney Bean never actually existed. He was made up, either to sell chapbooks or to help paint the Scots as something less than civilised. English propaganda in the eighteenth century.'

'Aye, that's what I told Doctor Graham.' Grumpy Bob slumped back in his seat. 'She's something of an expert on the subject too, oddly enough, but she reckons Bale's fixation on folk tales harks back to his childhood, and given what he did to his parents it's a part of his life that he needs to find a way to address. Or something like that anyway. I kind of tuned out after a while.'

McLean was tempted to do the same, but something was niggling away at the back of his head. 'Have you seen the PM results for the bones we found up on the moors?'

Grumpy Bob's confusion might have been because of the

rapid change of subject, but was most probably because he hadn't.

'Should I have?' he asked.

'Marks on one of the bones might tie in to an old missing-persons case. I spoke to Duguid about it. Meant to send him a couple of DCs to help search through the archives.' McLean pulled his laptop towards him, tapped away at the keyboard until the screen showed him Cadwallader's preliminary report. He didn't really need to read it; he'd been there after all. 'There was something else though, about the bones. They'd been de-fleshed completely before they were buried. And there were knife marks on them, as if they'd been butchered.'

Grumpy Bob ran a hand through his thinning hair. 'Jesus. And you think . . . ?'

'Sawney Bean. Scotland's infamous cannibal. And Bale insists that he was a Lothian man. He might just possibly have heard about the bones we found on the moors, but there's no way he could have known about the butchery marks.'

'Then how?' Grumpy Bob asked.

McLean sighed, picked up his mug and drained the bitter liquid. 'I don't know, Bob. But I'm going to have to find out, and there's only one way to do that.'

Having only heard her on the phone, McLean wasn't sure what to expect from Dr Millicent Graham. He'd imagined her to be young, and wasn't disappointed. Late twenties or very early thirties, she hid her face behind a veil of straight black hair and spectacles that were too large and too thick. She was dressed for an earlier century too, although that might have been a conscious decision to put her patients at ease. She met him at Reception discreetly branded with the Dee Foundation logo, and led him along institutional corridors to a surprisingly spacious office.

'I'm so glad to finally meet you, Detective Chief Inspector.'

She indicated a seat away from the desk. It was one of four arranged as casually as four chairs can be around a low table. A sickly pot plant sat dead centre.

'Call me Tony, please. Detective Chief Inspector's a hell of a mouthful.'

Dr Graham looked momentarily flustered, a slight blush tingeing what little of her face he could see. 'Oh, of course. Millicent. Can I offer you a coffee?'

McLean was more keen to get on with things; the sooner they started the sooner he could leave. But one lesson you learned early in the police was never to turn down an offer of coffee. He'd only had the one that day so far too. 'Thank you,' he said, then waited another five minutes for it all to be sorted. Finally Dr Graham sat down in the chair opposite him and placed a thick folder on the table.

'I'm very pleased you changed your mind and came out.' She brushed hair away from her face as she spoke, but it slid back again seemingly unnoticed. 'I really think I'm getting somewhere with Norman.'

McLean tried not to tense at the name, although he might have failed in that. 'Doctor Graham . . . Millicent . . . I realise that it's your job to help people like Bale, and in the main I think it's a good thing that you do. But I very much doubt you'll get anywhere with him he doesn't want you to go.'

Dr Graham recoiled slightly, as if she'd been slapped. 'Do you think I don't know my own patients, De— . . . Tony?'

'I'm sorry. That's not what I meant to say. It's just that I saw what Bale did. I know how long he'd been doing it too, before we caught him. His skill is inveigling his way into your life, winkling out your deepest secrets. He takes on the identity of his previous victim, like a penance. And then he begins the whole sick charade all over again.'

'I don't think that's how things are going to work out here.'

Dr Graham recovered her composure almost as quickly as she'd lost it, taking McLean's diagnosis in her stride. 'He hasn't tried to gain the confidence of anyone in the hospital, although he speaks very highly of you. In his own way, he considers you his intellectual equal. Not that he'd ever say it in quite so many words.'

'What does he say then? About me. Why is it so important he speak to me face to face?' McLean wanted to ask: 'Why am I even here?' and throw his hands up in the air, but that would have meant spilling his coffee for one thing. It was never a good idea to ask such questions of a psychiatrist, for another.

'Norman is a changed person. The first year here was difficult for him, as it is for many long-term patients, I expect. He's adjusted though, found his place and accepted it. I genuinely think he wants to be helpful as a way of atoning for his past sins. That's how he sees the world, after all, in terms of a deeply held religious belief. However flawed. He believed he was doing God's work, freeing the blessed from the temptations of mortal sin. You showed him that he was wrong about that. He wants to prove to you that he has understood. More than that, I think he *needs* to prove it to you. Not to me, or a parole board or anything like that. To you. His childhood friend and the man who stopped him. Who brought him back to his senses.'

It was a long speech, possibly rehearsed. McLean knew enough about psychology to see the truth in it, and the lie. People like Bale didn't change, not really. They adapted to the circumstances, but always with an eye on any chance to revert to their old ways.

'There's something I'd like you to see, before we go and meet Norman.' Dr Graham must have taken his silence as doubt, which to be fair it was. She stood up, and crossed the room to her desk. Grabbing the mouse, she woke her laptop and clicked away for a couple of moments. McLean drained the last of his coffee, but before he could go to see what was on the screen, she had brought the laptop over to him. This time she sat in the seat next to his, rather than across the table, put the laptop down and tapped the return key. The screen had been showing a still image, but now it sprang to life. A video of a room, a man sitting on a bed.

Norman Bale.

42

McLean remembered Norman Bale as a thin-faced man, a little shorter than average and in many ways unremarkable. He was still short, but clearly the food served at Bestingfield suited him. Either that or he'd never got the hang of feeding himself before. Now that he didn't have to, his sallow features had filled out, the start of a paunch gently straining at the lower buttons of his shirt. Seen from the high perspective of the security camera in his cell, Bale's greying hair had almost completely retreated from the top of his head. He wore thick-framed spectacles, pulled down to the tip of his rat-like nose. Sitting perfectly still on the edge of his bed, he peered over the top of them at an empty chair in the corner opposite.

'This isn't live, I take it?' McLean asked. He could see no timestamp on the video screen, but the washed-out black-and-white image was clearly taken with an infrared CCTV camera.

'No. This was from a while back. Every night's pretty much the same though.' Dr Graham reached out and tapped a key. The screen image jumped slightly, then a timestamp appeared in the top-left corner, seconds and minutes counting away. It was half past ten at night, apparently. Bale still sat motionless.

'He only sleeps for a few hours each night. Lights out is at ten, so he should really be in bed.'

'Do you have cameras in all the cells?'

'This is a secure mental-health establishment, not a prison,' Dr Graham said. 'We prefer the term "secure room".'

'What's he doing now?' McLean ignored the tone of disapproval in the doctor's voice, leaning forward as Bale did something similar on screen. A quiet mumbling noise drifted out of the tinny loudspeakers either side.

'He does this every night. It's a conversation of sorts. Only, as you can see, there's no one there for him to talk to.'

'Can you hear what he's saying?'

'Some of it, but it's very quiet. I'm not sure it's all actual language either. Something subvocal.' Dr Graham adjusted the volume up, a hiss showing that the microphone was at full stretch. McLean strained to make out the noises. It was a bit like listening to someone in another room speaking a foreign language. It sounded like words, sentences, questions and exclamations, but the intonations were all wrong.

'I think he's praying half of the time. The rest of it feels more like a conversation,' the doctor added.

'Have you confronted him about this?'

'I have, yes. He says he's talking to his friends. Says that's how he knows all the things that are going on out in the world. How he knew about the missing woman, and that she's still alive.'

'And you don't think he's just playing us all like a stage magician? Doing the old mind-reading trick of suggesting vague things and picking up on the ones that get a reaction?'

Dr Graham turned sharply, that face as if she'd been slapped again barely visible through her curtain of hair. McLean thought it had been a perfectly reasonable question, but obviously he'd stepped over some invisible line.

'I do know how to do my job, you know.'

He paused a moment before replying. His first instinct was

to argue the point, but he held back the sarcastic comment and counted a silent five seconds instead.

'I'm sorry. I didn't mean to suggest that you didn't.' Another count of five while Dr Graham stared at him unconvinced.

'Look, what about visitors? Talking to the nursing staff? He has to be getting information from somewhere, and I don't believe for a minute that it's an invisible fairy who comes in the night and sits in that chair.'

'He's had no visitors other than a lawyer since he arrived. He has no family of course . . .' Dr Graham's voice trailed away, and McLean couldn't help but remember the scene he'd found in the dining room of Bale's house. The desiccated corpses of his mother and father sitting at the table. Their meal untouched. Rotten.

'What about the staff here? Does he have any favourites? Maybe other –' McLean stopped himself from saying 'inmates', added instead 'patients?'

'There are a couple of nurses who deal with him most of the time, but they're not the gossiping kind really. You can talk to them, anyway.' Dr Graham reached out and tapped the enter button again, pausing the video and killing the mumbling noise. 'As to the other patients, well, they tend to avoid him. We've a couple like that. Keep to themselves. To be honest, as long as they're not being difficult, we tend to let them.'

McLean picked up his coffee mug, then realised it was empty and put it back down again. He didn't want to be here, but neither could he ignore it. If there was the slimmest possibility Bale could shed light on Anya Renfrew's disappearance, however he'd come by the information, then the visit would have been worth the discomfort. And if not, then he could rest assured that Norman Bale would have guaranteed his continued incarceration in this secure facility for the rest of his natural life.

'OK then.' He struggled to keep the sigh from his voice. 'Let's go and see what he's got to say.'

★ ★ ★

The interview room was rather more pleasant than those back at the police station in the city. It had a window that looked out onto parkland and trees. The walls had been painted in a calming shade of institutional beige, and a near silent air-conditioning unit pumped cool, fresh air through a vent in the ceiling. No odour of unwashed bodies and nervous farts in here.

McLean took a seat at the one table, noting as he did so that it was bolted to the floor. The single chair opposite was similarly fixed, although there was no ring set into the tabletop for securing handcuffs. Dr Graham fussed a bit with her folder while they waited, and then with a minimum of fuss the door opened. Two large men in white uniforms escorted Norman Bale into the room.

The video had only partially prepared McLean for the physical change. It was one thing to see him seated, in monochrome video on a tiny laptop screen. Quite another to see him in the flesh. All of it.

Oddly enough, the fuller face reminded McLean more of the six-year-old Norman from his childhood. Something of the puppy fat about Bale's neck and jowls harked back to the young boy he'd known. He was still not entirely convinced this wasn't some imposter though, a changeling monster who had taken on the identity of a dead child, and used it somehow to gain the confidence of still-grieving parents. And yet there was that DNA test result he couldn't ignore, however much he wanted to.

'Tony, you came! I'm so pleased.' Bale's voice was different too. Fatter like the man who spoke. His sibilant hiss had almost gone, the barest traces of it left. He tried to step forward, extend a hand or possibly even attempt a hug, but the nurses were too quick for him. The handcuffs made it difficult too.

'Sit,' one of them commanded. He gained a disdainful stare for his efforts, but Bale complied with no other hint of complaint.

The two nurses took up station behind him, which was a little intimidating but reassuring too.

'Doctor Graham, might I say you are looking particularly lovely this morning.'

'That's very kind of you, Norman. But need I remind you of the rules regarding personal observations?' The psychiatrist retrieved an A4 notebook from her folder, opened it on a blank page and took out a pen. McLean knew better than to look up at the cameras that were recording the entire interview.

'I'm sorry. This is all a bit exciting for me. I don't often get visitors,' Bale said. 'And we're running out of time too.'

This last comment he addressed at McLean directly.

'We are?' he asked. There was little point coming all this way and not engaging with Bale, even if that was the last thing he wanted to do.

'Did you get my message? What I told Detective Sergeant Laird?'

'That Sawney Bean was an East Lothian man?' McLean placed his hands on the table in front of him, fingers interlocked to stop him fidgeting with them. 'Yes, I did.'

'Good old Grumpy Bob.' Bale's shoulders slumped a little, his nervous energy abating. Then he sat up again so suddenly one of the nurses almost grabbed him. 'Sorry, sorry. I shouldn't have called him that.'

It was an act. A good one, McLean had to admit, but he could see exactly what Bale was doing. He had a knack, like any circus sideshow performer, of reading his audience. He could pick up information like a vacuum cleaner, and remember every last detail. Squirrel it away for a time when it might be useful. And he'd been years in this place now, with nothing much to do but think and plot, put all those little fragments together into a picture he found pleasing, build it all into a strange machine and then set it off running.

'Sawney Bean never existed of course.' McLean held Bale's gaze even though what he really wanted to do was get up and leave the room, drive out of the security gates and never come back to Bestingfield again. 'He's just a reflection of our worst nightmares. A horror story. But then you'd know all about that, wouldn't you.'

Bale shook his head slowly from side to side. 'Ah, Detective Inspector. No, Detective Chief Inspector of course. But no, you've got it all wrong. Alexander Bean was a real person. It's true his parents weren't ditch-diggers or hedge-layers or whatever the later tales have them being. They came from a much older and nobler tradition than that. They were cannibals only after a fashion, but Alexander had too much of a taste for human flesh. That's why he was banished, and how he ended up on the Galloway coast. If only his family hadn't cast him aside. If they had just tried to understand him, then none of it would ever have happened.'

'None of what? The thousand victims that there's no trace of in any contemporary records? The children and grandchildren held in a prison that wasn't big enough for more than a single convict? The fact that they were executed in Leith when their crimes were committed on the West Coast?'

McLean stopped himself, realising he'd been drawn in. What was he even doing here? The man had nothing to say that was going to help them find Renfrew.

'He was an East Lothian man. That's why they brought him home for his punishment. They could control what came out when he was confronted with his crimes. That's an old secret held by powerful folk, Detective Chief Inspector. They would go to any lengths to stop it being revealed in open court.'

McLean almost drummed his fingers on the tabletop, managed to stop himself at the last moment. Bale's eyes might have been set in a fleshier face now, but they were still pin-sharp, attentive, reading the whole room and the people in it as if they were open books.

'And you know this how?' he asked.

'I haven't always been locked up in here. Nice though it is to have three square meals a day. I've been a student of the esoteric all my life. A collector of tales like your old friend Madame Rose.'

McLean ignored the reference. 'Tell me about this missing woman you're so concerned about. Who is she? And how do you know she's missing?'

Bale smiled like a snake, tilting his head slightly to one side. 'She has secrets of her own. A double life, I think? Unusual appetites.'

'Maybe even a name?'

'That much I don't know. I can tell you though that she is destined to become the centrepiece in an ancient ritual. Something truly momentous. You might say life-changing.'

'Enough of the mumbo jumbo. Either you have useful information for me, or you don't. If it's the latter, then it's time I was leaving. Plenty else to be getting on with.' McLean stood up and turned towards the door.

'I'm only telling what I know, Tony. She's not pure yet. Too much sin to be so easily purged. But it won't be long now until she is ready, and then they will kill her. Her time – our time – grows near.'

'Enough of the bloody riddles.' McLean looked down at the still-seated psychiatrist. 'Doctor Graham. I know you meant well when you contacted me before, but next time he claims to be hearing voices might I suggest you increase his medication?'

'You never were much fun, were you, Tony. Always so bloody serious all the time. Well, when you find her bones out on the moors, don't blame me for not trying to warn you. The Fraternitas de Rosae Fontis have her, and the appointed hour approaches.' Bale stood, cuffed hands reaching out in a mockery of supplication. 'You have to find her, find them.'

Before he could do any more, the two nurses grabbed Bale by the arms, lifting him off his feet before he could even register what was happening. They carried him to the door as if he weighed nothing, and in moments he was gone.

'I'm so very sorry,' Dr Graham said once the door had closed. 'That's not how he usually behaves.'

'He got what he wanted, me dancing to his tune. I should have known better than to come here in the first place, but, truth be told, we are searching for a missing woman, and we have found bones up on the moors. It's not common knowledge. I'd imagine one of the psychiatric nurses or orderlies has been talking to a cop friend or something.'

Except that didn't fit well with Bale first trying to make contact over a week ago. McLean didn't want to think about that. Not now. Not ever.

43

Bale's words niggled at him all the way north from Bestingfield towards the city. McLean was certain the man was playing with them all, but he still couldn't shake the feeling that Bale knew something about what was going on. He'd couched it all in mystical mumbo-jumbo, sure. That was how he worked, after all. But there was more to it than that. Bale knew things he couldn't possibly know, which meant either that he had access to information he shouldn't have, or that he was somehow involved in Renfrew's disappearance. Neither explanation made any sense at all.

The sign for Penicuik had whizzed past before McLean realised where he was. Any chance to avoid returning to the station was a good one, even if he'd get shouted at by the DCC for it later. He indicated at the next turning, taking a narrow lane that led up to the moors. He'd pay a visit to the dig site, and if he was very lucky there might be some new information for him to justify the trip.

He parked a good half a mile from the scene, in a small lay-by that was well clear of the steady flow of forensics vans, squad cars, fire trucks and other vehicles that were turning the narrow road into something more like Princes Street during the Festival. For once he'd worn sensible shoes and a lightweight suit, but he was still panting and sweaty by the time he reached the police cordon. A constable in short sleeves signed him in, directing him towards a cluster of forensics vans. Here he found ill-fitting white paper overalls and shoe covers, taking his time to adjust everything as best he could before heading up to the moor itself.

The stink of burning had filled the air from the moment he'd stepped out of his Alfa, but as he walked along the designated path towards the gully and the excavation site, the stench grew ever stronger. At least it was a burned heather and whins smell. McLean had attended too many house fires in his time as a police officer, and there was something about the reek of burning plastics, singed carpets and all too often barbecued meat that made his stomach clench. This was more like an autumn bonfire, almost innocent in the way it reminded him of childhood.

The heat was another matter altogether. If there'd been a breath of wind it might have helped, but the lay of the land meant the air was still. The early-afternoon sun hit scorched black earth, the view shimmering at the close horizon. For once McLean was glad of the white overalls, especially the hood. He'd remembered sensible shoes, yes, but completely forgotten about a hat.

Up ahead, where the initial bones had been found, technicians had staked out the land with the sort of red and white tape he more usually associated with building sites than crime scenes. A small tent had been erected at the head of the path, presumably as some kind of holding and processing area for any finds. Most of the people on the site, and there were a lot of them, were higher up the hillside, kneeling in the dirt and sifting through it with archaeological precision. Only two figures stood at the tent, both of them with their heads down as they examined objects brought to a large table.

He set off towards them, recognising the shorter of the two as Professor Turner, but before he managed more than a pace, a commotion back at the roadside distracted him. The short-sleeved constable was holding up a hand to stop what looked like a taxi from coming any closer. He walked to the window and bent down to talk to the driver. McLean expected to see the taxi back up to the nearest convenient spot, make a three-point turn and go to its destination a different way. Instead, the constable stood up straight as if he'd been zapped with a cattle prod, went to the cordon tape and untied it so that the taxi could go through.

With a sigh that nobody else could hear, McLean set off back down the path to greet whichever senior officer or, more likely, politician had come out to make a nuisance of themselves. By the time he reached the road and its cluster of parked vans, the taxi driver had climbed out and gone round to the rear passenger door on the other side. McLean rolled down the hood of his white overalls, the better to see and be recognised. He was dimly aware of the Crime Scene Manager remonstrating with the uniformed constable a few paces away, but mostly he was trans-fixed by the figure being helped out of the car. Not a politician at all, nor a senior officer. At least, not one currently serving.

Ex-Detective Superintendent Grace Ramsay leaned on the taxi driver for support, but she looked far less frail than she had when he'd interviewed her a couple of days earlier. She stared up at the burned moorland for a moment, and then her eyes alighted on him.

'Ah. McLean. Good. Show me these bones you've found.'

In the end, he decided it was easier to give in than try to stand firm. Perhaps it was a memory of his days as the most junior of officers, when Detective Superintendent Ramsay had been someone you wouldn't even consider crossing. Perhaps it was the sheer effort that she had put into coming out here, that same dogged determination which had marked her career decades earlier. It helped that the site was more of an archaeological dig than a crime scene now, so it was unlikely Ramsay would upset any of the forensic technicians. She still had to wear white paper overalls like everyone else though, and it took a while to find a set that fitted her tiny, shrunken frame. Longer still for her to put them on.

McLean sent the taxi driver away while he waited for her to get ready; he'd take her back to the home himself. Then he led her slowly up the path to the tent and the professor.

'Thought I saw you earlier, Tony. Then you turned and ran.'

'Something came up,' he said. 'Or, more specifically, some-one. Professor Harriet Turner, meet retired Detective Superintendent Grace Ramsay.'

Like everyone else, Professor Turner was dressed in overalls, although she had tied the arms around her waist, exposing a tight-fitting T-shirt. Everything was smudged with soot and burned earth, even her face. She emerged from behind the sorting table and wiped her hand on her backside before offering it to be shaken.

'Pleasure to meet you,' she said, then before releasing Ramsay's hand added: 'Ramsay. Weren't you involved in the Jamesfield case?'

That got something like a smile from the old detective, but her posture was defensive. 'I was SIO on that one. How do you know about it?'

'Student days. I was working on the dig when they found the old man. It was one of your colleagues who interviewed me. Dagwood, I think they called him?'

Ramsay laughed, and the defensiveness melted away. 'Ha. Detective Inspector Charles Duguid, as he was then. He hated that nickname. But Jamesfield, yes. That brings back memories.'

'It was probably what set me on the path to here, in a way.' Turner released Ramsay's hand and waved at the hillside. 'Forensic anthropology's taken me all over the world, but it started when we dug up that old man and realised he'd not been there thousands of years like the other bones.'

McLean didn't know the case, which meant it probably dated back to before he'd joined what was then Lothian and Borders Police. Ramsay and Turner seemed to be getting on well enough without him though, so he kept his mouth shut.

'Talking of bones, I hear you've found some,' Ramsay said. 'Rather a lot of them.'

'Indeed we have, and fascinating they are too. Would you like a look?'

The professor led the retired detective chief superintendent up a narrow marked path towards one of the large squares marked off with red and white tape. A gang of a half-dozen or so suited technicians were carefully scraping at the burned soil, collecting it in buckets that another group were diligently carrying away to a sorting area around the back of the tent. McLean kept close enough to hear their conversation, but otherwise was content to leave the two women alone.

'The initial bones were found over there.' Professor Turner indicated the area in the gully where McLean had met Angus Cadwallader the previous time. If she hadn't done, he'd not have recognised it. All the burned vegetation had been stripped back, and the earth neatly dug away in narrow terraces that crept up the hill like a giant's staircase.

'Skeletons of three women, is that right?' Ramsay asked, and not for the first time McLean wondered where she'd got her detailed information from. Probably that same tweed-suited city pathologist.

'That's what I'm told, yes. They'd been carted off to the city mortuary before Tony called me in to survey the whole site.' Professor Turner managed to make this sound like an insult to her professional reputation, and the most appalling of rookie errors. She didn't quite turn to chastise him for his lack of foresight, but McLean could sense her wanting to.

'And what of the rest of it? How far back does the site go?'

'That's what we're here to find out. It's early days so far, but I reckon we've got another seven bodies so far.'

McLean felt a cold chill in his gut that should have been welcome given the afternoon heat, but wasn't.

'Seven? Nobody told me. We should be treating this whole area as a secure crime scene.'

'Calm yourself, Tony. None of the bones we've found are recent. Far from it. Given what's at the top of that hill there, I won't be at all surprised if we don't find more.' Professor Turner pointed up towards the brow of the hill, beyond the drystone wall that had held the fire in check long enough for it to be brought under control.

'What's up there?' he asked, wishing he hadn't missed the last briefing about the site.

'You don't know?' The professor raised an eyebrow. 'And here's me thought you were an educated man. That, Tony, is one of Scotland's more than fifteen hundred Iron Age hill forts. They call them forts, but really they were settlements. Back when the country was mostly forest and the high ground was the safest place to live.'

'So these bones are what? Neolithic?'

'I'd have to do carbon dating to tell that; but they're certainly old. I think this might be a sacred burial site, only it's not like any site I've ever heard of before. These bones have all been de-fleshed. Probably laid out for the birds to pick at, then collected once there's nothing perishable left. Normally you'd expect them to be in a stone barrow of some kind, but here they've been buried. And not whole bodies either. Sometimes there's half a skeleton's worth, sometimes just an arm or a leg.'

McLean cast his mind back to the first time he'd seen the place. 'But the bones we found initially were just lying on the surface.'

'Yes, that is odd. I've spoken to your friend Angus Cadwallader, and he tells me they're all relatively fresh too. Strange that someone chose to dispose of them right on top of something much older. Almost as if they knew what was down here. Only there's no way they could have done.'

'Not unless they've been doing it for a very long time.'

McLean had almost forgotten Grace Ramsay. The retired detective superintendent had wandered off towards the spot where they'd found the first bones, but was clearly still close enough to hear what he and the professor were saying. She had crouched down, and had one hand on the ground, knobbly arthritic fingers splayed. With a great deal of effort, she stood back up, her back not fully straightening however much she might try. McLean went over to help, and she took his hand gratefully.

'You'll find more, Professor,' she said as he led her back to the path. 'Trust me on that. You'll find more.'

44

'I've always wondered what became of them. Years I spent searching, hoping. And now I know.'

Ex-Detective Superintendent Ramsay stared out the passenger window of McLean's Alfa as they drove away from the excavation site. She was so old and wizened, sunk into the leather bucket seat, she looked almost like a child.

'What is it you know?' McLean had an inkling, a hint of what she might believe, but it was the sort of thing he needed to hear her say out loud rather than assume outright that she was as mad as Duguid had said.

'When I first joined the police, I was stationed out at Penicuik, you know? That's how I met my husband. He was garrisoned at Glencorse. Dashing Jack Renfrew, fair swept me off my feet.'

Renfrew. McLean wondered why Ramsay had kept her maiden name, or reverted to it after her husband had died. He knew better than to interrupt her though.

'We got married in seventy-five. Right after I'd made detective sergeant and he'd been promoted to captain. Anya came along soon after. She was always her father's girl rather than mine. Got his looks and his sense of mischief. You have children, McLean?'

The question brought him up short, and for a moment he

didn't know how to answer. Ramsay started up again before he could gather his wits.

'I don't suppose you do. Not the type. If you think about changing your mind, take my advice and don't. More trouble than they're worth.' She shook her head. 'I'm being unfair. Anya didn't take her father's death well. She was only eight years old.'

'I lost both my parents a few weeks before my fifth birthday. I can sympathise.'

'So you did. I'd forgotten that.' Ramsay looked at him with eyes clouded with age, but piercing nonetheless. 'Did you go off the rails?'

'I was four. I didn't really understand most of it. But there were times later on I probably behaved badly.'

Ramsay said nothing to that, and the road passed underneath them both in silence for a while before she picked up the threads of the conversation.

'Anyway, Penicuik. My first case after probation was a missing person. A young woman by the name of Charlotte McGowan. Twenty-six, I think she was. A little bit older than me. She'd come to Edinburgh for a holiday and just disappeared. Last seen at an outdoor party on the banks of the North Esk, down below Rosslyn Castle and the chapel. You know the spot, aye?'

McLean nodded. It would have been long before his time though. 'I take it she was never found.'

'Not her. Not June Christie four years later, or Angela McMahon two years after that. They found Jennifer Tennant's jacket, but nothing else of her. Then there were Mary Breacewell, Sharon Cartwright, Beatrice Cowan, Penelope Shepherd.' Ramsay began counting on her fingers as she spoke the names, but tapered off as she went past ten. A couple of them sparked the ghost of a memory in McLean's mind, but he couldn't say he recognised any of them.

'All missing?'

'Thirty years I was a detective, McLean. I dread to think how many missing-persons reports I came across in that time. There's thousands disappear every year. But those women? They were all last seen in this area. All of them were at a party or hanging out with a group of friends. All of them wandered off while nobody was paying attention. And none of them were ever seen again.'

Another mile of road passed under the wheels, more slowly this time as they approached the main road and its snarled-up late-afternoon traffic. Was this what Duguid had meant when he'd warned him about Ramsay being a couple of sandwiches short of the full picnic? McLean didn't know enough about the missing people she had named to make any decision about that. It wasn't unusual for a detective to have a pet obsession either. Christ alone knew he was bad enough in that department.

'You think that's them up on the moors then?' he asked as they crawled past the ugly blue and yellow box that was the IKEA warehouse.

Ramsay closed her eyes and let her head bump against the back of the seat in a manner that felt oddly like prayer. 'I know it.'

'So how did they get there then? Who killed them? And why?'

Another pause that saw them under the bypass and up the hill past Burdiehouse. 'That moor, you know what the locals call it?'

'Not really. I didn't even know about the hill fort until an hour ago.'

'It's not a hill fort. Not a classic one anyway. It's a sacred site for Druids. Cnoc nan daraich, they call it. Hill of the oaks. Even though there's not an oak tree for miles.'

And now they were straying into loony territory. 'Druids? I thought that was more of a Welsh thing.'

'Aye, and the language they would have spoken here before the Romans came was closer to Welsh than the Gaelic they speak in the Western Isles. There were Druids all up the East Coast, most likely one in every hill fort settlement. But Oak Hill was a teaching centre, somewhere the tribal chiefs sent their sons for an education.'

'You seem to know a lot about the subject.'

'I've been retired over twenty years now. You know what us coppers are like, McLean. We don't do hobbies. I've read pretty much every book about the history of the area I can get my hands on, trying to work out what happened to all those women. When I heard about those bones on the moorland, well . . .' Ramsay stopped talking, not because she'd run out of things to say so much as because they had arrived at their destination. McLean pulled into the kerb in front of the care home and switched off the engine.

'I'd like you to come into the station for a longer chat,' he said. 'Maybe have a look over some of the evidence we've uncovered so far. I know it's irregular, but I think your input might be invaluable.'

'Send a car for me. Eight sharp, tomorrow morning.' Ramsay unclipped her seat belt, and patted at the red leather seat. 'And thank you for the ride, McLean. Much nicer than that stinking old taxi. They obviously pay detectives better now than they did in my day.'

'There's a few back at the station would disagree with you there, ma'am. I have another source of income besides my Police Scotland pay cheque.' He climbed out of the car and walked around to the passenger side to help Ramsay out. She had already opened her door by the time he got there, but was struggling even if she didn't want to show it. She stared at him with something of that old venom he remembered from almost a quarter-century earlier, then relented and allowed him to help her to the front door.

'One other thing.' McLean pulled out his notebook and pen. 'You couldn't give me those names again, could you?

I'd like to run them past the Cold Case Unit.'

Ramsay arched an eyebrow. 'You checking out whether I'm a complete loony then?' She shook her head at the thought. 'Give me your card and I'll email them to you. I may be old, McLean, but I'm not a complete Luddite.'

The email pinged through a half an hour after McLean had finally sat down at his desk. He'd managed to avoid all of his superior officers only because they'd been called to a strategy meeting at Police Scotland headquarters. Judging by the increasingly strained messages on his phone, McLean was supposed to have been there with them. He couldn't help thinking his day had been better spent out in the field.

He toyed with the idea of forwarding the email directly to Duguid, but in the end it seemed a safer bet to print a hard copy and carry it down to the basement where the CCU had its offices. McLean found the ex-detective superintendent in conversation with Grumpy Bob. The two of them looked up at him like guilty schoolboys as he walked into the basement room.

'Thought you were over at HQ,' Duguid said as he peered over his spectacles. Despite the heat outside, the CCU office was pleasantly cool, one of the benefits of being underground.

'It was tempting, but I thought going to a secure mental hospital and talking to a psychopathic serial killer would be more fun.' McLean crossed over to Grumpy Bob's desk and handed him the printout. 'You couldn't get me some background on these missing-persons cases, could you, Bob? Some of them might be paper archives only, so concentrate on the computerised records first. Could well be our broken-legged woman in among them.'

The detective sergeant took the sheet of paper from him with a nod, then reached for his keyboard and mouse to wake his computer. McLean sensed the ex-detective superintendent's approach before Duguid reached him.

'What's all this? Another case for us?'

'I've just been out at the moorland dig. Slightly surprised to find Grace Ramsay there.' He told them both about what he'd learned, indicating the list of names with a nod of the head. 'She's certainly obsessed with it.'

Duguid barked out a single laugh. 'Obsessed? You clearly don't remember working under her command, do you, McLean.'

'Not really. She retired when I was still just a DC. She was running a special-investigations team before that, and I was in general CID.'

'Retired is the polite way of saying it. She was something of an embarrassment to the top brass towards the end. That's partly why she had her own team. What did they call them, Bob?' Duguid tilted his head at the detective sergeant.

'The polite name was the "Torphicen Street Irregulars".' Grumpy Bob looked uncomfortable at the question, and McLean wondered whether the old DS had been one of them.

'Aye, that's right. The "loony squad" was another. Mostly I remember senior officers just calling her "that fucking woman". She had a knack for putting people's noses out of joint.'

Has a knack, McLean almost added.

'Well, it looks like she might get the last laugh. I'm bringing her in for tomorrow morning's briefing too. I'd like to get up to speed on these missing-persons cases before then. Just in case we need to reopen them.'

'I'll get right on it, sir.' Grumpy Bob turned his attention back to the computer and began pecking at the keyboard with one finger on each hand, like a pair of hungry chickens.

'Thanks. I'll send a couple of DCs to help, shall I?'

Duguid stalked back to his own desk. 'As long as they're on your budget and not mine.'

45

There wasn't much afternoon left by the time McLean made it back to his office. Not that it was easy to tell by the harsh sunlight flooding through the window wall. He tapped a hopeful finger against the control panel for the air-conditioning unit, coaxing the noisy fan into life in a vain attempt to lower the oven-like temperature. Sitting in the room was not really an option if he wanted to get any work done, so he scooped a couple of important reports off the desk and retreated to the relative cool of the canteen.

His phone rang as he was halfway down the back stairs. A quick glance at the screen showed him it was someone he didn't really want to talk to, but also couldn't ignore. At least there was an empty room close enough to slip inside as he thumbed the accept button.

'I was wondering how long it would be before you called me, Dalgliesh,' he said.

'Fine, thanks. Good of you to ask. Not as strong as before I was almost poisoned to death by some cake meant for you, mind.'

It was a sore point between him and the reporter that she never failed to mention whenever their paths crossed. A couple of years back, she'd greedily helped herself to his cake in a café, both of them unaware that it contained rather more than chocolate, flour, eggs, butter and sugar.

'What do you want?' he asked. He didn't think he could ever bring himself to like the reporter, but he owed her for the cake. And the other time she'd saved his life.

'Wee birdie tells me you paid a visit to our mutual friend Norman Bale this morning.'

Of course she'd have an informant at Bestingfield. McLean had seen the string of sensational articles her newspaper had printed about the place over the past couple of years.

'What makes you think that?'

'Oh, come on, Tony. Enough of the back and forth. I know you went there, know you spoke to him. I think it's only fair you tell me what's going on there. Given I was the one stopped him from cutting you up with that butcher's knife of his.'

It hadn't been a butcher's knife. More the sort of thing outdoorsmen sharpened over a whetstone as they sat in front of a fire in the middle of nowhere. McLean glanced at his watch, noticed the reports he'd picked up. Had he really been meaning to read them, or was that just an excuse?

'Where are you now?' he asked, knowing full well it would be close by. That's how Dalgliesh operated.

'Café on the corner of East Preston Street. You know? The one that used to be a bank?'

McLean kept the sigh to himself. He'd learned down the years that Dalgliesh was a boil best lanced as soon as it appeared. 'Ten minutes,' he said.

'Excellent. I'll get a pot of tea ordered. And you can tell me all about the bones you've found up on the moors too.'

McLean could remember the building when it had still been a bank. He'd paid cheques in there, back when cheques were a thing. After it became a café, he'd often dropped in at the weekends when he'd lived a few hundred metres up the road.

The coffee wasn't quite good enough for Grumpy Bob's exacting standards, but the pastries made for a fine breakfast.

True to her word, Dalgliesh had ordered a pot of tea. By the look of the plates, she'd ordered cakes too, but not waited for him to arrive before tucking in. Probably wise to eat them before he got there, just in case.

'You said ten minutes.' She made a show of looking at the time on her phone. For all that she'd said she was fine, the reporter looked thin and weak. There'd never been much in the way of spare flesh to Jo Dalgliesh, but her brush with death had left its mark.

'Got caught up on the way out. I had to explain to a couple of detective constables why leaving before shift end was frowned upon.'

'Skiving? Can't be having that.' Dalgliesh poured tea into a spare mug and pushed it across the table. McLean helped himself to milk while she topped up her own mug and heaped several teaspoons of sugar into it.

'So then. What's your angle this time, Dalgliesh?' he asked.

'Call me Jo, why don't you? Dalgliesh makes me sound like some kind of footballer.' She grinned and gulped down a mouthful of tea, not waiting for it to have finished going down before she continued. 'And it's like I said on the phone. My wee birdie tells me you paid your old pal Norman a visit today. What's that about? And how does it fit in with your bones up there by Penicuik?'

McLean took a more measured sip of his own tea, swallowed properly and put the mug back down before answering. 'The bones on the moor are most likely Neolithic. Certainly ancient rather than modern. Professor Turner from the university Department of Forensic Anthropology is leading the dig. No doubt there'll be a series of learned papers, maybe a lecture tour and perhaps even a BBC docu-drama about it at some point. For

271

now, we're keeping an eye on it because finding human bones is something we take very seriously.'

'So Norman's nothing to do with that then?' Dalgliesh asked.

'With the bones on the moor? Why would you think that?' McLean studied the reporter's face for any sign that she was playing with him. More often than not she already knew the answers to all the questions she put to him. Far too often she knew more than he did too.

'You're also missing an admin support officer, last seen getting her end away in that vicinity, something like that. I'd have thought you'd have the whole of Police Scotland out combing the woods.'

'One of these days, Dalgliesh, we're going to have to have a long talk about where you're getting your information from.' McLean hid his worry behind his mug, taking another mouthful of tea.

'Oh, Tony. You're so naïve sometimes.' The reporter rubbed her finger in the chocolate icing smeared on one of the plates in front of her, then licked the mess off. 'And besides. If I gave you the names of my sources, you'd have to sack them. Then you'd have hardly any officers left and you're short-staffed as it is. Still one or two who refuse to divulge their secrets, mind. You inspire loyalty, you know?'

'Get to the point, will you? Only I'd like to go home soon. It's been a long day.'

'Home? Before it's dark already? That's not the Tony McLean I remember.'

McLean drained his tea and stood up. 'I've better things to be doing, Dalgliesh. If you need anything, call Dan Hwei in the press office, OK?'

He'd turned away, almost set off towards the door when she spoke more quietly. 'I know about the knife marks, Tony. Not the ancient bones, the more recent ones. Someone cut up people and ate them, didn't they.'

McLean could see the headline in his mind: 'Cannibal at Large' or maybe something even more sensational. Dalgliesh wasn't exactly known for her subtlety or restraint. Reluctantly, he turned back to her, pulled out the chair and sat down.

'I can't speak on the record. That has to go through the proper channels, you understand.'

The reporter smiled and poured more tea. 'And you can't confirm or deny. I know. But you know as well as I do, Tony, that this story won't stay buried. Much like those bones. I've picked it up already. Only a matter of time before everyone else does.'

McLean didn't know what was more annoying; that Dalgliesh already knew too much about the case or that she was right about the press. He'd have liked to have discussed the matter with the other senior officers before speaking to her at all, but by the time he managed to get them all in the same room together it would be too late.

'OK. I'll tell you what I can. But promise me you'll at least try to keep your headline-writer in check, yes?'

Dalgliesh shrugged. 'I can try.'

'You wanted to know why I'd gone to see Bale? Well, believe me, if I never set eyes on him again it would be too soon. He knows something about our missing support officer though. Don't ask me how. It's too much detail for him to be just playing us all along.'

'Seem to remember that about him. The way he could pick up on the tiniest detail and spin it so you'd think he knew everything about you.'

'That and dropping hints about weird things going on. Almost as if he'd set them in motion in the first place. Only this time I know he's been locked up. There's only so much he can get other people to do for him, and, to be honest, I don't think that's his game.'

'What is his game then?' Dalgliesh got to the heart of the

problem that had been worrying McLean all along.

'That's the thing. He's not going to get out of that hospital any time soon. Not ever, if I have any say in the matter. Nothing he does is going to change that. Apart from the sick joy he gets from making people dance to his tune, there's nothing to be gained from messing me around like he's doing right now.'

'Well, he was your friend a very long time ago. Maybe he's just trying to help.'

The thought had occurred to McLean, as he'd driven back from the hospital. He'd dismissed it almost as swiftly. 'If so, he's going about it in a strange way. Tell me, Dalgliesh. Does the term Fraternitas de Rosae Fontis mean anything to you?'

The reporter shook her head. 'Sounds like cod Latin to me. Never really was much cop at languages.'

'It means Brotherhood of the Red Spring, or something like that. I asked one of the constables to check it out, but it doesn't even warrant a Google entry.'

'And this is what Bale told you to look out for, was it?'

'Not in as many words. He dropped it as a name, knowing I'd pick it up. Made it sound like they were some kind of secret order or society or something.'

Dalgliesh shrugged. 'Never heard of it. I can ask around though.'

McLean stood up again, pushed his chair under the table. Dalgliesh already had her phone out, a small spiral-bound notebook and pen beside it.

'You'll let me know if you find anything, right?' he asked. 'A woman's life could be at stake here.'

She paused a moment before answering, thoughts hidden behind an inscrutable expression.

'I'll see what I can do, Tony. But you'll owe me, right?'

46

McLean noticed the shiny green Range Rover belonging to the deputy chief constable as he crossed the car park on his way to the back entrance to the station, half an hour later. Robinson had parked far too close to the Alfa for comfort, and he was tempted to go and check no one had dinged his paintwork getting out of the passenger door. Climbing in to drive himself home was going to require the skills of a contortionist too, unless he could persuade the DCC to leave first, but at least he knew the senior officers were back from headquarters.

The sound of raised voices leaked through the closed door to Robinson's office as McLean approached it. He considered going back to his own room, still uncomfortably warm despite a full hour and more of the air conditioning on max. On the other hand, he recognised Detective Superintendent McIntyre as the other half of the argument, which meant this was a perfect opportunity to talk to them both. And maybe stop them from coming to blows.

'Enter,' the DCC barked a moment after McLean had rapped sharply on the door with his knuckles. When he opened it, he saw Robinson standing on the business side of his desk, face flushed as if he'd run a mile. It didn't help that the office had clearly not benefited from an hour or more of air conditioning to lower the temperature. McIntyre, in sharp contrast, looked far cooler, and calmer, than the raised voices might have led McLean to expect.

'Hope I'm not interrupting anything,' he said, knowing full well that he was.

'Where the hell have you been all day, McLean?' Robinson turned on him like an angry headmaster.

'Pursuing cases, sir. Chasing down leads.' He knew as soon as he said it that it was the wrong thing to say.

'Dammit, man. That's sergeants' work. At best an inspector. You're meant to be here keeping everything under control.'

McLean put his hands behind his back, the better to hide his clenched fists. It was Robinson who had bounced him into the promotion to chief inspector in the first place. The constant suggestion that he should be some kind of manager rather than the experienced investigator his training and years on the job made him irritated him more than he'd care to admit.

'I'm not sure a sergeant could deal with Norman Bale, sir.'

'Norman –?' Robinson's thoughts took a measurable time to catch up with his mouth. 'Oh.'

'You went and spoke to him?' McIntyre asked. 'Thought you weren't going anywhere near.'

'I wasn't, Jayne. Right up until he started talking about the bones on the moors.'

McLean filled them in on his trip to Bestingfield and the unsatisfying interview with Bale, the forensic examination of the bone site, Grace Ramsay's unexpected appearance and the rest of the day's misadventures.

'And, just to top it all, I've spent the past hour or so talking to Jo Dalgliesh,' he added. 'That's what I was coming to tell you about.'

'You've what?' Robinson's response was predictable. 'You should know better than to go mouthing off to the press,

McLean. We sack junior officers for doing that.'

Every time. 'Actually, sir. I didn't tell her anything she didn't already know. This place leaks like a colander, and it's only going to get worse the shorter-staffed we are. Never thought I'd admit it, but actually Dalgliesh is a lot of help. Unlike some of the gutter press, she at least gives us a little heads up before telling the world we've a mass-murdering cannibal on the loose.'

The silence that followed his words lasted far longer than McLean thought reasonable. His attention was focused on the DCC, but he risked a sideways glance at McIntyre. Her eyes were as wide as Robinson's.

'That's the line they're going with?' she asked.

'The more sensational the headline the better, I expect. Thought you might want to know so we can make a start on our response.'

'Shit.' Robinson sat down heavily in his seat. 'I guess we were going to have to come clean sooner or later. They know we found bones up on the moor, and now there's a bloody archaeological dig going on up there.'

'They also know Renfrew is missing, and what she was getting up to in the car park.'

'You think any of them want a job?' McIntyre asked. 'They're way ahead of us on this one.'

'Don't joke about it, Jayne.' The DCC rubbed at his face with tired hands.

'Who said I was joking?'

'We'll need to set something up for tomorrow.' McLean unclenched his fists, began counting off points on his fingers. 'Nip the more lurid speculation in the bud. We can't put off telling people exactly what we've found up on the moors for ever, and knowing Dalgliesh she'll try to make a link between them and Anya Renfrew.'

Robinson glared at McLean in disbelief. 'Is there a link?'

'To be honest, I have no idea. The bones aren't hers, that's for sure. They've been up there too long for that. Of course, that means we've no idea who they belong to, let alone how they got there.'

'Do we know anything at all, McLean?' The DCC looked like he was about to start pulling his hair out. McLean knew how he felt.

'Not nearly enough, but I think Grace Ramsay might be able to help us.' That got him blank looks and silence, which on balance was the best result he could have hoped for. 'She's been tracking missing-persons cases in the area since the nineteen seventies. Duguid thinks she's obsessed beyond the point of madness, but I think she might be on to something.'

'Something how?' Robinson asked, his voice edged with disbelief.

'That's what I'm hoping to find out tomorrow, sir. She's going to come in and address the morning briefing.'

McLean walked down the corridor away from a worried deputy chief constable's office, McIntyre keeping an easy pace beside him. They had the vaguest of plans for a press statement to go out in the morning but he could see already that it was only going to lead to more questions. Right now he was more concerned with getting home on time, but he knew better than to glance nervously at his watch too often.

'How did the meeting at HQ go? I never did find out what it was meant to be about.'

McIntyre gave him a sideways glance that could have cut through steel. 'If you ever read your emails –' she started, then shook her head slightly. 'Probably just as well you were out there doing actual police work rather than sitting in a stuffy room listening to the NCA moan about their budgets being stretched.'

'NCA? I thought they were loaded.'

'Aye, they are. Still not happy, mind. Particularly since Operation Caterwaul looks like it's going to fizzle out before it's even started. And they've been keeping tabs on a few "Very Important People".' McIntyre made bunny ears with her fingers as she said the words. 'Seems there's a list you get onto by being obscenely wealthy or involved in crucial technology. It might surprise you to know there's a number of Scots on that list, although most of them live and work in the US these days.'

McLean tensed, certain that the detective superintendent was going to bring up the name of Jane Louise Dee at any moment. Life was complicated enough, without the enigmatic Mrs Saifre getting involved.

'Three of them have arrived in the capital in the past week,' McIntyre continued, unaware of McLean's anxiety. 'Apparently it's just a coincidence. There's no conference of evil supervillains or anything. But our friends at the NCA get nervous whenever two or more of them are on British soil at the same time. They're high-profile targets for kidnappers, state-sanctioned terrorists, that sort of thing. They want us to keep an unofficial eye on them while they're here, so that the public don't get caught in anything if it happens.'

'Do I know any of these people?' McLean asked.

McIntyre stopped mid-stride, forcing him to back up and face her.

'They want us to do their job for them, on our budget, and that's all you can think about?'

'Sorry. I figured that much out already. Just wondered who these people were to get the NCA all riled up. I've no doubt they gave you a superficially good reason why they need our help to deal with their problem.'

McIntyre stared at him as if she couldn't quite believe what he'd said. Then she shook her head. 'Jonathan Scanlan? Dominic Smythe? Gordon McTavish? I know you're comfortably well off,

Tony, but they're in a different league. Seeing as you're interested though, I'll send through all the details and you can coordinate with uniform to rearrange patrols around where they're staying. Hopefully whatever's brought them all home will be over soon and we can get back to the real job.'

McLean sighed. He'd walked into that one. 'Fine. But it'll have to wait until tomorrow. I'm off now before Emma chucks me out of my own home.'

'That bad, is it?' McIntyre asked.

'Not really, no. We're getting there. Early days though. And we're meant to be having dinner with Professor Turner and her wife. Em's got her heart set on studying forensic anthropology now, so my life won't be worth living if we're late.'

McIntyre patted him on the shoulder. 'Go home, Tony. Have a good evening. Try to relax, aye? The super-rich can wait until morning.'

47

Professor Turner lived in a small mid-terrace house in one of the quieter streets in Stockbridge. As McLean stood on the doorstep, the sound of the bell still echoing inside, he looked around at the leafy garden at the end of the road, the other buildings climbing three, sometimes four storeys into the evening sky. It wasn't far from here that he'd found the body of a dead hedge fund manager in his bath, killed by either a vengeful ghost or a heart attack. His old chief superintendent's son had died of a drug overdose just a few hundred yards away. Strange how the city presented itself to him as a series of crimes investigated. Cases solved, or at least closed.

'Tony, Emma, do come in.' Meg's voice snapped him out of his maudlin daydream. She waved them into a spacious hall, giving both of them hugs this time. 'Hattie's getting changed. She came in smelling like the bastard child of a bonfire and a grave, and only half an hour ago.'

Emma gave him a stare that silenced any comment he might have made. Not that McLean was that stupid. He'd been late enough home and been rushed through the shower and change routine himself. It was reassuring to know that it wasn't just him though. He handed over the bottle of wine they'd picked up on the way over, receiving an appreciative noise in return. Then they were both ushered through into the kitchen at the back of the house.

'We don't have a dining room as such,' Meg said as she busied herself making something that looked suspiciously like cocktails. 'Well, we do, but Hattie's filled it with bones and stuff. Not really the right atmosphere for eating. And besides . . .' She waved her hand across the room, seemingly unaware of the sharp knife she was holding. '. . . eating in the kitchen's so much more intimate, don't you think?'

McLean caught Emma's eye, and her expression was enough to stop him replying to Meg's rhetorical question. He would have been just as happy eating bought-in pizza in his own kitchen when the couple had visited them earlier in the week, but saying as much would not have been wise.

'How's the exhibition going?' he asked, thinking that was probably a safer topic for conversation. The kitchen walls were dotted here and there with some of Meg's less gloomy paintings, along with a few choice works by other notable artists.

'Early days. The *Scotsman* gave me a half-decent write-up, but the other papers haven't been effusive with their praise. Oh, and I had a very good review from Danielle Murray, of all people. She normally hates my kind of work, but she couldn't have been nicer.'

McLean considered what kind of response would be least incriminating or potentially condescending. Fortunately they were interrupted before he had to make a decision.

'I'm so sorry, everyone. It's been one of those days. No doubt Tony can tell you.'

All heads turned to see Professor Turner in the kitchen doorway. She was better dressed than the last time McLean had seen her, although the shower-damp hair and kaftan look was from a different decade, a different century. She strode into the room, picked up two of the strange-coloured drinks Meg had prepared and carried them over to where McLean and Emma stood.

'You look like you need one of these,' she said to Emma. 'You definitely need one of these,' she said to McLean.

'What –?'

'You never ask. That's the rules.' She went back to the counter and helped herself to another glass, lifted it in salute. 'Cheers.'

McLean felt that he had no option but to drink, even if what he really wanted just then was a nice cold beer. The cocktail tasted much like all cocktails tasted, of spirits, a bit too much sugar, and some unidentifiable fruit. At least it was cold.

'I know if I even mention work my life won't be worth living,' he said. 'Meg was telling me about her exhibition.'

Emma smiled, and all was well in the world.

It didn't surprise McLean to learn that Meg was the cook in the household. She was good at it too; her flare for the creative evident in the delicate dishes she served. He was glad to see that they didn't reflect her obsession with the horrors of genocide. Unless you considered meat to be murder, and counted eating langoustines as pillage of the sea.

They spoke of inconsequential things, skirting around the tricky subject of work. He, Harriet and Emma were all to some extent involved in the same job, which would have put Meg at a disadvantage anyway. Mass graves and charnel pits weren't his idea of a great supper topic either.

'Interesting piece on the news earlier,' Meg said as they ate pudding, the most delicate panna cotta McLean had tasted outside of an expensive restaurant. In deference to the summer heat, the food had been light and fresh, and this was no exception.

'Oh yes?' He tried not to sound wary, although news often meant crimes and misdemeanours, and that would mean the conversation inevitably turning to work.

'Apparently Gordon McTavish is back in town.'

'Isn't he a footballer or something?' McLean asked. He knew the name, knew exactly who they were talking about, but like mass graves and charnel pits, it wasn't something that he could get excited about. It was work, of course, too, even if he'd only found out earlier that evening. And he'd promised they wouldn't talk shop.

'Oh come on, Tony. You know perfectly well who he is.' Emma butted into the conversation a little more loudly than was necessary, perhaps aided by the large glass of white wine she'd consumed after her cocktail, and the half of its refill she had already downed too. When he gave her a look of bafflement she rolled her eyes. 'Only the third-richest man in the world. Or is it fourth?'

'Not just him either. Jonathan Scanlan somehow managed to get himself a table at Chez Innes in Leith even though the waiting list's meant to be something like eighteen months. Goes to show how the rich don't play by the same rules as everyone else.'

'Actually, I could get us a table there with just one call.' McLean pulled out his phone, half considered flicking through the menu to the contacts page and the number. He contented himself with holding it up as a visual aid to his point. 'Bobby's an old friend. He'd be hard pushed to better that pudding though.'

Meg laughed. 'Flattery will get you everywhere. But really? You know Bobby Innes?'

'I do, and I'd be happy to introduce you to him and his husband. Not spoken to either of them in far too long. And as to McTavish and Scanlan, yes, I do know who they are. I'm aware that both of them are in town because sadly it's my job to know.'

'Really?' Harriet's voice was all disbelief.

'I did promise Emma I'd not talk about work this evening. I'm sure there are more interesting topics of conversation than the comings and goings of the filthy rich.'

'Yes, but now you've mentioned it and we're all fascinated.' Meg topped up his wine glass even though McLean hadn't really touched what was already in it. Not that it wasn't as good as the rest of the meal; he simply didn't feel much like drinking.

'It's not all that interesting really. Just another routine part of the job. People of high net worth, that's the technical term for billionaires these days. They'd like to tell you they're just like everyone else, but really they're not. All that money makes them targets for every terrorist organisation, kidnap gang or just plain crazy out there. They've got their own security to deal with things like that, but we keep an eye on them so that ordinary folk don't get caught in the crossfire.'

'You learn something new every day,' Meg said. 'Still, it's a bit strange the two of them being in Edinburgh at the same time, isn't it?'

'Three actually. Dominic Smythe's on the watch list. You know, the tech guy? He has a big house out near Haddington he visits occasionally. According to my friends at the NCA he flew in on a private jet last night. Didn't bother letting anyone know he was coming.'

'What are they all doing here?' Meg asked. 'Is there some financial conference on?'

'Nothing official, that's for sure. Don't even think they know each other, particularly. Seems they all just decided to come home at the same time.'

'Maybe they're all part of some evil secret society, and their leader has called them all home to do his bidding.'

'Her bidding, more like.' McLean's words were out before he realised.

'Her? How very feminist of you.' Meg grinned. 'Equal opportunities villains. Excellent.'

'Actually, if the filthy rich expat Scots are gathering, I'm surprised Jane Louise Dee hasn't turned up already. Running a sinister cabal of billionaire sociopaths would be right up her street.'

That got him a raised eyebrow from Meg, a bark of laughter from Harriet and a strained cough from Emma, followed by a lengthy silence at the table.

'What?' he asked eventually.

'You sound like you know the woman,' Meg said.

'We've had run-ins. She's not what everyone might think.'

'She funded some of the work I did in Rwanda,' Harriet said. 'Well, the Dee Foundation funded us. It's all her money at the end of the day though.'

'Have you ever met her?' McLean asked.

'Can't say I've had the pleasure.'

'Pleasure's not the word I'd use. Horrible, horrible woman.' McLean had been going to say the same thing, perhaps a little less effusively, but Emma beat him to it. Another awkward silence fell on the room, broken finally by Meg's disbelieving voice.

'Do you really know Bobby Innes? I probably shouldn't say so in front of a policeman, but I think I'd kill to try some of his duck confit.'

'I did try not to talk about work. Honest.'

The taxi was warm and dark, and surprisingly didn't smell of stale vomit. McLean sat in the back with Emma leaning heavily on him, her head in the crook of his neck, her hair smelling of shampoo. He'd not drunk much over the course of the evening, but she'd made up for it. Not to the point of embarrassing herself in front of her soon-to-be professor, but enough that it was as well she had a day off tomorrow. He was too much of a gentleman to try and take advantage, but it was pleasant to be hugged all the same.

'You did very well,' she said, snuggling up against him in a manner he found most acceptable right up until the moment she pushed herself away. She stared at him, swaying slightly in the half-dark of the taxi's interior. 'Were you being serious about your lot following around all those famous rich people?'

'We don't follow them around, Em. Not like you think anyway. It's more a case of being aware they're here and the problems that might arise from that. Kirsty's dealing with it all anyway. That's the joy of being a DCI. I can palm off the rubbish jobs on my junior officers.'

Emma let out what could only be described as a girly giggle, and thumped him weakly on the chest.

'What?' he asked.

'You're so full of it sometimes, Tony McLean. "Palm it off on my junior officers". Like you've ever delegated anything.'

'Well, I've delegated this one.' He didn't have the heart to tell her that it had been Jayne McIntyre who had assigned the duty to Ritchie.

'It's weird though, to think that people are so important they need protecting, but they've not been elected or anything. They're just rich beyond sense.'

'We're not protecting them, Em. We're keeping an eye on where they are just in case . . .' He was about to say 'the little people' but had the sense to stop himself. '. . . ordinary folk are in any danger. It's nothing really. Just part of the job. They'll be away on their private jets in a day or two and we can forget they were ever here.'

48

She wakes from a dream of warm water, scented bubbles and lazing in the bath. For a moment she recalls that bathroom, the yellowing tiles and mould spots in the corner of the ceiling above the shower head. She almost recalls who she is too, a name attaching itself to her past experience. But before she can grasp it, the harsh reality comes crashing down on her once more.

It is not warm, but bitter cold. She is wet, and the blanket has gone. In its place, the rough, rasping tongue of the flannel works at her skin like some over-friendly dog.

'Awake? That's good.'

She remembers the voice from before. The old woman. How long has it been since last she heard another person's voice? It seems like a lifetime, a hellish eternity. She tries to move, but though she can feel no restraints around her arms or legs, nothing responds to her command. Not even her eyes. She remembers huddling in the corner, caked in her own waste. Now she lies immobile on the bed, no memory of moving whatsoever.

'Don't worry yourself, dear. You are blessed, chosen. But you must be clean in the eyes of the Lord. Purged of all sin.'

The words are not reassuring, but she is helpless as the rough washing continues. She can smell a heavy odour of soap, coal tar like they used to shampoo the horses with, back when she was a little girl infatuated with such things. Lathers well in cold water, that's one thing she can remember. It's a scent that never quite leaves. She remembers that too.

'Why are you doing this to me?' she tries to ask, but the words won't come out. Instead she feels a damp finger press against her lips.

'Shh now. Almost done, dear. Then you can rest and prepare yourself.'

She wants to ask what she must prepare herself for, but she has no control over her body. She can only lie there, eyes closed, and imagine what is happening to her. A strong hand lifts her head, then she feels her hair being gently pulled back. For a moment she thinks her jailer is going to wash it; the tugging sensation and familiar salon noise suggests something else entirely. There is no great skill as her hair is cut down to her scalp, and the strong-smelling soap stings the many small cuts as the stubble is shaved away. When the old woman is done, she has no hair left at all. Even her eyebrows are gone, and the cold air grips her newly bared head like a migraine.

'Wh-why?' This time she manages to squeeze the question out. As she does so, her eyes flick open to reveal the painted stone wall arching overhead, unfocused and far too bright. Whatever strength she mustered to action, it is spent now and she cannot even close them again, only stare as a thin film of tears builds up in each eye, then leaks out across her cheeks.

'You must rest. Prepare yourself. Don't struggle.' The old woman's blurred face moves into view. 'You are clean in body now, soon you will be clean in soul too. A blessed vessel for the spirit of the Lord.'

'I –'

'Soon.' That strong hand is under her head again, lifting it up as the old woman brings a cup to her lips. She would fight it, but there's nothing left in her. She can barely even swallow the trickle of bitter water poured into her mouth. And she knows now that she is truly lost. No one will come to her rescue. She will die here, starved and frozen. A part of her knows that she deserves no better. If only that part would tell her why.

49

McLean's thoughts were still stuck on the evening before, and that amazing pudding, when a knock at his open door distracted him from his reverie. He looked up to see a young uniformed constable whose name he couldn't remember, but before either he or she could say anything, she was elbowed aside and Grace Ramsay stalked into the room.

'Never liked this building. Gayfield Square was always a better nick.'

'Ma'am.' McLean was on his feet and across the room in moments, even if his hip protested at the sudden movement.

'Enough of the ma'am, McLean. I'm not your superior officer any more.'

McLean dismissed the constable with a quiet 'Thank you' and turned his attention to Ramsay. She had wandered off to stare out of his window at the view over the rooftops towards the castle.

'What should I call you then? Mrs Renfrew?'

'I dropped that name when Jack died. Anya kept it though. She always did take after her father.' Ramsay turned away from the view to face him. 'Grace is fine. Or Ms Ramsay if you're one of those old-fashioned types who finds it embarrassing to use a woman's first name.'

'I'll call you Ms Ramsay in front of the officers, if you don't mind. You're happy enough to address the briefing?'

'It's my bloody daughter who's gone missing. Course I'm not happy. It's important your people know what they're dealing with though. You got my email? The names?'

'I did, yes. Detective Constable Harrison's working on them now. Some of the earlier ones are in the paper archives. The filing's not what it once was.'

Ramsay made a noise that sounded like 'Hmph'. 'Sergeant Needham would never have stood for that.'

An image rose unbidden into McLean's mind. A man, dressed in a long cape like some latter-day Count Dracula, eyes wide and mad, flames all around him, leaping over him, devouring him. He shuddered. 'Needy's long gone, Ma— . . . Grace. We do the best we can without him.'

'And this Harrison. He's reliable?'

'She actually. And you can ask her yourself.' McLean waved an open hand back towards the door, where a suspicious-looking DC Harrison had just appeared. She held a thick pile of folders in one hand.

'The DCC's here and everyone's ready for the meeting, sir.' She noticed the small figure standing beside him. 'Ma'am.'

'Are those all the case files, Constable?' Ramsay asked in a voice that was unmistakably that of a detective superintendent. Harrison stepped into the room, arm raised to hand the paperwork over before she realised what she was doing.

'Everything I could find. Some of the earliest cases are a bit sparse.'

'I don't need to see them, girl. I wrote most of them. It's important your team are properly briefed though. Get copies of them to everyone working the case.'

McLean saw the way Harrison tensed at the word 'girl'. He was about to come to the detective constable's defence, when she simply nodded, smiled politely and took back the offered folders.

'Yes, ma'am. I'll see that it's done,' she said, then turned and left.

'I like her,' Ramsay said to McLean after Harrison had disappeared. 'You need to be careful though. Station like this, there's bound to be gossip.'

If he didn't know better, he'd have thought she'd been talking to the DCC. Or McIntyre. Or Grumpy Bob. They all had a point, but that didn't help the fact that the station was under-staffed and Harrison was the best of the new batch of detectives.

'Shall we get this meeting done then?' he asked, and ushered the retired detective chief superintendent to the door.

'Women have been disappearing in this area every few years for at least the last four decades. On the face of it, there's no pattern. They're not from any particular background, don't go missing to any discernible timetable. Sometimes two or more have disappeared in a single year, and the longest gap between reported disappearances is nine years. Note I said reported dis-appearances. Not everyone who goes missing is noticed. Remember that.'

For all that she'd retired two decades earlier, Detective Super-intendent Grace Ramsay knew how to catch the attention of her audience. Old and tiny, she nevertheless had the undivided attention of all the senior officers sitting around the conference table in Deputy Chief Constable Stevie Robinson's office. That might have had as much to do with the novelty value as anything, or perhaps a collective disbelief that she was both here and still alive. Of the officers present, Jayne McIntyre and Grumpy Bob would have known her best, and ex-Detective Superintendent Charles Duguid of course. He'd protested at being asked to attend, but was as captivated by the story as the rest of them. At least for now.

'The discovery of ancient remains up on the moor above Gladhouse is a worrying development,' Ramsay continued. 'It's true most of the bones you've found are historic, but not all of them. You'll all have read the pathologist's report on the first finds. They're none of them more than a few years in the ground. All female and in the target age group. As I understand it, the investigation into that is in its earliest stages, so you'll have hardly begun combing the archives for potential missing persons yet. Scope the size of the dig, get DNA samples where you can, approximate age, height, that sort of thing where you can't. Is that right, Chief Inspector?'

McLean was caught off guard by the question, his mind on other things. It took a moment to catch up, and he felt that horrible sense of being picked out at assembly by the headmaster. He looked at Grumpy Bob, but the old detective sergeant was no use.

'We've begun DNA sampling of the bones, ma'am, but they're badly degraded so it's going to take a while.' DC Harrison came to the rescue, and McLean was glad he'd asked her to sit in and take notes. She handed Ramsay a sheaf of papers, but the retired detective chief superintendent waved them away.

'I'd lay good odds those results will identify the bones as belonging to at least some of the women on my list. I suggest you reopen all those missing-persons cases. You might need to contact any known relatives for comparator samples. I doubt there'll be anything else you can work with.'

'Ms Ramsay, ma'am.' The DCC knew her only by reputation, and so far had trod more carefully than usual. 'What exactly do you suspect is happening here? Are you suggesting that these women have been abducted, killed and then . . .' He paused a moment, no doubt aware that Ramsay's own daughter was missing. They all knew what had happened to the bones before they'd been disposed of. '. . . then buried on the moors?

In a site that appears to have been used for over a thousand years?'

· Duguid's cough might have been an attempt to clear an obstruction in his windpipe, but McLean thought it far more likely the ex-detective superintendent was trying to cover up a laugh. Either way, it didn't fool Ramsay.

'Would you like a glass of water, Charles?' she asked. 'Or are you still having difficulty with basic investigatory principles?'

'I'm having trouble with a retired detective seeing patterns of evidence where there are none. Same as I did when she wasn't retired. Have you any idea how many people go missing in Scotland every year? How many people in Edinburgh alone?'

'Aye, I do. Probably better than most. This is different. These ones are different.'

'So you keep saying,' Robinson said. 'But I don't see how you can tell.'

Ramsay closed her eyes briefly, and McLean could almost hear the silent count to ten. It was a technique he'd used himself plenty of times before when dealing with idiots and bureaucrats, but he wasn't sure he understood her point any more than the rest of them. The links between the cases she'd given him were tenuous to say the least.

'Gentlemen,' Ramsay finally said, then after a slight pause added: 'ladies. Twenty years ago, when I retired, these missing-persons cases were all unsolved, filed away, forgotten. In those twenty years, another dozen or more women have disappeared from the same area in similar circumstances. And now my own daughter can be added to the end of that list.'

She let that last statement hang in the air for a while, judging the moment to resume with absolutely perfect timing. McLean could see both Duguid and the DCC beginning to speak, no doubt to object.

'What we can do now that we couldn't do back in the last

millennium is combine pattern analysis with mapping software and far more rigorous statistical analysis. I've spoken to experts at the university, and a few contacts I've made in the US over the years. As some of them are fond of saying, the math never lies.'

50

'You still think she's not a couple of sandwiches short of a picnic?'

McLean watched as DC Harrison escorted Grace Ramsay away from the DCC's office, the meeting having broken up not long after the retired detective had tried to explain her plan to use complicated data analysis to prove a connection between the many unsolved missing-persons cases she had collected over the past fifty years. Duguid stood in the corridor beside him, perhaps less fractious than he might have been but still dismissive.

'I'm not sure about her methods, but you can't deny we've got bones from at least three different women up on Oakhill Moor, probably a lot more to be discovered. And people have been going missing in that area for a long time.'

'Statistical inevitability.' Duguid shoved his hands deep into his trouser pockets, and, for the first time he could remember, McLean thought of his old boss as being childish.

'You really don't like her, do you.' It wasn't meant to be a question.

'We have . . . history. Never did rate her as a detective, and as for her people management skills . . .'

McLean laughed. He couldn't help himself. Only the thunderous look on Duguid's face stopped him.

'Look. I don't know about Ramsay's conspiracy theories, but we have got an ongoing investigation. Those bones belonged to people, and it's a fair bet some of those people are going to be in missing-persons records. At least we can start getting them into some kind of order so we know what to look for when the DNA results come in. And if nothing comes of it, then you'll have proven she's as mad as you say.'

Duguid's scowl would have made a clown cry, but he nodded his head minimally along with it. 'Aye, I suppose that's true. Best get on with it then.'

McLean would have wished him good luck, but his phone chose that moment to ring. He pulled it out of his pocket and stared at the screen stupidly for a couple of seconds before accepting the call.

'DCI McLean.'

'Ah. Morning, sir. Police Sergeant Donaldson. From Penicuik? Hope I've not interrupted anything important.'

'No, you're fine. Just out of a meeting, you know how it is.' McLean shut himself up before he started wittering on too much. 'What can I do for you, Sergeant?'

'More what I can do for you, sir. Ken you asked me about a lad named Bobby?'

McLean struggled to remember, then it came to him in a rush. The interview with Dan Forbes, the lost lighter, the fire out at Rosskettle, first in a series that had spread out around the southern edge of Midlothian like a plague. Anya Renfrew's burned-out car had been one of them, and it had been called in by a young boy with a friend called Bobby.

'Aye, I remember now.' He set off towards his office and something to write notes on.

'Well, I asked around, like you said. Seems there is a young Bobby known to some of the patrol officers. Name of Robert Wilkins. He's only thirteen, but the family's known to us.

Father's currently in Saughton, mother's an alcoholic and sometime drug addict. They live on the caravan site by Bilston, or at least that's the address we've got for them.'

'He have a history of arson?' McLean had to ask it, even if it was never that easy.

'Nothing any of the constables know about. His dad's away for GBH. Bottled his best mate in an argument at the pub.'

'Sounds charming.'

'Aye, well, the kid's got a mouth on him and all his old man's attitude apparently. He's not done anything worth more than a quiet word so far. Social services are aware of the home situation too.'

But they're as strapped for cash as the rest of us. Donaldson didn't have to say it for McLean to know.

'Email me that address, can you? I'll see if we can't set up an interview.'

'Already on its way,' Sergeant Donaldson said. 'Rather you than me, sir.'

McLean knew what he meant. Interviewing a minor was never straightforward, and if this Robert Wilkins's family situation was as bad as the sergeant described, they'd have to tread very carefully. Still, it was a lead maybe. And so far they'd drawn a blank on everything else regarding the fires.

He thanked Donaldson and hung up. By the time his laptop had woken up, an email with the address had come through. Plot 34, Bilston Caravan Park. Genevieve and Gordon Wilkins, son Robert, thirteen. No other children. Gordon currently in the second year of a five-year stretch for GBH at HMP Edinburgh, otherwise known as Saughton. McLean looked at the message, then at his watch. It was school holidays, so there was every chance young Bobby would be at home playing games on his computer. Or he could be out in the countryside setting fire to things. Only one way to find out really.

★ ★ ★

The caravan park sat on a patch of scrubland around the back of Bilston, not far from the Bilston Glen control centre. McLean recalled hearing there had been plans to redevelop most of the area into a Scottish Film Industry centre, including big-name studios and all manner of other support industries. The plan had fallen apart, as so many of these things did. Not enough funding, no tax breaks, disputes over changing land use and building on green-belt land. He couldn't remember which one had been the reason. Maybe it had been all of them.

The Alfa Romeo looked very much out of place as he drove past the lines of static caravans. There were few cars about, and those that were looked like they'd not moved in a while. He'd brought DC Harrison with him, even though he should really have passed the whole thing on to DI Ritchie. But then again, palming stuff off on his junior officers was never something he'd been good at; at least, that was what Emma had said. Ritchie was busy keeping an eye on the billionaire techbros too.

Harrison sat silent, staring out the side window as they tried to identify the correct address. 'My gran and grandpa have one of these. Up in Fife,' she said eventually. 'Used to go there for holidays when I was wee. Can't imagine living in one all the time, mind.'

'It's a roof over your head, I guess.' McLean heard the awkwardness in his voice. He could have fitted one of these whole caravans in his drawing room, a room in his house that he rarely even entered.

'Here. It's this one, I think. Plot 34, right?'

McLean stopped the car alongside a caravan that looked to his untrained eye to be exactly the same as all the others in this part of the park. Only when he'd climbed out of the car and approached the steps leading up to the door did he notice the faded number painted on the side. He checked his watch, looked back along the narrow road towards the park entrance. He'd arranged for a child support officer from social services to meet them, but it was anyone's guess how long it would take them to arrive.

'Think we should wait, or see if there's anyone home first?' No sooner had he asked the question than McLean knew it was unfair. Harrison was a detective constable; she would do what she was told. Decisions were his responsibility.

The problem was solved by the appearance of an elderly woman from the next-door caravan. She was dressed in the thinnest of tops over denim shorts that might have been made by cutting up a pair of old jeans worn at the knees, but equally might have been expensively manufactured to look that way. She had clearly been spending most of the summer sunbathing, as her skin was a colour and texture more often associated with Barbados than Bilston.

'Youse lookin' for Genevieve, yer out of luck. Took her off in an ambulance yesterday. Reckon she OD'd again, daft bitch.' The elderly woman raised a stick-thin arm to her face, pressing an e-cigarette to her lips. She took a long drag, the end glowing with a fake red light, then she let out a thick plume of sickly smelling vapour into the air.

McLean took out his warrant card, but it didn't seem to impress the woman. She raised a badly painted-on eyebrow and took another drag.

'What about her son, Robert?'

'Bobby? Not seen him today. Probably gone off with that mate of his. They're always whizzing around on their push bikes. Little terrors, they are.'

'He have a name, this friend? An address?'

'What am I? His secretary?' The old woman scowled and took another drag of her e-cigarette. The vapour must have calmed her down a little, as once she'd cleared it from her lungs she relented. 'Wee Gav, everyone calls him, but I know his mum Sheila. Does meals on wheels for some of the old dears round here. Sheila Mason. Lives in Roslin. No' sure where.'

With a name and the village to go on, it didn't take long to get a full address. McLean drove, while Harrison attempted to put a call through to social services redirecting their child support officer. She also tried to get through to the Royal Infirmary over in Little France, to find out what had happened with Genevieve Wilkins, but her call was still in a queue by the time they arrived.

Sheila Mason lived in a neat semi-detached house in a quiet corner of a seventies housing estate on the south side of Roslin. McLean knew the village mostly from its association with the chapel made famous by Dan Brown. The last time he'd been there was to investigate a dead body found in the River North Esk, where it cut its deep path through the sandstone of Roslin Glen. That had been winter, with snow on the ground, but as he stepped out of the car the summer heat squeezed the air and weighed heavy over the land. In the distance, he could see the black smear where the fire had raged across the moorland. Some-where over there, hidden from view by closer trees, lay Gladhouse Reservoir and the woods where Anya Renfrew had gone missing.

'Genevieve Wilkins was admitted to the ERI yesterday morning. Drug overdose, apparently. She'd been drinking too though.' DC Harrison still had her phone in one hand as she climbed out of the car to join him. 'She's not likely to be released any time soon. Report's gone to social services about her son.'

'Shouldn't he be in care? His dad's in jail and he's only thirteen years old.'

'Aye, he should. Apparently not though. He's —'

'Can I help you?'

McLean and Harrison both turned towards the front door of the house, where a middle-aged woman had appeared. She looked crumpled, hair awry and face a little puffy as if she'd been sleeping. Like the old lady at the caravan park, she was dressed for the heat, which was to say she was not wearing much at all. Her T-shirt had probably fitted fine when it was new, but now it sagged in some places and bulged in others. Her shorts would have embarrassed a girl a third her age.

'Mrs Mason?' McLean asked.

'No' since the divorce. Who's asking?'

McLean pulled out his warrant card, held it up for her to see and made the introductions. 'We're looking for Robert Wilkins. I believe he's friends with your son, Gavin?'

'Bobby? Is this about his mam?'

'In a manner of speaking.' McLean took the opening given him. 'Is he here?'

Not Mrs Mason scratched at her cheek with a fingernail that had to have been glued on. 'No' just the now. Him and my Gavin headed off this morning on their bikes. Probably out on the old railway somewhere.'

That seemed a bit casual, but then who was he to judge how people raised their children? 'Any idea when they'll be back?'

She shrugged, checked her watch. 'Twelve, maybe. Unless they're hungry. Or bored. What's this all about then? He's no' in any trouble, is he?'

McLean considered the options. They could have Control broadcast a message to all patrols to be on the lookout for two thirteen-year-old boys on bicycles. Then he could head back to the station and get on with all the other work that needed doing. Or they could sit and wait for them to turn up. He was only here on a hunch, a first name that wasn't exactly unusual in these parts. And yet the fact that Robert Wilkins and Gavin Mason were out unsupervised during the holidays fitted the theory that had brought him here in the first place.

'I don't suppose we could come in, could we?' he asked.

51

The inside of the house was mercifully cooler than the oppressive afternoon heat outside. Not Mrs Mason led them through a narrow hallway to a kitchen at the back. Big enough for counters and a central table with four chairs around it, the room was dominated by a window looking out over a garden bounded by mature trees. The top of the Pentland Hills could be seen poking above the canopy in the distance, set against a deep-blue, cloudless sky.

'Tea? Or is it a bit too warm for that? I've juice in the fridge. Unless you'd prefer something stronger?'

McLean didn't need to glance at his watch to know that it was a bit early for that, even if he wasn't on duty.

'I wouldn't mind a glass of water, if it's not too much trouble,' Harrison said.

'Mrs Mason,' McLean began as the woman went to the fridge and brought out a filter jug.

'Ms Underhill actually. Like I said, Mason was my married name. I've been divorced almost a year now.'

'Sorry. Ms Underhill. Your son, Gavin. He's been friends with Bobby Wilkins a while?'

Underhill passed two glasses of cold water to them, took up a third for herself. 'Since they were at nursery, aye.'

'And do they often go off together? On their bikes?'

'Rather that than they sat upstairs playing computer games all day. Do you have children?' Underhill's gaze swept over McLean's face, then down to his bare ring finger, before rising back up to his face again. He fought the urge to clasp his hands together.

'No.'

'Well, if you did, you'd know what they're like, aye? An' teenage boys're the worst. Never wash unless you tell them to, never pick anything up. They eat crap all the time and won't even look at a meal you've cooked for them. An' see if you let them, they'll sit in front of a computer all day and all night. Rots their brains. Well, it'd rot them if they had any.'

As an only child, raised by his grandmother, McLean had no reference to the life of a modern teenage boy. He risked a glance sideways at DC Harrison, who had two brothers if memory served. She raised an eyebrow, not quite smirking.

'I couldn't use your toilet, could I, Ms Underhill?' She held up her empty glass by way of explanation. McLean knew it was a ruse to have a look around the house, and possibly give him some time to talk to the woman alone. If Underhill had watched any cop shows on the telly she hadn't taken that nugget of information on board.

'Aye, back the way you came in. Last door on the left.'

Harrison thanked her and left the room, closing the door behind her. McLean waited a moment before speaking again.

'Do you think it's safe, letting two lads go off on their bikes like that?' he asked.

Underhill laughed mirthlessly. 'Safe? Aye, they're sensible enough not to get into trouble. And they've both got phones if they need to get in touch. That's more'n you had when you were a lad, aye? Bet you never thought twice about biking out to the hills or going round your mate's house for tea.'

McLean hadn't, but then he'd never really had mates to go round to tea with anyway. He'd been bundled off to boarding school before he was old enough to spend much time biking around Edinburgh, and he'd spent most of his holidays under the baleful eye of his grandmother or being smothered by Mrs Roberts the housekeeper. He'd not made any close friends until university. Well, apart from Norman, but he'd died when they were both six.

'I take it you work, Ms Underhill?' McLean tried to steer the conversation away from awkward subjects.

'Aye. Part-time just now, but it's still a struggle in the holidays. Easier now Gavin's turned thirteen. I couldnae leave him long before.'

'So going out biking with his friend, that's recent?'

'His father took him out last summer, Bobby too.' Underhill managed to inject an almost lethal amount of venom into the word "father". 'Now he's no' around any more, they have to make their own entertainment.'

The possibilities are endless. 'Have you any idea where they've gone? When they'll be back?'

'They like the old railway line. It's safer than the roads. Sometimes they go up towards Gladhouse and the hills, but I told them no' tae go there. What wi' the fire an' all. As to when they'll be back?' Underhill looked at her watch. 'Could be any time really. Depends how hungry they are.'

'What about Bobby? I've seen where he lives and we know about his parents.' McLean left the assumption unsaid, fishing for information on the boy and killing time until Harrison came back.

'Ach, wee Bobby's no' so bad. There's plenty worse my Gavin could be hanging oot wi'. An' the poor wee lad's no family worth the name. Gen, his mum, she used to be fine, aye? But Bobby's dad got a bit free wi' his fists, and she took to the bottle to cope.

Youse ask me if they're safe out there on their bikes? The real danger's at home half the time.'

A rattling noise came from the back window before McLean could say anything to that. He couldn't see what was making the noise, but Underhill, standing a bit closer, looked around. 'That'll be them now.'

A moment later the back door clattered open, and two young boys barrelled into the kitchen. The one in front was obviously Gavin, he had his mother's nose and eyes. The lad behind was thinner, a bit taller, and dressed like a street urchin from casting central. They didn't see McLean at first, didn't even acknowledge Gavin's mother, as is the way of teenage boys. Instead, they went straight to the fridge. It was only as Gavin was opening it that Bobby noticed they weren't alone.

'Hey, Sheila,' he said, which McLean thought was a bit informal. 'Who's the boyfriend?'

'Gavin, Bobby. This is Detective Chief Inspector McLean, from the polis.'

The effect would have been funny if it wasn't also tragic. Underhill's words took a few moments to percolate, but McLean could see the instant they registered. Gavin went rigid, and it was as well he'd not yet picked up the bottle of Coke that was in the fridge door, otherwise he'd surely have dropped it. Bobby betrayed his previous form by reacting more like a hardened criminal. The 'fuck' was barely audible, and then he was off.

Had he gone for the back door they'd both walked in through, he might well have got away. As it was, he sprinted for the other door, aiming for the hall and out the front. Too bad for him DC Harrison chose that exact moment to come back in. She was quick off the mark, as well, reading the situation in an instant. And she had experience growing up with two brothers.

'Not so fast, you wee – oof.' She caught Bobby in a tackle that would have got a cheer at Murrayfield, wrestled him to the floor and sat on him. Gavin could only watch, his face turned white with shock.

Given the circumstances, McLean felt that Sheila Underhill was very understanding, at least to start with. He hadn't told her why they wanted to talk to Bobby, happy to let her assume that it was something to do with the young boy's mother overdosing the day before. Her tune changed remarkably the moment he expressed an interest in speaking to Gavin too.

'He's no' a criminal. Youse can't treat him like one.'

'Ms Underhill. Gavin is, technically, old enough to be treated as a criminal. I could have him taken away for questioning, into custody even. I have no intention of doing that. I don't particularly want to treat Bobby any differently either. But I do need to talk to them, both of them, about some of the things that have been happening around here in the past couple of weeks.'

Underhill eyed him suspiciously. 'What is it you think they've done?' she asked. They were sitting at the kitchen table, her and Gavin and McLean. Bobby was through in the living room with DC Harrison for now, awaiting the arrival of the child support officer. McLean shouldn't really have been talking to either of them without social services; there were protocols for dealing with children, age of criminal responsibility or not, and he'd get into hot water for ignoring them. Well, it wouldn't be the first time.

'There was a vehicle fire in the woods up by Gladhouse Reservoir early last week.' McLean kept his focus on Underhill as he spoke, but he watched her son out of the corner of his eye too. 'It was called in to the control centre at Bilston Glen from the payphone at Temple. I've listened to the recording, and it's a young man's voice. He mentions his friend Bobby.'

The flinch was unmistakable. McLean knew in an instant that Gavin had made the call, even though he was yet to hear the boy speak. His mother wasn't going to let things go that easily though.

'And that's enough to come hassling folk, is it?' She puffed up like a blowfish prodded, prickly and poisonous. 'You come into my house accusing –'

'I'm not accusing your son of anything more than being an upstanding citizen and reporting a fire.'

Underhill turned her attention to her son, anger still there but momentarily deflected. 'Did youse call the polis, Gavin? What were you doing all the way up at Gladhouse anyway?'

The young lad squirmed in his seat as if he needed to go to the toilet. Given that he'd not been let out of his mother's sight since returning home, that might well have been the case.

'The car belonged to a colleague of mine.' McLean addressed his words at the young boy now. 'Not a police officer, but one of the support staff. A bit like a secretary, I suppose would be the best way to describe her. She went missing almost two weeks ago now, and we're all very worried about what might have happened to her. That's why we want to talk to anyone who might have seen that car before it caught fire, as well as whoever it was called 999 that day to alert us.'

'I didnae set it on fire.' Gavin's voice was quiet, almost a whisper. His mother put a protective hand on his shoulder and squeezed it gently.

'I never said you did.' McLean didn't add that it was more likely Bobby who'd lit the flame. Probably found Dan Forbes's lighter while mucking around at Rosskettle. Maybe caused that fire too, and the one on the moors. Or they could all be random, nothing more than might be expected from a hot, dry spell in the middle of the school holidays.

'There was rubber johnnies everywhere up there. Pure disgusting it was. Bobby flicked a bag of them at me. Got stuff on ma troosers.'

'Was this the same day you called us about the fire?' McLean asked, receiving a nod in answer.

'And can you remember anything else about the car park? Were there any other cars there?'

A shake of the head this time.

'How about people? Did you see anyone else while you were up there? Apart from Bobby?'

Another shake of the head. Gavin had been studying the tabletop, but now he looked up at McLean. His eyes were wide, and glistened with the tears he was trying hard not to cry. The poor lad was terrified.

'I didnae want tae go there, but Bobby dared us. The woods're haunted, right? Folk disappear in there and they's never seen again. I've heard the stories.'

McLean tried to remember what the world had been like when he was thirteen. He'd changed school that year, from the horrific prep school he'd have been happy to let Bobby Wilkins burn down, to a slightly less horrific public school. Still in the south of England, still a nightmare. The summer he'd turned thirteen had been a holiday between the two, and he'd spent most of it bicycling around the same places Gavin Mason and his friend now frequented. Only he'd not had anyone to share the experience with. Nor a purloined Zippo to set fire to things with.

'There's no such thing as ghosts, Gavin. And well you know it.' The young boy's mother squeezed his shoulder again, then looked at McLean. 'Are we done here?'

He was about to say yes, but they were interrupted by the doorbell.

'That should be social services. We'll need to take Bobby into care, at least for a day or two until his mother's been assessed.'

Gavin opened his mouth to say something, but McLean held up his hand for silence. 'Don't worry. You'll still be able to see your friend.' He put his hand in his pocket and pulled out a business card, placed it down on the table. 'And in the meantime if you remember anything else from the woods, however small and insignificant you might think it, you tell your mum and get her to give me a call about it, OK?'

52

Lunch had long since passed by the time McLean climbed the stairs to his office. He stopped at the vending machine on the third-floor landing; there wouldn't be much left in the canteen now, and he was realistic enough to admit he'd probably not eat any fruit if he bought it. A packet of crisps and a couple of chocolate bars would have to do. Washed down with some tarry coffee from the pot he'd put on at six that morning.

His phone buzzed in his pocket as he was walking back with his spoils, leading to a complicated shuffle until he managed to fetch it out. The name that appeared on the screen meant he had no trouble deciding to answer it straight away. Or at least as soon as he was able to juggle the food so he could lift the handset to his ear.

'Manda. How are you today?'

'Ugh. Tired mostly. Trying to get any usable samples for DNA analysis out of bones that have been lying about in the bushes for God only knows how long and then baked in a fire isn't easy, you know?'

'But you're a miracle worker so you managed, right?'

'Don't get your hopes up. We'll know for sure once the tests are all complete.'

'And how long'll that be?'

'Will you still like me if I say "a while"?'

McLean pushed through the swing doors and into the corridor that led back to his office. 'A while' wasn't what he wanted to hear, but Manda Parsons wouldn't have called him if she didn't have something more than that. She'd have called her flatmate, DC Harrison, and asked her to break the bad news instead.

'You know we're still missing a police admin support officer, right? This is high priority.'

'Aye, I know that. There's some things you can't rush though. Confirmation will have to wait until we've got the full sequence done, but I can give you a wee heads up. A possibility of a match with one of the more recent cases.'

McLean stopped walking, the corridor empty and silent. 'Go on.'

'One of the bones had an old fracture. Healed for a good few years, but there's always a mark, right?'

'Yes, I remember Angus showing it to me. Happened maybe ten years or so before death. What of it?'

'Well, I was going through the records Janie sent me. We need something to compare the DNA results to, after all. A close relative if we can't get an actual sample, which is unlikely at this distance. That's when I noticed that one of the missing women broke her leg when she was a teenager. Right tibia, same as the one we found.'

That cold sensation spread into McLean's gut again, and it felt almost as if the corridor was shrinking around him. 'Which woman?' he asked.

'Abigail Porter. Disappeared twenty-five years ago according to the file. There's an X-ray in there someone must have thought might come in handy during the investigation, which is lucky. No way her medical records would still be around after all that time.'

313

McLean saw the hand of Grace Ramsay in the inclusion of the X-ray, her obsession with missing-persons cases. She'd be delighted to hear that they had a bone match, even if it was tenuous at best. Certainly not enough to persuade Duguid and Robinson that she was right, but possibly enough for a more concentrated search of the area where the bones had been found. A few more detectives assigned to combing through the old missing-person files.

'That's great work, Manda. Thanks. Seems I owe you a drink.'

'Just the one?' Parsons managed to pout even over the phone. 'Maybe I'll not bother with the other news then.'

'Two drinks? Or will I just send Janie home with a bottle?'

'That sounds more like it. See those partial prints we got from the lighter you found under the car?'

McLean didn't think it necessary to remind her that it was the forensic technicians, and in particular their boss Jemima Cairns, who had found the lighter. 'You've got a match?'

'Ha. There's a joke in there somewhere, I'm sure. But, aye, we got a good positive from the boy you just picked up. Bobby Wilkins? Pretty sure he's had his grubby mitts all over that thing.'

'A word, McLean. In my office, now.'

He had only got in, barely sat down, certainly hadn't managed to do more than look at the pile of folders that had magically appeared on his desk in his absence. McLean had been hoping he might even manage to eat the chocolate still nestling in his pocket, but the DCC appeared to have other plans.

'Have a seat,' he said as McLean entered the room. That was never a good sign. A short, sharp bollocking usually meant standing in front of the desk like a guilty schoolboy.

'I wanted to have a chat with you about this morning's meeting, only you disappeared almost as soon as it was done.'

'Sorry, sir. I had a phone call from Penicuik. A development that needed following up.'

Robinson pulled out a seat on the same side of the conference table, settled himself into it with a weary sigh. It could have been the DCC's old bones complaining, but on balance it was more likely the pain came from outside.

'You're a good detective, Tony. I've seen you at work and I've seen the results. You've an eye for the pattern where nobody else can see it.'

There was a 'but' coming, McLean knew. He kept his mouth shut all the same.

'But lately you seem to have got yourself into a bit of a rut.' Robinson held his hand up to stop McLean from complaining. Not that he'd been going to. 'No, it's OK. Everyone has a rough patch now and again. And you've been through the mill these last couple of years, haven't you. Hardly surprising if it starts to affect your judgement.'

McLean sat sideways in his chair, the better to face the deputy chief constable. The twist put pressure on his hip, which twinged uncomfortably. A cup of tea and a biscuit would have made this dressing down a lot easier, but in the absence of those things, he reckoned keeping quiet and letting Robinson get whatever was on his chest off it would lead to the swiftest conclusion.

'It's been noticed . . .' the DCC began, then corrected himself. 'I have noticed that your control of budgets has been slipping lately. Overtime and shift arrangements are one thing, and I appreciate we're seriously undermanned at the moment, but over a hundred DNA samples from used condoms? On one case? Do you know how much that costs? And for what? You interviewed one person on the sex offenders' register and didn't even arrest him.'

Again, McLean remained silent. He could have pointed out that the sampling had been necessary, that the man in question had given them a list of names even now being pulled in and interviewed. He might even have mentioned that the DCC himself had said Anya Renfrew was one of their own, needed the full resources of Police Scotland to be brought to bear in finding her. He knew better than to do that though. The budgets weren't what was bothering Robinson. At least, they weren't the most pressing thing that was bothering Robinson.

'And then you go rushing off to the loony bin without telling anyone where you're going. You waste time interviewing petty vandals and chasing after children. Not to mention digging up random old missing-persons cases and trying to turn them into . . . what?'

'Actually, that's beginning to look like more of a possibility, sir,' McLean finally said, and told the DCC about the broken bone among those found on the moors. If he'd been expecting it to mollify Robinson, he was disappointed.

'That's my whole point. One bone out of hundreds that has a mark which might, just possibly, be in the same place as an X-ray from the possible victim's childhood? It's not even tenuous.'

Again McLean said nothing. They'd get DNA results from the bones soon enough, and he'd put the Cold Case Unit onto tracking down relatives of Abigail Porter. It was only a matter of time before that one bone opened up a whole can of worms, an investigation on a far, far bigger scale and with much greater ramifications. Was someone high up involved in some way? Was that why they were putting pressure on Robinson?

'It's not been officially announced yet, but Operation Caterwaul has been wound up. The NCA have some ongoing watching briefs, and our American friends will no doubt be making a nuisance of themselves as they always do, but the great multi-agency joint operation is a bust. Thanks to Ms Renfrew.'

'I hardly think that's fair, sir.'

'You don't?' Robinson seemed genuinely mystified for a moment, then shook his head to clear away whatever thought was blocking his mind. 'No matter. It's been almost two weeks now since she was last seen. We have to accept that she's gone. Most likely run off somewhere for Christ only knows what reason. By all means keep the investigation open, but I can't sanction the level of spending on it you've had so far.'

So that was it. Hidden behind a smokescreen, but there if you knew what to look for. Someone in a position of power had a guilty secret, all right. It wasn't bones buried on the moor so much as a potentially embarrassing addiction to outdoor sex with strangers.

'And the bones, sir? Do you want that investigation curtailed too?'

'Dammit, McLean, I don't want any of these things curtailed. But we have to prioritise. Hand the moorland dig over to the university. It's an archaeological site now, not a crime scene. Let's hope it stays that way.'

McLean nodded once, stood up. 'Very well, sir. I'll have status reports on your desk by the end of the week. And if anything else awkward comes up, I'll let you know.'

Robinson stared at him, but said nothing. He looked fed up, and McLean knew that feeling all too well. Without another word, he turned and left the room.

Bobby Wilkins had been taken to Fenton House, yet another social-care facility run by the Dee Foundation, and one he'd had reason to visit not many months earlier. Seeing the plaque at the entrance put McLean in a bad mood even before he and DC Harrison were led to the sparse room set aside for interviews, although his lack of lunch might have had something to do with it too.

At least Bobby was already waiting for them, sitting next to an older woman, her grey hair pulled back into a severe bun that did nothing to soften her sharp features. She introduced herself as Mrs Webb, and apparently had no first name or any other explanation as to why she was there, even if McLean could work it out for himself. Alongside her, a nervous young solicitor was there to make sure Bobby didn't say anything untoward.

'They looking after you OK, Bobby?' he asked, trying in vain to put the boy at ease. It was probably a bit daft, given that he would have only just arrived. According to the records, this wasn't Bobby's first brush with social care, and he clearly didn't want to be here now.

'Gavin was asking after you,' he tried. 'Said he hoped he'd see you again soon.'

'Why's he no' in here too, aye?' Bobby's young voice was all attitude and snarl. It reminded McLean of Dan Forbes. Was that what life had in store for Robert Wilkins too? Petty crime and repetitive incarceration. What a future.

'His mum's not in hospital. She said she'd look after you too, but we have to sort out a few things before that can happen.'

That got Bobby's attention more than anything else. 'For real? I could stay wi' Gav?'

McLean shrugged, tilted his head to one side. 'If we can get it sorted. I need to ask you a few questions first though.'

Alongside the young boy, McLean saw the lawyer sit up a little straighter, paying attention lest his client be tricked into something.

'Aye?' Bobby said.

'We know you and Gav were up at the forest car park, where we found the burned-out car.'

'I didnae –'

McLean held his hand up. 'I'm not interested in that, Bobby. Not now.' That could come later, if the Procurator Fiscal thought it worthwhile. 'I want to know about the car park, the forest, why you went there. Gavin told me you said it was haunted. What makes you think that?'

'Dunno. Stories, I guess.'

'What kind of stories? What's meant to be haunting the woods?'

'It's just stories. Ghosts dinnae exist. An' even if they did they couldnae hurt youse. It's just a creepy place. Wee Gav's a feartie.'

'Aye, I know that. But here's the thing about stories. Usually even when they're made up, that's for a reason. I'm interested in knowing why, and to find that out, I need to hear the stories, see?'

The lawyer looked at McLean as if he were mad, and Mrs Webb was on the verge of saying something, no doubt to admonish him for his foolishness the way his old matron at school had done so many times. Before either of them could interrupt though, Bobby gave a little shrug of acceptance and began to speak again.

'Was my da' telt me first. Back when I was wee. Y'ken how there's an old castle at the top of Oak Hill, aye?'

McLean assumed the boy meant the old Iron Age hill fort. This didn't seem the time to point out that such places weren't castles, as such. He nodded his understanding instead.

'Been folk living there thoosands a' years, ken? Warriors an' Droods and stuff. Theys used tae kill their enemies, cut 'em up intae wee bits and bury them a' over the hillside. A' the trees in that wood are growin' oot of the bodies, see? And when one falls doon, sometimes the bones come up an' the ghosts wi' them. Least, that's what my da' said.'

'Sounds quite horrible.'

'Aye, and there's this spring, see? Only it's no' water comes oot the ground but blood. No' all the time, like. Just when there's something special happening. An' there's the roons a' the monastery too. They's haunted an aw.'

Something about the way Bobby spoke made McLean think the boy would make a great actor someday, or maybe a novelist. At least, if life gave him a chance. Telling the stories brought him to life in a way the anger he wore like a cloak never had. And there was something creepy about the tales he spun too. Some underlying truth distorted into myth by time and repeated telling. After all, there were bones on the moors, and lots of them if Professor Turner's dig was anything to go by. And there was a spring in the woods, around which there had once been a monastery. Whether it had ever flowed with blood rather than sweet water was another question altogether.

'When your father told you these tales, did he also warn you never to go into the woods after dark? Not to go alone?'

'Aye, he did. He said the woods were a' wrong there. They lure youse in an' youse starve tae death. 'Less yer a local an' ken where y'are an' where yer goin'. An' he telt me aboot the folk who thought theys knew better, right? The folk who disappeared.'

'Disappeared?' McLean asked. 'What folk are these?'

'Jes' folk. I dinnae ken who they were. But they went intae the woods at night, see. An' the red monks killed them an' et 'em.'

53

'L ad's got some imagination, I'll give him that much.'
Traffic crawled all the way up the Old Dalkeith Road as
McLean drove from the care centre back to the station. Sitting
beside him, DC Harrison had said very little until they'd reached
Cameron Toll, keeping her thoughts to herself or maybe thinking the journey would only take a few minutes. Now it was clear
it would be quicker walking, she broached the subject of their
interview with Bobby Wilkins.

'I kind of feel sorry for him,' McLean said. 'Life's not exactly
dealt him a winning hand, but he's a smart kid. Quick-thinking
too. Might even make a good detective, come to that.'

Even though he was staring at the line of unmoving cars,
McLean could almost feel Harrison's raised eyebrow.

'You think he made all that stuff up? About the bones in the
ground and the red monks and all?'

'Half made up, half riffing on things he's heard, I'd guess.
The bones found up on the moor are hardly a secret any more,
and he knows we're looking for a missing person. I never really
expected to get any great truth out of him.'

'So why go speak to him then?'

McLean stared silently as a bus a few dozen metres ahead
eased itself into the queue despite there being no space for it.

The readout on the screen in his car's dashboard said the temperature outside was already more than thirty degrees, the air in between the tenements shimmering with it. Tempers were bound to fray in this weather, and sure enough the horns began almost immediately.

'First off, we have evidence of his presence at the scene of the burned-out car, and good reason to believe he was the one who actually set it alight. We had to interview him, and will probably have to do so again soon enough. The Procurator Fiscal needs a report whether she decides to pursue the case or not.'

'But you didn't actually talk to him about the fire, sir.'

'No. Not yet. I'll need to set up an interview with Gavin Mason about that too, and at the moment that's a little down my list of priorities. What I wanted to know was why they went there in the first place. I know they're a couple of bored kids kicked out of the house during the school holidays, but why there? What's the attraction?'

'Looks like he wanted to scare the crap out of his best friend,' Harrison said after they'd moved forward half a car's length. 'Strange how boys are like that.'

McLean remembered that the detective constable had two brothers. Chances were she would know better than him what boys were like.

'The stories though. That's what I found fascinating. I don't believe a word about ghosts and red monks and the like, but there's always something behind these tales. People have been going missing, that's the truth of it. Bones have been found too. It's part of the local folklore. Even Sergeant Donaldson at Penicuik nick mentioned something similar, remember?'

'So, what? You want to go and speak to Donaldson again?'

'No. I think I need to get closer to the source.'

'And the boys? Chances are they're behind all these recent fires. The car, the moors even. It's a miracle nobody's got hurt yet. You think we should just let them off with a caution?'

Something about Harrison's tone made McLean glance at her briefly, one eye half on the slow-moving traffic ahead. She was staring forward, a grim set to her face that spoke of something in her past that still bothered her.

'We gather the evidence, present it to the PF's office. Leave it to them to decide. It can wait for now though. Bobby Wilkins isn't going anywhere, and the chances of Gavin Mason being let out of his mother's sight any time soon are slimmer than mine of being made Deputy Chief Constable.'

That brought a slight smile to Harrison's lips, a distinct improvement on her frown. 'They're still a pair of wee scrotes,' she said, then added 'sir' for good measure.

'Aye, they are. But right now I'm more concerned with finding out what's happened to Renfrew. If I have to take my clues from wee scrotes, then so be it.'

He dropped Harrison off at the station, but carried on alone through improving traffic to the other side of the city. HMP Edinburgh wasn't McLean's favourite place in the city, so he was pleased at the businesslike way he was escorted swiftly to an interview room. He had to wait only a few minutes before Gordon Wilkins was ushered in.

There were traces of the son in the father, although prison food and a largely sedentary life had softened Gordon Wilkins's edges a little. He wasn't fat like Norman Bale, but neither was he whippet-thin like Bobby. His face was cleanly shaved, but nevertheless he managed to look dishevelled. Perhaps it was his mop of thick unruly hair, or the rumpled creases in his prison fatigues. Or maybe it was the way he slouched in his chair, eyes slightly out of focus as if he were stoned.

'They said youse wanted to see me. Din't say why.'

He had the same accent as his son too. Only deeper and more

drawn out. That sense of anger barely contained, but dulled by whatever it was he was on. Not a narcotic, surely? Although it wasn't exactly unheard of in prison. Maybe it was simple boredom, worn down by day after day of nothing to do.

'Your boy, Bobby. He's been getting up to mischief.'

'An' youse came all this way just tae tell me?'

'Actually, no. I wanted to ask you about the stories you used to tell him. Back when he was just wee. About the woods on Oak Hill, the bones in the ground, that sort of thing?'

Colour rose up Wilkins's neck and into his cheeks. The dullness in his eyes turned to a sharp focus, and he stiffened in his seat. 'What you talkin' about? Don't know nothin' about bones inna ground.'

'They don't let you see the news in here? Don't read the papers?'

A shrug. 'Cannae be bothered readin' that stuff. No' as if any of it's important to me, aye? Stuck in here.'

McLean couldn't argue with that. Wilkins still had a couple of years to go before he could even be released on licence. Most prisoners he'd met clung like limpets to any information about life outside, hungry for any sense of normality. There were a few who went the other way. He'd not have pegged Wilkins as a patient man though, and usually it was the quiet, thoughtful types who accepted their lot and concentrated on doing their time with minimal fuss.

'You grew up in Rosewell, is that right?'

The change of subject caught Wilkins off guard. 'Aye. Whut of it?'

'Nothing particularly. Just establishing a few facts. Has your family always been in the area? Grandparents, great-grandparents?'

'Far as I ken, aye. Why?'

'Those scary stories you told your son. Did your father tell them to you? His father to him?'

Again McLean saw that tensing in the shoulders, the slight twitch in Wilkins's fingers as he tried not to fidget. It could be that he had a drug habit, that this was a sign he needed at the very least a cigarette. Or it could be something else.

'They's just stories. Folk tales meant to scare you when you're a kid, aye? Nothin' to them really.' Wilkins slumped back in his seat again, defeated. 'Dinnae ken why they're so important to youse.'

It was McLean's turn to shrug. 'Possibly because there are bones in the ground up on Oak Hill. Lots of them. Some of them have been there a very long time indeed, but others are much more recent. That could be a coincidence, Mr Wilkins, but I'm a detective and we don't really believe in coincidences.'

'You're no' tryin' tae pin anythin' on me, are youse? I've been banged up in here you know?'

'No. I'm not trying to pin anything on you, Mr Wilkins. Some of the bones we're finding have been there centuries, maybe longer. Even the most recent ones were put there when you were even younger than Bobby is now. But you know the stories about that place. You told them to your son, like your father told them to you. All I want is for you to tell them to me, and then I'll leave you alone.'

Wilkins sneered in disbelief for a moment, then seemed to understand that McLean was telling the truth.

'I only ken what I told Bobby. Back when the whole of Oak Hill was covered in trees, the whole of Scotland an' a'. There was a castle, aye? Right at the top. That's where the Druids lived, where they taught their magic and made their sacrifices. Human sacrifices, aye? The story goes they used to kill folk an' eat them. Then they'd take the bones and bury them, deep in the ground.'

McLean leaned back in his chair. He knew better than to interrupt now. Like listening to old Mrs Roberts in his grandmother's kitchen, you waited until the end before asking questions.

'Only, they was greedy, see? They killed so many folk the blood seeped into the earth. The spring ran red with it. And they a' went mad too. Started killing each other till there was a' but one left, and he could never die. Nor could he ever leave the place, cursed to roam the moors for ever. They say nothing grows proper on the hill any more, and the ghosts of all those deid folk wander the woods. An' the last o' the Druids, when the hunger comes on him, lures wee boys intae the woods, kills them an' eats them. An' the spring runs red again wi' their blood.'

As ghost stories to scare children into not wandering off alone went, it was a good one. If a little gruesome. How long had people been telling it, and how had it mutated and evolved down the years? The only thing that surprised McLean was that he'd never heard it before.

'And what about the red monks?' he asked, checking off the other story Bobby had mentioned from his notes. A puzzled frown worked its way across Wilkins's brow, followed by a half-smile of recognition. Not a man who kept his emotions hidden.

'Ach, tha's a Penicuik tale. Youse'll have tae speak tae the boy's mother about that one.'

54

The contrast couldn't have been more marked between HMP Edinburgh and the Royal Infirmary on the opposite side of the city. Both were public institutions, of course, but their aims were very different. It was far easier to park outside the prison too. McLean finally found a space for his Alfa ten minutes' walk away from the main building, which meant he was dripping with sweat by the time he reached Reception.

A harassed-looking administrator directed him to a ward at the back of the building, and he was surprised not to bump into any nursing staff or doctors he knew on the way there. Maybe they were all on their tea break. He could have certainly done with one himself, although the air-conditioned chill was welcome.

Genevieve Wilkins was the other half of the mix that made up her son Bobby; there was no doubting the young lad's parentage. She lay motionless in a bed in a busy ward, and if it hadn't been for her open eyes staring fixedly at the ceiling, McLean might have thought her asleep. As he came closer, he could see the corner of her mouth twitching, as if she were singing along to a tune only she could hear. He came close enough to see the lines on her face, the pale blotchiness of her skin and the dark shadows around her sunken eyes before she noticed him.

'Who're you?' She rolled her head in the pillows to look at him, the most minimal of movements as if anything more strenuous was beyond her.

'Tony McLean. I'm a detective.'

'Polis?'

McLean didn't show his warrant card, but nodded instead. 'I wanted to have a word about your son, Bobby.'

He might reasonably have expected some reaction to that, maybe Mrs Wilkins sitting up straight despite her obvious exhaustion, a hand to her throat, a look of concern. Instead she slowly blinked her eyes.

'Oh aye? What's he up to now?'

'You do realise you left him to look after himself. A thirteen-year-old boy.'

'Aye.' Wilkins clearly mistook McLean's chastisement for praise. 'He's a braw wee lad. Takes after his father, only wi'out the fists, ken?'

McLean recalled Sheila Underhill's words about Gordon Wilkins, the reason he was in Saughton in the first place. Was that enough to drive someone to drugs, or had Bobby's mother been an addict before then?

'He's being looked after by social services now. What happens to him after that . . . well, we'll see.' If they pressed charges, he'd be in a young offenders' institute until he was old enough to look after himself. Except that he was already old enough to look after himself, just not in the eyes of the law.

'Is he no' stayin' wi' Gavin Mason?' Finally Mrs Wilkins struggled to sit upright, the plump pillows making life difficult for her. After a very short while she gave up again.

'He was. But now he's helping us with something else.' McLean held up his hand to forestall the question he could see forming on the woman's lips. 'No, he's not been arrested. He's fine. But he did tell me some interesting stories about the woods up at Gladhouse, and Oak Hill. Stories I'm given to understand you told him?'

Confusion knitted the woman's brow, no better at hiding her thoughts from her face than was her husband. 'What stories?'

'I know about the Oak Hill Druids, the buried bones. I'm interested in the red monks. Is that anything to do with the ruined monastery?'

This time Wilkins made more of an effort to sit up, and as she did so McLean could see how thin were her arms. Old track marks pocked the insides of her elbows, but the only fresh injection site was the catheter for her saline drip. She scratched at it absentmindedly with crooked, claw-like fingers, her nails raising red welts on the almost translucent skin of her forearm.

'Who did you say youse were?' she asked, suspicion replacing the confusion on her thin face.

'Detective Chief Inspector McLean.' He pulled out his warrant card and showed it to her. 'I'm conducting a missing-person investigation. A woman, last seen in the vicinity of the woods near Gladhouse.'

The focus changed in Wilkins's eyes, as if someone had just broken some terrible news to her. McLean had seen that look many times before, when he'd told people their loved ones had died or otherwise been the bearer of bad tidings. It was a necessary but uncomfortable part of being a police officer, and he recognised the reaction. When she spoke again, it was barely a whisper.

'Oh Christ. No' another one, surely?'

An eerie quiet fell over the ward as the thin, pale woman let her head sink back into her pillows. McLean waited a while for her to speak, but she seemed unwilling.

'Another one?' he asked. He had put Genevieve Wilkins in her mid-thirties, possibly younger. It was always hard to tell with drug addicts, and Bobby being thirteen didn't necessarily mean anything. The eyes she turned to him now seemed far older.

'Are you a religious man, Inspector?' she asked.

'Not especially. Hard to be when you've seen the things I've seen.'

'Fair enough. I was very religious when I was wee. Good Catholic girl. Might have been a nun at one point.' Wilkins laughed, then descended into a coughing fit that lasted long minutes. McLean gave her all the time she needed, surprised that no nurse came to see what was happening. .

'It's no' the red monks, that's just Bobby getting confused. My mother used to tell me about the Red Abbot. She says her family used to work up at the monastery before it was knocked down, but I reckon she made that up too. The way I remember it was they were an order much like any other. The monastery had land, Oakhill Moor and all the farms down towards Temple. No' the best, but good enough. Hundreds of years they were there, and nobody paid 'em much attention. They just did what they did. An' every few years someone would go missing. A local girl would wander off and never be seen again. A traveller passing through would set off for the Border towns and never reach their destination. No' enough to raise much in the way of suspicions, you understand. Girls disappear all the time, always have done. Run off wi' their beau an' end up in a whorehouse in the Old Town, aye?'

Wilkins fell silent again, as if the words had exhausted her. She looked even more ill than a recent overdose and an ongoing habit could account for. Some underlying sickness was eating away at her.

'Only one of the local girls came back. She claimed she'd been lured in by the monks, trapped in their monastery and given nothing but plain bread and water. They'd prayed over her, told her she was being purified, aye? That her blood was becoming

Christ's blood, her flesh Christ's flesh. They called her blessed, but she knew she was cursed, that they weren't men of God but of the devil. The locals all owed their living to the monastery, and might have turned a blind eye, but the magistrate found out, took the young woman and her story to the king.'

McLean knew better than to ask which king, and when this was all supposed to have happened. He was also fairly sure he knew where the tale was going, and it wasn't any more a happy place than it was real.

'The king went to the monastery and searched it top to bottom. He found bones piled up in the crypt that weren't the remains of monks, and he found other things too. When he interrogated the abbot, the truth came out, just as the young woman had told it. They took in young girls, used some occult ceremony to purify them. And then like good wee Christians they drank of the blood and ate of the flesh.'

McLean shuddered as he listened to Genevieve Wilkins's words. He'd heard enough ghost and horror stories to recognise the tropes, but this was the sort of thing to give a child night-mares, not any kind of warning to stay away from the woods. Even told here in the modern, clinical setting of the hospital, bright daylight, sun shining through the windows, it chilled him more effectively than any air conditioning.

'Why are they called the red monks?' he asked, after a lengthy silence assured him she had finished with her horrible tale.

'No' red monks. It's the Red Abbot. And it's no' real, you know? Just a story, aye?'

'Stories always come from somewhere.'

She looked at him with those hooded, ancient eyes again. Better educated than her husband, probably from a family that might once have been from a higher class. Her name, Genevieve, wasn't exactly common. Had she run away with her beau? If so, it hadn't worked out so well for her either.

'Aye, that they do. An' he's called that because of what the king did, see? He put the monks all to death. Hung, drawn and quartered. 'Cept for the abbot. He was flayed alive and the monastery demolished. Its lands went to the crown, of course, so that's your reason for the story there. Nothin' like a bit of diabolical controversy to justify a land grab, aye? An' it's the abbot's ghost as walks the woods, luring in any who stray his way. He's red on account of having a' his skin peeled off.'

'But girls kept on going missing, even after the monks were gone, the monastery destroyed, right? You knew someone, didn't you. That's why you said "another one".'

'My best friend. Sally Wainwright. Would have been, what? Fourteen years ago? Something like that. There was a party, up by the reservoir. Was a summer like this, now I think about it. Hot and dry. Gordy an' me, we'd not long been together. Young love, aye? We sloped off for a bit of privacy. That's probably when Bobby was conceived.' Wilkins choked back a sob, tears beginning to well in the corners of her eyes. She didn't seem to have the strength to reach up and wipe them away.

'Nobody noticed Sally was missing till the morning. We reported it, searched for her. You lot were useless.' She turned her head and stared at him again. 'An' I never saw my best friend again.'

55

McLean drove back from the hospital with the radio turned off, his phone still in silent mode, thinking through what Mr and Mrs Wilkins had separately told him. The two of them knew similar stories, which was unsurprising given they had grown up within a few miles of each other. It was strange to think that folk tales still had any coinage in this internet age, where everything was filmed and spread around social media the instant it happened, where the improbable antics of the rich and famous were more interesting and more easily seen than the deprivation on your own doorstep. And yet those scary stories were still told, still handed down through the generations. They resonated far more than the instant-fix ephemera of the digital age.

He still wasn't sure why he was interested in them either, except that the events of the past few days were somehow echoed in the mythic tales of ancient times. It was fanciful to think that some malevolent spirit, the wandering ghost of an undead Druid from Neolithic times, haunted the woods south of Gladhouse. Madame Rose would maybe think it fascinating, but even she wouldn't believe that an ancient evil would, every so often, call out to anyone who might hear, lure them into the trees and . . . what? Kill and eat them? And as for an order of monks, executed for their literal interpretation of transubstantiation, their souls shackled to the stones of their ruined monastery, waiting for the last trump, when they would be judged by God for their wicked ways? Well, that was almost as stupid as the rest of it.

Except that there was a ruined monastery, and people had gone missing. He would have to add Sally Wainwright to the list the CCU was preparing. What if it was her bones they had found on the moors? Dumped alongside Abigail Porter and God only knew who else?

And Anya Renfrew was still missing.

He knew as soon as he entered the station that something was up. The usual end-shift bustle of officers milled around, but he could feel an atmosphere about the place, a sense of a storm brewing. Or was he simply letting his imagination get the better of him, fuelled by the scary stories he'd heard?

Reaching into his pocket, McLean pulled out his phone and checked for messages, but the screen showed nothing except the time. He'd successfully spent another entire day away from his desk, more or less. No doubt Robinson would have words to say about that, Jayne McIntyre too. For once they'd be right. He couldn't really say he'd achieved much.

'Ah, sir. You're back.' He met DC Harrison at the top of the stairs. She had a thick sheaf of papers in her hands that may or may not have been a prop to stop anyone from asking her to do something for them. She also had a worried expression on her face.

'Yes, I'm back. Did somebody need me?'

'The detective chief super wanted a word, sir.' Harrison wasn't saying something, which worried him. No point in pestering her for information though. McLean nodded his thanks and carried on along the corridor to McIntyre's office.

The door was open, which meant he could see the DCC, Grumpy Bob and DI Ritchie in there, all standing, all talking over each other. None of them noticed him until he knocked on the doorframe.

'Anyone in?' he asked, then saw the looks on their faces as they all turned towards him. Not the time for joking. 'What's up?'

'First thing, Tony. Emma's safe. There's a couple of uni-formed officers at the house and another squad car patrolling the area.' Detective Chief Superintendent McIntyre stepped out of the crowd and crossed the room until she was directly in front of him.

'Emma's safe? Why wouldn't she be?' He looked past her at the others, their faces all identical pictures of horror. 'Why wouldn't she be?'

'It's Norman Bale,' McIntyre said, her voice low. 'He's escaped from Bestingfield. He's disappeared.'

The journey to Bestingfield had taken him over an hour the day before. With a police escort and his Alfa unshackled from the speed limit, McLean was standing in the reception area in less than forty minutes. He might have made it there faster, but he didn't want to leave the squad cars behind. The officers who had come into the building with him looked a little wild-eyed after their high-speed drive, which no doubt added to the alarm on the face of the facility administrator who had been unlucky enough to be on shift when the disappearance was discovered. A small, round-faced and sweaty man, he had introduced himself as Giles Staunton. Of Dr Graham there was as yet no sign.

'We've absolutely no idea how this can have happened, Detective Chief Inspector. I can assure you we maintain the highest security standards here.' Staunton wrung his hands like a penitent.

McLean could see the high security standards in the large number of burly male nurses milling around the reception area.

It had the feel of stable door and bolted horse to him, but he kept that to himself.

'When was the last time anyone saw him?' There was no need to say who 'him' was.

'Norman was supposed to be having a therapy session this afternoon, but Doctor Graham had to cancel. She's not well apparently. Some nasty tummy bug that's doing the rounds, I'm told.'

'That's not an answer to my question, Mr Staunton.'

'No, no. Sorry.' Staunton wrung his hands some more. The sweat prickled his brow as if he'd run a mile to get here. The air in Reception was cool and fresh compared to the heavy heat outside, so it was more likely nerves. He cleared his throat with a noise like a small dog being choked to death before speaking again.

'He had his lunch at midday in the refectory on C wing. That's when we got the news about Doctor Graham, so he was taken back to his room. There were no other scheduled activities, but he said he was happy enough to be left there until it was time for the evening meal.'

'Who took him there? I'd like to speak to them.' McLean looked around the room at the collected staff. Who was looking after the patients if they were all here?

'I'll have them brought to the conference room. Is that OK?'

He nodded. 'First I'd like to see Bale's room.'

'Of course, sir. This way.'

Accompanied by a pair of male nurses, Staunton led McLean along a bewildering number of corridors, through a collection of locked doors until finally they arrived at what looked more like the door to a hotel bedroom than a prison cell. It took several minutes to get there, and nowhere along the route did they meet any other people.

'You've got the whole place locked down?' he asked as one of the nurses unlocked the room door and pushed it open.

'For now, yes. Some of our patients are very sensitive to change, new faces, that sort of thing. It's for the best if we keep them to their quarters until you're done.'

McLean thought that a bit presumptuous. If he asked a forensics team to go over the room they might be there for days. He said nothing, but stepped inside.

It wasn't much of a surprise to him, since he'd seen it on CCTV footage a few days earlier. Instinctively he glanced up at the point above the door and saw the smoked-glass bulb behind which the camera sat. It was perfectly placed to take in the whole room with a wide-angle view.

As prison went, it wasn't a bad place to be. The window was small, and didn't open, but it looked out on a view of trees and distant hills, fading as the evening came on. The single bed sat against one wall, a stainless-steel basin and a toilet in the opposite corner. Bale had a desk fitted to the wall, a shelf with a few books on it, a chair to sit on. A narrow wardrobe held a change of clothes, a couple of pairs of slip-on shoes. No television, nor a radio, McLean noticed.

The air smelled mostly of toilet cleaner, a fake-lemon scent that was both sickly and sweet. But underneath it there was something else, a kind of electric tang he couldn't place.

'Can you smell that?' he asked DC Harrison, who had pushed her way past the male nurses to join him in the room. She sniffed a couple of times, brow wrinkled in concentration.

'The urinal cake, or the burned fuses?'

'Burned fuses. Electrical fire. That's what I thought I could smell.' McLean turned his attention to the door. On the inside there was a handle as you might expect, but no lock. The mechanism could only be operated from the outside, remotely. He crouched down close and sniffed again.

'Was the door locked when you found him gone?' he asked of

Staunton. The administrator stared helplessly at the nearest male nurse.

'I think so. I'm not sure. We'll have to check with Billy. You want to do that now?'

'In a moment.' McLean went to the bookshelf and looked at Bale's collection. Scottish history texts in the main, although he had a couple of collections of folk tales. Opening one, McLean found the stamp of South Lanarkshire Libraries. It was due back soon. One book had been left on the desk beneath the shelf, alongside an A4 pad and a couple of HB pencils, all arranged as neatly and squarely as if Bale had used a ruler.

The cloth-bound hardback book had long since lost its dust jacket. McLean opened it to see the somewhat unimaginative title: *A History of Scottish Myths and Legends*. Written by someone called Barnaby Fortnum, it had been published in 1935 by an Edinburgh company he'd never heard of. He flicked through the thick, yellowing pages until he found one with its corner folded over as a place marker, something that would have caused actual physical pain to his grandmother. It didn't surprise him to find the bibliographic desecration marked the beginning of a chapter, the title almost certainly intended as a message for him. 'The Legend of Sawney Bean'. Of course Bale was playing games. That was what he did.

Placing the book back down at an unruly angle, McLean concentrated on the pad. He ran his fingers over the top, and felt where words had been written on the sheet above before it had been torn out, along with several others by the look of it. Forensics could try and work out what Bale had written, but it was almost certainly not important, most likely gibberish. There was nothing here; that was the whole problem.

'OK. Let's go and talk to this Billy. Maybe he can tell us how someone can just up and walk out of a maximum-security hospital without anyone noticing.'

56

Billy turned out to be she, not he. She stood up from where she had been sitting at the conference table when McLean, Harrison and Staunton entered the room. In a poor light, McLean reckoned you could be excused for the gender confusion, as she stood as tall as the two male nurses who'd escorted them back from Bale's room. Her short-cropped hair probably made sense in a profession where it might be grabbed at any moment by an unstable patient, but combined with her square-set jaw and broad shoulders, it made her look more William than Wilhelmina. At least until you saw her in profile.

'The door was definitely locked, sir. Both when I took Bale back to his room and when I went to check on him later.'

McLean had barely been introduced before Billy was stating her position, but far from it coming over as needlessly defensive, he found himself believing her all the more for it. She had a certainty about her that was probably her way of coping with difficult patients, and maybe the male nurses too. It couldn't have been easy, dealing with the likes of Bale and some of the other high-security patients he knew were here. Something as fundamental as making sure a door was locked would be drummed in so deep that forgetting was unthinkable.

'So you're sure you had to unlock it to get back in then?'

Staunton asked, before McLean could tell him to go away. Billy's gaze flicked from her boss to the scary detective and back again, but she held her nerve and her certainty.

'Aye. I'm sure.'

'Mr Staunton, could you give us a minute?' McLean asked. The administrator looked at him for a moment as if he didn't understand what the request meant. Then he nodded once, turned and left the room. McLean waited until the door had clicked closed before turning back to Billy the psychiatric nurse.

'First off, I'm not here looking for someone to blame,' he said as he settled into one of the other chairs at the conference table. DC Harrison did likewise, taking out her notepad and a pen. Billy started to speak almost immediately.

'I did everything by the book, sir. I –'

McLean raised a hand to stop her. 'I'm sure you did. Like I said, not here looking for blame. What I'm trying to do is find out what state of mind Bale was in, who he'd spoken to, whether anything might have set him off. Anything that might give me some insight to where he's gone. We can worry about how he escaped later.'

That seemed to mollify the nurse, at least she kept her mouth shut, merely nodding her understanding.

'So. You last saw Bale when you escorted him from the refectory back to his room after lunch. Is that right?'

'Aye, sir.' Another nod.

'Did he speak to you over the course of that? Ask any questions, make any observations?'

Billy shook her head this time. 'No' really, sir. Bale's no' like that. He hardly ever speaks to any of us unless he has to.'

'What about the other patients? Does he speak to them? Does he have any regular contacts, acquaintances?' McLean hesitated a moment before adding: 'Friends?'

The answer was clear before the nurse even spoke. 'He eats

alone, sir. Never mixes with the others unless he has to, same as speaking to us. I know Doctor Graham's been working with him on that, trying to get him to interact with others. He does too. When she's there and watching. But soon as she's away, he's back to his old self again.'

McLean couldn't help noticing that Billy referred to Bale in the present tense, as if he was still sitting in his room a short distance away. Not out in the wilds, free to do as he pleased.

'His old self?' he asked.

'Aye. Silent. Withdrawn. Always watching you though. Like he can see right through your skull and read the thoughts in your head. Fair creepy bastard, so he is.' Billy seemed to remember herself then. 'Begging your pardon, sir.'

'No, I'm with you there. Fair creepy bastard sums him up well enough. I always thought he was playing with the doctor too. And I don't think she's stupid, but I don't think she knows what she's dealing with in Bale either.'

'If he spoke to anyone regularly, it'd be the librarian,' Billy said.

'This place has a library?'

'No' really. Not unless you count a wee trolley wi' all the latest Val McDermids an' Ian Rankins on it. No. We've an arrangement with the local library up in the town. The patients, well, those that're well enough behaved, get to make requests. No' many do, aye? But Bale always has a list when the librarian comes.'

Out of the corner of his eye, McLean saw Harrison making plenty of notes. He recalled the book on the desk in Bale's room. It had been close to its due back date. 'When was the last time they were here?'

'They come once a week. Think they're due tomorrow, but I could check.'

'And it's always the same librarian?'

Billy frowned. 'I'm not really sure. Think so, aye. It's the same mobile library as goes round the villages.'

'Get on to that, can you, Constable?' McLean asked Harrison, but she already had her Airwave set out and was putting the call in to Control. A quick glance at his watch confirmed that library hours were over. He wasn't sure that the connection was anything more than a red herring, but it needed to be checked. Bale's MO was taking on the identities of his victims, after all. No real hope that he'd mended his ways.

He turned his attention back to Billy, tuning out Harrison's softly spoken words behind him. 'Apart from the librarian, was there anyone else Bale spoke to except when he absolutely had to?'

'Can't think of anybody, no.' Billy shook her head slowly. Then she brought her hands up to her face, covered her mouth. 'Oh God. What if he does it again? What if he kills somebody?'

McLean and Harrison left the psychiatric nurse to her despair and went in search of the administrator. The local police were already combing the area, the circumference of their search growing by the hour. He had a horrible feeling it was all in vain. If Bale could walk out of a cell, an entire secure hospital, without being seen or indeed bothered by such insubstantial things as locks and three-metre-high, razor-wire-topped fences, then a few bobbies in squad cars weren't going to slow him down, wherever he was going.

'Control's chasing down a list of names and addresses for all the library staff, sir. Should have a lead on whoever it is supplies Bale with his books soon enough.'

'I want them brought into protective custody. Anyone outside of this place who's had contact with him in the past month, for that matter.'

Harrison nodded and took out her Airwave again. McLean disliked the chunky handsets, but they had their uses. Especially out here in the sticks, where mobile coverage was patchy at best.

'All done, sir. I've had word back from the officers going round to Doctor Graham's too. Seems she's been at home all day in her bed. When she's not been throwing up. Reckons she caught the flu from a colleague.'

'We'll still need to speak to her soon as she's feeling up to it.' McLean didn't much fancy the interview though. 'Let's have a look at this CCTV footage first.'

They found Staunton's office after a couple of wrong turns and locked doors. The man himself was on the phone, shrunken in on himself as some superior gave him a bollocking McLean could hear even from the other side of the room. He looked up with an expression of deepest relief as he noticed the two of them waiting, muttered, 'Sorry, ma'am. Have to go. It's the police.' The silence that fell as he cut the call was like closing a door on a noisy crowd.

'My boss,' he said by way of explanation, then shrugged. 'Though who knows for how much longer, eh?'

'Is the CCTV footage ready for viewing?' McLean asked. He didn't enjoy a bollocking any more than the next man, but so far Staunton had done little to gain his sympathy.

'CCTV?' A moment's confusion, then understanding bloomed across the administrator's face. 'Yes, of course. This way.'

He led them back out into the corridor and down to a room full of screens. McLean tried to suppress his impatience as the controller, a young lad called Steve, fussed with buttons and some form of custom-built scroll wheel. Images flickered on the main screen, disappearing before McLean could make any sense of them. Rooms, corridors, the front gates, the car park, where a small group of uniformed officers had clustered around his Alfa Romeo for a gawp. Finally it settled on a familiar view of Bale's room. It was obviously earlier in the day, as sunlight flooded in through the window and Norman Bale sat at his desk, pencil poised over his pad.

'Here you go, sir,' Steve said, clearly unaware that this was supposed to have been cued up and ready for him.

'Play it then,' McLean said.

Steve tapped a button and the screen sprang into life. Which was to say, Bale's hand moved and he wrote a few lines on the open page of the pad, paused, consulted the book he had beside him, then wrote a few more lines. This went on for five minutes before McLean told Steve to hit fast forward. Apart from Bale's writing becoming frenetic, this didn't change the scene much. Only the angle of the light spilling through the window betrayed the rushing minutes. That and the timestamp readout in the bottom corner of the screen.

And then everything changed.

For a moment McLean thought Steve had touched a key to pause the image, but the clock kept scrolling forward at the same, accelerated speed. Bale sat absolutely still, hands on the desk, pad full of writing in front of him, for a full half an hour of real time. Then he stood up and disappeared so swiftly several minutes of camera time sped past before any of them realised what had happened.

'Go back,' McLean said at the same moment as Steve realised he'd missed it. A swift rewind got them to the point where Bale was motionless.

'This is half actual speed,' Steve said as he hit a button and the image began to move again. This time they watched as Bale swiftly closed the pages he had written on and ripped them from the pad. In what must have been a matter of seconds, he arranged the desk the way McLean had found it hours later. Then he stood up, turned to the door. The camera angle showed it open and Bale walk out. The timestamp read twenty-seven minutes and fifteen seconds past four in the afternoon.

'Well, at least we know when he left,' Harrison said, perhaps unhelpfully.

344

'Have you got the footage from the corridors at the same time?' McLean asked, but Steve was already tapping away at his console. Images flipped and they were looking at the door to Bale's room. McLean couldn't think of it as a cell. The timestamp was one minute before Bale had opened what Billy the psychiatric nurse had sworn was a locked door.

'Should see him coming out any second now. Still no' sure how that's possible, mind,' Steve said. They watched as the clock counted the seconds. Twenty-seven minutes past four, twenty-eight minutes, twenty-nine.

'You sure this is the right camera?' McLean asked.

'Aye, I'm sure.' Steve twisted the control wheel and the timestamp went into reverse. He kept it spinning backwards until a quarter to one in the afternoon, when Billy the psychiatric nurse walked backwards down the corridor, carefully checked the door was locked, opened it and walked backwards inside. Moments later she and Norman walked out backwards together and disappeared off screen in the direction of the refectory.

'What the bloody hell?' Harrison leaned forward past McLean, one hand on the back of Steve's chair as she peered at the screen.

'Go back to the bit where he leaves, can you?' McLean asked. There was only a short pause to get there as Steve had marked the point on the video somehow. The miracle of modern technology. They watched as the timestamp counted the minutes from twenty-five past four to half past. It was like watching a still image. Not even a flicker of interference.

'I'll need copies of all camera feeds for the whole of yesterday. All of the hospital, OK?'

'No problem.' Steve tapped at the keyboard in front of him. 'Got an email address I can send the link to? It's all in the Cloud these days.'

57

Coordination of the search for Anya Renfrew had initially warranted no more than a whiteboard in the CID room and a small team of officers. Even when the DCC had sanctioned extra resources after her secret double life had been uncovered, it was still a fairly small-scale operation. Norman Bale's escape and disappearance by contrast had the major-incident room and the full works. Fair enough, the man had killed at least five people they knew about, and attempted to murder three others, McLean and DI Ritchie included. He was a danger to the public, and an embarrassment to the authorities for as long as he remained at large. McLean walked into a bustling hub of activity, the beginnings of a full-scale, nationwide manhunt.

'Ah, you're back. Good. Any news?' Deputy Chief Constable Robinson greeted him with a serious face. It was a measure of how important this case was that he hadn't gone home already. True, there was still light in the night sky, but only because at this time of year in Edinburgh it never truly got dark.

'Half past four this afternoon, Bale got up and walked out of his locked room as if it was no more secure than my wardrobe.' McLean gave Robinson the edited highlights of the past few hours, leaving out the bit where the CCTV footage showed the man leaving his room, but not emerging into the corridor beyond. That was a puzzle for the technical bods to solve, although he didn't much fancy their chances.

'We've got his likeness out to all patrols across Scotland and the north of England. Airports and ferry terminals are on full alert. He'll not get far.' The DCC's words would have been more convincing if he'd really believed them. McLean could tell from Robinson's tone that he didn't. And, besides, that wasn't Bale's style.

'I don't think he'll try, sir.'

Robinson opened his mouth to say something, then closed it again. His expression was enough.

'What do we know about Bale? What he does, his motivations and methods?' McLean asked. He'd not expected an answer, carried on when the DCC continued to stare.

'He's a psychopath, for sure. A dangerously deluded individual who believes he is here to hasten the passage of the truly blessed into heaven. That's his mission, given to him by God, along with the power to tell who is actually at that moment of apotheosis, their soul ready to pass through the Pearly Gates unchallenged.'

'So what you're saying is he's bonkers.'

McLean smiled at that, even though it wasn't really funny. 'In a nutshell, yes. But what I mean is he's obsessive to a terrifying degree. When he gets some new idea in his head he will not let it go. Not until he's killed it.'

'And which poor bastard's in his sights now?' Robinson ran a hand through his thinning hair.

'That's what I'm not sure about, sir. I don't believe for a minute he's not dangerous, but he seems to have fixated on a cause this time. I think he broke out of the hospital to go and find Anya Renfrew.'

It might have been a simple coincidence, an accident of timing, but as McLean said the words, the entire room fell silent.

He glanced at the clock over the door to see if it was quarter past the hour and an angel was passing overhead. Not that he had much time for angels. Or demons for that matter.

'How do you figure that?' Robinson asked as the noise in the room slowly began to build again. McLean knew that he couldn't say it was his gut telling him, but the sequence of events that had brought him to this point didn't exactly court logic. He'd spent the best part of an hour thinking about it as he drove back from the psychiatric hospital, and it still only made sense on an instinctive level.

'He first tried to contact me the day we noticed Renfrew was missing. Best we can tell that was at least two days after she left her car in the woods up by Gladhouse. I didn't want anything to do with him, and said as much. But he seemed to know stuff he couldn't possibly know. I asked DS Laird to have a sniff about, but he couldn't find out anything. Certainly nobody was passing on classified intel, but Bale's always been good at making connections, second guessing. That's how he got away with what he did for so long.'

'Jayne told me he'd been trying to get in touch, and that you weren't going to respond.' Robinson leaned in close, as if he didn't want the rest of the room to hear what he was saying. McLean couldn't help but feel it was a bit too late for that now.

'I thought it was a bad idea, sir. I told his psychiatrist as much, but he has a way of manipulating people. Even quite intelligent people.' It occurred to him as he said it that he'd not yet spoken to Dr Graham. She was safe; he knew that much. At least, as safe as anyone could be with that madman on the loose. It seemed unlikely that Bale would attack her anyway. That wasn't the way he worked, although he'd shown quite staggering disregard for women in the past.

'OK. Assuming there's a connection, if Bale's trying to find Renfrew, how's he going to go about that?'

McLean noticed that the DCC didn't ask why. 'Bale's been using the case to get me to talk to him. It worked too. You know I went down there a couple of days ago and met with him and his psychiatrist, right? It . . . didn't go well.'

'You surprise me,' Robinson said, although McLean couldn't tell whether that was a comment on the meeting or on his having finally given in.

'The information he had could only have come from someone who knew about our investigation into Renfrew's disappearance. Either he was being told things by someone with a connection to this station, or he's much, much better at wheedling information out of people than even I thought he was.'

'Wheedling?' Robinson raised an eyebrow at that.

'You know what I mean, sir. He works you like a stage show mindreader. It's all leading questions and vague predictions, but he does it so very well. I think he's been playing the staff at that hospital ever since he was sent there. What I don't know is why he's made his move now. Except that maybe he's fallen for his own tricks, got himself so caught up in the Renfrew case he can't leave it alone any more.'

Robinson stared at him with sceptical eyes, but McLean didn't care. Let the DCC think him mad if it helped. As long as they caught Bale and put him away for good this time.

'Search teams will be out again at first light,' Robinson said after a while. 'We've got tracker dogs working the ground, and a helicopter with infra-red cameras in the air. I'll put DI Ritchie in charge of that, and you can lead the search based on what he was doing prior to his escape. OK?'

McLean stifled a yawn as he watched the major-incident team go about their night-time business. A glance at the clock above the door told him he should have gone home and got some sleep hours ago. It was unlikely there would be any great developments

349

in the next few hours, but, if there were, someone would be sure to wake him and let him know.

'You still here?'

He turned to see DI Ritchie striding towards him. She looked as tired as he felt, and dragged a couple of detective constables in her wake who were surely up way past their bedtime.

'Can't quite get my head around it all yet. I'm not sure I can leave until I know what's going on.' McLean studied Ritchie's face for any signs of the strain he knew she must be under. She'd been affected by Bale as much as any of them. More even. 'You holding up OK?'

'Let's just say I've had better days and leave it at that.'

'So "Call-Me-Stevie" has given you your marching orders then?' McLean nodded his head towards the thick sheaf of papers Ritchie was holding.

'Aye, and then some. We've search teams heading out in . . .' She checked her watch. '. . . approximately four hours. I need to be down at the hospital for the briefing. Doesn't look like I'm going to get much sleep any time soon.'

'Now I feel bad for considering heading home.'

'Don't. You look done in, Tony. Go and get some sleep. At least then one of us will be fresh in the morning.'

'You're right. Not sure I'll get much rest knowing he's out there though.'

'Aye, I know what you mean. Could do without this hassle. Busy enough as it is.'

McLean wondered what she meant for a moment, then remembered. 'Oh, right. The Very Important People.' He made little bunny ears with his fingers around the words. 'They behaving themselves?'

Ritchie smiled at his joke, but it was a tired effort. 'Pretty much. It's mostly uniform keeping an eye on them. And they're all at Scanlan's place at Nine Mile Burn right now anyway, which makes me think the whole thing's some hush-hush business deal nobody's supposed to know about. Seems they forgot that doesn't mean us too.'

'Nine Mile Burn?' McLean knew the place well enough. Not so much a village as a loose association of houses on the A702 road to Biggar and the Borders, he'd driven through it to and from Bestingfield. It was barely a hop, skip and jump from Penicuik, nestling in the eastern lee of the Pentland Hills and staring across the Esk valley towards Oakhill Moor. Coincidence? Probably. Except he didn't believe in coincidences. Not any more.

'Scanlan's family farm that area. He grew up there.' Ritchie seemed oblivious to his suspicions. 'Odd to think a farm boy could turn out to be one of the richest men on the planet. But then I guess everyone has to come from somewhere.'

58

He was at the bottom of the stairs, had his hand out to open the back door and walk to his car. Home, perhaps a wee dram to settle his nerves, and then bed. Having checked all the locks first of course. But before McLean could make that last step, the door swung inwards. Grumpy Bob, DC Harrison and two uniformed constables led a bewildered-looking middle-aged lady into the station.

'Looks like we made it just in time,' Bob said, although whether the words were addressed to him or Harrison, McLean couldn't be sure.

'Who's this?' he asked, although he had a suspicion he knew. There was the fact that she was here, for one thing. And she wore the unofficial uniform of her kind, the sensible, comfortable and yet nevertheless presentable clothes of the librarian.

'Agnes Braithwaite, this is Detective Chief Inspector McLean.' Grumpy Bob made the introduction. 'Agnes drives the mobile library that visits the psychiatric hospital.'

'Pleased to meet you, Detective Chief Inspector.' Agnes even had the librarian's voice, a soft mix of Morningside and the Borders. Despite the pleasantry he could hear the edge of worry in it though.

'I take it they told you why you're here?' he asked, aware that,

352

now she was, the prospect of home and bed was fast receding.

'Yes. Came as quite a shock, to be honest. I never thought Norman would do such a thing.'

McLean tried not to wince, but there it was again. He could hardly bring himself to think of the man as Bale, still doubted it was his old childhood friend despite whatever the DNA analysis might say. And yet people referred to him as 'Norman', as if he was just some ordinary bloke you might find a bit boring down the pub. Not the man who had killed his parents and then sat their preserved bodies in his dining room so he might have someone to talk to at mealtimes.

'Indeed, but we should maybe talk about this somewhere a little less public.' He looked at the two detectives who had brought the librarian in. 'Bob, if you could show Ms Braithwaite to interview room one?'

Harrison beat him to his next request, but then she had always been quick on the uptake. 'I'll see about getting us all a cup of tea, aye?'

'How long have you been driving the mobile library, Ms Braithwaite?'

They sat in interview room one, the last light of the long day painting the sky outside an eerie orange-red that should give any shepherds a restful night. McLean held his mug of tea in both hands, not quite willing it to be something stronger. Beside him, DC Harrison munched quietly on one of the biscuits she'd somehow managed to find, her notebook at the ready as ever.

'Well, now, there's a question. That'd be, what? Twelve years now? No, I tell a lie. Thirteen.' Braithwaite sat upright like a finishing-school girl, her back straight and hands folded neatly across her lap. Most people who found themselves in a police interview room, even the nice one with the window and proper furniture, tended to act a little nervously. Even if they tried to suppress their nervousness it usually showed through in little ways. A slow twitching of one foot, perhaps, or a difficulty in looking directly at the person talking to them. In McLean's experience, an absolutely relaxed manner was generally as good as an admission of guilt, but, of course, the woman sitting opposite him had done nothing wrong. It was still a little unnerving how utterly unfazed she seemed.

'And you've been going to the hospital all that time?' he asked.

'Oh gosh, no. They only opened it about five years ago, didn't they? I've been going there about eighteen months now, I suppose. They used to have an onsite library, and we'd rotate our collection through there. We never had much in the way of special requests though. A lot of the patients either don't read or can't. I think that's probably why they closed theirs and asked us to take the mobile there instead. There just wasn't the demand for books.'

'Except from Bale.'

'Except from Norman, yes. He was always testing us with obscure titles. I should think he's quite the expert on Scottish history by now. Particularly the folk history, you know? What the common people got up to, not the lairds and kings.'

'Did you meet him then? Bale?'

'Not at first, no. One or other of the nurses would bring me request lists, and some of the staff came in for books too. Most of the patients weren't allowed out without supervision, particularly not the high-security ones.' Now Braithwaite looked a little uncomfortable, one hand going up to her face before she noticed and dropped it back to her lap.

'You say "not at first", and you speak of him as Norman, so I take it you have met him though.'

'I . . . that is to say, yes, of course. But I'm not sure it was properly sanctioned and I wouldn't want to get anyone in trouble. They were only trying to help rehabilitate him.'

Rehabilitate for what? McLean wanted to ask. It wasn't as if Bale was ever going to be released back into society on purpose.

'Tell me how that worked then. Did they bring him to the mobile library, or did you go into the hospital?'

'Like I said before, they used to have their own library in the hospital. It's still there, but it's only shelves. There's a rack with maybe a couple of dozen bestsellers on it, but nothing like the stock they used to have. Mostly that was enough, for the patients who wanted books and the staff too. But when I started getting requests for more . . .' Braithwaite searched for the right word. '. . . unusual books, well, I must confess I was interested in who wanted to read them. Why they wanted to read them. That's the part of being a librarian that's most satisfying, you see? Finding the spark of interest and nurturing it.'

'And you did that with Bale?' McLean tried to keep the incredulity out of his voice. He could tell Braithwaite was passionate about her job, but even so she must have known what the man was in hospital for.

'Well, nurture's perhaps a bit too strong. But the topic he was interested in is a particular hobby of mine too. So we had that in common. And I was able to suggest a few books to him. I even lent him a couple from my own collection.'

'That topic being Scottish folk history, I take it.'

'The very same. He said he was working on a book of his own, a review of all the literature, as it were. Quite an undertaking, although I suppose he didn't have much else to keep him occupied.'

'And did he say how that was coming along?' McLean asked.

'Well, it's funny you should ask that, Detective Chief Inspector. You see, he had become somewhat fixated on a particularly grim set of folk myths of late. Not one particular period in our history, you understand, but a recurrent theme that pops up every so often in the oral records. He was fascinated by tales of cannibalism and what they represent. From the earliest stories thought to be Pictish in origin, or even earlier, right up to our most famous cannibal, Sawney Bean.'

McLean winced at hearing the name again, although given what Bale had said both to him and to Grumpy Bob, it was hardly surprising that Agnes Braithwaite would know about it too. He recalled the book on the desk in Bale's room, its page corner folded at the beginning of the relevant chapter. Another message, but why?

'Did he ever say why he was so interested in that subject?'

'Well, not in so many words, but I know a little bit about his . . . how might I put it? Psychosis? I read the papers, and of course I've spoken with him. I think he has a morbid fascination for the evil that men do. Where it comes from and how it manifests itself. He wants to understand it so that he can overcome it in himself. He wants to be pure of spirit.'

'And you still agreed to meet him? To help him?' McLean once more had difficulty keeping his voice level.

'I was never in any danger.' Braithwaite paused and only then seemed to understand where she was, why she was there. 'At least, I never felt like I was in any danger.'

'So, why do you think he was interested in Sawney Bean?'

'Oh, it was much more than just that. And anyway, that tale's largely discredited. There's no legal record, for one thing, and the story is full of inconsistencies. It's nothing more than horror meant to entertain and frighten us. Norman knew that of course, but he was fascinated by the background to it all. He began researching all sorts of equally gruesome tales. "The Druids of Knockdarry", for instance, and "The Red Monks of Oakhill Priory".'

Two stories, or variations of two stories, that until a day ago McLean had never heard of. Another coincidence he didn't like.

'That's useful to know, Ms Braithwaite. Thank you. It might

suggest why Bale absconded, and maybe even where he's going. Hopefully we'll catch him soon, but in the meantime we'll keep a constable stationed at your home, just to be on the safe side.'

The librarian raised a hand to her throat, no longer quite so sure of herself. 'Of course. But he wouldn't . . . I mean, why would he?'

'I'm afraid with people like Bale it's almost impossible to know.'

59

A patrol car took up his usual parking space when McLean finally arrived home, much later than he had wanted. A quick glance at the downstairs windows on the front side of the house showed that someone had gone around and closed all the shutters. How effective a deterrent that would be should Bale choose to break in and kill him in his sleep was a point he didn't desperately want to debate with anyone.

Two uniformed officers, Sergeant Stephen from Torphicen Street station and a constable McLean didn't know, sat at the kitchen table with mugs of tea and a plate of the good biscuits. They both stood up hastily as he entered, but he waved for them to sit.

'No need for that, Kenny. Enjoy your tea, you've earned it.'

'Thank you, sir.' The sergeant sat down and helped himself to another biscuit. The younger constable hesitated a moment before taking his seat again.

'I saw the shutters closed. Your idea, I take it?' McLean asked.

'Just as a precaution, aye, sir. Don't think Bale's going to try and come here, but a big old house like this, he could be in one end and you'd never know. Least the shutters will slow him down. You'll set the alarm when you go to bed, right enough.'

McLean looked across to the Aga, where Mrs McCutcheon's

cat would normally be sleeping even in the heat of summer. She was nowhere to be seen, doubtless affronted by the arrival of strangers in her kitchen.

'I'll need to find the cat and make sure she's shut away in here, but, yes, I'll be setting the alarm.'

McLean considered making himself a cup of tea, but it wasn't all that long since he'd drunk one while interviewing the librarian, Agnes Braithwaite. Bad enough that he was unlikely to sleep tonight; the last thing he needed was to be getting up every half-hour to go to the toilet. And there was a dram in the library with his name on it too.

'A search team's been through Bale's house, haven't they?' he asked, even though he knew they had.

'Aye, sir. No sign of anyone having been there any time recently. Well, apart from the decorators. You know it's up for sale, right?'

'Yes, I saw that. Surprised it wasn't done earlier, to be honest. But I guess Bale was sectioned, so they'd have to sort out powers of attorney and all that nonsense. Can't imagine he's too happy about it either. Family's owned that place almost as long as there's been McLeans here.'

Sergeant Stephen merely raised an eyebrow at that, drained his tea and sneaked the last biscuit off the plate. The constable's Airwave set gave a squawk in the silence and he stood up swiftly with an 'I'd better just check this' before disappearing through to the utility room at the back.

'We'd both best be getting on, sir. Now you're back.' Stephen levered himself out of the chair with all the reluctance of a beat sergeant who knows a nice cup of tea and a biscuit when he sees one. 'We've extra patrol cars in the area tonight. Everyone's on high alert. We'll catch the bastard.'

'Thanks, Kenny. I know we will. Just hope it's sooner rather than later.'

★ ★ ★

Emma lay on her back on the sofa in the library, one arm crooked across her eyes to blot out the ceiling light. The room felt strange with the shutters closed, somehow smaller and less welcoming. The heat of the day still lingered, and McLean would have liked nothing more than to open the French windows onto the garden, let the night air in. A decent summer was rare enough, after all. Yet another thing Norman Bale had spoiled for him.

'That you, Tony?' Emma stirred, blinking as her eyes adjusted. 'What time is it?'

'Late. I thought you were asleep.' He walked over and sat down beside her as she swung her feet out and onto the floor. She was still wearing the clothes she'd left for work in that morning, her hair mussed up from lying on the sofa and sporting far more grey than he remembered in the black.

'I couldn't. Not upstairs anyway. Why do you live in such a big old creepy house?'

'Never really thought of it as creepy. It's always felt safe to me.'

Before the words were even out of his mouth, something moved in the shadows by the shuttered window. McLean was on his feet in an instant, hand already reaching for the phone in his pocket, as if it would be much use in a fight. A moment later, Mrs McCutcheon's cat leaped onto the arm of the sofa and arched her back. Emma smiled, put her hand out and the cat nuzzled it, a deep rumbling purr soon following.

'Wondered where you'd got to,' McLean said to cover his embarrassment. The cat ignored him, leaping lightly onto the seat he'd just vacated, then into Emma's lap. 'Don't get too comfortable. Sergeant Stephen wants me to set the alarm, so you're confined to the kitchen tonight.'

'Actually, I'd rather she was upstairs with me.' Emma lifted the cat with ease and stood up. 'Think I trust her to keep us safe more than any alarm system. No offence to the sergeant.'

McLean knew better than to argue, and he had to admit Emma had a point. Mrs McCutcheon's cat had been something of a good luck charm for him ever since he'd rescued her from the burned-out remains of his Newington tenement. Not that he was prepared to admit in public to trusting in luck. Or cats. Knowing she'd be prowling the upper floors, keeping an eye out for would-be assailants, was curiously comforting though, even if it was more likely she'd be curled up asleep at Emma's feet, oblivious. He wasn't quite ready for bed yet himself though, cat or no cat.

'I'll be up soon,' he said. 'Thought I might sit and think for a bit.'

'With a dram to help the process along?' Emma gave him a knowing look, but there was no malice in her words. Another plank in the bridge they were slowly rebuilding. 'Don't be too late, OK?'

'Half an hour, tops.' He walked over to the bookcase and opened the hidden cabinet where the good stuff lived. Emma carried the cat across the room with her, something that would have earned McLean an unreasonable number of painful scratches, but seemed to present her with no danger whatsoever. She gave him a light kiss on the cheek, her closeness and scent both pleasant, and then she walked out into the hall.

He poured himself a thumb of cask-strength Balblair that he couldn't remember buying, sniffed its heady aroma for a while, then topped it up with what was almost certainly too much water from a bottle that should probably have been thrown away weeks earlier. Retreating to his favourite armchair, he settled down in the silence to think.

Bale's escape was a disaster, a headache for all of them and an added complication he could have well done without. The man was dangerously delusional, completely amoral, and would do whatever he needed to get to where he wanted to be. Heaven help anyone who got in his way.

McLean let out a brief bark of humourless laughter, almost spilling his whisky. Heaven help. That was the point, wasn't it? Bale had believed he was gifted by God to see the state of people's souls. His victims were chosen for their purity of spirit, their single-mindedness and focus. At least, those of his victims who had been his actual target, rather than the poor nurse who'd been unfortunate enough to get in his way. He truly believed he was doing God's work. With a capital G. Sending those pure souls to heaven by killing them at their moment of apotheosis. Being caught, stopped from carrying out his sacred mission, had shaken his faith, at least for a little while.

Leaving his chair, McLean went to the desk in the corner of the library and fired up the computer. It took a while to log in, but eventually he found what he was looking for. Transcripts of the early psychologist's interviews and assessment following Bale's arrest. Dr Millicent Graham hadn't been involved in any of that, although presumably she had read it all in preparation for his therapy. The report he read had been prepared by a more familiar name. Dr Matthew Hilton hadn't seen any hope of recovery or redemption in his patient, only a disturbing intelligence. 'An almost preternatural ability to know what a person is thinking after only a few minutes of conversation with them' was a phrase that popped out. What had Billy the psychiatric nurse said? 'Like he can see right through your skull and read the thoughts in your head.' She'd also called him a right creepy bastard, and she had the measure of him far more than Dr Graham, at least in McLean's opinion.

'What are you up to?' He asked the question out loud, not expecting an answer and not surprised when none was voiced. It was only one of many that swirled around in his head. Why was Bale interested in Scottish folk history, cannibalism, Sawney

Bean? What did it have to do with Anya Renfrew's disappearance? Or was that just Bale's way of dragging McLean into his latest insane plan? If that was all there was to it, then why did he want McLean involved? Was it some strange kind of revenge? It had to be a trap of course. There was no way Bale would actually be trying to help. Unless something really had changed in him, taken him back to the lonely boy who'd been McLean's friend so many years before.

He reached for the glass, tipped it to his lips and only then realised he had already finished the whisky. Tempting though it was to help himself to another, McLean knew better than that. He needed a clear head in the morning – later in the morning, he corrected himself after a quick glance at the clock in the corner of his screen. There was nothing to be gained from sitting up into the wee small hours as the thoughts tumbled and fought. Better to try and get some sleep, even if it would be fitful. The problem would still be waiting for him when he woke.

60

There are no days, no nights. There is only time. Time and
an emptiness that gnaws at her like rats sewn up inside her
stomach.

She has no idea how long she has been here, in this dark and
foetid hole. The cycle of wake and sleep is more like a continuous
nightmare than a progression of time. She knows only cold and
hunger, a punishment for something she has forgotten, like she
has forgotten who she is.

The thin blanket that covers her must be a new one. There is
no odour from it, and none from the bucket across the room.
The floor looks like the same, dry, hard-packed earth that it has
always been, there is nothing to suggest where she might have
thrown up and worse. Was that all a dream?

She reaches shaking hands to her face, feels her skin. Her
fingers trace over her cheeks, then up to her eyebrows. They are
gone, along with all the hair on her head, and she remembers the
scrape and sting of the razor, the smell of the coal tar soap. She
can smell that still, under her fingernails when she brings them
close to her nose.

She feels no pressure in her bladder now, only a terrible
parched dryness in her throat to match the utter emptiness of her
stomach. She has had nothing but water for what feels like a

lifetime. Water laced with something to make her vomit, and something to make her empty what little there might have been in her bowels. She remembers that much even as the core of her identity eludes her. A word floats across her semi-consciousness, spoken in the voice of an old woman. Purged. They have taken everything from her, even who she is. Left nothing but an empty vessel.

Does she sleep? She can no longer tell the difference between sleep and wakefulness. She lies on her side, knees pulled tight to her chest, blanket tighter still, and lets her mind go blank. Nothing will happen here. She will die here. Maybe she already did.

The light goes out, plunging her into darkness that is almost instantly shattered as the door swings open. Rough hands grab her, force her arms behind her. She could no more fight than run, but they hold her tight all the same. She is lifted off her feet, carried from the room that has been her prison. Up swift stairs and then she is blinded by brilliant sunlight, so bright it sears deep into her brain. She screws her eyes closed, but the light still burns.

Blind, the plunge into water comes as such a shock she feels certain her heart will stop. It doesn't help that she is still held, that whoever is carrying her has come into the water with her. All she can feel is the panic as her head goes under, the urge to breathe and the choking as she takes in a mouthful of liquid instead of air. She is held down for long enough for her to wonder why they are doing this to her? Why starve her for what feels like weeks, only to drown her now? And then she is hauled up into the air again.

'Christ is with us this day. He is with us every day. His blessing is upon us.'

The words are chanted, a deep male voice that almost sings but not quite. He is the one holding her, arms pinned behind her

365

back. She pukes out water, gasping for breath, risks opening her eyes against that harsh, bright light. Only now it's not nearly so painful. She has barely moments to take in a round pool, its dark surface reflecting the rippled image of trees overhead, before she feels a hand at the back of her head and she is forced under again.

She would fight, but she has no strength left. Her arms are held tight behind her, and that strong hand is like a mountain, pressing her ever deeper towards the bottom. She can see only the bubbles of her escaping scream, then more water forces its way down her throat, choking into her lungs. She is doomed, dying, and all she wants is for it to end.

And then with a heave she is in the air again, spewing water from mouth and nose as she splutters and gasps for breath.

'In the name of the Father, of the Son and of the Holy Ghost. Bless this empty vessel. Purify it so that it might become one with the Lord.' The man's voice roars, his words running through her like hot knives. She is aware of nothing save the hold he has on her, the crazed surface of the pond and the silent trees that witness this strange ceremony. She coughs up yet more water, lets out a moan as her lungs struggle to find room for air. But before she can even begin to breathe, she's plunged under again.

This time whatever holds her hands behind her is released, only the pressure on the back of her head keeping her down. It makes no difference. She has nothing left. Let it end now, let her have peace.

She closes her eyes and surrenders to the darkness.

61

An ugly quiet filled the major-incident room when McLean entered at a quarter to six in the morning. He was used to early starts, but even so this one felt worse than most. The night shift had been hard at work doing what they could, but there had been no sightings, no reports of suspicious break-ins anywhere near the hospital, nobody missing a crucial appointment or failing to come home on time. At least none that had been reported yet. It was as if Bale had opened his locked cell door and stepped into another world.

'He's out there somewhere. We'll find him soon enough.' Detective Chief Superintendent McIntyre joined him as he stared at the map of the Lothians and Borders that had been pinned up on one wall of the room. A big red circle marked the site of the not-so-secure psychiatric hospital, with pins where all the local police stations were around it.

'I wish I had your optimism, Jayne. He's the worst kind of slippery wee bugger. Cunning and totally without remorse.' Well, maybe not so wee any more: a couple of years of minimal exercise and good food had seen to that, but the rest was true.

'Aye, he's cunning. Which means he has a plan. And that's got to mean accomplices, connections, places he needs to go. We work that out and we've got him.'

McLean wasn't sure it was that easy. 'Oh, he has a plan all right. It's just not one based on any logical sense.'

'You have a theory then?' McIntyre turned to face him. Behind her the room was beginning to fill up with more officers, come for the morning briefing or simply an update on what had immediately become their top priority.

'I went over his initial psychiatric evaluation again last night. I've a few ideas that don't really fit together yet.' Hours spent lying in bed staring at the ceiling, listening to Emma and Mrs McCutcheon's cat both snoring had given time for the whirl of thoughts to begin to coalesce. 'I need to talk to a couple of people first.'

'Oh aye? Anyone in particular?'

'Jo Dalgliesh for one. We took her into protective custody last night, didn't we?'

McIntyre rolled her eyes. 'Christ, you should have heard the fuss, but yes. She's in a safe house with an armed unit. You want her brought here?'

'Would probably be easiest. I don't actually think Bale's going to go after her, even if she was the one stopped him from gutting me like a fish.' He could see it in his mind's eye, the gloomy inside of the church, scaffold holding up the roof, builders' detritus everywhere, a young trainee priest nailed up on a makeshift cross and Norman Bale with an evil-looking hunting knife and the practised skill of a man who'd used it many times before. If it hadn't been for Jo Dalgliesh and a stout piece of steel pipe to the back of the head, McLean most likely wouldn't be worrying about anything right now.

'She ever let you forget that?' McIntyre smiled at her joke, but not for long. 'I'll get the team to bring her in. Sure that will be popular with everyone. Who else do you need to speak to?'

'Grace Ramsay.'

McLean had expected a reaction to the name, so McIntyre's wasn't a surprise.

'Ramsay? Why?'

'It's something I've been thinking about since I spoke to the DCC last night. Too many coincidences for my liking. Bale knew someone was missing, used that to get me to speak to him when he knew nothing else would. I thought that was all there was to it, at first. He so desperately wanted to get me to do his bidding, and that was his only way. But I think I misjudged him.'

'How so?' McIntyre asked. 'He hates you, doesn't he? You locked him up, after all.'

'Dalgliesh was the one who stopped him, when you get down to it. But he doesn't hate and he doesn't love. That's not how he works. Revenge means nothing to him. He just wants to get back to doing what he was doing.'

'Killing people in horrible ways?'

'God's work. That's what he believes it is. Only he made some mistake somewhere along the line. "God" . . .' McLean put deliberate emphasis on the word. '. . . was protecting him, guiding him, making him invulnerable. In his twisted way of thinking, the fact we stopped him means that God was punishing him for getting something wrong. Or maybe testing his faith, like Job. For him, we're just instruments of divine justice. In many ways taking revenge on us would only make things worse for him.'

McIntyre raised both eyebrows, then let out a long, slow breath. 'Have you spoken to anyone else about this . . . theory?'

McLean almost laughed. 'Of course not, Jayne. It's as insane as Bale. Which is why it's probably right.'

'OK. So Dalgliesh I can understand. We need to talk to the press anyway, and she'll need special handling after last night. Why Grace Ramsay though? What can she possibly know that we don't?'

McLean paused a moment before answering. This was where

369

his internal logic had started to break down as he'd finally succumbed to uneasy sleep.

'It's to do with the disappearances, and possibly the bones we found on the moor. I think she was very close to uncovering something, and Bale knows about it too. Or thinks he knows, and thinks it will get him back where he was with his god.'

McIntyre looked at him as if he was mad, which was probably a fair enough assessment at that moment. Then her expression changed as she considered his words. McLean was considering them too, and perhaps they were both coming to the same conclusion. A horrible sensation crept over him as the implications that had eluded him in the night now started to line up.

'You don't think he's going to try and speak to her himself, do you?' McIntyre asked, but McLean was already shouting orders to one of the sergeants.

'I want a full team at the Deal Street care home right now. Lock the place down if you have to, and make sure Grace Ramsay is OK. Contact me the moment you have her safe.'

'On it, sir.' The sergeant bustled off, calling constables from the crowd that had begun to build in the incident room.

'You going with them, Tony?' McIntyre asked as he stared towards the door. He stopped, turned back to face her.

'Not the care home just now, although I'll need to speak to Ramsay soon. I've a hunch I want to play out first.'

'Oh yes?' McIntyre crossed her arms and stared at him until he relented.

'Her house in Joppa. It's where Ramsay lived until she went into the home. If he doesn't know about her fall, he might have gone there looking for answers.'

The detective chief superintendent considered this for a moment, then shrugged. 'What's the point. You'll go anyway. But take a full team with you, Tony. And for God's sake be careful.'

★ ★ ★

Two patrol cars blocked the end of the cul-de-sac, a third swinging around the back to cut off escape through the neighbouring garden. McLean parked a good distance away to avoid having his Alfa driven into by one of the Transit vans full of officers. Everyone wore stab vests and head protection, causing a certain amount of alarm as they went swiftly from house to house, knocking on doors, waking residents and telling them to keep inside until everything was over. Finally there was only the house at the end left.

The forced-entry team approached with caution, waiting for the call from the officers at the back before opening the front door with their big red key. McLean winced at the sound of it, imagining the earful he was going to get from Ramsay when she found out. Nobody wanted to take any chances with Bale though, and fiddling around with the lock would have taken too much time.

Officers piled in through the smashed-open door, and after maybe ten seconds of waiting for a response he remembered to breathe. Another thirty seconds passed, with only the occasional thump and muffled voice shouting 'Clear' to break the silence. Then, finally, one officer stepped back out into the front porch, unclipped his helmet and took it off before giving McLean the sign for OK.

'That'll be our cue,' he said to Harrison, and together they made their way down to the house.

'All clear inside, sir. But someone's been here. Recently too. Must have only missed them by an hour or so.'

McLean nodded his understanding, stepped inside. Broken splinters of the front door crunched underfoot, but once he was past the hall, the house was much the same as he remembered it from his last visit. At least for the front rooms. Further back it was a different matter altogether. A pull-down loft ladder reached from a hole in the ceiling by the kitchen door, and McLean could

371

see a sizeable attic space lit by a bare incandescent bulb.

'Like that when we came in, sir. No one up there, but judging by the look of it the boxes have been searched through.' A uniformed officer in full riot gear stood at the base of the ladder. McLean thanked him, then climbed up just far enough to poke his head into the space.

Any estate agent deserving of the name would have described the attic room of the bungalow as having massive development potential. A couple of dormer windows and there would have been space for two more bedrooms up there, perhaps with a small bathroom in between them. Other houses in the cul-de-sac had already been extended, but clearly Grace Ramsay hadn't needed the room. Instead her attic was a glory hole, filled with a lifetime of accumulated junk.

Archive boxes that looked suspiciously like they might have been lifted from the old Lothian and Borders Police records store were stacked neatly along one gable end. Or at least they had once been stacked neatly. Now half of them were lying open, their contents rifled through and strewn around the wooden floorboards. He climbed all the way into the attic, then stepped carefully around the mess, hunkering down to get a better look.

As he had suspected, they were case files. More particularly, missing-persons case files, most probably copies as the sheer quantity of them would have been noticed if they'd gone missing from the archives. Even so, the collection represented a serious breach of security protocols. Like mother, like daughter.

McLean knew that Ramsay had been obsessed with the missing women; he'd spoken to her about it, after all. Seeing the boxes of files, the uncounted names, was a stark reminder of just how common it was for people to simply disappear. Given the age of some of the cases, the people they referred to were almost certainly dead now. But had they died soon after they went missing, or had they lived long lives away from whatever caused them to run away in the first place? It was madness to believe that every single one of these files was a murder unsolved, and yet something had persuaded Grace Ramsay to add each and every one of them to her collection.

'Ah, you're up here, sir. I did wonder.'

McLean looked around to see DC Harrison's head appearing through the hatch.

'I'm surprised nobody noticed these when we came here the last time,' he said. 'Did nobody think to look up here?'

Harrison frowned. 'I'm no' sure, sir. I can check, but you might want to see this first.'

Reluctantly, McLean left the mess of missing people and clambered back down the ladder. Harrison led him to the bedroom at the back where they'd assumed Anya Renfrew had slept when she was staying there. The wardrobe hung open, drawers gone through carelessly, but it was the bed that caught his attention. A set of Anya's work clothes had been laid out on one side, arranged to look a bit like a woman sleeping on top of the covers. On the other side, a clear depression in the duvet showed where someone heavy had lain down, and a few dark hairs flecked the pillow. Bending close, McLean sniffed and caught a scent he couldn't quite place. Pine trees, perhaps, and something earthy. He also noticed an additional book on the bedside table that he was certain hadn't been there before. Neatly placed on top of Renfrew's copy of *Persuasion*, an old Penguin paperback with the title *Scottish Folk and Horror Tales* collected by someone called Preston MacCauley. Neither title nor editor were of any great interest to him, but McLean knew a deliberate clue when he saw one. He pulled on a pair of latex gloves before carefully picking up the book and studying its edge. Sure enough, a page corner had been folded down. He didn't even have to open it to know what would be marked there. 'The Legend of Sawney Bean'.

62

A couple of police cars were parked outside the nursing home when McLean arrived, and he was greeted at the door by a pair of uniformed constables sweating in their heavy stab vests. Inside, the tension hung in the air like the growing heat of the day. No sooner had he stepped through the door than a fierce, middle-aged woman in a tweed skirt and matching top came striding across the room towards him.

'Are you the officer in charge? This really is quite intolerable.'

McLean tensed, then forced himself to relax. It wasn't her fault that her quiet nursing home was suddenly under almost military lockdown.

'Detective Chief Inspector McLean.' He put on his most polite manner, held out his hand to shake, smiled. 'And I do apologise for the disruption. We wouldn't do it if it wasn't absolutely necessary.'

It seemed to work, the fierceness fell away from the woman's face and she took his hand with a slightly limp grip of her own.

'Dorothy Elmsworth. I'm the senior manager here. This is about Grace Ramsay, is it not?'

'It is indeed, Ms Elmsworth. We have reason to believe that a very dangerous individual might seek to contact her, possibly even threaten her with harm.'

'Can you not . . .' Elmsworth did a half-shrug, half-wince. '. . . take her to a safe house or something?'

'We could, yes. I'm actually here to try and persuade her to do just that. But we would still need to leave a substantial police presence here. Just in case.'

'The man you're looking for. He's an escaped convict, is he?'

Technically Bale had never been convicted of a crime. He wasn't deemed mentally fit to stand trial, and so wasn't a convict. McLean considered that the distinction would probably be lost on Dorothy Elmsworth. 'Yes,' he said.

'And he's dangerous?'

'Very.'

Elmsworth glanced past McLean's shoulder to where another uniformed constable stood by the door through to the residential part of the nursing home. 'You will catch him soon, won't you?'

'Yes,' he said again, even though he wasn't sure. 'But the quicker I talk to Grace, the sooner I can work out where he might be.'

It took the senior manager a moment to parse that sentence, but the message finally percolated through. 'Of course. She's in the dining room just now. I'll take you there. And we can see about getting you a cup of tea while we're at it.'

Ramsay sat at the same table as the last time he had visited, although she appeared to have abandoned the wheelchair in favour of a stick. She was staring out of the window at the sun-bleached garden beyond, but turned when she heard them enter. The frown she directed at Elmsworth turned into a genuine smile when she saw McLean.

'Detective Chief Inspector. Tony. How good of you to come visit.' She stood up slowly, using the table for support, then came over and clasped his hand in both of hers. 'Is it true what they're saying? Norman Bale broke out of the hospital and spent the night in my old house?'

'Norman Bale?' The senior manager's voice was an octave higher than when they had spoken moments earlier, which suggested she knew who they were talking about and what he had done.

'Oh do calm yourself, Dorothy. We're not in any danger. Not with so many fine officers of the law here to look after us. Come, Tony. Let's sit down, shall we? I'm sure you've lots to ask me, and I've questions for you too.'

McLean allowed himself to be led to the table, where he helped Ramsay into her seat. When he looked around, Elmsworth was still standing where they had left her.

'I don't suppose we could have that cup of tea, Ms Elmsworth?' he asked.

She snapped out of her stupor as if she'd been poked with a stick. 'Oh. Yes, of course. I'll send one of the nursing staff.'

McLean waited until she had left the otherwise empty dining room before he pulled out a chair and sat down beside Ramsay.

'So, you've been talking to the constables.'

'Of course I have. What do you expect me to do when you come here mob-handed and tooled up for a fight? So tell me, has he made a terrible mess of the place?'

'Who?' McLean took a moment to understand what Ramsay was asking. 'Oh, Bale. Not really. Well, he's been up in your attic going through all those missing-persons case files you probably shouldn't have.'

'Am I going to get my wrist slapped?' Ramsay held out her hand as if to accept her wrongdoing and subsequent punishment. That tremor he had noticed the first time they met was back, perhaps even worse than before. The stress of the past week had not been kind.

'Duguid might have a word or two, but only because he'll be

the one who has to go through them all.'

'They're copies. The originals are all still in the archives. Not that being there does the poor souls much good.'

They were interrupted from any further conversation by the arrival of tea, brought by a tidily presented young nurse who also had Ramsay's medication with her. It took a surprisingly long time for her to work through the stack of pills, some so large McLean was amazed the old lady could even swallow them. He did his best to wait patiently while the performance lasted, even if there was a potential killer at large.

'I take it you didn't come here simply to tell me off,' Ramsay said once the nurse had finished fussing and left them to their tea.

'I didn't come to tell you off at all. Although you probably should have had those files destroyed once you came here.'

'I probably should have, yes. You'll know I fell and broke my pelvis. Bloody stupid of me, but we all get old. I only came here to recover. It's just taking rather longer than I thought it would. Never intended it being permanent.' Ramsay lifted both hands to indicate the room in which they were seated, the nursing home as a whole. 'Anya, bless her. She did her best to look after me, and that was fine. But she had her own life to live, her own particular hang-ups.'

McLean must have reacted to that, even though he thought he had kept a straight face.

'Oh, I know about the sex, Tony. It's distasteful and I can't begin to see the appeal myself. But she grew up without a father, and I wasn't perhaps the best of mothers. She was never going to be a normal adult really. As peccadilloes go, it's fairly harmless. Well, it was.'

'Bale seems to think that she's still alive. That she's being held by something called the Brotherhood of the Red Spring. Does that mean anything to you?'

Ramsay's concentration deepened the wrinkles on her face, then she shook her head slowly. 'Sounds like the sort of nonsense someone like him would make up. "Red Spring" is interesting though. Do you know why Rosewell is called that, Tony?'

The question took him by surprise, both because it was a bit of a non-sequitur and because he'd never thought about it. Driven through the place plenty of times, yes. Seen it on maps, written in reports, mentioned in dispatches. It was just a name, same as Roslin or Penicuik or Bilston Glen. Except that names always meant something.

'Can't say that I do.'

'The town itself isn't all that old. It grew out of a mining village in the mid-nineteenth century. Not much more than a dormitory for the city these days, but you know what? It doesn't have a well and it's not renowned for its roses.'

'So why the name then?' McLean asked when he realised that was what was expected of him.

'There is a well – a spring, I should say. It's said to run red with the blood of the sacrificial victims slain on Oak Hill by the Druids in ancient times. Hence the colour rose, nothing to do with the flowers.'

'I've heard that story. Recently too.' McLean tried to recall all the details Mr and Mrs Wilkins had told him, but it was nonsense mostly. 'And later there was a monastery built on it, and a rather questionable abbot. But that's all myths and legends, scary stories to frighten children. And, anyway, it's miles from Rosewell. Up in the Moorfoot Hills.'

'It's a local legend, true. And not much told these days at all. I remember my mother telling me, when I was small. And she swore blind it was true. She also said the man who built Rosewell, who owned the mine that changed it from a wee farmstead into a village and then a town, was a local man who knew the legend well. That's why he chose that name. It wouldn't surprise me if he'd been a member of your so-called brotherhood. Not Red Spring, but Rose Well? All the well-to-do were members of secret societies in those days. It was the only way to get on in life.'

Sooner or later, McLean knew, it was bound to get back to secret societies. Illuminati, Freemasons, the Knights Templar were just down the road, after all. This was Ramsay's obsession given new life, and he had to take most of the blame for encouraging her. Except that all the mad things she talked about were coming true, in one way or another. Was it time to take the conspiracy seriously?

'Just how long have people been going missing in that area?' he asked.

A night in protective custody hadn't done Jo Dalgliesh any favours. Granted, she normally gave scruffy a bad name, but now she looked haggard with it. Or maybe that was just age and a bad nicotine habit finally catching up with her.

'Always said they should've locked that wee shite up an' thrown away the key' were her first words on seeing him when McLean entered the interview room. She'd been pacing back and forth; he could tell both by the chair still tucked under the table and the way she stood, awkwardly, halfway to the window, mid-turn.

'That's exactly what they did, remember? I'm sorry it's not quite worked out the way we both hoped.' He indicated the chair for her to sit, but Dalgliesh stayed standing. She shoved her hands in her pockets, brought out her e-cigarette, twirled it in agitated fingers, then put it away again. Fidgety and unfocused.

'You needing a smoke?' McLean asked. 'Come on, I'll take you out to the car park. Don't think Bale's going to try anything on here.'

Dalgliesh stared at him uncomprehending for a moment,

then broke into a broad grin. 'You beauty. I'd kiss you, only folk might get the wrong impression.'

McLean grimaced at the thought, then held open the door for the reporter. They walked to the back door and out into the car park. Around the corner, the perspex-covered bus stop that had been erected to keep the smokers sheltered from Edinburgh's more normal climate was now acting as a small greenhouse. Nobody was using it, either because it was too hot to even think about going outside, or because they'd seen the detective chief inspector coming.

'Christ, but I needed that,' Dalgliesh said after she'd drawn deep on the e-cigarette a half a dozen times, breathing out plumes of sickly-smelling vapour into the stifling air. 'So, you found our boy Norman yet? Only nobody'll tell me a thing.'

'Sorry about that. They're all terrified of talking to the press, particularly on this one. After you dug up all that stuff about the bones and our missing admin officer, the DCC came down hard on everyone.'

'Aye, well. Fair enough.' Dalgliesh took another drag, so deep she ended up coughing out the vapour and thumping her chest. McLean waited as patiently as he could until she was able to breathe properly again.

'Didn't see your name on any of the bylines in the weekend papers,' he said. 'Guess I should be grateful for that.'

'Plenty of time yet, Tony. Don't you worry. Didn't seem the right moment.'

Either that or she'd not managed to find an editor brave enough to take the story. Dalgliesh was freelance these days, McLean remembered, which was something of a mixed blessing.

'Was that what you wanted to talk to me about?' she asked after another, more careful drag.

'Not exactly. Although I guess in a way it's all connected.' He told her about Bale's obsession with Sawney Bean, and how he'd somehow managed to get from the psychiatric hospital all the way to Joppa without being seen. 'No idea where he's gone, but he left this for me to find.' He pulled the paperback book from his pocket, still slightly sticky from where it had been dusted for fingerprints.

'MacCauley, eh? Had no idea they'd published a modern edition.' Dalgliesh held out her hand. 'May I?'

He passed the book over. Dalgliesh tucked away her e-cigarette and started riffling through the browned pages. She tutted at the folded corner, stared briefly at the beginning of the Sawney Bean chapter, then flicked forward to the index. A moment of peering myopically at the tiny print, and then she thumbed her way back to an earlier chapter. 'Ah, the wee scunner's turned down the page corner here too. What kind of animal does that to a book?' She opened it up and showed it to him. 'Here you go. "The Red Abbot of Oakhill Priory".'

McLean couldn't say he was surprised. Bale might think he was being subtle with his clues, but actually it was more annoying. 'Aye, I've heard of it.'

'You have? Well, so has Norman by the look of things.' She turned a couple of pages, and McLean saw scrawled handwriting in the margins, tiny loops of words he couldn't begin to read. Passages in the text had been underlined too.

'Why did you go looking for it?' he asked, although the fact that she had was already setting off alarm bells as various disparate thoughts began to collide. He'd known as soon as he'd seen it that this was another of Bale's little trail of breadcrumbs to whatever sick ending the psychopath had in mind. That it had been left on Anya Renfrew's bedside table was no coincidence either.

'What you were saying earlier, the Fraternitas de Rosae Fontis. MacCauley's the only reference I managed to track down. It's a footnote to the legend of the Red Abbot.' Dalgliesh closed the book and handed it back. 'You had a good read of that then?'

'I've not read it at all. Only just got it back from Forensics.'

'So how come you know about the Red Abbot? It's no' exactly a well-known tale, even round here.'

'Oddly enough I was told it just the other day by a drug addict recovering from an overdose.' Another coincidence McLean didn't like, but not one he could fit into the ever-growing picture. 'You any idea what it might mean to Bale? The story, that is?'

Dalgliesh shrugged, pulled out her e-cigarette again, shoved it in her mouth but didn't switch it on this time. 'Who knows? It's a bonkers story anyway. Almost as bad as Sawney Bean.'

'Bale seemed to think the two were linked. He kept on saying that Bean was a Lothian man, as if that was important.'

'Well, Oakhill Priory is presumably on Oak Hill, up where you've found all those bones. That's in Midlothian, so I guess the two might be connected that way. I mean, neither of them actually existed in history, they're just folk tales to scare the kiddies with.'

'What's the book say about the brotherhood?' McLean asked. It was probably quicker than trying to read it for himself.

'Only that there was an eighteenth-century secret society of the name. Not as famous as the Hellfire Club or the Beggar's Benison. There'd be more in the literature about it if it was. MacCauley reckoned it petered out before 1750.'

McLean looked at the book, well read, extensively annotated in a tiny scrawl it would take hours to decipher if they could manage it at all. Bale's obsession, his latest obsession. His way of atoning for whatever sin had made him fall from God's grace.

'What if MacCauley was wrong?'

63

Mclean was sitting at his desk, thinking about Jo Dalgliesh's words, and what Grace Ramsay had told him too, when his phone rang. He recognised the name as one only recently added to his contact list. Thumbing the button to accept the call, he lifted the handset to his ear.

'Harriet. How are you?'

A moment's confused silence, then the voice came through loud and clear. 'Ah, modern technology. I always forget you know who's called before you even answer. Very useful that. I'm fine, Tony. It was lovely to see you and Emma the other night.'

From the background noise, McLean could tell that Professor Turner was outside, probably up on Oakhill Moor at the dig site, breaking in new students and uncovering yet more Neolithic remains. Was this just a social call? Another invitation? Not that he didn't enjoy the company, and it made Emma happy too, but he was in the middle of a manhunt.

'It was fun, thank you. We'll have to get you and Meg over again some time soon. Maybe see if I can persuade my old flatmate Phil and his wife to come over, if they can find a babysitter.'

'Or they could bring the baby. Meg's a sucker for other people's kids. Just never wanted any of her own.'

Unlike Emma, who had done and now couldn't. One reason

why he'd not seen much of Phil and Rachel and young Tony Junior of late.

'Sounds busy where you are. You up at the dig site?' He changed the subject before it became too awkward.

'Aye. That's what I was phoning about.'

For a moment McLean fancied everything went quiet. He glanced up at the clock just to be sure that angel hadn't flown over again. 'There a problem?'

The professor laughed. 'When is there not? But, no. It's not that. Well, sort of that. I'm usually fine getting my head around a site after a day or two, but this one's . . . I don't know. Weird?'

'Weird?' McLean asked. 'Weird how?'

There was a pause during which he imagined he could hear someone shouting in the distance, the scream of some disturbed raptor, a car horn. Then Professor Turner was back. 'Well, the mapping's all off for starters, and geophys are giving me grief as if it's my fault.'

'Geo fizz?' McLean wondered if he sounded like an echo.

'Jesus, Tony. Have you never watched an episode of *Time Team*? Geophys. Geophysics. Ground-penetrating radar, electrical-resistance measuring, that sort of thing. Helps us see what's down there without actually having to dig first.'

'I don't get to watch much television these days.' The old excuse was out before he realised the professor was teasing him. Her laugh, even over the phone, took him straight back to being seventeen.

'Me neither, Tony. Look, I know you're probably knee-deep in it at the moment, but it would be much easier to explain if I could show you. Any chance you might be able to swing out this way some time today?'

McLean checked his watch, even though he'd only seconds ago looked at the clock on the wall. Knee-deep in it wasn't exactly accurate, unless you counted the paperwork piled on his desk and overflowing to the conference table. Operation Caterwaul was dead in the water, the search for Renfrew had pretty much stalled, and any investigation into the bones on the moor was going to have to wait now until they'd found Bale. That was constable and sergeant work, not something he could be much help with beyond what he'd already done. On the other hand, the trail of crumbs was leading inexorably towards Oakhill Moor, so any excuse to head out there was a good one, surely?

He checked his watch again. Thanks to the day starting far too early, it still wasn't lunchtime yet. Well, he could pick something up on the way.

'Sure. I'll be with you in about an hour.'

'It's a date then,' Turner said, and before he could protest she had hung up.

In the end it took nearer two hours to get there. Partly because he'd run into Detective Chief Superintendent McIntyre, who had insisted he take at least one detective constable with him, partly because it had then taken him twenty minutes to find one. There had also been the small matter of the canteen running out of sandwiches due to a large influx of uniformed officers involved in the search for Bale. McLean wasn't unhappy with the alternative picked up at the M&S Food Hall on the outskirts of Loanhead. It was just as well DC Harrison had been with him, otherwise he'd not have noticed and most likely ended up with a dodgy lukewarm meat pie from a corner shop in Penicuik. Or gone without, if he was being realistic.

'Ah, Tony. You're here at last.' Professor Turner met them at the roadside as they were eating cheese and ham baguettes. She took one look at Harrison and stuck out a slightly grubby hand. 'You'll be Janie then. I'm Hattie.'

'How . . . ?' Harrison mumbled through an awkward mouthful.

'Emma's told me all about you. Tony's new protégée. And the rumours, well . . .' She waved a hand in McLean's direction. 'If I'd not known him since he was fifteen, I'd be very worried.'

'Did you want to show me something, Professor? Or did you just ask me out here to make fun of me in front of the junior detectives?'

'Professor. Honestly.' Turner waved them in the direction of the path leading up to the main dig site. 'Come on then. We'll start in the command centre.'

McLean looked around for forensics vans and white-suited technicians, but there were none to be seen. The few people digging and shifting earth he could see were dressed in shorts and T-shirts, which made more sense given the heat. As he followed the professor to the tent, he could see the area where the more recent bones had been found still taped off as a crime scene, but the rest of the dig, spreading upwards through the charred moorland in the direction of the Iron Age fort at the summit, was an archaeological dig. Nothing coming out of the ground here would need to be presented as evidence at a trial; anyone involved was long dead, perhaps by a thousand years or more.

'I think the problem's with the maps. Nothing's quite where it's meant to be.'

Professor Turner led them into the tent, where the temperature immediately spiked a good ten degrees, even with the sides tied open. A couple of semi-naked archaeology students sat at a trestle table, peering at laptop computers and sweating profusely. Everywhere smelled of char, but inside the effect was almost overpowering.

'You work in this?' McLean waved his hand across his face. Harrison had wisely decided to stay outside.

'You get used to it. And the shower at the end of the day feels wonderful.' The professor beckoned him over to another table, where a map had been spread out, weighed down in each corner with interesting rocks from the dig. Not quite a military campaign, but the impression was there.

McLean stepped around the table to get the orientation right, and took a little while longer to identify the positions of the reservoir, the woods where Renfrew's car had been found, the moorland and the dig site. This last one was at least marked, with a big red X and some smaller squares drawn, presumably, to mark the actual excavations.

'See here?' Turner obscured a good couple of acres with the tip of her right index finger, her short fingernail cracked and blackened with burned earth. 'That's the remains of the hill fort, up at the summit of Oak Hill over there.' She took her finger from the map and used it to point out of the tent in a vaguely uphill direction. 'This here's the road where you've parked that ridiculous midlife crisis of a car of yours.' She stabbed the narrow pair of parallel dotted lines on the paper where they snaked around the lower slope. 'Those woods climb up to a point here.' She indicated the green shape, that now McLean looked at it very much seemed to be an arrowhead pointing towards the hill fort. Glancing out the open side of the tent, he could just make out the green tops of the pines through the wavy heat haze.

'And the problem is?' he asked.

'The problem is it's all wrong. The hill fort's a good five hundred yards further west than the map shows. Or if it's in the right place, then the road isn't. And as for the woods? I've looked at those trees, Tony. They've been growing there since long before this map was last revised. But if they're where the cartographer put them, then somebody's moved Gladhouse Reservoir a quarter-mile north.'

McLean stared at the map again, unable to tell whether it was right or not. He didn't doubt the professor though. 'What about aerial maps? Isn't it all digital these days anyway?'

'I've got Angie on that right now.' The professor tilted her head in the direction of one of the students working at her laptop. Hearing her name, she looked up and smiled, wiped sweat from her brow. Then she turned her computer around so they could see the screen.

'I've been working with the most recent photographs, and they show everything in the right place, at least. But the resolution's not good enough to be useful for what we're doing here. And the overlay's just as wrong as the paper map, see?'

McLean peered at the image, too small for his old eyes. 'I'll take your word for it, but why's it wrong? More importantly, how is it wrong?'

Angie shrugged. 'Bad mapping data to start with, maybe? Most of this stuff's been locked down by GPS now, but if they're still working on old OS data for this area . . .' she tailed off, shook her head. 'No. OS is solid. I've never heard of it being wrong.'

Something niggled at the back of McLean's mind. The search teams looking for Renfrew had complained about the maps not fitting the terrain well, but they'd put that down to the woods obscuring the old land features. 'Easy to get lost even with a map and compass' was how Sergeant Donaldson had put it. But Bobby Wilkins had mentioned it too, in his childish, roundabout way. 'The woods are all wrong there. They lure you in an' you starve tae death, 'less you're a local an' ken where y'are an' where yer goin'.'

'What if someone had made it wrong on purpose?' He gestured at the paper map.

'Why would anyone do that?' Angie asked, her talents clearly wasted in forensic anthropology.

'Presumably to hide something, or make it less likely people would go somewhere you didn't want them to go.' McLean looked out the open side of the tent again, bending slightly so he could see up the burned moorland to the top of Oak Hill. It wasn't that far really. And a walk would do him good, even in this heat.

'I couldn't borrow that, could I?' He pointed at the map again.

Professor Turner removed the stones from the corners and folded it up expertly before handing it over. 'Going somewhere?' she asked.

'Thought I might have a look around from the summit. Try to see what's in the wrong place and why.'

'Then you'd better take this with you too.' She bent down and guddled in a box underneath the table for a moment, coming out with a compass. 'You do know how to use one, right?'

'Grid to mag add, isn't it?' McLean took the compass and slipped it into his jacket pocket. He couldn't confidently say he remembered how to navigate with one, but that particular gem had stuck in his head from school geography lessons. Mr Collier would have been proud.

'Very good, Tony.' Turner smiled, picked up a small pair of binoculars and shoved them into the soft case lying beside them. 'Take these too. Just don't lose them, OK?'

64

With hindsight it was probably a mistake, climbing a steep hill in the early afternoon of one of the hottest days of a year already breaking records for hottest days. By the time he and a stoically uncomplaining DC Harrison made it to the top, McLean was damp with sweat. He'd shed his suit jacket, trailing it over his shoulder with one crooked finger. His shirt stuck to his skin, and a sizeable puddle had formed at the base of his spine too. Now he understood the reason most of Professor Turner's workforce wore barely any clothes. The view was worth it though. Of the countryside from the top of the hill, not the professor's students.

'I'd forgotten how far you can see from up here,' he said as he reached the Ordnance Survey trig point and tapped it for luck. He'd done the same at the top of every hill and mountain his grandmother had forced him to climb in the course of countless holidays in the Highlands. Now it was an ingrained habit, not only to touch the brass plate in the top, but to do it before anyone else on the walk and thus claim some kind of imaginary prize for getting there first. Harrison breathed heavily but said nothing. She stopped a few paces short of the concrete pillar too, which felt strangely wrong.

'You get a good view of the reservoir from here.' McLean

shielded his eyes against the glare rising off the unnaturally still water. He turned a slow 360 degrees, seeing the distant Pentland Hills to the west, the continued rise of the Moorfoots to the south, the horizon speckled with slowly turning wind turbines. To the east he could make out North Berwick Law and the Bass Rock, then the Isle of May out in the Firth of Forth, and across to Fife in the north. Somewhere in the sun-baked brown was Traprain Law too. Another Iron Age hill fort, and one-time capital of the Gododdin, if he remembered his ancient history correctly.

'Is that the castle?' Harrison asked, and for a moment McLean thought she meant the hill fort they were standing on. That's what Bobby Wilkins had referred to it as, a castle. Then he realised she was looking out towards Edinburgh, where a grey-brown haze of pollution hung over the city. Castle Rock and Arthur's Seat both rose up out of the murk like knees in dirty bathwater.

'It is, yes. Here, you can get a closer look if you want.' He passed over the binoculars Professor Turner had pressed upon him. Harrison took a moment to work out which end she was supposed to be looking through, but was soon scanning the horizon.

McLean unfolded the map and spread it out next to the trig point, orientated so that north was in approximately the right direction. A quick check showed that the castle was on the right bearing from their position, according to both map and compass, but when he lined up one of the two islands in the reservoir, it was out by five degrees. It was the same for the woods that climbed up the slope towards them like a very slow advancing army. Looking south-east, he could make out a series of low mounds that looked like barrows, where only a few stubby trees grew. The long, dry spell had kept the grass short, and he imagined he could see stone ruins in among the whins, which he took to be the remains of the monastery. Except that according to the map they should have been much further away, and considerably more to the south of where he was standing.

'Can I have those binoculars back a minute?' he asked. Harrison was still staring through them towards the city, maybe looking for her flat. From here it would be hidden behind Braid Hill.

'Found something?' she asked as she handed them over. McLean took a moment to adjust them, then focused on the ruins.

'I think that's the remains of the old monastery. Only it's in the wrong place.' As he spoke, so the magnified image began to come together. Most definitely worked stone, the bases of pillars perhaps, a piece of an archway, all overgrown with gorse and broom, brambles and wild raspberry. Not an easy place to get into. Scanning back and forth, he saw again the low mounds with their twisted and stubby trees, in sharp contrast to the towering mature pines that grew around them. And then he noticed movement, a car making its way along a track he couldn't quite see.

'Where's Woodhill Farm from here?' He took the binoculars from his eyes, noticing as he did that it had a zoom function. A quick glance at the map showed where the farm was supposed to be, but he wasn't entirely sure he could trust that any more.

Harrison bent down to peer at the sheet as McLean once more lifted the binoculars. With the zoom, he was able to get a clearer view of the woods, and make out a fence beyond the trees that must have marked the track leading to the farm. As he stared, another vehicle moved through his field of view, a shiny black Range Rover with dark-tinted windows. He followed its passage through the trees, and as it disappeared down below a rise, he noticed the unmistakable triangular shape of the old open barn's corrugated iron roof.

'Should be that way, about a mile and a half.' Harrison's voice interrupted him, and when McLean looked she was kneeling by the map, one finger in the middle of the paper, the other hand pointing somewhere clearly different to where the farm buildings stood.

'Well, it's actually over there, and no more than a few hundred yards.' He crouched down, the better to see the map. Now that he had the points of the farm and the ruins of the monastery in his head, McLean could see why it was upsetting Professor Turner. They were much closer together, for one thing. Far from being separate to the monastery, Woodhill was almost its kitchen garden. They were closer to the Iron Age hill fort, and not far at all from the site where the bones had been discovered.

'We searched the farm buildings thoroughly, didn't we.' McLean stated it as fact. He'd been there after all, drank tea with Mr and Mrs Bayne, Harrison herself and Police Sergeant Donaldson. He'd not been in the buildings himself, but the sergeant had said his team had been through them.

'Twice, aye.' Harrison was just as certain. 'Looks like they've got visitors, mind.'

He looked up from the map just in time to see a flash of light where a car windscreen reflected the sun through the trees. Three vehicles in as many minutes tripped his finely tuned policeman's sense of suspicious activity, even if it was probably nothing.

'I think I'll go and pay them another visit.' He stood up, fetching out his phone as he did so. The icon at the top of the screen showed no signal. 'You got your Airwave with you?'

Harrison produced the chunky handset from her jacket pocket, prodded a button to bring it to life, then frowned at it in puzzlement. 'No signal, sir. Thought these things worked everywhere.'

'Thought these did too.' McLean waved his useless phone.

Harrison put her Airwave away and fumbled for her own mobile.

'Must be a black spot. It was fine back at the car.'

'OK then. You take these.' He folded up the map and passed it, the compass and binoculars to the detective constable. 'And this.' He shoved his hand in his pocket and came out with his car key. 'Get back into signal range and call in a search team. Then you can meet me at the farmyard. We're going to go over the whole place again. And the monastery ruins.'

Harrison made everything disappear into pockets except the binoculars. 'Do I need to ask what you're going to be doing in the meantime?'

'I'm going to see if I can persuade Mr and Mrs Bayne to give me a cup of tea. Looks like they're already entertaining a crowd, after all.'

Another car bounced its way along the rutted track to the farmyard as McLean struggled through the thick undergrowth around the mature trees. He wasn't as up to date with these things as once he had been, but he recognised the impossibly clean SUV as one of the new Bentleys. North of a hundred grand's worth, it wasn't the sort of vehicle he would immediately have associated with Sandy and Morag Bayne. Their battered Series 1 Land Rover might have been worth a bit, but only because it was old and rare, and that more by accident than design.

Fighting through the brambles was a fool's errand, so he worked his way around the thickest bushes, taking a zigzag route to the farmyard that brought him close to the barrows. There came a point where he was prepared to admit, albeit only to himself, that this was a really stupid idea. A detective chief inspector had no place hacking his way through jungle that would have thwarted Tarzan, and procedure would have dictated putting together both a plan and a team of fit young detective sergeants and constables to carry it out. On the other hand, he would have had to explain his reasoning to them all before sending them into this place, and that would have required there to be some reason behind it all. Instead he had gut instinct and a horrible feeling that all the strange things that had been happening this past week and more were somehow connected.

There had once been a fence between the woods that spread up towards the summit of Oak Hill and the area where the barrows lay. McLean could tell that by the lone rusted iron post that poked out of the ground like some broken vertebra. That and the change in the vegetation. On one side, it was thick and lush and threatened to ruin an otherwise fine suit. On the other it was twisted and stunted, starved of nutrients or blighted by something evil. As if to hammer home the idea, flies buzzed around the hot air and a scent of rotten meat hung like a miasma of decay.

As he struggled through the scrub, McLean caught his foot on a heavy rock, almost tumbling headlong into the weeds. On closer inspection, he could see the ground was strewn with building rubble, carved lintels and bits of arch. At first, they appeared to be scattered randomly, but the more he looked, the more he saw that they formed a wall, perhaps an ancient cloister. Only where he might have expected there to be the remains of a chapel in the centre, instead stood the three low earth mounds.

A vague path followed the line of one wall, giving him the option of heading towards the farmyard or away from it. He'd told Harrison he was going to speak to Sandy Bayne, maybe find out who the visitors in the expensive cars were, but he wanted to get the lay of the land first. Something was happening here, and he'd rather find out what before confronting anyone. The more time he gave the detective constable to bring backup the better too. And there was the small matter of that smell. It wasn't quite full-on rotting carcass, but there was something about it that set him on edge.

Taking the path away from the buildings, he skirted around what must have once been a sizeable cloister, now he was able to get the layout in his head. At the farthest corner, a tumble of stones and hacked-back weeds marked an entrance of sorts, and one that had been used recently. What little breeze there was passed over the barrows and on to where he stood, bringing with it that cloying odour. He knew he would have to find out what it was, but not just yet. McLean pressed on, following a path that showed ever more signs of regular use as it headed back to the farmyard. Soon the rusted steel and corrugated iron shed rose up through the trees, the path leading past the knackered old tractor and on to the stone steadings.

The sound of an engine had McLean ducking down behind one large tractor wheel on instinct. He peered up the track, and soon enough a car appeared over the rise, weaving back and forth in a vain attempt to avoid the worst of the potholes. When it came closer, he almost stood up and waved it down, recognising the Police Scotland markings on the bonnet and sides. Something stopped him though. It was too soon, and there should have been more than one. When it crunched slowly past him, he was able to spot the driver, alone rather than accompanied by a squad of burly constables. Police Sergeant Donaldson had the look of a man who's late for the party, and McLean could think of no reason why he would be coming out here alone. No good reason, at least.

The dust kicked up by the tyres stung his eyes and tickled his nose. Stifling a sneeze, he worked his way along the hay shed, then ducked across the lane to the steadings. Inside was a little cooler than out, but not much. It smelled of disuse, and all McLean could see in the shadows was broken farm machinery of a vintage his great-grandfather might have recognised. At least none of the doors were locked, and the various interlinked byres and stables brought him to the courtyard at the back of the house.

Through a missing pane in a glass window otherwise opaque with grime, he saw a dozen or more cars neatly parked in rows. Some were expensive, like the blacked-out Range Rover and the ugly Bentley SUV, but others were nothing special, nothing new. A mix of the wealthy and the common folk had come to whatever gathering this was. And Sergeant Donaldson.

'You're late, Andrew.' Sandy Bayne's voice drifted across the yard. McLean saw the old man standing at the back door as Donaldson weaved through the cars towards him. He said something in reply, but with his back to McLean the words were lost. Then the two men greeted each other like old friends. A warm embrace, a step back, a curiously formal bow, and a handshake straight out of the Freemason's handbook. Except that McLean had met enough Masons in his career and this wasn't any one of theirs. A secret society, just as Ramsay and Dalgliesh had suggested, and very much active. But why were they meeting here? Now?

'I was beginning to think you'd never get here, Tony.'

He spun round, already knowing who'd spoken, but spooked by how quietly he'd crept up all the same. A figure shuffled forward out of the shadows.

Norman Bale.

65

The first words that came to him were 'You're under arrest', but McLean managed to stop them from spilling out. For a start, he didn't want to make any noise that might alert Sandy Bayne and Police Sergeant Donaldson to his presence. It was pointless anyway, since he had no cuffs, no way of easily overpowering the man, and no phone signal to call it in.

'I left enough clues for you. Really thought you were smarter than that.' Bale sat down on a wooden packing crate that creaked ominously under his weight.

'What are you doing here, Bale?' As questions went, it wasn't much better than trying to arrest him, but McLean was still coming to terms with the situation. The last time it had been just the two of them, Bale had been intent on killing him. Then, he had been filled with a religious fervour, a mad zealotry that would brook no interference. Now he sat like a fellow drinker in the local pub. Not one iota of menace in his chubby face and sloped shoulders. It could have been an act, most probably was. Still, it was disorienting.

'I'd have thought that would have been obvious, Tony. Same thing as you. I'm here for Anya Renfrew.'

Not here to save Anya Renfrew, McLean noticed. Only here for her.

'And what makes you think she's here? What makes you think she's even still alive? It's been two weeks since she disappeared.'

Bale shook his head like a disappointed teacher. 'She had to be cleansed of all her sins. Purged. That takes time. She's ready now, her soul pure. That's why they've all come.'

'I've absolutely no idea what you're talking about,' McLean said, but that was a lie. He had an idea; he just didn't like where that idea was taking him.

'Oh, come on, Tony. The Brotherhood of the Rose Well? The Red Abbot? The Oak Hill Druids? It's all connected. You've even found bones up on the moors over there.' Bale waved a hand in the approximate direction. 'That should never have happened of course. Bury them deep. That's what old man Bayne always said. But his son couldn't be bothered. Chucked them in the gorse and hoped no one would ever notice. Probably for the best he came to a premature end, him and his sister both. The Baynes throw up a bad 'un every few generations.'

'How do you know all this?'

'Frankly I'm surprised that you don't. It's all there, in the stories and the news. If you know where to look. Grace Ramsay knows, or at least part of it. All those missing girls, and now her daughter among them.' Bale made a noise that might have been a laugh, although there was no humour in it, no humanity.

'So what you're trying to tell me is that these people are . . . what? Some kind of secret society of cannibals?' McLean couldn't help himself. He shook his head in disbelief even as the implications of Bale's words began to knit together in his mind.

'The blood and the body of Christ, Tony. It's not cannibalism. Least, not to those who have faith. They will come from this ceremony pure of spirit and soul. Cleansed in a way your narrow atheist mind can't hope to comprehend.'

Something of Bale's words sparked a memory then. A few days earlier, when McLean had been sitting in the kitchen at the rectory, talking to Mary Currie. It wasn't revenge that drove this lunatic to do the horrific things he did. He truly believed this nonsense about sin and forgiveness, about doing God's work. Did he think of these people as kindred spirits? Is that why he wanted to join them? But that couldn't be it. He'd said he was here for Anya, not the rest of them.

Movement in the corner of his eye dragged McLean's attention away from Bale for a moment. The back door to the farmhouse had opened and a line of people were walking out into the sunlight. More like a group of ramblers than anything, they moved slowly across the yard, through the closely parked cars and out towards the old shed. Fifteen, maybe twenty of them. They disappeared from view before long, but he had no difficulty guessing where they were going. He also recognised three of the men from the briefing notes DI Ritchie had shown him. Gordon McTavish, Jonathan Scanlan and Dominic Smythe, all flown in on their private jets at short notice. They didn't lead here, but mingled with the others as if they were all equal, all friends together and heading off on some grand adventure.

'What the hell are they doing?' He turned back to Bale as he asked the question, but Bale was gone.

For a moment McLean wondered if he'd not caught too much sun and hallucinated the whole thing. He stepped away from the window, over to the packing case where he'd seen Bale sitting. There wasn't much light filtering into the dark room, but it was enough to see the mark in the heavy dust left by someone's ample buttocks.

He took out his phone again, only there was still no signal. What he should do was work his way back out of the old stone steadings, off up the track towards the road and find help. Something was going on here, something bad. It made no sense to go poking his nose into it before backup arrived. On the other hand, trying to get off the farmyard would take him the same way as all the people he knew were up to no good. Some of them knew the area, the woods and fields around here, far better than him. He could stay put and wait for Harrison and the cavalry to arrive, but Bale knew where he was, and Bale had some plan in mind. That couldn't be good. He had to do something, if only to avoid the nutcase coming back with a knife while he hid in the shadows.

There were three doors out of the room. One opened onto the courtyard where all the cars were parked. He'd have known if it had been opened. Bale certainly hadn't gone out the way McLean had entered through, as it was close by the window. That meant he had to have gone deeper into the complex of interlinked buildings.

Stone steps led down to a larger shed that must once have been used to store hay, back in the days when it was made by gangs of men wielding scythes and pitchforks. Insufficient light filtered in through small, grimy skylight windows, casting more shadow than illumination. The packed-earth floor smelled strange, a fishy scent overlaying the dirt, and, as he noticed it, so too did McLean hear the faint sound of running water. He remembered the first time he'd been to this farm, the strange pond around the front of the house, and the stone building from which Sandy Bayne had emerged, a large fish clutched in his arms like a sleeping infant. What had the man said it was all built for? Cleansing the fish before eating it. A week in the stone-lined pond, no food. Fresh water and nothing else.

'Fuck.' McLean wasn't much given to swearing at the best of times, but there, in the darkened hay barn, as all the hints and clues began to fall into place, he felt like it was justified. He followed the sound of running water, finding doors and passageways, one after another. He'd seen old farm steadings before, knew how complicated and confusing they could be. The longer the farm had existed, the more additions, lean-tos and extensions were grafted onto what might once have been a simple design. Old doorways blocked off, narrow passages formed that led seemingly to nowhere, big open barns and small storerooms in random succession. Woodhill Farm, by all accounts, had been here since the time of the monastery. A thousand years of building had turned it into a terrible labyrinth. And somewhere at the heart of it all, he knew, was a monster as horrific as any minotaur.

McLean paused a moment to get his bearings, something that wasn't easy given the turns and dead ends. Somewhere close by a door creaked, then he heard the click-clack of a latch. Heading in that direction, he came to another room, this with a concrete floor, a raised plinth in its centre. Some kind of engine house, he guessed, and sure enough up in the eaves he could just make out the shapes of wheels, and gaps in the stone walls where pulleys would go to ancient threshing machines and the like. The sound of water was louder here, spattering as if from a great height. It came from a frameless window, more a neatly lined hole in the wall that opened onto almost complete darkness. Peering in, he felt the dampness first. As his eyes adjusted to the gloom, he saw the cast iron spokes that made up a huge water wheel. Its wooden buckets had long since rotted, water cascading over the frame and away into the bowels of the earth.

Further along from the water wheel, he found the creaking door. It opened onto stone steps leading down into darkness. He pulled out his pen torch and played the light over glistening, moist walls. The steps themselves were dry enough, dust-free and worn in the middle by the passage of many feet. A rope handrail looped between iron sconces on one side, but the steps themselves weren't so steep that it was needed. At the bottom, even flagstones lined a narrow corridor, with alcoves to each side at regular intervals. McLean could tell by the cool dampness of the air that this was underground, and after a few dozen steps he worked out, more or less, where he was.

The alcoves housed water troughs, each fashioned from slabs of slate big enough to be used to make snooker tables. Most were empty, but towards the end of the corridor he found a half-dozen filled almost to the brim with water. At first he thought that was all they were filled with, but then a fin broke the surface of one. Playing the light on it, he saw a fish, a carp if he'd learned anything, swaying from side to side as if it were moving against a current. Was this one ready now? Cleansed of all taint by a week of starvation in the pool outside, then left here to stay fresh until it was time for it to be eaten?

McLean shuddered at the implications of that thought. He hurried on down the corridor, and eventually came to another set of steps leading upwards. The daylight was almost blinding as he emerged at the top. He had to blink and squint to see that he was where he thought he would be, at the edge of the pond. The trees across the other side swayed in a gentle breeze, and looking up he could see a few wispy clouds, the first in weeks. He pulled out his phone and checked the screen again, but there was still no signal. Perhaps unsurprising given that he'd not moved far from the last place he'd looked, but it felt suspicious all the same. The last time they'd been here, both Donaldson and Harrison had received calls on their Airwave sets, after all.

A scream overhead had him shrinking back into the doorway of the fish house, but it was only a buzzard wheeling in the hot sky.

Looking back down at the pool, he noticed something strange about the water. As still as glass, it mirrored the movements of the bird and the slow build of clouds, but there was a scum clinging to the edges where the surface met the stone. McLean crouched down, dipped a finger in the water and brought it back up to his nose. The faintest whiff of coal tar. A little further along, he saw wide stone steps under the surface, disappearing into the depths, and the scum around the edge there was thicker. Something had been washed here, in this supposedly pure water. Someone?

Suspicious, he traced his footsteps back to the entrance to the fish house. A switch at the top of the steps turned on lights all along the corridor below. Back down under the ground, the lone fish still swum lazily in its narrow slate tank, unaware of its inevitable fate. Moving along the corridor, McLean paid a little more attention to the other alcoves, now that the lights were on and he wasn't relying on the faint beam from his torch. Most of them were filled with tanks, either dry or empty but filled with still, dark water. A couple of them, facing each other on opposite sides of the narrow corridor, had heavy wooden doors leading to small chambers, and it didn't take a genius to see how much they looked like cells. Both doors were locked, but each also had a heavy iron key pushed into the hole. He opened the first, clicking the light switch beside it as he peered inside. A low-watt bulb hung from the centre of an arched ceiling that matched the shape of the alcove. An iron bedstead stood against one wall, and in the far corner, a bucket with a lid on it made for a toilet. That same scent of coal tar soap came to him, stronger here.

Taking the key from the lock, McLean stepped further into the room. The floor was hard-packed earth, darker in the middle where it had been scuffed by recent feet. Crouching down, he peered more closely at the stained mattress and thin blanket, sniffed the damp, cold air. There was nothing to prove it, no carelessly discarded evidence, no clothing rolled up and left under the bed, but nevertheless he was certain that this was where Anya Renfrew had spent the past two weeks. He couldn't begin to imagine what hell that must have been. Standing again, he carefully retraced his footsteps to the corridor outside. It was time to get out of here and fetch a team of officers he could trust.

He closed the door on the cell, locked it and put the key in his jacket pocket before heading back along the passage towards the steps leading up to the pond. As he did so, a change in the light alerted him to the presence of someone at the top. Turning to go back the other way, McLean realised too late the mistake he had made. Another man, larger than him, stood at the other end of the passageway.

'You really shouldn't be here, sir.' Police Sergeant Andrew Donaldson hefted his extendable baton, just in case McLean had any ideas of making a run for it. Instead, he turned in time to see Sandy Bayne appear at the bottom of the steps.

No way out.

He was trapped.

'I'm very disappointed in you, Sergeant. Didn't you swear an oath to uphold the law?'

They had taken his phone, pen torch and the couple of pairs of latex gloves he always kept in his pocket, but left McLean his wallet and warrant card. If Donaldson had noticed the lack of car keys, he'd not said anything about it. Neither had the police sergeant done anything more violent than cuff McLean's hands behind his back and push him in the direction of the steps up to the pond, but he was in no doubt as to what they intended.

'What did you hope to achieve by coming here, sir?' the sergeant asked as they stepped once more into the sunlight. 'I mean, I know you have a reputation for ignoring procedure at every turn, but . . .' He shook his head, said nothing more. In front of them, Sandy Bayne led the way back towards the house. The path took them close to the edge of the pool, the steps leading down into black water.

'I was trying to track down Norman Bale, if you really want to know.' McLean played for time. Harrison and a team of officers couldn't be all that far away, surely. But would they find him in time? Would they find him at all? The place was a rabbit warren. He'd have to leave some kind of trail, but how?

'Bale?' The sergeant stopped. 'Why would he be here?'

'Oh, come on, Sergeant. It's obvious, isn't it? He wants in on your little secret society. The Fraternitas de Rosae Fontis? Christ knows he's been dropping hints about it for long enough. Partake of the hallowed flesh and sanctified blood and all his sins will be wiped clean? Then he can go back to doing God's work like he's always wanted to.'

'It doesn't work . . . You don't . . .' Donaldson stopped walking. McLean felt the grip on his arm loosen and he pulled away. He made it two paces before the sergeant caught a hold of him again, a heavy hand grabbing the fabric of his jacket, a second one snatching at the cuffs, missing. McLean tried to time it, although it had to look unintended. Swivelling as best he could, he shoved at the sergeant, one foot in to trip him over. They struggled briefly, and then both of them went over the edge into the pool.

Hands tied behind his back, McLean fought to keep his head above water. It didn't help that Donaldson was bigger than him and on top. Fortunately the pool wasn't deep, and he'd tried to make it so that he was close to the steps anyway. Spluttering he hauled himself up and out as the sergeant came up behind and smacked him hard in the side of the head.

'The fuck was that for?' Donaldson shouted through the roaring sound in McLean's ears. Then Sandy Bayne was standing directly in front of the two of them, his face grim.

'Enough. We're late already. Bring him.'

'But he's not one of us,' the sergeant complained. 'And I'm soaked through.'

'He's here. He was called. Bring him.' Bayne turned his back and set off up the path. McLean allowed himself to be pushed forward, then fell into step a couple of paces behind. He hoped to hell that Harrison arrived soon, and that she had her wits about her. Even with clouds finally gathering, the trail of water the two of them left behind them wouldn't last long.

66

It didn't surprise him when he was half led, half pushed through the farmyard and back out along the route he'd come in by. Through the ruined cloisters, the path snaked around fallen masonry until it arrived at the middle of the three barrows, and there a dark hole opened in the ground. The arch of its entrance was far more ancient than anything built by monks, and the stone steps leading into the depths were worn with the passage of millennia. That sweet, cloying scent of decay wafted up from the earth like a desecrated grave. McLean shivered as much from the look and feel of the place as from his sodden clothing, although he did his best to pause long enough for a half-decent puddle to form on a bare slab of paving before allowing Donaldson to prod him forward. Resisting meant that the soaked police sergeant added his own damp to the mark too, even if it resulted in another painful blow to the ear.

The stench disappeared the moment they crossed the threshold, and along with it the nagging dread that had urged McLean to keep away. They descended deep into the earth before he saw the first light, a flaming torch shoved into an iron sconce set in the hewn rock of a tunnel. Their route took them ever downwards, and back in the direction of the old farmyard, the farmhouse and the pool beyond. As if the thought of it were a cue, McLean began to hear the sound of running water again. And soon enough, the source of it became clear.

It reminded him in many ways of the man-made caves at Gilmerton Cove; an unhappy memory of the case that had first brought Norman Bale back into his life. The cavern he stepped into was far bigger than that whole complex, hidden beneath those suburban streets. Rough-hewn stone walls climbed up in an almost perfect dome to a point far over his head in the middle. Not that he could have stood in the middle, as that was where the water bubbled up from the ground in a constantly flowing spring. It filled a circular pool, raised up from the gritty stone floor like a font the size of a jacuzzi, then overflowed at one point to gurgle away down a drain. If it was red, McLean couldn't tell. Everything was painted in shades of orange and yellow by the flickering torchlight reflecting off the sandstone. The smoke must have been escaping through a hole somewhere in the ceiling, as there was no smell of it in the cave. Instead a kind of sweet odour pervaded; not the reek of death and decay from outside, but something equally unsettling.

'Bring him.' Bayne moved forward and the people parted like the Red Sea before him. All adults, as far as McLean could see. There were men and women in the crowd, so it was an equal-opportunities cult at least. They were dressed in street clothes, not particularly tidy, not Sunday best, and certainly not robes or something similarly wacky. He recognised again the faces from Ritchie's surveillance files, and a couple of others whose names didn't immediately spring to mind but would once he managed to get hold of current photographs of all the city's great and good. Some stared back at him, faces questioning as he was led through the crowd. Others wisely ducked and turned away.

'What is this?' a voice demanded, but Bayne cut it short with a glare. Clearly he was in charge. The high priest for this unusual gathering.

'The spring purifies, and the spring calls. We have all heard its summons. It has brought us our salvation, as it always has done, since people first walked this land.' Bayne passed through the crowd as he spoke, and McLean could only follow, pushed as he was by Sergeant Donaldson.

They emerged into a clear space in front of the pool, its surface gently distorted by water rising from deep below. That wasn't what grabbed McLean's attention and held it though. That would have been the low stone altar on the far side, a single slab left behind when the rest of the cavern had been carved out of the rock. The light from the torches dotted around the room made it a focal point, casting everything else into writhing, sinister shadow. He hesitated, quite sure he wanted nothing to do with this place. Where the hell was Harrison?

'Kneel, sinner.' Sergeant Donaldson's voice sounded different in the cavern, cruel and on edge. Something heavy slammed into the back of his legs and McLean fell to the floor. Unable to steady himself, his knees cracked on the hard stone and he slumped sideways to avoid smashing his head against the altar, a bright flash of pain as his shoulder took the brunt instead. Dazed and winded, he stared up at the stone ceiling high overhead, until his vision cleared. Then closer in, at the faces of the sergeant and Sandy Bayne as they peered down at him like giants.

'Calm yourself, brother.' The old man put a hand on Donaldson's arm. 'This one is no threat to us. Quite the opposite. He seeks the same blessing as we all do.'

'I know his type. He's beyond redemption.' Donaldson turned away, as if he might spit on the floor to rid himself of a bad taste. 'He wants to deny us what is rightfully ours. We've waited years.'

'You know as well as I do that it is the spring which calls, Andrew. And when it does, those who answer are welcome. Those who are not welcome cannot enter. This one has been lost a long while, it's true. But that only means that his need for

410

salvation is greater than ours. He will join us willingly. You'll see.'

'At least let me restrain him.' Donaldson sneered at McLean as if he was some wet behind the ears constable. Bayne considered the request for a second or two, then nodded his assent. Before McLean could do anything, the burly police sergeant grabbed him by the arm, dragged him away from the altar towards the back wall of the cavern. Hidden in the shadows, a heavy iron ring had been set into the stone, a length of chain dangling from it. In a swift move, Donaldson smacked McLean across the head, and while he was still reeling, bent to the cuffs holding his hands together. There was the briefest moment when he might have been free, but before he could react, his arms had been wrenched around in front of him, and the cuffs replaced, this time looped through the last link in the chain. Finally, the sergeant shoved McLean hard in the chest. He fell to the floor again, winded, his vision darkening in pain as he banged his shoulder again.

'Stay there.'

Chained to the wall and his head still ringing with the blow, McLean could only comply. He dragged himself into a slightly less uncomfortable position, back to the cavern wall, and stared past the edge of the altar towards the gathered people. Donaldson took up position beside Bayne, both with their backs to him. The older man opened his arms in welcome to the congregation, his voice commanding.

'Brothers, sisters. Are there any besides the inspector who are newly called?'

A shuffling of feet, and then a man stepped forward, hands on the shoulders of a teenage boy, steering him past the font and into the space between it and the altar. Judging by the shape of their faces, they were father and son, and McLean recognised the man from Ritchie's surveillance files. Gordon McTavish, the Penicuik lad who'd moved to Silicon Valley and made several fortunes. Rich, powerful, he had the ear of many a head of state. And, it would appear, a taste for human flesh. He stopped a few paces from Bayne, then bowed his head. After a moment, the boy did the same, but not before McLean saw the fear in his eyes, the tremble in his lips.

'My son. Alexander,' McTavish said. 'He turned sixteen a week ago.'

Bayne lowered his hands, held them out for the boy to take. 'Welcome, Alexander. We share a name, you and I. Today we will share much more besides.'

Something clicked in McLean's head as he listened. Sandy Bayne. Alexander Bayne. Alexander Bean. Sawney to those who wrote about him. A family line and a grisly tradition then. And maybe there was something to Norman Bale's obsession after all. He managed to choke back the bark of mirthless laughter that rose up in his throat. There was nothing remotely funny about any of this.

'You shall bear witness, Alexander.' Bayne embraced the boy, kissed him once on each cheek, then led him to the altar. McLean shifted his weight, meaning to get to his feet, but Donaldson stepped forward and kicked him in the ribs hard enough to drive all the breath out of him. Followed it up with a second blow to the head which had him sprawling on the ground.

'Stay down. Your turn will come.'

McLean rolled over, felt blood in his mouth and spat it out onto the floor. By the time he'd gathered himself enough to shuffle onto his knees and look up, Bayne had produced a knife he must have stolen from the film set for a Hammer horror movie. Long, pointed and obviously very sharp, it gleamed strangely white in the reflected torchlight, sparkles running down its cutting edges as he turned it gently around and presented the handle to the boy.

'Take it, Alexander. This blade is blessed by God. Passed

down the generations since the time of the Druids.'

The boy hesitated, but Bayne took his hand, pressed the handle into it and folded his fingers closed. From his position on the floor, all McLean could see was the startled, frightened expression on young Alexander's face. Then Bayne turned him around so that they both faced the congregation. All eyes were on the old man as he lifted his hands towards the ceiling and began to chant words that had no obvious meaning. It reminded McLean of those few unfortunate times he'd been forced to attend Catholic mass, the Latin no more than gibberish even if the sing-song voice and rhythm of the intonation might have had meaning for some.

It went on for as interminably long as those dull canticles, but a heartbeat after Bayne fell silent, a tremor ran through the floor, a great cracking noise, and the door at the far end of the cavern inched open. For a moment McLean thought it was the cavalry finally arrived to save the day, but it wasn't Harrison and an armed-response team who entered.

She was mostly obscured by the congregation, slowly parting to let her through. Even so, McLean knew who it was without a doubt. At first he thought she was alone, and he couldn't understand why she didn't turn and flee. Then he noticed the short figure behind her, one hand firmly gripped around an elbow. Morag Bayne gently piloted Anya Renfrew through the crowd, past the spring and up to the altar. The closer she came, the more McLean could see of her, and the deeper his shock.

They had shaved her head, even her eyebrows gone. Tiny cuts and abrasions dotted her scalp, her face, her shoulders. She stood naked, but it was her eyes that drew his focus. Black holes, they stared at nothing, lifeless. She must have been drugged to be so compliant, but she might simply have been too weak to fight. McLean's memory of her was of a thin woman, but not so thin as you might comment on it. Now her cheeks were sunken hollows, her arms like flesh-bound sticks. Her collarbones strained through her skin as if she'd been in a concentration camp for years, not locked up in a cell for almost a fortnight.

'Welcome, blessed one. Vessel of our Lord.' Bayne's voice boomed out in the cavern, and the congregation took up the chant like good cult members.

'Vessel of our Lord. Vessel of our Lord.'

The sound was almost hypnotic, drilling deep into his head. McLean struggled to keep his mouth shut, not to join in as the voices rose in unison. The shape of the cavern echoed the noise, reflecting and building, louder and louder until it was painful, the words themselves lost in a jumbled roar. He tensed against the chain, focused on the pain in his shoulder. Leaning it hard against the wall brought a sharp stab to his senses and he clung to that like driftwood in a storm.

'Vessel of our Lord. Vessel of our Lord.'

The congregation were more of a mob now, chanting as one, caught up in the ritual. Only McLean held on, and Renfrew. She stood motionless, oblivious to the cacophony, staring at nothing. Almost as if she was waiting for something to happen.

It began as more of the noise, a low rumble that might have been made by a combination of human voice and cavern acoustics, except that McLean felt it rise up from the floor and into his bones. The ground shook beneath him, a long, low rumble that grew in intensity until it was louder than the chanting. For a moment he feared that the roof would cave in and bury them all, but with a clap that left him deafened it ended. The crowd fell silent, and in that same instant Renfrew's eyes swivelled upwards. She began to crumple like a puppet whose strings have been cut, but before she could hit the ground or even smack her head on the altar, Bayne caught her up as if she weighed nothing.

414

'Vessel of our Lord,' he said, so quiet that McLean could barely make it out over the ringing in his ears. He watched as the old man carried Renfrew across to the font, partially obscured by the altar. Without another word, he bent down and gently lowered the unconscious woman into the water.

67

'The grace of God be with us. Come forward, my brothers and sisters. Be witness as this empty vessel becomes the body and blood of Christ.'

McLean struggled to his feet, the better to see what was going on. Across the altar he could make out the stone font, and Renfrew floating on the surface of the water, held by the current that bubbled up from deep in the earth. Bayne had his back turned, and beckoned the congregation forward. One by one they came. Each bowed their head, and the old man dipped his hand in the font before touching wet fingers to their brow. Thus blessed, they took it in turns to push Renfrew's unresisting body beneath the surface, some no deeper than their hand, but others rolling up a sleeve and immersing an entire arm. A few pushed her down with both, and it was as one emerged, dripping, that McLean finally noticed the red glow that suffused the water.

Once he'd seen it, he couldn't understand how he'd missed it before. The only reason he could make out any detail of what the crazy people were doing was because of the light that played over their faces and arms. It painted the ceiling high overhead, a whirling mess of shadows and shapes formed by the bubbling water and Renfrew's body. Looking back, McLean could see marks on the foreheads of the people Bayne had touched, etched a darker red in their flesh as if the water burned like acid. Arms dipped in the water had that hue too, and the congregation moved differently. Those yet to be blessed shuffled and shifted, nervousness or excitement in the way they held themselves. After contact with the spring, they were more like Renfrew, compliant and placid.

Sergeant Donaldson lumbered up to the font, bending low so that Bayne could splash water on him. It came as no surprise to McLean when the big man pulled off his shirt, splayed both hands wide and pressed Renfrew's motionless form deep. He held her far longer than the others, and when he released her there was a red gleam in his eyes far deeper set than the reflected glow from the spring, as if an oily fire burned in his soul. In contrast, Morag Bayne approached with ill-disguised reluctance. She accepted her husband's benediction, but only laid a hand lightly across Renfrew's chest, and then for less than a heartbeat.

McLean searched the crowd for the boy, Alexander, saw him at the back of the group who had already undergone their strange initiation, clutching the knife in a nervous hand. It was clear he'd not been anywhere near the font, so maybe there was some hope for him after all. Bayne seemed too caught up in his job as high priest to notice, and everyone else had that drugged look about them. He had to hope that they'd forgotten about him too. If there was something in the water making all these people act like sheep, he wanted nothing to do with it.

The whisper in his ear almost made him scream. Only the pudgy fingers clamped across his mouth stopped him.

'Say nothing. Not yet.'

The hand over his mouth slid away, and he was able to look around to see his unlikely saviour. Not that he needed to. He'd recognised the hissed whisper of a voice, so wasn't at all surprised when Norman Bale slumped down beside him.

'Do you think it will work? I think it will work.'

Bale's eyes were wide with an excitement that bordered on intoxication, but it wasn't madness. More the wild enthusiasm McLean remembered from their childhood friendship. Hair thinned almost to nothing, face chubbed up with too much institutional food and not enough exercise, Bale even looked more like the six-year-old boy he remembered. The six-year-old boy who had fallen out of a tree they had both been climbing. The six-year-old boy whose cut knee never seemed to stop bleeding. Leukaemia, they'd called it. A word that had scared McLean all his childhood. A disease that couldn't be cured.

'You died,' he said.

'True. Can't say I recommend it.' Bale tilted his head as if to concede the fact.

'What are you doing here?'

'Keep up, Tony. This is my salvation. You know the legend. The spring turns red and any who bathe in it become one with the Lord. No, it's more than that. They become the Lord. I fell so low, but you showed me I'd strayed. And this is how I get back onto the true path. I owe you a great debt.'

Bale laid a hand briefly on McLean's shoulder, then ducked away into the shadows. In moments he was gone, more competently camouflaged than any jungle predator. McLean tried to follow his progress, but he was distracted by the sight of the congregation still clustered around the font. The red glow seemed brighter now, although that might have been down to his having looked away. Renfrew's body floated, face up, glistening and wet. All eyes were on her naked flesh. Hungry eyes.

'God has blessed us all this day.' Bayne's deep voice echoed in the sudden silence. As he spoke, so he stepped forward and lowered his hands into the water, up to the elbows as he bent to lift Renfrew out. She flopped like a rag doll, head tilted back, eyes still closed. No sign of life in her, but as Bayne turned, McLean saw that her skin had been stained red by the water, like all the others. The old man's arms were tinted too, although not to the same extent as Renfrew. As he carried the inert body back to the altar, the congregation followed, shuffling like some B-movie zombie horde. The old man lifted Renfrew high as if in offering to some unseen god, then laid her gently down on the cold stone.

'Christ is in her. Christ *is* her.' He laid a hand over Renfrew's sternum, closed his eyes and murmured something incomprehensible. McLean thought he might have caught snatches of that same cod Latin he had heard before, but it might have been nonsense for all he cared.

'Come, Alexander. It is time.' With his free hand, Bayne waved the young boy forward. He came, reluctantly, as if something beyond his control was moving his legs, lifting his hand that gripped the knife so tight McLean could see the whiteness of his knuckles. Unlike the others, he held his head up, eyes darting from side to side, struggling against some invisible bond as he came closer and closer to the woman lying on the altar. The bare skin of his hands was pale, and no mark scarred his forehead like the others.

'When the spring runs red with the blood of the earth, then is the Lord with us. Then is He inside us. Then must we eat of his flesh and drink of his blood, so that he might cleanse us of all our sins.' Bayne reached out, gently took the boy by the elbow and steered him close. The gathered congregation still held their heads low, but their chanting began to rise again, words like those the old man had mouthed, meaningless and yet painful to hear.

'The wisdom of the divine be with you, Alexander.' Bayne lifted the boy's hand up high, that blade of bone jutting from it in lethal fashion. If she wasn't already drowned, Renfrew would soon be bled.

'You don't want to do this, Alexander.' McLean heaved at the chains around his wrist, pulled at the ring set into the wall. One last desperate attempt to free himself, to do something rather than witness this needless murder. There was no way they were going to let him go after they were done with Renfrew, but he'd take a few of them with him if he could.

'Do not give in to temptation, my son.' Bayne wrapped his free hand around the boy's, and McLean could see the tension build in his muscles as he readied himself to guide the knife down to its target. Alexander's eyes widened in shock and fear. He struggled against that pull, not yet ready to commit to the same madness that gripped everyone else here.

Then with a crack like thunder, the iron loop came out of the wall. At the same moment, McLean saw movement in the shadows, a running figure. The stupefied congregation barely reacted, but Bayne turned, as did Donaldson, anger burning like hellfire in their eyes.

'Christ is not in her. He is in me. I am the one who will be sanctified this day.'

Norman Bale stood on the stone edge, naked as the day he was born. Even at this distance McLean saw the old madness in his face once more. No longer the boy who had been his friend, but the impostor, the man who had killed so many and blamed it all on his faith. The light from the font grew stronger, the red turning a paler pink as the water began to roil and foam. Those of the celebrants closest began to shake off their stupor, move towards him. But they were too slow, too late.

With a smile and a wave, Bale stepped off the edge and into the spring.

68

He might have expected a splash. Perhaps something more apocalyptic. As it was, Bale disappeared into the font with barely an extra ripple on the surface. If anything, McLean imagined the water climbed up him in a manner water had no right to do. Almost as if a million tiny hands reached out and grabbed the intruder, dragging him down into the depths.

In moments Bale had disappeared completely. The water continued to bubble and roil. Even the light shining from it barely changed, as if whatever was causing it was no single point that might cast shadow. McLean counted long seconds, waiting for the man to resurface. Everyone else in the chamber was the same, frozen in place, expectant.

But nothing happened.

Bayne reacted first. He had dropped his grip on the boy with the knife, pulled his other hand away from Renfrew as he turned to see what was happening. The stunned silence changed to murmurs, and then cries of alarm. The collective stupor that had spread over the congregation was dissipating fast. Then the old man shouted at Sergeant Donaldson.

'Get him out of there. Now.' He didn't wait to see if his order was carried out, instead turned back to the altar. This time he grabbed the boy's hand more roughly, but the magic was swiftly dissipating, the moment lost. Alexander fought him for control of the knife, until Bayne cuffed the boy across the face. With a high-pitched yelp of pain, Alexander fell to the floor, relinquishing his grip. The old man caught the knife, spun it in his hand like a professional, and raised it high again. He mouthed a silent prayer, placed his other hand back on Renfrew's breast, thumb and index finger spread to mark the position of her heart.

McLean was already swinging the heavy chain around as Bayne brought the knife swiftly down. Iron met bone, and the blade shattered. A sound far louder than any explosion reverberated through the chamber, shook the ground under their feet, rattled the nearby hills and distant mountains. Cracks ran through the stone walls and ceiling, meeting at the high point above the font. Dust and small rocks fell to the ground.

'What have you done?' Bayne stared at the remains of the knife in his hand. A solid handle fashioned from old wood and leather, and poking from it like a bad fracture, the ragged stub of bone that was all that remained of the blade. Then the old man lifted it high again, his other hand moving up towards Renfrew's neck, sizing it up for a slicing cut.

This time McLean's chain and ring hit him square in the face. His head snapped around, blood spraying from mouth and nose, along with something that might have been teeth or might have been dentures. Bayne toppled sideways, falling to the floor with a noise like breaking sticks.

McLean paused, panting at the exertion, then looked up to see the congregation staring at him. They all faced him from the other side of the altar, and they all had a mad, angry gleam in their eyes that didn't bode well for either him or Renfrew. The boy, Alexander, lay on his back on the ground where he had fallen. His face was a picture of fear and confusion. Everyone else looked murderous.

'You're all under arrest. Conspiracy to murder.'

Even to his own ears, it sounded weak. He might as well have shouted at a herd of cattle. They moved in slowly at first, hesitant, eyes on his swinging chain. But then someone who might have been a senior civil servant he had once met at a police liaison committee meeting lunged forward with an animal snarl on his lips. McLean hefted the chain and its ring, swung it round and caught the man in the side. He grunted, doubled over as the weight knocked the wind out of him, but the others were already spreading out. They circled around the altar and towards him; no way he could fend them all off, and he didn't like the manner in which some of them were eyeing up Renfrew either. She had to be dead, he was sure, but they looked like they might rip her apart anyway.

A young woman leaped at him from the side, and he was forced to duck back to avoid her outstretched, claw-like fingers. As if that had given them permission, the rest of them fell upon the body lying on the altar like vultures. Something collided with the side of his head, a glancing blow that darkened his vision even as his reflexes kicked in. McLean dropped low, lashed out with his still-bound hands. There were bodies everywhere, too many for an effective attack, and half of them focused solely on the woman laid out on the altar. Roaring in defiance, he sprang up, speed his best weapon in the confined space. He pushed hard at the chest of a woman with mad eyes and unkempt hair, hardly waiting to see her fall backwards and take out three other people before he swung around and swept the heavy chain into a group coming at him from the other direction. It snagged around an outstretched arm, snapped bone. As someone screamed more in frustrated rage than pain, McLean saw the young boy, Alexander, back on his feet and desperately trying to pull his father away as he clawed at Renfrew's body. At least someone still had their wits about them.

He pulled at the chain, and another scream erupted from the

man around whose broken arm it was wrapped. McLean stepped forward, smashed his forehead down, felt the man's nose explode. No point in trying to fight fair, he tugged the chain free as the man went down, then let out a quiet 'Fuck' as he saw who had stepped in to take his place.

Police Sergeant Andrew Donaldson was a big man, fully six foot four and with the heavy build of an active lifestyle despite his advancing years. Any thought McLean might have had of appealing to his professionalism disappeared as he saw the sergeant's face. The spring water had painted it a rosacea red, matting his grey hair to his skull like bloody bandages. He bared his teeth like a wolf. A low animal growl rumbled up from his throat as he advanced.

McLean took one step back, foot wobbling on something uneven. He tensed his arms, felt the weight of the chain that was both his only weapon and his biggest restriction. Hands tied together, he could only swing it, and that took time to get momentum. Donaldson's eyes might have been wide and mad, but he was still smart enough to know it too. He crouched low, ready to close in. Another step back, and this time McLean's foot slipped, forcing him down onto one knee. Off balance, there was nothing he could do as Donaldson pounced except fall backwards, put his hands up to try and stop the killing blow.

The cavern echoed with the grunts and screams of a mob turned animal. McLean lashed out with a foot, but the sergeant dodged the blow, pinned him down. Large hands reached in and grabbed him round the throat, choking the breath from him as he struggled to free himself. Too heavy, too strong, Donaldson had the upper hand. Even as McLean tried to smash his clenched fists into the sergeant's side, he could feel the weakness in his arms, see the light grow dim as his brain was starved of oxygen. He was going to die here, in this hellhole cavern hidden underneath the Moorfoot hills. He'd never see Emma again.

Never have the chance to apologise for being so useless.

'I'm so sorry,' he tried to say, even though he had no breath left.

Then something erupted on the other side of the altar and the world lit up in painful, brilliant light.

Shielded by the rock, McLean was spared the brunt of the explosion. Donaldson wasn't so lucky. One moment he was there, squeezing the life out of McLean's neck. The next he was tugged away by some unseen hand, picked up and thrown against the wall a few metres away. If his neck went crack as it twisted too far, McLean didn't hear it. The blast was so loud it had turned almost instantly to muffled silence, and the sergeant slumped to the ground without so much as a word, clearly dead.

Others nearby weren't so lucky. Rocks thrown by the explosion had smashed heads, broken arms, punched holes in bodies. McLean struggled to his feet, the dust-filled air choking him even as he desperately needed to gasp it down. It was only as he leaned his still-cuffed hands on the altar for support that he realised Renfrew was missing. She lay at his feet, rolled off the altar either by the throng or by the explosion. Her body was twisted almost as badly as Sergeant Donaldson, but as he watched, she spasmed, retched, began to spew out what seemed like gallons of dark red liquid. Not blood, but the water from the spring.

The silence morphed into a high-pitched whine, his ears beginning to recover. McLean bent down, doing what he could to gently ease Renfrew into a better position. How she was alive, he couldn't begin to understand. Unconscious in the water she should surely have drowned. And yet she flinched at his touch, if only weakly. Her skin was still stained red, darker bruises and scrapes beginning to form where she had been attacked by the mob.

'Shallow breaths. Take your time.' He barely heard the words, doubted she did either. Fuzzy, indistinct noises that might have been shouts began to fill the cavern. He risked a peek over the altar, and saw through the settling dust to the entrance across the other side.

Only there was no entrance.

Where there had been a neatly carved arch, fitted with stout iron-banded oak doors, now there was a gaping, irregular hole. Rocks piled around the floor like broken teeth punched from a drunk man's face. Cracks zigzagged through the arch of the ceiling, wide enough to shove a fist in. Half of the flaming torches had gone out, along with the strange glow from the font. As he shook his head to try and get rid of the water in his ears, McLean saw pinpricks of brighter light spear through the dust from the tunnel beyond the entrance. In moments they resolved themselves into the beams from torches strapped to the side of semi-automatic weapons, carried by a fully tooled-up armed-response unit. He let out an inaudible sigh of relief. DC Harrison might have gone a bit over the top with the backup, but it looked like the cavalry had arrived just in the nick of time.

69

'Hold still a moment, sir. There. That should do it.'

McLean leaned over the stone altar, arms out as if he were in prayer while an ARU officer freed him from his chains. He hadn't appreciated quite how much they weighed until they dropped to the floor with a clang even he could hear, albeit as if underwater. His arms rose upwards of their own accord, in supplication to whatever bizarre version of God the people now being taken away for questioning had worshipped.

'Thank you. That's much better.' He rubbed at the chafe marks around his wrists, then winced in pain as the pins and needles set in.

'Might want to get that seen by someone, sir,' the ARU officer said, then wandered off to the far side of the cavern. Despite the ominous cracks, the ceiling hadn't shifted at all. The dust had settled, matting everything but the bubbling surface of the spring as it filled the stone font.

'We should get you out of here, sir.' DC Harrison stood close by, her nervousness all too apparent. McLean agreed with her, but there were a couple of things he needed to do first. Still rubbing at his wrists, he walked over to where Sergeant Donaldson lay, head at an impossible angle. He pressed a finger to the sergeant's neck to be sure, but he was certainly dead.

427

'I thought he was one of the good ones, which just goes to show.' He stepped carefully around the rubble strewn across the floor until he reached the prone form of Sandy Bayne. Unlike Donaldson, he lay on his front in a pose that was almost natural. To the casual observer he might merely have been unconscious. The pasty texture of his skin said otherwise; that and the lack of any discernible breathing. He had no pulse and was cold to the touch already.

'Give me a hand here, will you?' McLean gestured for Harrison to help, and together they rolled Bayne onto his side. He had trapped his arm underneath him as he had fallen, the ceremonial knife with its shattered nub of bone blade pierced his breast, exactly where his heart should have been. Poetic justice? Maybe. It would save the cost of a trial, at least.

They lowered his body back down gently as, nearby, a pair of paramedics attended to Anya Renfrew, making sure she was stable before they took her away. Face covered by an oxygen mask, and a saline drip already in her arm, they had covered her nakedness with a blanket. Her head flopped over to the side and she looked straight at McLean, but there was no recognition in those eyes, and neither was there any sense of fear or alarm. It could have been whatever they had given her to help with the pain of course.

'What . . .' Harrison paused as if unsure how to voice her question. 'What exactly happened here, sir?'

McLean stood up slowly. His hearing was still recovering from the blast, and he knew that technically he should be handing the crime scene over to someone else to process. He was too close, too involved, and possibly too concussed to be of any use.

'He might've been able to tell us.' He waved a hand at Bayne's prone figure. Then he turned slowly and pointed at Donaldson. 'I reckon he was second in command. So I guess we'll have to piece it all together from the statements we get from everyone else. But basically they were going to sacrifice Renfrew, drink her blood and eat her flesh. Apparently that makes them pure or something.' He didn't add that they'd been doing it for centuries, possibly millennia, generation upon generation of the Bayne family. Formerly Bean, which derived from the Latin, *bene*. The root of benevolent, good, blessed, sacred. He'd have laughed then, if there wasn't the horrible chance that once he started he'd not be able to stop.

'I saw her skin,' Harrison said. 'Their hands are the same. Is that blood? Paint?'

McLean looked over to the font, the spring water now running clear. If what Bayne had said was true, then the time for the ceremony had passed. Would it ever run red again?

'Bale.' He was striding towards the font before the word was even out. How could he have forgotten?

'Bale?' Harrison echoed him, catching up as he reached the stone lip. In the poorly lit cavern, the depths were black, impossible to make out anything in there. No more the strange glowing light from the depths.

'He was here,' McLean said, even though the whole episode had the feel of a dream about it. Everyone else in the cavern had been acting as if they'd been on a bad acid trip, so maybe some of it had rubbed off on him too. 'He went in there. I didn't see him come back out.'

If Harrison thought him mad, she kept it to herself. She called one of the ARU officers over and had him point his torch into the water. The stone sides disappeared down further than the beam could penetrate, but something floated in the centre, only a few feet below the surface. Something large that spun slowly as the current eddied around it.

'Fetch a rope or something, can you?' McLean asked. The words were hardly out of his mouth before the object began to shift from its slow circle. Inch by inch it rose towards them, but he knew well before it broached the surface what it was. Who it was. The ARU officer packed away his torch and reached in to haul the body out. No miraculous recovery, no spluttering up of mysterious red liquid. Norman Bale's skin had that puckered look of having spent too long in the bath, and unlike Renfrew, he was pasty white. No miracle of transubstantiation for him. No redemption from his god.

They laid him out on the dusty, rubble-strewn ground, and the ARU officer felt for a pulse. He left his fingers at the wet neck for long moments before finally pulling them away, prised open one eyelid and shone a torchlight into the pupil.

A shake of the head.

Norman Bale was truly dead.

It took McLean a while to pick a route out of the cavern through the fallen stone and remains of the door. He stared for a while at the heavy boulders before realising he was looking at a body crushed by the fall. Morag Bayne had gone the same way as her husband, it would seem. She must have been dead, or a paramedic would have been trying to revive her. Had she been fleeing the mob? He recalled her reluctance to join in with the ceremony, the way she no more than touched Renfrew's body where others had pushed the sacrifice deep under the water. It was a puzzle they would never solve now.

A couple of soldiers stood to one side of the ragged entrance, staring at the mess and arguing among themselves about something.

'Maybe went a bit heavy on the explosives, lads,' McLean said to them in passing. 'Not that I'm complaining, you understand.'

'You were in there when it happened?' The soldier who asked the question looked at him with a quizzical eye, then past him to see if there were any arresting officers about.

McLean stuck his hand in his pocket and pulled out his

warrant card. It was damp, like everything else about him, but he showed it to them anyway. Both soldiers still looked at him as if he might attack them at any moment, so he added: 'I'm one of the good guys. Glad you arrived when you did, even if the explosion was a bit . . .' He shrugged.

'That's the thing, sir. We only used enough to shatter the lock. It's almost as if the door was already rigged to explode if it was interfered with. Like a booby trap. Only we can't see how they could have done it. There's no residue, no wires.'

McLean shrugged again. Yes, it was a mystery, but it was someone else's mystery. He had no energy or enthusiasm for such questions. He left them to their quiet argument and carried on up the wide tunnel.

When he emerged at the top of the steps, he was surprised to find it was still full daylight. Somehow it felt as if much more time should have passed than that. There was something else strange about the scrubby ground around the barrows too. Apart from the milling groups of police officers and yet more soldiers. He took a deep breath of pine-scented air, and that was when he realised what it was. The foul death stench that had permeated the place before had vanished. He no longer felt the urge to flee deep in his core. Of course, that might just have been the bone weariness that blotted out everything else.

'Tony?' The familiar voice had him turning to see Detective Chief Superintendent Jayne McIntyre. Her eyes widened as she saw his face, so he reckoned he must have looked quite a state. Standing beside her, leaning on an elegant cane, Grace Ramsay merely raised an eyebrow and tutted.

'I'd heard you weren't much of a one for following protocol,' she said, just loud enough for him to hear. The ringing in his ears from the explosion had only begun to dissipate, although at least outside the echoes no longer hurt his brain.

'What are you –?'

'Grace was filling me in on the details of her investigations when word came through about what you were up to. It was her who suggested calling in the soldiers from Penicuik, seeing as they were closest.'

'Helps that their commander's an old friend too.' Ramsay hobbled up to him as she spoke, her final question a hopeful whisper he could hardly hear above the whining in his ears. 'Anya?'

McLean looked back at the entrance to the underground complex as the first of the paramedics emerged, stretcher between him and his colleague. Before he could say anything, Ramsay had moved across to them with a speed that belied her age and fragility. He kept well back, scarcely able to hear the conversation over the whining in his ears, not sure he wanted to be involved in it anyway. After the shortest of debates, the paramedics continued along the path towards the farmyard, where presumably an ambulance awaited. They moved more slowly, so that the retired detective superintendent could keep pace, one hand clasped around her daughter's.

'I should tear a strip off you for going in there on your own, Tony, but it's hard to do that seeing as, well . . .'

'Not much point in shouting at me right now, Jayne.' McLean pointed at one ear. 'Can't hear a thing.'

The worried smile that brought to her face gave him hope the inevitable enquiry and case review wouldn't be too bad.

'What about Bale?' she asked.

'Dead. Stupid bugger drowned himself.'

McIntyre's raised eyebrow demanded more detail, so McLean told her the whole story as best he could, interrupted by the steady stream of officers, wounded and dead either walking or being carried from the underground chambers.

'What the hell was he thinking?' McIntyre asked as the last bodybag, holding Bale's corpse, was carried away to the mortuary and an appointment with Angus Cadwallader. McLean paused a while before answering. The clear skies of the past few weeks had given way to clouds, scudding in off the sea on a breeze that chilled him to the core. He wanted nothing more than to go home, have a hot shower, and climb outside a stiff measure or two of fine single-malt whisky. Reports and justifications could come later. Except that McIntyre was here, now and on his side.

'Don't ask me how he knew about all this.' He waved his hand towards the opening into the barrow. 'Same as I've no idea how he walked out of a maximum-security psychiatric unit as if it was nothing more than a hotel room. Bale is . . . was . . . not normal. But he believed strongly in his god. You'll recall that from our first encounter with him. He was trying to send the pure to heaven before they could become corrupted again. And, yes, I know that's bonkers, Jayne, but that's why he was in Bestingfield. The point is he believed it, and he believed he'd fallen from grace. Us catching him was God's way of telling him that. All those years of good behaviour? That was him looking for a way to get back into God's good books. And he found it. Right here with this bunch of equally mad bastards.'

'So this lot . . . ?' McIntyre's frown was directed at the barrow, but McLean knew what she was referring to.

'The Fraternitas de Rosae Fontis. Brotherhood of the Red Spring, Rose Well, whatever. Christ, where to begin?' He tried to recall the details of the ceremony, but it was all a bit of a blur. 'They thought that whatever they did to Renfrew down there infused her with the holy spirit. She became the body and blood of the Lord. They were going to kill her and eat her, much the same as their sick little secret society's been doing for generations. Religion, eh?' He shook his head wearily. 'Always said it was overrated.'

McIntyre said nothing for a while, then she looked slightly to

McLean's side. He followed her gaze to find that DC Harrison had sidled up to him unheard. She wore an expression of worried concern he had become used to lately.

'Janie, can you see that the detective chief inspector gets home in one piece?' McIntyre asked.

'Yes, ma'am.' Harrison almost curtsied, settling instead for a nod of the head. McLean felt like a schoolboy being dismissed by the headteacher, but at that moment he was too tired to care.

For some reason, it didn't surprise McLean to find the sleek Jaguar parked outside his house when they pulled into the usual space alongside Emma's rusty blue Peugeot. DC Harrison was driving, a small treat for her perhaps, but he was also beginning to feel the strain of the afternoon and didn't trust himself not to fall asleep at the wheel.

'I-Pace? Nice.' Harrison handed him the key before climbing out of the car. 'About time Em had something decent to drive.'

'It's not hers,' McLean grumbled. 'Stealing our bloody electricity, mind. You want to come in?' He nodded his head towards the back door.

'Think I'll head home, sir. Been a long day, and I reckon tomorrow'll be longer.'

'You want to take the car?' He held up the key, saw a glimmer of something pass across Harrison's face before she shook her head.

'Thanks, but there's nowhere to park outside mine, and I'd hate to scratch her.' She looked back down the drive towards the gate, hidden behind thick rhododendron bushes. 'Besides, I had a squad car follow us. They'll be waiting to pick me up.'

McLean was quietly relieved. He'd meant it when he'd offered the loan of his car, but he'd have worried all the same. 'You did good work today, Janie. Thank you.'

Harrison said nothing, maybe blushed a little at the praise, then turned and walked away. McLean leaned against the roof of his Alfa and watched her go, not quite sure whether he was ready to face Emma's inevitable wrath at his recklessness. There was no way she didn't know what had happened if Professor Turner was here already.

'Good detectives are hard to find. You should keep an eye on that one.'

He turned a little too swiftly, felt a jab of pain shoot up his hip. At least it dulled all the myriad other pains. It took a moment to recognise the figure who emerged from the shadows, a little longer to put the right name to the face.

'Mr Fenwick. Why am I not surprised to see you here?'

'Brad, please.'

'Brad. OK. You want to come in? Only I'm overdue a meeting with a bottle of beer.'

'So I hear. And no, thanks. I'll not keep you long. Just wanted to let you know we're grateful.'

That surprised him. 'Grateful? I thought Operation Caterwaul had been closed down.'

'Yeah, that.' Fenwick shook his head. 'It was never going to go anywhere. Too much politics. We were aiming high. Maybe too high. But that little secret society you uncovered?' He let out a theatrically low whistle. 'Three techbro billionaires who'll do anything to keep themselves out of the limelight. Man, that's all my Christmases come at once. Heard you were a disruptive influence. Keep up the good work.'

Fenwick flicked a mock, single-finger salute in McLean's direction, then turned and sauntered off down the drive. Too much to hope Harrison would still be there, maybe arrest the man. It wasn't difficult to see how it played into the CIA's hands to have such leverage over Gordon McTavish, Jonathan Scanlan and Dominic Smythe, they were all big players in Silicon Valley, after all. McLean would rather they were where they should be, locked up in a Scottish jail, but he was old enough and jaded enough to know that was never going to happen.

Wincing at the pain any kind of movement made, he limped slowly to the back door and whatever fate awaited within.

70

'I'm told they've been getting some strange tox screen results. Reckon most of the folk down in that cavern were drugged up way past their eyeballs. Probably had no idea what they were doing or even where they were.'

Monday morning, and McLean's hearing still hadn't quite settled back down to normal. At least in the examination theatre of the city mortuary the background noise was at a minimum. He found it hard to filter conversations out of the general noise.

'Any idea what with?' he asked. Across the examination table from him, Angus Cadwallader was preparing to carry out the post-mortem on Alexander Bayne. The old man lay naked on the slab in a manner oddly reminiscent of Anya Renfrew laid out for her sacrifice. She was still in intensive care, either too traumatised by her experience to speak, or suffering brain damage after her time in the water.

'That's the thing. It seems to be something different for each of the people involved. Or left different metabolites in their bloodstream, at least. I've only heard second-hand from a couple of colleagues at the Royal Infirmary. The patients are mostly still alive, after all. No doubt there'll be a report waiting on your desk when you get back.'

McLean did doubt it. He was currently in something of a

limbo. Not exactly suspended awaiting the outcome of an enquiry into the investigation, but not expected to have anything to do with the clean-up either.

'I wouldn't bet on it. I'm not even supposed to be here.' He nodded at the dead man, ready to reveal his secrets. 'But he did try to kill me, and I'd like to know why.'

Cadwallader paused a moment, head tilted slightly to one side as if he was trying to make his mind up about something. It didn't take him long. With a minimal shrug, he set about his work.

'Subject is male, Caucasian, approximately two metres tall. Age according to the records is seventy-two, although he looks younger. Death appears to be due to a stab wound to the heart, but we'll know better once we've opened him up.'

McLean only part listened as his old friend worked his way swiftly around the cadaver. He took a couple of steps back when the Y incision was made and Cadwallader began taking bits out for a closer look. There wasn't much reason for him to be at the post-mortem really. It was just nicer here in the mortuary than back at the station right now, and he'd never quite got the hang of sitting around doing nothing at home.

'As I thought. The wound in his chest carries on through. It's punctured his heart. Death would have been pretty much instantaneous, I'd guess. Not that he'd have noticed anyway if he was drugged up like the rest of them.'

'Have we got tox results for him?' McLean asked.

'Have we, Tracy?' Cadwallader passed the request on to his assistant. Dr Sharp rolled her eyes, then went off to the terminal on the workbench at the side of the examination theatre. The keyboard had a rubberised plastic cover over it to stop blood and gore getting in the mechanism, which was a nice touch.

'He's clean,' she said after a few moments. 'Remarkably so for a man of his age.'

Cadwallader made a 'hmph' noise, shrugged his shoulders

and went back to his examination. McLean was grateful for his half-deafness when the bone saw came out to open up the old man's skull. Swift and efficient, the pathologist didn't take long to finish the whole thing. He stood up straight and stretched his back with a noise that was half groan, half sigh of relief. McLean knew how he felt.

'If it wasn't for the stab wound to the heart, this man might have lived another fifty years. Don't think I've ever seen a healthier specimen.'

'Healthy? How?'

'Just everything in general. His muscle tone's good; apart from the wound his heart wouldn't shame a twenty-year-old; lungs don't look like they've ever seen a city, let alone a cigarette, which is unusual for a man of his age. He's just in really good shape all over. Maybe the cannibal diet has something going for it after all.'

'Don't even joke about it, Angus.' McLean didn't move from his position a good few paces from the body, but he nodded in the direction of Bayne's head. 'Brain OK? No signs of kuru or mad cow disease?'

'Like the rest of him. Rude health.' Cadwallader pulled his gloves off with a dull snapping noise. 'Apart from the whole dagger to the heart thing.'

McLean wondered if any normal dagger would simply have bounced off Bayne's chest, but he kept that thought to himself. This wasn't his case any more. Someone else could worry about the whys and wherefores.

'You had a chance to look at Bale yet?' he asked.

The pathologist raised a greying eyebrow. 'He's up next. Why? You want to stay for him too?'

It was tempting, just to make sure the man was really dead, hadn't somehow faked it all. Again. But there was only so much he could take.

'Think I'll give it a miss,' he said. 'I can always read your report if I need cheering up.'

Cadwallader gave him a worried smile, then waved him away. McLean was halfway to the exit when he stopped, turned back to see his old friend still standing there.

'Do me a favour will you, Angus?'

'Of course. Anything.'

'See, when you open him up for a look? Maybe forget to put his heart back in there after you're done.'

He'd meant to walk back to the station, slip as unobtrusively as possible upstairs to his office, and do his best to get on top of the paperwork that would inevitably be waiting for him there. Instead, McLean found himself driving out of town towards Little France. The black smear of burned moorland still dominated the distant view to the south. In time the heather would regrow, and soon enough it would look no different to the rest of the hillside, but for now it was a reminder of all that had happened these past couple of weeks. All that had been happening for so very long before that.

It took a while to park, walk to the main reception and then find his way to the Intensive Care Unit. When he finally reached the room where Anya Renfrew lay, he was surprised to find Grace Ramsay sitting in a chair beside the bed, even more surprised by the knitting needles in her hands and ball of wool in her lap.

'It helps with the shaking,' she said as she carefully folded up whatever it was she had been making and put everything away in a cloth bag beside her chair. 'Not a word to any of my old colleagues.'

'The thought never crossed my mind. Any updates on her condition?' McLean stepped further into the room, taking in the minimal machinery attached to Renfrew. A saline drip still fed into her arm, and a breathing tube had been slipped up one nostril. The wire from a heart rate sensor clipped to a finger stretched over to a silent monitor beside the bed. Her skin had lost the red tint from the spring, at least that part of it he could see, and there was no sign of the cuts and scrapes he remembered from the cavern. Rather, she looked rested, well. Even her hair was beginning to grow again, a dark shadow over her scalp. The starved hollowness of her cheeks had filled out, smoothing the angles and making her face almost childlike.

'She's been speaking in her sleep.' Ramsay stretched like an elderly cat. 'Well, sort of speaking. No words I understand, anyway. Doctors can't find anything wrong with her. Reckon she could wake up any time. What she'll be like when that happens . . .'

'I'm sorry.' McLean looked around the room for another chair, but there was only the one Ramsay sat on.

'What on earth for? The way I hear it, you found her, saved her from being cut up and eaten.'

'We visited that farm days ago. Searched it twice. Well, I thought we'd searched it, but –'

'Don't wallow in self-pity, McLean. It's not pretty in a detective constable, even less so in a chief inspector. I've been working this case for over forty years and got nowhere. You cracked it in a matter of days.'

'Not me. If you want to thank anyone, thank Harriet Turner and her team. They're the ones who noticed the maps had been altered.'

'And you were the one who put it all together. And went in there single-handed to keep an eye on things until the backup could arrive. Not strictly correct procedure, but then I've heard that about you, McLean. Surprised you made it as far as DCI, if half the things I'm told are true.'

Who had she been talking to? Duguid, probably. Maybe

Grumpy Bob. Not much point arguing with it. He shrugged. 'Let's just call it a team effort, shall we?'

Ramsay nodded once in approval, folded her ancient, wrinkled hands across her lap, fingers locked tightly together. 'Do you suppose anyone will be charged?' she asked after a while. It reminded McLean of his discussion with the spook, Brad Fenwick.

'I think it's safe to say the billionaires won't go to jail. That's not to say they'll get away with it though. As for the rest, my best guess is they'll try to pin most of it on the Baynes and Donaldson, since they're dead and can't make any excuses. The rest of them will probably say they were tricked or drugged or something. Maybe claim they had no idea there was any kind of sacrifice involved. We'll get some of them as accessories to the fact, but those who can afford good lawyers will almost certainly walk away.'

'One law for the rich, another for the rest of us.'

'Isn't it always the way?'

Ramsay reached up and laid a trembling hand on her daughter's. 'You put a stop to it though. They won't be taking anyone else ever again.'

It wasn't a question, so McLean made no answer. In truth, he wasn't sure he could. He stared at mother and daughter for a moment longer, wondered what else to say. As he turned to leave, Renfrew began to stir, woken perhaps by the touch on her hand or the noise of their conversation. Ramsay struggled to stand, so he went to help her, then stood back rather than be in the way.

'Anya?' The ex-detective chief superintendent leaned over the bed as her daughter opened her eyes and blinked at the bright ceiling. It took a long time for her to focus, longer still to move her gaze to her mother's face. McLean expected a smile of recognition, maybe a sigh of relief as the realisation dawned that her ordeal was over. That she had survived. Instead she said nothing, only stared at her mother as those slight tremors ran through the old woman's frame.

Then she reached up with her free hand, cupped Ramsay's face and whispered something unintelligible. For a moment everything was still, so silent McLean could hear his own heartbeat. And then Ramsay let out a little 'Oh!' She stepped back as if she'd been stung, slumped into her waiting chair slightly breathless.

'Are you all right?' He crossed the room to her side. Ramsay held one hand to her chest as if clutching her pearls, the other covering her mouth. When she placed them both on her lap, McLean couldn't help but notice the tremor had gone. She looked up at him with a startled expression, but eyes far clearer than he remembered. Then she reached up and removed her spectacles, gazed across the space to where Anya had gone back to staring at the ceiling.

'Actually, I'm fine,' she said, a note of incredulity in her voice as she raised her hand and stared at it as if it were something she had never seen before. 'I'm absolutely fine.'

71

Gav doesn't like the place. It reminds him too much of school. That ugly concrete with the pebbles splattered all over it to make it hard for the graffiti artists or something. He stays close to his mum as she walks up to the door and presses the bell. Doesn't quite reach out to take her hand; he's no' five any more after all. Feels like it though, staring up the sheer wall towards the sky.

'Aye?' A bored woman's voice, tinny through the intercom.

'It's Sheila Underhill. I'm here about Robert Wilkins?'

Gav looks back down at the door when he hears the name. How many days is it since the polis man came and took Bobby away? He's hardly slept a wink, worried the truth will come out, that it was him who set fire to the heather that made the whole hill go up. Will they bang him up too?

The lock buzzes and Gav's mum grabs his hand as she pushes it open. He'd complain, but now he's scared. She's got a bag over one shoulder that looks a lot like the one he had the last time they went on holiday. Before his dad ran off with Wendy the secretary.

'Mum? Why're we here?' he asks, but she ignores him. She's been ignoring him a lot these past few days. It's good because he's had all the time he wants on his Xbox, but she's been on the phone too. Shouting sometimes. There was a polis man came round late one evening. Not the one who took Bobby away, mind. But Gav knows his mum's keeping secrets from him.

A sour-faced old woman meets them inside. She looks like she's sooking on a lemon, and her hair's pulled back so tight her skin's all stretched around her eyes. Gav tries not to stare, but she pays him no heed anyway, leads them down a long corridor that smells of boiled cabbage and wee. They stop at a door near the end. The old woman knocks once, then goes in before anyone answers. Gav wants to run back to the front door, out to his mum's car, hide. They're going to lock him up here like they locked up –

'Bobby?'

His friend's sitting on a cheap sofa on the far side of the room. He's got an old Sega game or something, staring at it so hard his tongue's poking out the side of his mouth. Gav had forgotten how stupid Bobby looked when he got like that, and seeing it now makes things a bit better.

'Hey, Gav. Where you been?' Bobby drops the game console onto the sofa, stands up. He looks almost as sour as the old woman, and he's wearing the same clothes he had on when the polis man took him away, which might explain the rank smell in the room. How many days has it been? Have they even let him wash?

Gav's mum's let go of his hand, which is a good thing. He'd not want his mate to see him looking feart like that. She walks across the room to where Bobby's standing, takes the bag off her shoulder and puts it on the floor.

'Thought you might need a change of clothes, Bobby,' she says, then unzips the bag and takes out a pair of Gav's jeans, T-shirts, his favourite hoodie. 'We'll get you your own stuff soon as we can, but that'll have to do for now.'

'This is all Gav's. I cannae wear this.'

'Well, you can't wear that. Not if you're coming with us. You fair stink, Robert Wilkins.'

It takes Gav a moment to understand what his mum's just said. Takes Bobby a bit longer. Then the grin spreads across his face, mad like the light in his eyes.

'I'm coming wi' you? They's letting us go? Wicked.'

72

He was staring sightlessly over the stacks of paperwork, out through the glass window wall at the city beyond when the knock at his door distracted him. McLean looked around, a feeling of guilt stealing over him as if he was back at school. Seeing the DCC standing in the open doorway only added to it.

'Sir.' He started to stand, but Robinson waved for him to stay seated. He looked back down the corridor before stepping into the room. Made sure that the door was firmly closed before he spoke.

'I want you to know that I've told them I'll have no part of this.'

McLean stood up this time. Asked 'Part of what, sir?' even though he was fairly sure he already knew.

'The cover-up. It's started already. There were probably plans in place long before any of us knew what was going on. Before Renfrew even disappeared.'

'I'm not surprised, to be honest. Something like that? People like that? Of course they've got it covered should anything go wrong. That's why they dragged old Sawney back to Edinburgh and put his whole family to death.'

Robinson frowned in confusion. 'Sawney?'

'You know the story, sir. Sawney Bean. The infamous cannibal?'

'Aye, but that's just a story. And it all happened on the West Coast. Galloway, wasn't it? Hundreds of years ago, and all made up anyways.'

Just a story of course. 'He was a Lothian man, you know. But for whatever reason, he headed west, found himself a wife, spent all those years killing people and eating them. It was only bad luck that he was caught, but when he was they didn't try him in Ayr or Dumfries. They dragged him and his whole family back home to Edinburgh. Put them all to death without a trial. Why do you think they would do that?'

Robinson's confused frown had grown even deeper. He looked like a man who had thought he had come to terms with some bad news, only to find that it was much, much worse. McLean didn't wait for an answer.

'They've been sacrificing people up on those moors for centuries. Possibly millennia. Harriet's – Professor Turner's – team are finding more and more bones by the day. Ancient bones. The only way to keep something like that a secret for so long is to have powerful people in your circle. Time was that would have been the abbot of the local monastery, the landed gentry. Now it's the rich industrialists and tech billionaires, and a few useful folk to make sure the secret stays that way. Some of them were up there in the cavern, but I'd bet it wasn't all of them.' McLean shook his head, worn down by the predictability of this meeting. 'You're being leaned on by the chief constable, sir. And he's being leaned on by the politicians. They're being prodded by the people in the shadows. The wealthy folk who really run the show. We'll get a few unimportant heads for the block, a half-plausible explanation for what happened, a few folk bribed, a few blackmailed. They'll find out Sandy Bayne and Sergeant Donaldson were cousins and string a story out of that.

Bad from the start, a tragedy it took so long to find out, but now we know. And the whole sorry mess goes away. Except that it doesn't.'

The DCC pulled a chair out from the conference table, slumped into it with a weary sigh. 'I was a fairly easy-going person before I met you, Tony,' he said. 'All I wanted was a nice run-down to my retirement. Maybe a nod in the honours list one year.' He stared off in the same direction McLean had been looking just minutes earlier, paused for a long while before speaking again. 'Well, the retirement's coming a bit sooner than I'd thought. End of the month, same as Grumpy Bob. Maybe we can both ride off into the sunset together, aye?'

It was meant as a joke, but McLean could hear the sadness in the DCC's voice. He opened his mouth to say something, but Robinson stood up, waved him to silence as he headed to the door.

'Just thought I'd let you know. You're a good detective. Not so much with the politics. I can't stop them from sweeping this all under the carpet. I'm sorry.' And then without another word he left.

McLean sat back down again, forearms leaning on the desk. His wrists still ached from the chains, and if he shrugged his arms out of his shirt cuffs, he could see the red marks where they had chafed his skin. It didn't surprise him at all that the events out at Woodhill Farm were going to be quietly glossed over. In many ways he could see the sense of it too. When powerful and influential people were caught doing outrageous things, it was always everyone else who suffered. Lock up a couple of tech billionaires and who knew how many pension funds would suffer? And as for politicians, it seemed they could do pretty much whatever they wanted these days and the voting public wouldn't even raise an eyebrow. Being a member of an ancient secret society that engaged in ritualistic cannibalism would probably gain more votes than it would lose.

It took him a while to realise that his unfocused gaze had come to rest on a small plastic package lying in between two stacks of folders. For a moment McLean could only stare at it in incomprehension, but then he recognised the clear plastic evidence bag, and inside it Anya Renfrew's mobile phone. He reached forward and picked it up, unzipped the bag, pulled out the slim handset. Mike Simpson in the IT lab downstairs had unlocked it, and against all expectations there was still a charge in the battery when McLean clicked the button to switch it on. There was nothing to see on the screen that he hadn't looked at before, but there was a clear signal.

He dialled the number from memory, wondering how it was that he knew it well enough to do that. It rang four times, no doubt the person at the other end debating whether or not to answer an unknown caller. One chance. He'd not leave a message.

'Hello?' A female voice, husky and in need of a cigarette. McLean almost hung up, but then he remembered the look on the DCC's face.

'Dalgliesh? Hi. It's DCI McLean. Tony. Listen. You fancy meeting up for a coffee?'

Acknowledgements

You would think that after writing ten Inspector McLean books I would have got the hang of the acknowledgements section by now. You list all the people who have helped make the book a thing, and you thank them. Job done.

And yet for some reason I always manage to forget someone, or worry that I've spelled someone's name wrong. I wonder, too, if many people actually read the acknowledgements other than those of us in the industry who want to see if we've warranted a mention.

All that said, there are some people who most definitely deserve my thanks, even if they never know I've given them. My agent, the amazing Juliet Mushens, is certainly one. Seventeen books on, Juliet. Who'd have thought it? And to Liza DeBlock, who keeps Juliet in line, thank you for the cheery emails!

It was the wonderfully talented Anna Mazzola who brought the legend of Sawney Bean back to my attention just as I was beginning to think about a new adventure for Tony McLean. I am extremely grateful to her for that. You should all look out her books; they're awesome and contain very little actual cannibalism.

This is a Wildfire book, and I owe a huge debt of gratitude to the Wildfire and Headline teams who have made it a thing, rather than simply a random assortment of words in my head. Alex Clarke, Ella Gordon, Jo Liddiard and Jenni Leech – thank you all.

I have dedicated this book to the people who work behind the scenes. I get my name on the cover, but there is an army of people who support me along the way. First and foremost among them is my better half, Barbara. It's nigh on a quarter century since I first stole her surname for my detective. Thank you for putting up with such endless abuse of your name.

And last of all, if you are reading this then chances are you've also read the book. Or at the very least picked it up and riffled through a few pages. My thanks to you for doing that. Without readers I'd probably still carry on writing these stories, but it wouldn't be half as much fun.

Biography

James Oswald is the author of the *Sunday Times* bestselling Inspector McLean series of detective mysteries, as well as the new DC Constance Fairchild series. James's first two books, NATURAL CAUSES and THE BOOK OF SOULS were both short-listed for the prestigious CWA Debut Dagger Award. BURY THEM DEEP is the tenth book in the Inspector McLean series.

James farms Highland cows and Romney sheep by day, writes disturbing fiction by night.